Nightfall

Blood on the Stars X

Jay Allan

system 7
publishing

Also By Jay Allan

www.jayallanbooks.com

Nightfall

Nightfall is a work of fiction. All names, characters, incidents, and locations are fictitious. Any resemblance to actual persons, living or dead, events or places is entirely coincidental.

ISBN: 978-1-946451-11-8

Chapter One

Planet Calpharon
Sigma Nordlin System
Year of Renewal 263 (318 AC)

The screaming was almost deafening, the shouts of the fleeing—the dying—filling the air, assaulting her ears like a relentless
tide. The streets were flooded with the terrified throngs, howling
in vain for deliverance from the unimaginable nightmare that
had descended on them…at least where the shattered roadways
hadn't begun to buckle under the impacts of the orbital bombardment and buried them beneath incalculable tons of rubble.

Children were wailing in their high-pitched tones, clinging
desperately to the hands of parents, siblings, anyone they could
find, until they, too, succumbed to the massive bolts of energy
striking the ground or the avalanche of steel and concrete as
the buildings of the city came down. All around, rising into the
darkening sky, were great, billowing fireballs of nuclear oblitera-
tion. And below the great rising clouds of doom, all conceived
and built by mankind vanished, reduced to molten slag and gray
dust, with barely a hint remaining that an intelligent and sentient
race had dwelt there.

The world was dying, and its people with it.

A small boy ran across this vision of hell, his face covered
with tears and half-dried blood, clutching the tattered remains
of a cherished stuffed animal of some sort. There was no more

1

left of the toy than an arm and the scorched half of a tattered body. Akella thrust her arms out to him, seeking to draw him away from the fury, to pull him closer, keep him safe, but he was beyond her reach. And then he was gone.

There were blasts of energy firing up into the sky as well as those coming down, and volleys of rockets and missiles ascending as well, but their intensity and numbers were rapidly diminishing. The world's defenses, once mighty, were now mostly blasted into wreckage and radioactive slag.

It was a scene of unimaginable despair. Her eyes filled with water, and tears streamed down her face. There was nothing to feel but a sense of doom, no emotion save utter and complete despair.

Then there was a sudden change. The images were gone in an instant, replaced by near darkness, illuminated only by the vaguest hints of dawn sunlight trickling through the window. And something else, too. Peace. Near silence. The explosions, the screaming…they were all gone. All that remained was the solitude of her private chamber.

Akella turned abruptly over to her side. She reached out, frantically at first, to the small comm unit, thinking to call for help for the child she had seen. But she stopped herself before she called her guards or servants. *It was just a dream*, she realized. *A dream of hell.*

The same nightmare had plagued her for weeks now.

She blinked, trying to clear her head. Yes, it had been a dream. She was alone, in her bed in the villa, nude save for the light, gauzy cover she always wore at night, the thin and plush material now pasted to her skin with sweat. She pulled herself up, raising her head and shoulders above the pillow, and she reached again to the small table, more slowly this time, grabbing for the pitcher of water she always had placed there.

The dreams weren't new, but they were definitely getting worse. Horrible visions of the death of the old empire, of the billions who had been exterminated when that great polity had collapsed in on itself. When its technologies and great ships of war were turned on its own people like the wrath of an enraged deity whose thirst for blood defied quenching.

She took hold of the elaborate crystal decanter and poured herself a glass of water. She'd have been as happy with a simple container, but her position as the Hegemony's Number One had surprised her in no aspect so much as the virtual requirement for waste and decadence. The notion that those who wielded power should also indulge their every whim was a disturbing attitude that survived from imperial days, and she saw it manifesting itself ever more deeply in Hegemony culture.

She did not like it, not one bit, and she saw it as one of the seeds of decline, of a path that led the empire to destruction. Now, she feared, such impulses pushed her own people not toward the enlightened dominance—and protection—of mankind that they sought, but to a replay of the subject of her recurring dreams, the firestorm of warfare and bloodletting known in the Hegemony as the Great Death.

An overwrought title, drama masquerading as history, she might have called it…if the deadly series of conflicts and disasters had not rated it in every particular. Humanity had come close to extinguishing itself entirely almost four centuries before, leaving the galaxy—all of it known to human exploration, at least—a somber and silent graveyard.

She drank the water—gulped it, more accurately—and took a few deep breaths, compelling relaxation and feeling her heartbeats gradually slowing. Then she stood up, pulling herself out from the light cover and walking toward the great windows overlooking the ocean. Sleep was impossible now. She knew that from experience. It was close to time to rise anyway, and there was little point remaining in bed.

She looked out at the crashing waves below the low cliff behind her villa. The sea was her vice, and the one luxury she had gladly accepted. Past Number Ones had resided in the city, near the centers of power over which they ruled. Akella preferred the calm of her villa. She spent most of her time there, residing in her apartment in the capital only when affairs of state compelled her presence.

Which had become far too often since the Rim dwellers were

discovered. Her people were at war, a crusade to undertake their sacred duty. Hegemony forces had fought many times to bring the wild and untamed survivors of humanity's attempted suicide under its protection, but the conflict far out on the Rim was orders of magnitude vaster and deadlier.

She stared out as night continued its daily retreat, driven back by hazy shafts of fresh morning light. Her nightmares once again pushed aside, she plunged deep into thought. Chronos's report weighed heavily on her mind, as it had since she had first read it. She had to make a decision, and she had put it off for too many days already. It would not wait any longer. She would have to send back her response, and she would have to do it before the day dawning outside her window had ended.

But she still had not decided what her answer would be.

The commander of the Grand Fleet, and her colleague on the Supreme Council, Chronos had been clear and concise, and he had pulled no punches in his analysis. Refreshingly, neither had he made excuses for himself nor tried to overstate the gains he had achieved.

The fleet had seen success, by every conventional benchmark of war imaginable. Chronos's ships were only two transits from the Confederation capital, and there seemed no doubt the Confederation forces would soon be defeated, and their capital occupied. A substantial delay to refit damaged ships and modify more escorts to the new anti-small-craft configurations meant it would come later than she had hoped…but it would come. If she let it.

But what then?

Would the enemy collapse when its primary system was taken, as most of her advisors expected? Would the Rim dwellers sue for peace, and their leaders accept their places within an expanded Hegemony?

When she had issued the orders that sent Chronos and most of the Hegemony's military might far out to the Rim, she had believed as earnestly of any of her colleagues that the answer to that question was yes. Now, doubts began to form. She saw strength in the Rim dwellers she had not expected, a power of will that her people had not seen in any other pockets of human habitation they had yet encountered. The Confederation forces were outnumbered, outgunned, overmatched in every way... and yet they continued to fight.

The Hegemony had absorbed many worlds, including one from which some of her own ancestors had originated—but in almost every case, faced with the overwhelming might and technology of the Hegemony, those planets and polities had quickly yielded. Wars—save only for the one against the Others—had been quick, relatively low-cost endeavors, and even the delays normal logistics might have imposed had been largely eliminated by the great support fleet. So it had seemed to be in the Confederation, too, as Chronos's forces pushed ever forward, across distances no Hegemony fleet had been compelled fight over before. Yet now, even with the vast supporting forces, he'd been forced to slow his advance, to prep more ships to face the enemy small craft—*fighters, they call them*, she reminded herself—and to repair damage the fleet had suffered in amounts that had exceeded all expectations.

All of that meant delays, and yet more delays. Akella had hoped to receive word that the Confederation had surrendered by now. Instead, she had the fleet commander's vague assurance he would finish the campaign as quickly as possible after the pause...along with a request for authorization to do just what he had already done on his own. Push back the timetable.

Chronos wants to cover his ass...he wants me to tell him to go forward, not to cancel the operation and fall back.

She'd always liked Number Eight, and she considered him a capable commander. Indeed, he was one of the top ten genetic specimens in the whole of the human race...yet he'd always been a bit cautious in how he conducted things, and he'd never failed to make sure his own interests were protected.

Does he resent me? Akella knew Chronos had desired to mate with her, and she wondered for an instance if some kind of wounded pride had intervened in the fleet commander's actions, even subconsciously.

No, she decided almost immediately. Not Chronos. He would

never do less than his best, no matter what factors pulled at him.

And he does not hate me. Wounded pride or no, he will follow my orders to the best of his ability, even as he will rush to my bed if ever I agree to his desired pairing.

Whatever fight the Confederation, and the other Rim dwellers, might put up, they *would* be conquered. The Others…they were the true worry in her mind, and one she wasn't even sure was real, the return of a deadly enemy she herself had never faced. Few alive had faced the Others, the nightmare from the outer reaches of explored space.

It was to face this threat that the Grand Fleet had been built… and now that great force was hundreds of light-years away, fighting an entirely different—and previously unknown—enemy.

And, by all accounts, suffering significant losses in the process.

Akella stared out at the growing light, at the waves reflecting the morning sun, and pushed back against her thoughts. There had been no sign of the Others, almost within living memory, and she reminded herself that Chronos's delays were not long in the scheme of such a massive conquest. Would another year really matter? Was not the addition of billions of new humans, of DNA branches that had been spared the grievous damage of radiation and bacteriological warfare, worth the extra time, and the small risk the continuation of the campaign carried?

It was, of course, worth it. She knew that, in every way she could logically analyze the situation. And yet she had to fight the unease in the back of her mind.

The nightmares weren't helping.

She turned and walked back to the bed, sitting down and activating the comm unit. "Basha, I will have a communique ready in ten minutes. Order orbital command to have a *Tachyon* ready to depart immediately."

The Tachyon courier ships were the fastest things in space. Antimatter-powered, they could accelerate at over two hundred G. The lack of a human crew—the vessels were entirely AI-controlled—eliminated many impediments to extremely fast travel. The Grand Fleet was many months away in terms of large-unit maneuver, but the *Tachyon* would make the journey in a bit over three weeks, just as one had brought her Chrono's report had done.

She knew what her orders would be, deep inside, though she still had to force out the words once she activated the comm.

"Commander Chronos, you are authorized to continue your campaign, as much in accordance with the established plan as possible. In all matters, you are to use your judgment and remember our sacred duty to steward all humanity, even in the face of their foolish resistance. I support you fully in all things, and I wish you a speedy victory and a triumphant return. Akella, Number One, speaking for the Hegemony."

Chapter Two

"I still can't believe Striker's gone." Tyler Barron sat in the plush chair, staring at the now stone-cold coffee he'd barely touched.

The executive officers' club on Prime Base was luxurious, to say the least. The tables and deeply upholstered chairs lined up in a single row along a clear hyper-polycarbonate wall that offered a stunning view of the blue disc of Megara down below the high planetary orbit of the great Prime Base. No flag officer was denied a magnificent view, nor tasked to endure the head of a fellow admiral blocking his or her sightlines. The top navy brass had shown little sign of controlling wasteful expenditures any better than the politicians down on the surface.

"I can't either. I keep expecting him to walk through the door." Gary Holsten's tone matched the grimness of Barron's. Holsten wasn't supposed to be in the club, not officially, but in the aftermath of the civil disruptions that had almost brought down the Confederation government, the chief spy went just about anywhere he wanted to go, even more than he had before.

Admiral Striker had been one of the great heroes of the Confederation, and he'd been shot down in the street just days after Holsten's people had rescued him from captivity. He had been the last victim of Ricard Lille, the greatest assassin ever to have served Sector Nine and the Union.

Barron seethed with rage, with searing hatred for the Union. He'd been opposed to the peace treaty that had stopped the navy from pushing forward several years before. They could have recovered the systems lost in the first Union War, and made sure the despotic regime never threatened the Confederation again. Now, in the midst of an even more desperate threat, the Union proved yet again it could not be trusted. Even before it could rebuild its shattered fleets to the point where they could pose a credible threat, their machinations and plots still struck hard and caused irreparable harm.

He didn't discuss his thoughts, though. There was no point with Holsten, not again. The reinstated head of Confederation Intelligence agreed with him in every particular. Barron would have known that, even if Holsten hadn't made it clear more than once. But, as much pain as he still felt for the death of his mentor and friend, Tyler Barron knew his own sorrow was irrelevant. He had a job to do, one that would be even more difficult without Striker.

"Are you satisfied with the defenses?" Holsten changed the subject, just as Barron had been planning to do.

"No." Barron had worked tirelessly to bring the Olyus system to a state of preparedness for what would almost certainly be the greatest battle in Confederation history. "The asteroids are almost ready. It took just about every tug in the system to move them into place. They're not as built up as I'd like—and I wish we had more of them—but they'll be tough. I doubt even a couple of railgun hits will take one out of action."

Barron had directed the fortification of a dozen asteroids from the Olyus belt, and had every reactor and weapon system he could lay hands on installed on the huge chunks of rock. There was no elegance or sophistication to the design, but the makeshift forts would be rugged, and they would pack a punch.

They were also expendable, something that had troubled him, as he'd signed the personnel transfers sending crews to take their posts there. The bases were manned by volunteers, and that made it a little easier, but he couldn't help but feel as though he was signing death warrants. He'd been grateful when Admiral Nguyen arrived and took that particular duty from him.

Holsten paused for a moment. "Are you sure about Nguyen, Tyler?" It was almost as though Holsten somehow knew what Barron had been thinking about. "He is a hero, without question, but he's been retired for a long time. I could push your assignment through the Senate, put you in the top command."

Barron shook his head. He knew his friend could very likely do just what he claimed he could. Barron probably didn't even need Holsten to secure the top command. The Senate had been scared to death of him since he'd come close to opening fire on Megara. Between their fear of provoking him and their recognition that they needed the navy united and ready to face the coming threat, they would likely refuse him nothing.

That was one of the reasons he couldn't command the fleet. Barron had his scores to settle, and his frustration and anger toward the often corrupt and foolish actions of the Senate, but he was sure of one thing: he didn't want to be remembered in history as the dictator who destroyed Confederation democracy, however poorly that representative government functioned. Stepping aside, accepting his role in the chain of command, would send a signal. He was a loyal Confederation officer, and not a would-be strongman.

"It has to be Nguyen, Gary. You know that as well as I do. Clint Winters has done an incredible job, but he's junior to me, if barely. I commanded one faction of the fleet that came close—very close—to fighting it out with another, and I almost ended up attacking Megara myself. Nguyen will be above any resentments that still exist out there. He's the one officer the entire navy can follow, a man with the unquestioned record and stature to lead us into this fight."

Holsten nodded. Barron knew the intelligence chief would have preferred to force him right into the top command, but the truth was that he knew he just wasn't ready. In his heart, he was still a ship's captain, and for all that his dedication drove him to assume the responsibilities that had been thrust on him, he still imagined sitting on *Dauntless*'s bridge—*his Dauntless*, still, though she was years gone now—issuing orders to his crew. He was almost overwhelmed commanding the massive fleets he'd come to lead, and stepping fully into Van Striker's shoes, accepting the final, crushing responsibility for defending the Confederation and its billions…it wasn't time. Not yet.

If it will ever be…

"You are your grandfather's heir, Tyler, in every way," Holsten said. Barron always hated comparisons to his famous relation, mostly because they were usually platitudes with varying, and usually minimal, degrees of sincerity behind them. But he knew Holsten meant what he said, and he appreciated his friend's confidence.

He still wasn't ready.

"Dustin Nguyen *served* with my grandfather. He fought in the campaigns I studied at the Academy. He's the man we need now." *Striker is the man we need, he thought,* sighing softly as a fresh wave of grief hit him.

"Well, he should be here in two days." Nguyen had been roused from a comfortable retirement on his home world of Ghavion and recalled to Megara to take up the top naval command.

Barron sat quietly for a few minutes. Finally, Holsten broke the silence. "I assume you're taking a shuttle down to Troyus City later today?" The spymaster managed a slight smile. They'd been talking about grim topics all morning, and Barron figured even the grizzled head of Confederation Intelligence needed a few minutes of a cheerier topic.

He nodded before he answered, and despite the gloom that had dominated him while he worked to prepare a defense he believed was doomed to defeat, he returned the smile. "Yes… she's getting out of the hospital early tomorrow, and I'd like to be there." There was the slightest hint of guilt, as though Barron didn't believe he should take even a brief time away from his duties for what could only be considered a personal matter.

Though orders and duty and decrees from the Senate would

all be insufficient to keep him away from that afternoon's rendezvous.

"Make sure you're on that shuttle. They can spare you for a day. She'll never admit it, but she'll need you, Tyler."

Barron looked across the table, showing no reaction at all. But inside, he realized Holsten was right. However tough Andi's exterior, however determined—and pigheadedly stubborn—she could be, she wasn't a pillar of stone, she was a human being. She'd been through hell, and she'd come out the other side. Whatever duty demanded of Tyler Barron, it would stand aside for a short time.

He was going to be there when Andi Lafarge was discharged from the hospital, and it would take nothing short of Hegemony battleships streaming through the transit point to stop him.

* * *

"The numbers just don't add up. I thought if we increased the flow rate...but that just brings up another batch of problems."

Carson Witter was silent as his colleague spoke. Lucinda York was a gifted scientist and a brilliant woman, but sometimes she had trouble breaking free from the academic orthodoxy that so weighed down his colleagues. The technology they were studying was well beyond anything possessed by the Confederation. Much of it seemed to be direct application of imperial science, and there was just no way to analyze that within the constraints of Confederation academia.

Especially when they had to accomplish *something* useful, and do it damn quickly.

Witter had let his mind go in his work, reaching beyond what he *knew*, to what he could imagine was possible. It took a different approach to look at something and ask, "This shouldn't work, but it does. How is that possible?"

How *could* it be possible?

"Lucinda, this is beyond our basis of knowledge. We have to break free, to consider things that might not seem feasible to us. You've done the calculations, and you know the energy flows that must have run through these things. It *works*. We know that, whatever we were taught, whatever we've seen in our own work." His voice turned somber. "We've got the dead spacers and shattered hulls to prove it. If it works for them, it can work for us, too."

York looked as though she was going to respond, but she didn't for a considerable time. Finally, she said, "I don't know where to go next, Carson. We've tried everything I know."

"Then it's time to move on to what we don't know." He paused. "The navy needs this stuff. You know that. The Confederation's future hangs in the balance."

"I know." There was sadness in her voice. Witter knew York had a brother in the navy. He was still alive, which was no small achievement after the battles that had already taken place, but Witter knew, as virtually everyone in the system did, that the Hegemony was coming to Megara. There would be a battle around the capital, throughout the entire Olyus system. By all accounts, it would be the largest, deadliest, bloodiest conflict the Confederation had ever seen.

And it will be a defeat...unless we can get some of this stuff into Tyler Barron's hands.

Witter headed up the greatest collection of scientific minds the Confederation had ever known. The usual staff of the Institute, already at the pinnacle of the scientific community, had been supplemented by every leading physicist, engineer, and weapons designer who'd been able to reach the Olyus system. They even had Anya Fritz, the fleet's most renowned engineering officer, and probably the single person with the most field experience dealing with Hegemony technology.

And, for all that brainpower, all we've got is a dozen half-finished projects.

Witter pushed back against the despair hovering around him and redoubled his commitment. *We* will *do this. We will get the fleet the tools it needs to win this war.*

To save us all.

* * *

"Harder. You have to drive them harder. Even the veterans." Jake Stockton stood in the small conference room, looking out at his four colleagues, the best pilots in the Confederation. The best pilots in all of human space, as far as he was concerned, and perhaps the greatest that had ever existed. "Especially the veterans."

"I understand, Jake, but there is only so much they can take. If we drive them to exhaustion, to the verge of nervous break-downs…what shape will they be in when the enemy gets here?" Dirk Timmons's voice was calm, even tentative. Timmons had once been Stockton's rival, and he remembered arguments between them, times he'd outright despised the cocky pilot. But Stockton had matured since then, and so had Timmons. They'd long been friends now, and they treated each other with a respect each reserved solely for the other. Stockton knew they were the two best pilots in the service, and any doubts he'd had that Timmons had retained his ability through the loss of his legs and years behind a desk had been washed away. The veteran ace was as good as he'd ever been. Better, perhaps.

Stockton paused. He'd worked himself up into a tirade after watching the most recent maneuvers. By any measure, the wings had conducted themselves brilliantly…but Stockton knew it wasn't enough. Not against the Hegemony.

"You're right, Dirk. Or, in any other situation, you'd be right. But this is no ordinary enemy. They're way beyond us in tech. This battle fleet of theirs isn't only massive; it has an enormous support fleet. Cargo ships, mobile shipyards, factory vessels. They used it to reconfigure hundreds of escorts for anti-fighter ops…and they took down almost a thousand of our fighters in the battle at Ulion." Stockton cringed slightly as he spoke of the losses his people had suffered in the fight a few months earlier. "We managed to hurt them enough to buy some time, but they'll be here soon enough. And we've got to be ready. That means new tactics…and getting damned proficient with those muni-tion pack cluster bombs."

Stockton knew he was riding hard on the four people in all of Confederation space who were likely as aware as he was of what the fighter wings would face in the next battle. But he'd seen too much death already, too many old veterans—friends—killed, and young pilots, brimming with potential, shot down by the hundreds. Thousands.

He was thankful the enemy didn't have fighters. If they'd possessed their own squadrons, he suspected the war would already be over. But the blood of his pilots had staved off final defeat, at least so far.

There was one other thing the enemy didn't have, besides just squadrons. They didn't have his Four Horsemen. Dirk Timmons, Olya Federov, Johannes Trent, and Alicia Covington. Four of the greatest pilots the Confederation had ever produced.

Four cold-blooded killers in the cockpit, striking at the enemy like the very shadow of death.

He was grateful for them all. Because his massed fighter wings, veterans and fresh recruits alike, were the only thing buying time. The only thing giving the Confederation any hope at all.

And the cost was becoming more than he could bear.

Chapter Three

Andrei Denisov sat in his office, silent, staring at the large screen on his desk, but seeing nothing save for his own thoughts.

Dark thoughts.

His orders were clear. To stay where he was, to wait for word from the diplomatic team. But his fleet had been on station for more than three months, and there hadn't been any word at all from the ambassador. Montmirail had sent only a command to remain on station until further notice.

Denisov was struggling to fight against the morose feelings that threatened to take over his thoughts. He'd achieved the command of his dreams, a position he'd never dared to believe was in reach. He commanded the entire navy, a fact that guaranteed him either a retirement awash in luxury and riches…or one resulting from a pair of shots to the head. Service in the upper ranks of the Union armed forces carried many dangers, and the enemy was only one of them.

He was thrilled with the job. He loved the fleet, and he was dedicated to its personnel and proud of the professionalism they displayed, despite the corruption and disorder that riddled

16

every layer of Union society. But the current mission troubled him, as it had from the moment the orders had left Gaston Villieneuve's mouth.

Denisov didn't object to a rematch with the Confederation, or at least part of him didn't, the martial side of his personality that craved glory and revenge from the humiliations of the last war. But he knew what the cost would be, the thousands, perhaps millions, who would die. Worse, the fleet wasn't ready. The Union wasn't ready. It would take years to get the navy back to the strength it had boasted before the losses of the war. Any move against the Confederation before then was premature and dangerous, regardless of the new struggle that seemed to have come upon the Union's rival.

He understood Villieneuve's desire to capitalize on the fact that the Confederation was at war, apparently with a powerful and advanced civilization from beyond the Badlands. It made sense, tactically, strategically, in every way possible.

Save one.

Denisov didn't trust this enemy or its motives. He knew almost nothing about them, and worse perhaps, he was pretty sure Villieneuve didn't know much more. He'd dreaded receiving an order to advance into Confederation space, to begin another war while relying almost entirely on an unknown and untested ally. That fear had receded slightly as the official comm lines remained silent.

His worries had shifted to the ambassador, why nothing had been heard in almost three months. His crews were getting edgy. They could see the fleet massed, and they had to wonder why. He suspected even the lowest-grade spacers knew they weren't a match for the Confeds. Not yet.

By all accounts, this new enemy is pushing the Confederation forces back, which means they're strong. Villieneuve sees them as an ally, but what if…

He let the thought stop. There was nothing to be done. He couldn't leave the system without violating his orders, and as edgy as he was about what might happen, he wasn't ready to end up in a Sector Nine black site somewhere.

People's Protectorate, he reminded himself, reeling once again at the hypocrisy in the new name of the Union's feared secret police agency.

"Admiral, we're picking up energy readings at the Outremer transit point." The tactical officer's voice crackled slightly through the comm speaker. Like everything of Union manufacture, it was inferior to its Confederation equivalent. It worked, but not quite perfectly.

Denisov's head snapped around toward the screen on the far wall of his office. His first thought was a courier ship. Perhaps he was receiving word from the ambassador.

Finally.

But something was wrong. The energy levels were too high. Far too high for a single ship or, he realized as he continued to watch, even for a small flotilla.

Could the Confeds have discovered that Villieneuve was planning to attack? Had they managed to put together a force to strike first? It didn't feel right. That wasn't the Confederation's way, a fact that had often hurt them strategically.

The Confeds don't have enough free forces now anyway, not if half the intel we're getting is accurate.

But then what?

He felt his stomach tighten, a cold feeling taking hold, as another possibility came to mind.

* * *

"Our forward units have begun the jump into the Sigma-6 system, commander." The Kriegeri stood before Raketh's elevated chair, looking up at the Master as he made his report. "The completion of movement into the target system is projected in one hour, four minutes."

Raketh nodded then waved his hand, dismissing the officer. But before the Kriegeri had reached the door, he called him back. "Kiloron…"

"Yes, commander?" The officer turned back and bowed his head, a repeat of the respectful salute he'd given when he had first entered Raketh's sanctum.

"All ships are to transit at maximum velocity and accelerate at full power as soon as their systems have recovered from the jump."

"Yes, commander." The officer waited again, leaving only when Raketh repeated the dismissal gesture.

The Master watched the Kriegeri leave and the doors slide shut behind him, though he was barely seeing any of it. He was deep in thought, reviewing every aspect of the battle he was about to fight. Ideally, he would assemble his fleet into formation after all the vessels had jumped, but he had no scouting data, no idea where the Union ships were positioned in the target system.

He would normally have sent scouts through to gain that information, but he did not want to give the enemy—and the Union was about to become as much an enemy as the Confederation—any warning. The star maps seized from the Confederation data systems told him he was moving across the border, and that the systems on both sides were demilitarized by treaty. That meant the Union forces would be without fixed fortifications. He intended to close as quickly as possible and crush their entire fleet, before they had a chance to figure out what was happening. All the data he had been able to access from Confederation records suggested the Union forces were somewhat inferior. Slower, not as maneuverable, their crews less experienced.

Though they also have the small attack craft...

Everything he had read suggested the Union squadrons were demonstrably less efficient than the Confederation wings, but Raketh was not sure whether that was accurate, or simply the Confeds trashing their enemy.

Regardless of the truth of the matter, he suspected even less capable squadrons would prove to be a problem for his own units.

He was determined to hit the Union forces, and hit them hard. If the information from the interrogated ambassador and his staff proved to be true, Raketh had secured an incredible stroke of luck, an astonishing accommodation by the Union in

massing their forces together in one location, where they could
be destroyed in a single attack. One quick victory could eliminate months of costly system-hopping, and it would open the
way for a relatively easy conquest.

And it would erase forever any hint of disgrace for his initial retreat from Dannith. Raketh had not been disciplined or
demoted for that incident, nor had he been judged to have acted
wrongly. None of his superiors had even criticized him for the
withdrawal he had ordered, but he knew there was hushed talk,
suggestions that fear and not tactical analysis had, at least in part,
directed his decision. He was determined to shove those words
down the throats of those who uttered them, to return home in
triumph and glory, as befitted one with his status among the top
one hundred specimens of the human race.

* * *

That's no ambassador's retinue...

Denisov had already come to that conclusion, looking at the
first energy spikes, but now, there was no doubt. A dozen ships
were through already, and from the looks of the readings coming in, there were more behind those.

A lot more.

"All ships report reactors at full power, admiral."

"Very well, commander." Denisov looked over to the tactical station as he spoke. Guy Lambert had come along with
his promotion to fleet command, and the officer had proven
himself almost indispensable as an aide. Denisov had been a bit
suspicious at first. He didn't have a doubt his fleet was riddled
with political officers, there to watch him and report back to Villieneuve. Service to the Union was a complex calling, and one of
the first things a successful officer came to understand was this:
you were always being watched.

Lambert wasn't a Sector Nine plant, though. Denisov was
almost sure of that. He'd always considered himself a good judge
of people, and at some point, he just went with his instincts.
Besides, a few weeks before, he and Lambert had talked long

into the night and, after enough wine had flowed, the topic of likely political officers on *Illustre* came to the forefront. Denisov didn't entirely discount the possibility that it was a topic a particularly clever agent might raise, fishing for suspicious responses. But it was dangerous talk, and Lambert had shown the same resentment the majority of officers felt about being spied on while they were risking their lives in battle.

Lambert was legit—or, at least, Denisov was willing to bet on it.

Even if the stakes of that bet were his commission and posting. Or even his life. In the end, everything came down to educated guesses on probability.

"All ships are to engage engines, five G thrust directly toward the Valciennes transit point."

"Yes, sir." He could hear the hitch in Lambert's voice. Uncertainty. Even fear.

Denisov knew that command might raise some suspicion, especially to any officer planted on his ship to spy on him. His orders were clear. He was to remain in the Pollux system, and if for some reason he was compelled to leave it, he was to return to Montmirail. Valciennes led away from the Union capital, along the border toward another route into the Confederation. He wasn't sure why he was drawn there. The Confederation was his enemy, had always been his enemy. Their fleet had defeated and humiliated his beloved navy. His hesitation to start a war before the navy was ready didn't mean he didn't crave a rematch someday. But he had a feeling, somewhere deep in his gut, and it pushed him away from Montmirail. It was instinct, but it was strong...and his intuition had rarely led him astray.

"Fleet order. Arm all main guns. All fighter squadrons are to scramble and prepare to launch." He'd configured his wings half as interceptors and half as torpedo bombers. He'd heard rumors that the new force battling the Confeds didn't have any fighters of their own...but he didn't even know what he was facing, and he wasn't about to gamble on unconfirmed intelligence and leave his ships open to a devasting bomber attack.

You don't even know these ships are from the Confederation's new enemy, not for sure.

The words echoed in his mind, but the thought proved unpersuasive, and the answer in the depths of his consciousness was simple and to the point.

Yes, you do.

Chapter Four

Hegemony's Glory
Orbiting Planet Ulion
Venga System
Year of Renewal 263 [318 AC]

Chronos stared at the reports moving across his screen, and he listened to the endless, droning reports of his officers until the stream of text turned to a fuzzy blur, and the voices of his staff to something akin to the buzz of a swarm of Calpharon Red Flies. He relished his position as commander of the Grand Fleet, and he craved the place in history that would certainly befall the conqueror who brought the vast population of new subjects into the Hegemony. Glory was seductive, but his subconscious offered him a warning in simple, direct terms.

First you must secure the victory.

He had reviewed the numbers. He had considered every tactical possibility, reviewed seemingly endless projections. That victory he needed seemed assured. The enemy was just too weak, too technologically inferior. Their small craft had offset some of their disadvantages, allowed them to continue the fight far longer than they might otherwise have done.

But now I will take their capital. I will dictate the terms of peace, offer mercy in exchange for surrender.

He had felt better about that plan earlier in the campaign. It was one thing to look at numbers and technology, to compare weapons and tactics. But the Confeds were unlike any enemy he had faced, any he had read about in the annals detailing the Hegemony's conquests and absorptions of lost human populations. The Confeds fought like wild animals, and they sent their small craft in again and again, almost without regard for the losses they suffered.

He'd never seen such viciousness, such a warlike adversary, and he wondered if the Rim dwellers retained the savagery in combat that had helped to lead to the empire's destruction. He had been nervous about committing the Grand Fleet to the Rim conquest, and that worry had only increased as the time and losses of the campaign increased. Now, he had begun to wonder if it was fortunate that the Rim dwellers had sent their exploratory fleet toward the old imperial core and announced their presence. What might these wild beasts have done with another century or two to grow, to find and adapt imperial relics and technology? Chronos tried to imagine a future where the Rim dwellers were united and armed with imperial tech, where they launched their own attack. The Hegemony, and its sacred mission to unite and protect all of mankind, could have been snuffed out and replaced by a new empire, one ruled by wild Rim savages and destined for another tragic fall.

"The ground operations are proceeding at a pace that—"

"Enough." Chronos had let the single word out of his mouth unfiltered, his impatience and irritation on open display in his tone. Then he reasserted full control over himself and restored his voice to the emotionless norm to which his people had become accustomed.

He was standing on the bridge of the flagship, near the main command station. Masters tended to command from raised chairs in their dedicated sanctums, while officers came and went, delivering reports and information.

Chronos had enjoyed such trappings once, and as fleet commander, he had a massive chamber available for his use. But age and experience had caused the allure of such—*nonsense* was the only word that came to his mind—to diminish. He demanded obedience from those under his command, and the respect due to the eighth best genetic specimen in all humanity, but he'd lost his taste for pointless formality. He had found that being right in the center of things kept him on the edge of information coming in…and it reminded his people he was right there, watching.

The group clustered around him, a few other—far junior—Masters, and a clutch of high-ranking Kriegeri, both red and gray. They had gone silent at his single word, and they remained that way, waiting for guidance from the fleet's commander.

"Continue with the analysis," he said, his cool demeanor restored, hiding the growl he wanted to unleash on them all. He knew he was not being fair, that his officers had not done anything wrong. He had been worried about the time the campaign was taking, and the losses. Such things had been on his mind for some time, but now there was something else tugging at his thoughts, a confusing mix of emotion and reasoned concern.

He had not heard back from Akella yet.

He had sent his fastest courier ship back to the Hegemony's capital with a request for further instructions. He wasn't sure if it had been the desire for self-protection, an impulse to insulate himself from any negative effects of a prolonged campaign, or if he just wanted reassurance that Akella was still with him. It was unseemly for one of his stature to display any lack of purely personal confidence, but it would help him to know he had her fresh authorization.

And if he did not, if she ordered him to call off the attack…

That was the risk he had taken, but he didn't think it would happen. Akella knew as well as he did that the Hegemony *had* to absorb the Rim dwellers, both for the advantages they offered, and because it would be reckless to allow them to continue to grow stronger, to one day become the threat Chronos knew they could be.

"Get Megaron Illius on my private channel. Now!" He snapped out his words, particularly the last one. He was out of patience with them all, he wanted to speak directly with the commander of ground operations, and he wanted to do it immediately. "I will be in my sanctum."

He was beginning to understand at least part of why so many of his peers spent so much time in their grandiose chambers.

At least it is quiet in there…

* * *

"We have secured the capital, as well as all power plants and other support facilities servicing it. I have followed standard protocols, erected a circular line of defenses around the city, and positioned a series of supply dumps inside the defensive perimeter. Regular patrols are sweeping the area twenty kilometers out from the perimeter line around the clock. We have also taken the four other largest cities on the planet, with similar precautions taken at each."

Chronos listened to the officer's report. Illius was a megaron, an officer commanding a million or more ground troops. He was also a Master of considerable distinction, rated number nine hundred and two. Chronos was not taking any chances with this world. The population was vastly larger than that of the first occupied planet—Dannith, the Confeds called it—and that border world had become an immense headache, its pacification horribly behind schedule. When Chronos had seen the population estimates for Ulion, he had prepared himself for a nightmare, even for the dreaded necessity of resorting to intense orbital bombardments. The planet's population was over ten billion, larger than that of any planet in the Hegemony itself. But Illius's forces had secured their primary objectives faster than he had dared hope, and with fewer losses. Whatever spirit existed in the inhabitants of the frontier world, it clearly did not extend to this central and massively populated planet.

Perhaps what we saw on Dannith is not indicative of the entire Confederation. Maybe they are just rugged borderers of some kind, and the populations of the inner worlds are softer.

He liked that idea, but while he suspected there was some truth to it, he remembered the tenacity of the Confederation's fighting forces. Even on Ulion, where Illius's troopers had so far encountered the enemy regulars and not the multitude of planetary defense units, the fighting had been savage. Fortunately, however, there appeared to be few of those frontline troops so deep inside Confederation space. At least on Ulion.

"You have done well, Illius. My congratulations. With fortune, perhaps the pacification will be sufficiently advanced to spare you by the time the invasion continues. I would have you lead the ground assault on the enemy's capital if possible."

"You honor me, commander."

Chronos nodded. Though Chronos was far above anyone else in the Grand Fleet, Illius was a Master, too, and a member of the top one thousand. He was due a certain level of respect, even from a superior, and his success had only increased the call for proper handling.

"Not at all, Illius. Your skill and ability will be needed there, and there is no other officer I would have leading what will likely be the most crucial invasion of the campaign." Megara was the Confederation capital, the seat of its government, and, hopefully, its fall would compel an overall surrender. Chronos suspected some elements would fight on no matter what happened there, but if the legitimate government capitulated, any residual resistance would be scattered and relatively easy to mop up. If he had to conquer the entire Confederation, over one hundred inhabited worlds, fighting desperate battles at each of them, the war would last for years.

"I thank you, commander. Indeed, I am seeing preliminary reports that the planetary government here is already seeking terms for the cessation of hostilities. Perhaps the struggle on this world can be concluded even more quickly than we had hoped."

"Perhaps." Chronos had received vague intel to the same effect. He was not sure what to expect, especially since the local government had surrendered on Dannith as well, and that capitulation had done little to disarm the most effective defensive units. "Report to me at once if anything comes of that."

"Of course, commander."

"I will leave you to your duties, megaron. Fortune remain with you."

"And you, commander."

The line went silent, and Chronos sat for a moment, slipping back deep into thought. If Ulion could indeed be pacified so quickly, what did that portend for the rest of the campaign? He had been concerned about what resistance like that he'd seen on Dannith would look like on worlds with twenty to fifty times the population of that frontier planet.

The door alarm buzzed.

"Enter," Chronos said, pushing aside the wave of annoyance he felt at the intrusion. He had been clear he was not to be disturbed unless something crucial came up.

"Apologies, commander." A Kriegeri officer slipped inside the room and bowed his head. "A courier ship has just transited into the system, and it is transmitting a message from Number One. I believed you would want to know immediately."

Chronos found the way the Kriegeri said "Number One" to be amusing, almost as though he was speaking of some kind of deity. *We have done well to secure the respect of those beneath us. I hope we have done as well at guiding civilization forward, and that we have not just set up echo chambers and supplicants to bow and scrape before us.* There was some doubt in his mind as those thoughts moved through, but that was an internal philosophical debate for another day.

"On my line, kiloron, as soon as it is received and decrypted." He paused. "The *instant* it is decrypted."

"Yes, commander." The officer nodded respectfully, turned, and left the room. The doors closed, leaving Chronos alone again, with his thoughts, and his anticipation of what Akella had decided.

Chapter Five

"The field stretches from the point marked alpha one, all the way to delta nine." The officer extended a hand, moving it slowly across the large screen on the wall of Barron's office. It was an imperfect explanation, a two-dimensional representation of three-dimensional space, but Barron and Clint Winters understood what they were seeing. The minefield covered almost the entire area directly in front of the Olyus system's third transit point, the one from which the Hegemony forces would almost certainly emerge when they launched their expected attack on Megara.

The layout had a curvature to it that didn't appear clearly on the screen, not quite semicircular, but enough bend to wrap around the expected enemy line of advance. There hadn't been enough mines to cover every possible angle of approach, but avoiding the mines would require the invading forces to come almost to a dead stop, and then change their vectors ninety degrees along the Y or Z planes. It was an unlikely tactic, for all kinds of reasons, and it wouldn't be possible at all unless the Hegemony ships came through with almost no established velocity.

And if they did that, Barron knew the fighter wings would hit them like the fury of an ancient god of war.

"That should be perfect." Barron turned toward Winters. He outranked his fellow admiral, if only by a few months of seniority, but the presence of Dustin Nguyen in command of the fleet had spared him from the need to enforce such an insignificant difference. In fairness, Winters had given no indication that he had any problem following Barron's orders, but Tyler was just as happy not having to go down that road.

Not yet, at least.

"Yes, I think the fields will do their job. I can't see them avoiding it. Honestly, even if they knew about them, they'd have a hard time coming in slow enough to sidestep the field before coming into range. And their formation would be a mess. Stockton and the wings would tear them to shreds."

Barron nodded. The enemy ships didn't even have to move into the field itself. The term "mines" wasn't even accurate, at least not technically. The weapons weren't explosives waiting for enemy ships to strike them; they were bomb-pumped x-ray lasers, and the powerful one-shot devices would target their devastating rays on any ship that moved into range. The lasers were enormously powerful, stronger than a Confederation primary beam. Perhaps even a match for the enemy railguns. They were a deadly danger to any ship that moved into their zone of effectiveness, even the largest Hegemony battleships.

The only problem was...there weren't enough of them.

Barron had scraped up every bit of heavy ordnance in the Olyus system, and on any planet within half a dozen transits, but the worlds of the Core, and even those of the inner Iron Belt, had long felt safe from any imminent attack. Many—most—had allowed their defense grids to decay from lack of maintenance, and their supplies of ordnance and weapons to dwindle over time.

Megara's defenses were strong, at least, as befitted the Confederation's capital, but even the massive forts orbiting that central world had turned out to be poorly supplied for a full-scale fight.

Barron stood for a few more seconds. The minefield was done, the laser satellites deployed. There was nothing to be gained standing around guessing how they would work. There was more work to do.

More work than seemed possible. Barron didn't really believe the fleet could hold Megara against the overwhelming power of the Hegemony forces. But he was damned sure of one thing.

The enemy was going to get one hell of a fight.

* * *

Andi Lafarge walked across the room and into the bathroom. She looked in the mirror, trying to figure out who it was she saw. She looked okay. Better than she'd expected. At least the dark, drawn look was gone. She'd definitely come a long way from the zombie who'd stepped tentatively out from the hospital that had come to feel almost like home.

She'd spent almost three months in that facility for broken bones, concussions, and more internal injuries than she could easily recall. The time had been an ordeal all its own...and that terrible struggle for recovery followed the worst, most trying and painful battle she'd ever fought.

She'd been surprised when she awoke in the hospital. Her astonishment wasn't that she was in the hospital, but that she'd awakened at all. She hadn't had any clear memories at first, just a hazy confusion, but then it began to come back to her. The long hunt for her enemy, the desperate struggle on the roof, and then falling, dragged over by Ricard Lille as he, too, plunged to the street below.

Lille was dead. She hadn't known when she'd awakened, and as soon as she'd come to her senses, she'd almost lost control, flailing about in the bed, searching for anything to use as a weapon, and reopening fused wounds as she did. She had trouble believing her enemy was dead, even after three or four people told her. It was only when Tyler Barron got there and confirmed the story that she'd allowed it to truly sink in. She had succeeded. She had set out to take her vengeance, to kill the assassin no one thought could be defeated, and she'd done just that.

There had been some satisfaction in that knowledge…but not the catharsis she'd expected. The realization that he'd broken her, that she was not as invincibly hard as she'd imagined, was still there, if perhaps now manageable enough for her to press on with her life.

She'd told herself she'd been willing to die to kill her enemy, and she'd meant it. But as she'd lain there in her bed those first days of consciousness, Tyler standing above her, his face a mask of pain and worry, she'd decided she'd been wrong. She *had* to live. She was still badly injured, and though the doctors had told her she would likely be fine, she didn't believe a word of it. She'd seen through too many liars in her life, better ones than the medical staff at Troyus City's military hospital. She'd figured they'd given her about a fifty-fifty chance when outside her earshot. That was enough to terrify most people, but as far as Andi Lafarge was concerned, odds like that were a piece of cake.

She'd battled hard, gritted her teeth and virtually willed her way back to health. And the day she'd been released, Tyler had come for her and taken her back to his quarters. She'd had around-the-clock attendants, doctors stopping by two or three times a day to check on her…and a cluster of marine guards outside the door, a precaution that remained despite her repeated reminders to Barron that Lille was dead. The admiral, her lover and her best friend, had just nodded sweetly each time she'd raised the issue, calmly ignoring her. The couple of times she'd pressed the matter, he had said he wasn't taking any chances. She'd argued a bit, but in truth, she was relieved, at least while she was still recovering. Lille was dead, and by all accounts, Sector Nine activity on Megara had disappeared. But it wasn't hard to imagine some protégé of Lille's lurking in the shadows, consumed with the need to avenge his master's death, as Andi had been with her own lust to kill the master assassin himself.

She ran her hand through her hair once or twice, and then she pulled away from the mirror and walked back out into the main room, just as a soft bong announced that someone was coming in.

"Andi...it's me. I've got Gary Holsten with me."

She smiled when she heard Barron's voice, and lost only a little of it when she realized he wasn't alone. That was a shame. She was feeling much better, physically at least, and she had all kinds of thoughts about what she could do with Tyler if they were alone. Still, Holsten was one of her best friends, and she was happy to see him as well.

She walked up toward the door, just as the two men came in. She managed a smile, not a forced one, not even the crooked, weak grin that so often filled in, but a full-fledged "I'm back from the dead" smile.

"Andi, I'm so glad to see you looking back to form. What you did was amazing, and to survive that fall was incredible. I'd never have bet against you before, but now...I think there's nothing you can't do."

"You are quite the smooth talker when you want to be, Gary." She took a step toward him and planted a sisterly kiss on Holsten's cheek.

She was genuinely glad to see him, but she could tell immediately that the visit was more than a social call. She kissed Barron as well, a bit more pointedly, but still appropriate for public consumption, and a quick glance told her that whatever was going on, he was in on it too. They were two of the very few people in the world she trusted, so she suspected whatever was about to follow would have something to do with their ideas of how to help her or keep her safe. She wished she cared about that as much as they did.

"So, let's cut to the heart of things. I love you both, but you're here because you want me to do something." The last time Gary Holsten had visited her with that look on his face, she'd ended up on Dannith, and then in a Sector Nine torture chamber. She knew the guilt he felt about all that, and she was pretty sure the last thing he would have done now was come to her with was something dangerous. *Which means they want to protect me...*

Holsten paused, the normally unshakable spy seeming a bit lost. Barron stepped up and put his hand on Andi's shoulder. "If you feel up to it, we'd like you to take command of a ship. There *is* something we'd like you to do, something very important."

"I've already got a ship, Tyler."

"Yes, but *Pegasus* isn't big enough for this. She isn't fast enough either, not for what we have in mind."

Andi wasn't happy about being asked to command another ship, but she was intrigued. *Pegasus* was small, but she was a pretty damned fast vessel, and she couldn't imagine what they wanted her to do that required more speed.

"I thought we were getting to the point." A little impatience slipped into her tone, half genuine, half by design.

"The ship is called *Hermes*, Andi. She's new," Holsten said, beating Barron to the punch. "And we want you to take command of her, and go to the Institute. The research facility is in the outer system, as you know. You'll be on the other side of the enemy fleet there, and you'll be in a good position to evacuate the key science teams working on the Hegemony tech…if that becomes necessary." His tone suggested he didn't really see that as a question mark.

"You want me to load them onboard and run? While the battle is going on? While you, and most of the people I care about, are in the thick of the fight? Forget about it."

"Andi, please…" It was Barron again, and she felt her stomach tighten. She'd never had trouble saying no to anyone about anything, at least until she'd met Tyler Barron. He was looking at her, his eyes boring into hers, pleading with her to go along with what he was asking. She knew the stress he'd been under, the almost impossible workload that had fallen on him. She tried to say no again, even managed to shake her head ever so slightly… but she felt her resolve buckling as she stared into his eyes.

* * *

"Sara, thank you for coming." Gary Holsten gestured toward one of the chairs opposite his desk, and then he waited while

Eaton sat down before he dropped back into his own seat.

"Of course. If there's anything more I can do to aid in the defense, you just have to let me know."

Holsten nodded slowly. Eaton had been immersed in the defensive preparations, acting as Tyler Barron's right hand and blasting from the orbital fortresses, to the minefields, to the fleet waiting in its formations…and then around the circuit again. But what Holsten had in mind had nothing to do with the expected battle, and everything to do with a chance of winning the war itself.

It was also something Eaton was going to hate, and most likely resist with considerable effort. He *had* to convince her, because if he couldn't, he was going to have to ask Barron to order her, and that wasn't something he wanted to do.

"I'll get right to the point, Sara. We have several new fast cruisers, the quickest things in the fleet. Andi Lafarge is going to command one of them, and she's going to use it to evacuate the research teams at the Institute, if that becomes necessary."

"That sounds like a good plan, but I'm not sure what it has to do with—"

"We want you to take one of the others…and go out to the Far Rim."

"You want me to what?"

"There are inhabited planets out there, Sara, nations, smaller than the Confederation—but combined, they likely possess considerable military strength. We have some relations with these, others are barely known to us, but Imperator Tulus and his people have given us a complete breakdown, as well as a few likely places to start."

"Start what?"

"Looking for allies. The Hegemony isn't here to conquer the Confederation. They've come for the entire Rim. This is every-one's problem, and quite frankly, we need all the help we can get if we're going to win this fight."

"I agree with that, but what does it have to do with me? I'm no ambassador. And besides, wouldn't this be something for Imperator Tulus and his people? They're much closer to these worlds than we are."

"You know Alliance history as well as I do, Sara," Holsten said. "Every nation on the Far Rim is scared to death of the Palatians."

"You want me to leave the fleet…before the battle?" There was anguish in her voice.

"I know that will be difficult, but this has to be someone we can trust, and someone with the stature to get the Far Rim nations to pay attention." He reached down, scooped up a small box, and handed it to her. "You're getting your bump up to admiral, Sara, whether you agree to go or not. It's well deserved and long overdue. But if you really want to do all you can to help, please…consider this."

Holsten saw the pain in her eyes. It was clear she'd rather face any nightmare than leave her comrades before the coming battle. But there was something more, a deep sense of duty, and the analysis born of a strong intellect. After the near civil war, Holsten didn't trust any of the Confederation's career diplomats, and he was pretty sure Eaton didn't either. Besides, the Far Rim was dominated by small polities, most of them consisting of the conquests of gifted warriors, either present or past. They would listen more attentively to an admiral than they would to an ambassador.

She didn't answer, not for a long while…but, as he watched her expression, saw the thought in her eyes, a realization began to form.

I've got her.

* * *

"Thank you, Andi. I know you don't want to go, but we really needed someone we could trust to get the scientists out… assuming it comes to that."

"Shh." She put her lips to his ears and pulled closer to him. She knew why he *really* wanted her to take command of *Hermes* and get the research teams to a safe place, and it had *nothing* to do with her being the only person who could do the job. She was

a good pilot—a damned good pilot, if she did say so herself—
but she was far from the only one who could ferry the research
teams to whatever safe haven still existed out there.

Tyler wanted her out of the system, period. He wanted *her*
safe while everything else was slipping into the fires of hell...
and she loved him for it. But she still would have said no, refused
to leave his side, sworn to stand by him to the last—save for one
fact that bored into her brain like a drill.

If she stayed, he would worry about her. He would be distracted. And if his mind was on her, it wasn't where it needed to
be. For the battle to be won. For him to survive.

She would do anything to stay by Tyler's side, to live with
him—in peace, if she even believed such a thing existed—or, if
need be, die with him...but she would not allow herself to add
to the desperate danger he faced. She couldn't bear the thought
of him dying when he might have lived, of wondering if it had
been the distraction of his concern for her that had killed him.

She wanted to scream. Part of her wanted him to leave, so
she could lose her composure somewhere all alone and let the
tears come. But she wouldn't sacrifice the moments they had for
anything. He was with her now, and she would enjoy that. She
would get a lifetime's joy from it, because she knew very well
the enemy could come at any time. And when that happened...

The night could well be the last they had together for a long
while. Possibly forever. All she wanted now was to feel him next
to her, to know he was there.

To forget about what was coming.

Chapter Six

Denisov stared at the scanner, trying to make sense of what he'd just seen. *Vandaum* was gone. Just gone. One instant, the battleship had been there, holding its position as ordered, and the next, it was dust and radiation.

And nine hundred dead spacers…

Denisov had heard rumors of the enemy's great main guns, but he hadn't been prepared for the power he'd just seen at such extreme range.

"The battle line will pull back. Full thrust…now!" The orders came out of his mouth, even without conscious thought. He'd intended to hit the enemy hard, before they could organize their formations after the transit, but now he realized, with a shock that made him almost numb, his entire fleet would be blasted to scrap before he got off a decent shot.

"Yes, admiral." Lambert's tone suggested the aide was well on the way to reaching the same conclusion.

The range difference is going to be a huge problem in fighting these…whoever they are.

Denisov's mind raced, trying to come up with tactics—any

38

tactics—he might employ. The system was barren, stripped of any defenses by the treaties with the Confederation. There were two inhabited worlds, but both were barely colonized, with less than two hundred thousand people in the entire system.

Still a lot of men and women to abandon to an enemy…

Union doctrine placed a very low value on the lives of citizens, especially on peripheral worlds of no real value. Notwithstanding the fiction and propaganda that permeated every government proclamation, the population of the Union was expected to serve the state, without hesitation.

There were definitely some officers in the fleet who secretly differed from that point of view—Denisov was one of them. But that didn't matter. He could decide to hold the enemy back, to stand and protect the Pollux system's sparse population. All that could achieve would be the destruction of his fleet.

He stared at the screen in front of him. The rumors about the enemy main guns were true; he took that as proven fact. Another bit of unsubstantiated intel also appeared to be accurate.

They don't have fighters…or, if they do, they're holding them back.

His eyes moved to his own squadrons, even now closing to attack range. He'd armed a larger-than-normal number of the fighters with torpedoes, but now, as he stared at the formation, he realized he'd sacrificed half his attack strength.

"All interceptors are to break off at once, commander, and return to base."

"Yes, admiral." Lambert repeated the order into the fleet-wide comm.

"I want those squadrons armed with torpedoes and relaunched, and I want it done in record time." Denisov's voice was hard, an almost implicit threat in it toward anyone who did less than his or her absolute best to see it happen.

"Yes, sir." Lambert nodded as he responded. The aide clearly agreed with Denisov.

The Union admiral looked out across the bridge, seeing the fear rising in his people. They were all beginning to realize what they faced, the magnitude of the threat bearing down on them. He felt it as well, and he took a deep breath and pushed it back, deep into the darkest recesses of his mind. He was the commander, sitting in the seat he'd craved for so long. Now, he realized the crushing burden his long-desired position carried. He was as scared as anyone, and as uncertain of what to do…but no one else could know that. His people couldn't see him scared or indecisive. He wasn't sure what it would take to defeat this enemy—or even survive against them—but he knew his spacers had to believe he did.

"Interceptor squadrons decelerating, sir. Project return in sixty-two to ninety-one minutes."

"Very well, commander. Advise all bays to be ready. I want ordnance in position when those ships land." That was the first nonstandard risk he was putting his people through. A flight deck stacked with plasma warheads wasn't the safest place for fighters to land. Or for flight crews to work.

But there was no time for safety. No time for anything except getting a second strike out before the enemy could close and blast his fleeing battleships to atoms.

"Yes, admiral."

"And all ships, advise medical staff. I want stim doses for all pilots as they land." His fighter jocks were likely to have quite a protracted series of battle ahead of them. Losses would probably be high, and the stress unbearable. There was nothing he could do about any of that, but he would damn well make sure they were all wide awake and alert.

Even if they were still running nonstop sorties twenty-four or forty-eight hours later…

* * *

Raketh sat in his sanctum, the massive screen on the far wall aglow with blue and yellow and red symbols. Those icons—circles, triangles, and a dozen other shapes—all had bits of tiny print next to them, but even his sharp eyes were too far away to read it.

That did not matter. He could ask the AI for information any time he needed it, but right then, he knew all he had to know.

He had taken a risk—somewhat mitigated, at least politically, by obtaining Chronos's approval before following through—and now it looked as though it might come to fruition.

All he had known about the Union and its fleet was what he had gleaned from captured Confederation data banks and records. The Confeds had destroyed the majority of their historical, navigation, and other records before they'd withdrawn. While the Kriegeri had recovered significant information, it was a stunningly small amount to be obtained from an entire world.

He'd gotten enough to give him an idea of what to expect from the Union forces, at least to the extent he believed the intel. Their ships were similar to those of the Confeds, but not quite as good, and they lacked the heavy primary weapons the Confederation battleships possessed. Their numbers were badly reduced from the recent war, and they were still in the early stages of rebuilding. One other thing had become abundantly clear from the data sweeps: the Confederation had a very impressive economic machine, and its production outstripped that of the significantly larger Union.

The Union small craft were inferior as well, both in design and in the skill and capabilities of their pilots. But Raketh wasn't sure how much stock he placed in that. Battles between the Rim powers appeared to have focused heavily on engagements between the squadrons of attack ships, and much of the quantification of force quality appeared to focus on such dogfights. Bombing runs against major capital ships were entirely different, and for all the skill and experience required for success, he suspected they were… He was not sure if "easier" was the right word.

He had reviewed the status updates from the main fleet. The reconfigured escorts had been quite effective in inflicting losses on the enemy's small craft. But he did not have any. The reserve's escort contingents had been depleted to reinforce the main fleet. If the Union pilots were anywhere close to as good as their Confed enemies, his battle line was going to take some damage.

But if they could run down the Union fleet, destroy it in

place, it would be worth the losses…and the war for the Rim would be that much closer to won.

He waved his hand over the sensor to call in his aide. A few seconds later, the doors at the end of the room slid open, and a Kriegeri officer, a kiloron, stepped in.

"Yes, commander?"

"The forward line is to increase acceleration to full." The Union forces were overmatched, outnumbered, and outgunned. But they could still escape.

Raketh had no intention of allowing that to happen…even if it meant pushing his lead elements directly into the approaching enemy strike craft. The first wave of attack ships had caused considerable damage, but it was clear the Union forces lacked the Confederation's newfound experience at using their bombers effectively. The reserve could afford to take some damage, especially if the reward was the utter destruction of the Union fleet.

There were two transit points behind the enemy formation, and the Union ships were roughly equidistant from them. But Raketh had valuable intel, comprehensive maps of the Union, courtesy of the archives on Dannith. One of the points led along almost a direct line to the Union capital, while the other only skirted along the Confederation border.

The Union commander was obviously capable…and he was clearly trying to mislead Raketh's forces about which way they might go. But they did not know Raketh had the intel he did, and that would be their downfall.

"All first-line ships are to set a course for jump point A." He'd send his leading ships to get between the Union forces and their line of retreat. "Second-line vessels to adjust vectors to 120.260.090 and increase thrust to eighty percent." The second line would move as though it planned to try to cut off the other escape route, the decoy point that led away from the vital Union systems. Then, at just the right instant, they would change course again and press the disordered enemy against the force behind them.

It would not be success. It would not be victory.

It would be annihilation.

* * *

Denisov watched as his fighters sliced into the pursuing Hegemony formations, groups of four and five, sometimes all that remained of entire squadrons cut down by defensive fire, pushing to ranges far closer than normal. The absence of defending interceptor squadrons opened the door for bombing runs to point-blank range, but the accuracy of the enemy's point defense fire made such strikes costly.

He'd directed the AI to feed him data on squadron loss ratios, and the conclusions, however preliminary, were startling. The inexperienced squadrons were getting torn to shreds, and the veterans, while suffering losses, were adapting quickly to the new situation. They were handling evasive maneuvers better, and their casualties were correspondingly lower.

"Commander, all wing leaders are to stay on top of their squadrons. Evasive maneuvers at max for all ships going in for attack runs."

"Yes, sir." Lambert repeated the command, with all the force in his voice that Denisov had put into his.

The Union admiral stayed focused on the screen, his attention almost entirely on the fighter wings. His battleships were already pulling back, trying to stay away as long as they could from the longer-ranged heavy weapons of the enemy vessels. The Hegemony ships were faster, but the need to deal with his bombers was slowing their advance, buying his capital ships time to...

To what? Escape? No war has ever been won by running away.

And yet what else could he do? His squadrons were fully committed. The second wave—the ships launched first as interceptors—was attacking, while the initial strike force had returned to the launch platforms, their ships already halfway through being refitted and rearmed. They'd be back out and headed into the fight in less than thirty minutes. Minus the fifteen percent of their number that had never returned from the first attack.

Denisov knew already that whatever course he took, however the Union fought this new enemy—and there was no longer any doubt the Hegemony was an enemy and not a potential ally—the fighters would be the most effective weapon in the arsenal. He remembered the Confederation wings from the past war, and he imagined they had developed all sorts of new tactics for facing the Hegemony. His people were behind, but he wasn't going to let them stay there. Not if the Union was going to have a chance. Any chance at all.

Hell…this isn't a Union problem. These people are here to conquer the entire Rim.

Chapter Seven

The sky was dim, the shafts of early morning light mixing with residual fog to create a thick gray haze. Holcott could barely see through it, and he was grateful, for once, to endure such a handicap. A lack of visibility was a negative in almost any operation in war, but he was there, looking through the lenses of his scope, to see something he'd just as soon miss.

Still, even such a fleeting mercy was not to be his. The dawn light was intensifying, and the heavy fog began to dissipate in the warming air. Gaps opened up in the field of view, and from where he lay, he could see what he'd known he would, what he'd desperately hoped was a mistake.

At least a dozen figures stretched along a line in the valley below, a stretch of low grasslands just outside Port Royal City.

Fourteen, he thought, as he finished his count.

They were all clad in the same dark gray uniforms. They stood like statues, and not one showed any sign of fear or desperation. They were marines—his marines—and they were behaving as such.

Right to the end.

They stood there, lined up against the remains of an old

masonry wall, as a row of stocky soldiers stood in a line twenty meters away. The Kriegeri looked strange to Holcott. Their implants gave them a different profile than normal human beings, a sinister hint of something alien. But he knew a firing squad when he saw one.

The men and women in that line, standing so stoically, facing death with grim courage, they were *his* people...and they were there because they had followed his orders.

He'd sent them in, along with over a hundred of their comrades, on a strike against one of the Hegemony convoys. It was a normal operation, no different than a hundred others he'd planned and executed since the defense of Dannith had turned from a military operation into a partisan resistance. No different, save in the outcome.

Other attacks had failed, a few miserably, with vastly higher casualty figures. Losses had been heavy even in the most successful strikes, but this was the first time he'd seen his people captured, and witnessed the grim reality of what that meant.

The resistance was failing.

He lay on his stomach, looking down at fourteen of his marines about to be executed, and his stomach roiled with hateful intensity. He wanted to vomit or scream...something. What he really wanted to do was kill Kriegeri, and the Masters who commanded them. But he remained quiet. It had been a risk to come at all, to venture so close to the city. It was closer than he'd dared to send anyone in months. He had no hope of saving his people.

He was a fool to take the chance he had in coming there. He was the leader of the resistance—what was left of it, at least—and the dozen marines with him were all veterans, and a meaningful segment of what little strength remained to his cause. His first reaction had been even more insane, a stirring declaration that he would, in fact, mount an operation to free the prisoners. He'd blurted it out without thinking, a slip in discipline he knew was only one symptom of his own crushing exhaustion and declining mental state. He'd never have let his marines see such a display months before, but the constant losses, the drop to half rations, and then again to one-quarter—it was all too much. Marines were tough, but they were men and women, too. They had their breaking points, and Holcott suspected his people were all near theirs.

As he was dangerously close to his.

He'd realized almost immediately that his impulsive promise to free his captive people was not only unfeasible, but that it was virtually guaranteed to cost the lives of the marines required to mount such a foolish operation. Still, he'd needed his closest comrades, the few remaining senior officers who still survived at his side, to pull him back from the precipice.

So, why had he come? Why was he there, taking an insane risk so he could watch his people die? He didn't have an answer, none save the meaningless, yet uncontestable fact that he *had* to be there.

He stared down, lying still, fully aware that anything that drew attention to his small group would provoke a deadly response. He felt the urge to leave, but he couldn't do it. Perhaps it was self-flagellation, but whatever force was at work, it was irresistible.

He *had* to stay. He had to watch these fourteen men and women die. He owed it to them.

Then he and his small band of comrades could make their way back to HQ, back to the day-to-day duties of running a dying resistance operation.

* * *

Kaleth stood on the flat section of ground, his boots covered with mud created by late-night rains and early-morning fog. He was a kiloron, an officer commanding a thousand soldiers. His rank was well beyond that suitable for the commander of an execution detail—and, indeed, he commanded far more than the twenty Kriegeri lined up before the captured enemy fighters.

His soldiers were in every building within five kilometers, hiding in patches of woods, behind rock outcroppings, even crouched down behind ridgelines…anywhere they could lie in wait for the resistance fighters he hoped would come.

He'd been skeptical. Any rescue attempt would be foolhardy, even in the seemingly exposed spot he'd chosen for the executions, and the commander of the defense forces turned resistance fighters was anything but a fool. His resources *had* to be dwindling, his forces on the verge of starvation, and yet they fought on, and they had caused massive disorder among the occupation forces.

He would simply have killed the prisoners inside the city if it had been his decision. But the orders to try to entice the partisans had come from Develia herself, and the Master in command of ground operations was to be obeyed without question.

Kaleth felt some resentment when a Master like Develia refused to heed the advice of her far more experienced Kriegeri subordinates. He did not dispute the system that valued genetic quality, but he sometimes felt frustrated by the arbitrary line that seemed to divide the highest of one level from the lowest of the next. He, himself, had almost achieved Master status when he'd submitted to the Test, and he had a cousin who had actually succeeded in advancing to the exalted rank—a great honor for the family, though one that gave Kaleth pause. He'd always thought Teleth was a bit slow, and Kaleth had never lost a game of chess with his cousin, at least before the Test put a great gulf between them, and advanced one of them to a life of great opportunity while relegating Kaleth to the hard life of a Kriegeri combat officer.

He looked around, disregarding such thoughts. Old frustrations offered little of productive worth, and he had a job to do. "You may proceed, hectoron," he said grimly, still looking around the surrounding hillsides, not quite convinced the enemy hadn't foolishly taken the bait he'd laid out.

"Sir!" The officer turned on his heels and stepped forward, next to the line of executioners. "Ready," he snapped, slapping his boot down hard on the still-wet ground. It made more of a wet, splashing sound than the hard click Kaleth suspected the officer had intended.

The soldiers brought their weapons up, all twenty moving

almost as one, with the practiced efficiency of a group born and bred for combat.

"Aim!" The officer's voice grew in volume and intensity. The troopers stood still, their silhouettes bulky with implants against the rising light.

Kaleth stood and watched, even as the hectoron said, "Fire," and the entire squad discharged their weapons in unison. He would have looked at the line of stakes, and confirmed what he knew was the virtual certainty the prisoners were all dead, but he'd seen something.

Or, at least, he thought he had.

"Hectoron," he said into his comm unit, speaking to another officer of the same rank as the firing squad commander. "Coordinates G302/092. I saw a flash, possibly a reflection. Investigate at once."

"Yes, sir," the officer snapped, his voice pure discipline, without a hint of weakness or emotion.

Kaleth let his hand drop, still holding the comm unit, and looked back, his enhanced eyes scanning every meter, looking for what he'd seen.

What he thought he'd seen.

* * *

"Colonel Blanth, I admire your tenacity, I really do. You are a warrior, as I am. I respect your dedication to your people still in the field…though I would be lying if I did not say you might have saved many of them if you had helped us end this costly resistance sooner. Now, most of them are dead, and the rest soon will be. They are at the end of their resources. I cannot imagine the misery and suffering their continued refusal to disarm inflicts on them. If you were to order them to lay down their arms, perhaps I could see to some leniency for their past actions, some exception from the mandatory death sentence for captured rebels."

Blanth looked over at the Master and smiled. It wasn't an indication of joy, nor of friendship; though while he certainly didn't consider the Hegemony Master to be a friend, despite his best efforts, his hatred for Carmetia had diminished. The Hegemony commander had been entirely humane with him, and she'd spared him even from enhanced interrogations.

That was, as much as anything, he suspected, because she knew he had very little useful information. He'd been a prisoner for months now, and wherever his marines were, and whatever they were planning, he knew no more about it than she did. All he could do was to help her disrupt their operations by ordering them to stand down—and he was fairly sure he'd made it clear that was something he would *never* do, even if she took off the kid gloves and brought out the thumbscrews.

"Carmetia." He'd been uncomfortable calling his jailor by her name, but she'd insisted so many times that he'd finally given in. Now, it seemed almost normal. "We both know I am not going to help you hunt my people down."

"But you might be able to save some of them. If you do nothing, they will die, Steven. All of them."

Blanth sighed, not an indication of boredom, more of surrender to a difficult truth. "Most of them are dead already. And you could never spare those who are still in the field, not after the damage they've done. We both know that. I may not be a Master, but I am no fool." He suspected Carmetia just might have been willing to grant clemency to any survivors, but he couldn't imagine her superiors, who *had* to be riding her about how long the pacification was taking, would go along with it. She would have to show them that she'd exterminated the defenders who had so upset operations on Dannith. Blanth's only question was: would he be the final body in that mass grave?

He didn't know, but after all that had happened, he didn't think he cared. He wanted to live, but death would also be a release from the guilt, the grief, the anguish at all he had seen. And he didn't particularly relish living a long life as a hostage of his Hegemony captors.

She looked as though she was going to say something further, a final effort to convince him, but before she spoke, the doors opened and a Kriegeri officer stepped inside.

"Forgive the intrusion, Master Carmetia, but Commander Develia is on the comm line."

Carmetia paused then answered, "I will take it in here." She reached over to a small table and picked up a headset.

Blanth was surprised when she didn't leave the room—or have him removed—and despite the fact that it was certainly no surprise she wasn't letting him listen in, he found himself disappointed. He was starved for information from the surface, on any clues he could get as to the status of his marines.

"Yes, commander. Report." Her tone was sharp. Not quite angry, but very matter-of-fact. Carmetia's relationship with her immediate subordinate, also a Master, though a far more junior one, had deteriorated with the ongoing resistance operations on the planet, and the junior officer's failure to put an end to it in a timely manner.

Blanth couldn't hear what Develia was saying, but he could see a brief touch of excitement in Carmetia's expression.

"That *is* good news, commander, at least potentially. If you are able to find the enemy's remaining strongholds, perhaps this seemingly endless nightmare will finally come to an end."

Blanth wondered if what he was watching was the truth, or a charade concocted to convince him to give in to Carmetia's demands. His skepticism told him that was exactly the case, but there was something in the Master's voice, her expression. He wasn't sure, but was it...sincerity?

His stomach clenched. *Holcott has performed magnificently...but have they finally cornered him?*

In some ways, Blanth imagined an end to the fighting would be a relief. But it would also be defeat, as bitter and soul-killing as such things could be.

Blanth knew one thing: if the end came, down on the surface, he would mourn the dead.

And part of him would envy them.

Chapter Eight

CFS Dauntless
Orbiting Megara, Olyus III
Year 318 AC

"We've got energy readings from the transit point, admiral." Atara Travis sat in her chair, the captain's seat on *Dauntless*'s sprawling bridge. She'd commanded the vessel for several years now, and if *Dauntless*'s role as Admiral Barron's flagship had muddied the waters between them, she didn't mind. She knew Barron worried that he overshadowed her, that his presence robbed from her the true experience of independent command. But she was proud of what they had done in their years together, and for all her early years as an intractable individualist, she realized she'd become an immovable part of the team. It was where she belonged…and where she wanted to stay.

Her portfolio of duties was an extensive one, and included the command of the massive battleship, as well as wearing her other hat, as Tyler Barron's aide and tactical officer. It was somewhat out of the ordinary, perhaps, for an officer to take on so much, but she and Barron worked together almost as though they were linked telepathically. Sometimes she thought she *could* actually hear him thinking, before he even spoke, and the fruits of their flawless teamwork had been evident in an almost uninterrupted string of successful operations.

"One of the scouts?" Barron's tone was cautious, some tension bleeding through, but nothing too upsetting. Everyone on *Dauntless*—hell, everyone in the entire fleet and the system— knew the Hegemony forces would eventually come through that transit point. So far, there had also been considerable traffic, but it had been limited to movements of the scouting forces positioned on the other side of the jump. Admiral Nguyen had ordered reports every four hours, a fail-safe, just in case an enemy move somehow managed to knock out the scouting force before it could get the word back to Olyus.

There was nothing scheduled for several hours, but Travis was no readier to assume the invasion had come than Barron was. It was far likelier something mundane.

But her stomach felt differently.

She glanced at the screen, checking the readings. It definitely wasn't enough energy to signal a fleet transit, at least not yet. It wasn't even enough for a scout ship.

"Low-level readings, admiral. Looks light, even for a scout. A shuttle, maybe? Or a drone?"

Neither of those would be optimistic signs. The scouting force's orders were clear: transit back immediately and report any contact with Hegemony forces. She couldn't imagine why Captain Elsinore would disregard her instructions.

Unless a drone was all she could get back.

An instant later, she had the answer. A drone came ripping through the transit point at high velocity.

A battered, battle-scarred drone that had clearly *just* made it. "Admiral…"

"I see it, Atara. I think we all see it—and we all know what it means." Barron turned and looked across the few meters between their posts, and his eyes connected with hers, a silent communi- cation of the kind they'd shared for more than a decade. Then Barron's face hardened, a stony expression taking shape. "Patch the report through to me as soon as it is decrypted. And send a communique to Admiral Nguyen immediately. Advise him indi- cations are strong that the enemy is on the move."

"Yes, sir."

Barron leaned back in his chair and drew a deep breath,

holding it for several seconds before exhaling. Then he looked back toward Travis's station.

"Issue a fleet order, commander."

He waited for her to look up, for her gaze to meet his one more time. Then he spoke, almost softly, with no emotion save a gentle grimness.

"Battle stations."

* * *

"All right…you all know where we are. You all know why we're here, what will happen if we don't stand and hold this line. The four of you are veterans, and I say that only because I don't know a stronger word to describe your experience and quality. Crack, elite…they all apply to each of you. I have fought alongside you, some of you for a very long time. I could give you a speech, try to work you up for battle, but there is no need of that. Not with the four of you."

Stockton stood on *Dauntless*'s flight deck, completely ignoring the cacophony of the battleship's launch crews working feverishly to prep the ship's six squadrons for the battle that had long been coming, and now seemed to be almost upon them. The drone data was fairly comprehensive, and it left little doubt the enemy was on the move. Still, there had been no sign of additional energy readings at the transit point, and normally, Stockton would have waited until that confirmation to launch. But nothing about the present situation was normal, and he couldn't afford to wait. His wings *had* to hit the enemy as hard and as often as they could, and the fight he intended to give those Hegemony bastards right there, at Megara, started with slamming into their formations just after they transited and went through the minefields.

Then the fight would just continue, through the hours, days…longer. There would be no sleep, no food, save an occasional sandwich wolfed down while a fighter was being refitted. There would be no end to the carnage and exhaustion. This was *the* battle, the one he'd seen in his mind in the distance, through the smoke and fire of the terrible fights he'd already led his pilots through. This was the fight that would save the Confederation...or lose it. It was a simple truth, and words poured into his mind, forming one rallying cry after another. But the two men and two women in the room with him did not need such encouragements. They would do what they had to do, what he'd commanded them to do, because he doubted any of them even knew how to give less than one hundred percent.

"We're ready, Raptor," Dirk Timmons said. He'd known Stockton the longest, and he was the only one there who'd ever really challenged the fleet's top pilot for supremacy. "We're ready to follow you...wherever you lead."

The words were meaningful, especially coming from the one pilot who'd been a true *rival,* a man Stockton had once casually despised, and one who'd returned the feeling in full. They were well past that now, of course, and Stockton considered Timmons one of his few true friends. And in the return to duty of the badly wounded pilot, Stockton saw a flicker of justice in an otherwise dark and terrible nightmare. It had taken the terrible threat of Hegemony invasion to override the navy's regulation relegating Timmons and his prosthetic legs to the Academy classrooms. Now one of the best pilots who ever lived had been returned to the cockpit, where he belonged.

"It's an honor to lead you all." Stockton's response was heartfelt, but it still felt strange to be in command...of anything really, beyond his old Blue squadron, but especially of the vast force of fighters assembled in the Olyus system, almost five thousand strong.

His rise since his Blue squadron days had been dramatic and unsettling, driven in part by the increased importance of the squadrons in the fight against the Hegemony. Even as he sat in the small room, alone with his top four comrades, he thought of his last true pilot-commander he'd known, and the closest friend he'd ever had. Kyle Jamison had been gone for years now, just one of so many thousands of men and women Stockton had known who'd been claimed in the endless battles of the past decade. He mourned all his lost comrades, but the loss of

Jamison was still an open wound, and he still thought of his friend every day.

Kyle would be here now, if he was still alive, where I sit... and I would be facing him, a fifth horseman, sitting with Warrior and Lynx and the others.

There was no time for such thoughts. Rumors were sweeping through the fleet that a drone had transited in. Tensions had been high, and every crew member in the fleet, whether pilot, gunner, or engineer—even a fourth-rate spacer who cleaned out reactor cores—knew the word could come at any time that the enemy was there.

"I think it would be smart if all of you transferred back to your base ships now, just in—"

He never got to finish the sentence. The room was bathed in the red glow from the two lamps on the wall, and the battle-stations klaxons sounded.

The enemy was there.

* * *

"If you have a moment, Tyler, I'd like to have a word with you." Dustin Nguyen was old, by far the most aged officer in the active fleet. He'd been retired when the last war with the Union had begun, the fourth such conflict, but he had served in both the second and third incarnations of the long struggle between rival nations. He'd fought alongside some of the most renowned officers who'd served the Confederation, and he'd won no small amount of acclaim for his victories. He was the only active officer in the navy who had served with Tyler's grandfather, the legendary Admiral Barron, who stood like a giant in the Confederation's history.

Barron didn't have a moment, not even part of one, but Nguyen was his commander, and a tenuous link of sorts to his lost grandfather. He wasn't capable of refusing.

"Of course, admiral. Let's step into my office."

The two men walked toward the back of the bridge and down the short corridor that led to the two private workspaces, one for *Dauntless*'s captain and the other for the admiral flying his flag on the battleship. They both stepped inside, and Barron gestured toward one of the chairs.

"No, Tyler. Thank you, but I only need a minute, and I suspect that's all we have. I just wanted to tell you something before the battle begins, something I want you to know now…in case we do not meet again." The admiral paused. He was weak, that was clear, and although Barron still believed in his reasoning for turning down the top command in favor of the reactivated Nguyen, he worried whether the aged officer had the physical stamina to endure the likely long and difficult fight ahead.

"Yes, sir. Of course." Barron didn't know what Nguyen wanted to tell him—they'd already discussed every aspect of the battle plan more than once—and he was well aware of everything he had to do to attend to his task force before Hegemony ships started pouring through the transit point.

"I just wanted to tell you what a tremendous job you have done, what a fine and brilliant officer you've grown to be. Your missions, your successes, have rivaled those of your grandfather…and even exceeded them. I knew the admiral well, Tyler, as you are aware, and I just wanted you to know how deeply and profoundly proud he would be of you if he was here."

Barron hadn't known what to expect from the old admiral, and that definitely hadn't been it. The words took him by surprise, and he stood for a moment, just staring back in some sort of shock. He'd always strived to live up to his famous grandfather's reputation. He wanted to honor the lost hero, and also to emerge from his shadow, to stake his own claim at renown. Hearing Nguyen's words, delivered with a striking sense of sincerity, he almost lost his iron grip on his emotions.

"Thank you, admiral," he finally said, his words coming slowly and with some difficulty. "I miss my grandfather, and have always sought to honor his memory. For one of his comrades to speak as you have…" He didn't finish the sentence. The words just didn't come, but the expression on Nguyen's face told Barron he'd gotten his meaning across.

"My shuttle is waiting, Tyler. Fortune go with you, my

friend." Nguyen was flying his flag on *Vanguard*, one of the new, enhanced *Repulse*-class battleships.

"And with you, admiral." Barron nodded and then snapped off something close to a perfect salute. "I'll escort you to the launch bay, sir."

"No, Tyler…you have much to do. I will not take an admiral from his bridge when the fleet is on battle stations. Your people need you, and I am not so old and fragile that I can't make it to my shuttle unassisted." The admiral bowed his head slightly, and then he turned and walked back out into the hall, leaving Barron alone with his thoughts.

Nguyen's words still echoed in his mind, and he wondered if the old officer had just worked him a little, rallied him with the skill and dexterity he'd always used to draw the best from his own people.

Or if the words spoken had been truth, if Nguyen had been not only helping him, but discharging an old debt of sorts, speaking for a lost friend in his absence.

Or was it both?

Barron didn't know, but if the last Admiral Barron was watching over him, he hoped it would give him the strength he would surely need.

He would do all he could, give every trace of energy and skill that remained to him to the fight.

He would not fail the Confederation.

And he would not fail his grandfather.

Chapter Nine

Denisov watched as the second wave of bombers steaked toward the approaching Hegemony battleships, moving into attack range and launching their runs. It still seemed strange to send in massive groups of torpedo ships with no fighter protection at all, but he'd become entirely convinced the intel was correct.

The Hegemony didn't have fighters.

What they did have was a powerful line of capital ships, larger, stronger, and more technologically advanced than anything his fleet possessed. Those vessels were closing rapidly, their great engines putting out thrust levels he could barely imagine, and certainly couldn't match.

He'd been pulling back his battle line, keeping his big ships out of range of the enemy main guns, but he knew that was no plan for victory. He could only fall back for so long before the enemy caught him, and it was time to decide. Should he stand and fight? And if he chose instead to break and run, which way should he go?

He'd maneuvered his forces as cannily as possible, trying to confuse the enemy as to whether he would fight it out or run, and which way he would go if he did retreat. He had to assume the Hegemony commander had significant information on the transit routes in the Union, and it was a good bet his counterpart expected him to retreat on Montmirail.

That made sense. It was tactically correct. But Denisov wasn't sure he was going to do it.

Retreating on the capital *did* made sense, at least according to the normal standards of war. But Denisov knew his fleet couldn't defeat the enemy force. Not in Pollux, nor sitting under the guns of the Montmirail fortresses. The enemy was just too strong.

If he fell back on Montmirail, the Union would soon be cut off from Confederation space, and the enemy would have split the two greatest Rim powers more permanently than a century of war and hatred already had.

The Confeds were his enemy. The Union had fought four wars with its neighbor in a century, and resentment and bad feeling were deeply implanted in the minds and hearts of his crews.

And himself.

But now, he was imagining something different. A Confederation that was not an enemy, but an ally. Was such a thing even possible?

He thought of the great Confed battleships, with Tyler Barron and the rest of the grim veterans commanding them…as comrades and not adversaries. His mind reeled. But he held grimly to the image.

The thoughts were fuzzy, still forming, but the feeling inside him was strong, powered by a need he could not doubt. Even with what little he knew of this new enemy, looking out at the force closing on his ships, he was sure of one thing.

The Rim had to unite if it was to have any chance at all.

If I fall back on the line to Montmirail, we will never have the chance to link up with Confederation forces and meet the enemy in strength.

As alien as the concept was to him, his mind began to formulate strategies around it. A combined Confed-Union fleet could almost certainly defeat the force there in Pollux battling his ships. He didn't know what other fleets the Hegemony possessed, how great a numerical advantage they had, but it didn't take advanced analysis to figure the stronger a force the Rim could field, the better chance it had.

But if I fall back on the other course, along the border and into the Confederation, I'll be cut off from the heart of the Union. I'll be at the mercy of the Confeds.

The idea horrified him. Denisov still saw the most recent war as a conflict that could have been won rather than lost. Years of Sector Nine harassment, even the murders of officers who'd come under some kind of suspicion—or, in one case he remembered bitterly, whose wife a member of the Presidium wanted for himself—had drained away the skill and professionalism of the officer corps. The Confeds had fought well—Denisov grudgingly admitted that, at least to himself. But he still truly believed the Union forces could have won the contest... if they'd been left alone to do it, if the most skilled and capable commanders had been given free rein to conduct operations as they'd seen fit.

There was another concern with the route toward the Confederation. Denisov's orders were clear. In the event of any problems, return to Montmirail. Retreating in the other direction would be a direct violation of orders. Even if Villieneuve was likely to approve such a strategy—and it seemed virtually a certainty he wasn't—there was no time to get a message to the capital. Denisov had to make a decision, and he had to do it now. His heart told him to head toward Confederation space. His mind did, too.

But the knot of fear in his gut held him back. He would be openly breaking with Gaston Villieneuve. That would have been dangerous enough when Villieneuve had been the head of Sector Nine and a member of the Presidium, but now, he was the sole and unchallenged dictator of the Union. If Denisov disobeyed, he would be relieved the instant he returned to Montmirail.

Relieved? That was putting it lightly. If he took off toward

Confederation space and Villieneuve caught up with him, he'd be as good as dead. At best, he could hope for a quick bullet to the head.

At worst…

Villieneuve doesn't have to catch up with me. How many undercover political officers are in this fleet? And what orders do they have if I do anything unauthorized? Gaston Villieneuve was both a genius and a fool to Denisov's way of thinking, but more than anything, he was paranoid. He'd have imagined a hundred ways his admiral could betray him.

A hundred ways I am being watched…

Denisov stared at the screen, trying to take his mind off that upsetting fact, at least for a few minutes. *You're never going to make it out anyway. Those ships are too fast.*

Unless…

His eyes fixed on the map of the system, on the outer planets. Maybe, just maybe…

He did calculations, his fingers running rapidly across the small workstation at his command chair. *It just might work.*

"Commander, fleet order. All ships are to engage maximum thrust, course toward the Avignon transit point." The way back to Montmirail.

But the fleet wasn't going to Montmirail.

Denisov's eyes were fixed on the map, focused on the large gas giant in the outer reaches of the system. Its gravity well was huge, and enormously powerful.

Strong enough for one hell of a gravity assist…

He would take the fleet toward the Avignon point, show all signs he was running back to Montmirail, as the enemy no doubt expected. And once they'd changed their own vectors, he would issue new navigation orders. If the calculations were dead-on, the fleet might *just* manage it, a rapid vector change, and one that put his ships on a direct course toward the Sauvon transit point.

And the Confederation.

Assuming they made it out at all. If the enemy thought that he was falling back on his lines of communication, the ruse would give his people a chance. But it would still be one hell of a race to the point if those Hegemony monsters opened up at full thrust and pursued.

And assuming I make it out. He had no doubt there were political officers planted in the fleet, covert ones backing up the ones he knew about. He'd have to find them, somehow...because if his instincts about Villieneuve were correct, the Union leader would almost certainly have at least one operative planted on *Illustre* with orders to assassinate Denisov if he veered too far from his orders.

And heading toward the Confederation was about as far as he could get, short of surrendering outright to the Hegemony.

* * *

Raketh felt the distant rumbling under his chair, his feet. *Omadias* was accelerating at full thrust, directly toward the retreating Union fleet. He had expected to eventually be compelled to pursue the enemy in order to finish the battle, but he was surprised at how quickly the force had broken formation. The enemy bombing strikes had been less effective than the Confederation's, but then, this was the first time the Union had faced Hegemony forces. The Confeds had been fighting for more than a year, and they had had time to maximize their tactics against an enemy that did not possess small craft of their own.

As he watched the enemy flee, he began to believe the data from the Dannith banks. The Confederation's analysis of Union capabilities had not only been fair, but perhaps too generous.

Maybe the last war broke their spirit.

Whatever was at play, it did not matter. Raketh knew he could catch their fleet before they could transit...and when he did, he would destroy it. Any small number of damaged ships that made it through would be scattered fugitives, far too weak to oppose any invasion that followed.

The actual invasion of the Union would have to wait, of course, until the Grand Fleet had crushed the Confederation. Raketh could not keep the reserve tied up deep in Union space for long, and he lacked the ground forces needed for a true invasion and pacification. But with their fleet obliterated, the Union would be defenseless, waiting helplessly for the Hegemony forces to return and finish the job.

He had studied the intel on the Rim powers, analyzed their strengths and the dangers they might present. The Alliance, a polity out on the Far Rim, was somewhat of a concern. They were fierce, no doubt, but their technology was behind even that of the other Rim nations. And the rest of this far-out cluster of human habitation was divided into several dozen small entities, ranging from independent planets to federations and kingdoms of up to a dozen or so systems. They were fractured and weak, and once the Confederation and Union were gone, they would fall rapidly.

Then he would return at Chronos's side, and glory and esteem would wash away the shame of his retreat from Dannith.

* * *

"Commander Auverge...I am sorry, sir, but you are under arrest."

"I don't know what this is about, lieutenant, but I have neither the time, nor—"

The officer facing Auverge nodded sharply, and two of the spacers standing next to him moved forward and took hold of the officer's arms. Two others, standing off to the side, drew their sidearms.

"Lieutenant, I do not know who sent you, but—"

"I sent him, Pierre." Andrei Denisov stepped out from behind the bulkhead.

"Admiral? I do not understand."

"Sure you do. Did you really believe I didn't know you're Sector Nine?" Auverge had been easy to spot. He'd never been Denisov's worry. It was the more junior political officers, the ones that didn't stand out quite so blatantly that worried him. If he missed even a single one, it could easily prove fatal.

"Admiral...I don't know what's behind this, but I insist you release me immediately."

"Take him to the location we discussed, lieutenant."

"Yes, sir." The officer's voice was firm, no sign of hesitancy. That was probably foolish. Throwing in with Denisov now was dangerous. The admiral had chosen his people carefully, and as afraid as he was of disregarding Villieneuve's orders, he'd found the tensest part of the whole thing to be trying to decide whom he could trust.

Whom he could *really* trust.

Friendship was one thing, but involving others in a plot that could lead only to death for all involved if it failed was difficult. Suddenly, doubts appeared when considering those he thought of as friends. He questioned just how far they would go, how absolute their loyalty was to him.

The lieutenant was good, Denisov was almost sure of that. He'd plucked the officer from the ranks after the Battle of the Pulsar, and he'd obtained a commission for him. He was confident in his judgment, as sure as he could be of the officer's gratitude and loyalty.

He was less comfortable with the guards themselves, though the lieutenant had assured him they were reliable. Denisov had no reason to doubt that, but since he was effectively betting his life on it, he was still edgy.

"Commander Eustus is waiting in the designated location to...*interview*...Commander Auverge."

"Yes, sir." The officer waved to the guards, and they pulled the struggling Auverge down the hallway.

"You will pay for this, admiral. I insist you release me at once!"

Denisov turned and walked back toward the lift. He'd been gone from the bridge for too long. The Hegemony forces were closing rapidly, and the gravity-assist maneuver would begin soon. It had to be perfectly executed, or all his planning would be for naught.

He could still hear Auverge screaming, demanding release, his voice growing quieter as he was led farther down the corridor. Denisov detested the idea of using harsh methods to question members of his crew, even when they *were* Sector Nine agents and political officers who would think nothing of throwing him from one of the airlocks. But he had no choice, and even less now that he'd involved those he trusted. They *had* to make it work…or they would all die for their loyalty to him.

* * *

"Well done, commander." Denisov had intended more enthusiasm in his commendation for Lambert, but he was constrained by the need to hold back the contents of his stomach. The gravity assist had worked, at least for the sixty percent of the fleet that had so far completed it, and his ships were now on a vector more or less toward the Sauvon transit point.

Toward the Confederation border.

The ride had been a rough one, even to career spacers used to free fall and combat acceleration and deceleration. Union ships lacked dampeners and compensation systems as sophisticated as those in Confederation vessels, but even the newest ships rolling out of the Iron Belt shipyards would have been hard-pressed to offset the wild pressure the close pass by the gas giant had exerted on the Union ships, and on the men and women inside.

The bridge reeked of vomit, and at least half his officers were, at the very least, doubled over their stations and looking somewhat green. But such visible distress was a luxury that availed itself to normal spacers, even to bridge officers. Denisov was in command, and he was leading his people not only though desperate danger, but, from many points of view, into mutiny. He had to be above such things as being sick or seeming afraid. He had to be an inspiration, keep his people's attention focused on him…so it wasn't on the overwhelming strength of the enemy pursuing them, or the cold reality of what their actions meant to their futures and to their families back home.

He turned his head, slowly, closing his eyes for a few seconds until the bridge stopped spinning wildly in his field of view. He focused hard—an act far more difficult than it seemed—and he looked at the Hegemony ships on the scanner.

The enemy fleet was still on the same vector, still chasing the route the fleet had abandoned. Their vessels fired their engines, decelerating hard to change their vectors to follow his forces. But they couldn't copy the gravity assist; they were out of position. They would have to adjust course conventionally, and that gave Denisov's ships time—enough of a head start to just make it through the transit point.

Or just to miss it.

Exact calculations required better information than he had, especially on the levels of emergency thrust the Hegemony ships might be able to draw upon. If those ships were faster than he was guessing, if they could push just a little bit harder, Denisov and his people would still die in the Pollux system.

If his estimates were spot-on, they just might escape, for a while at least. A transit from Pollux would lead to a wild dash toward the Confed border, and beyond, to some system where he could contact the Confederation government…and somehow try to negotiate an alliance with his former enemy. A treaty he had no legal authority to propose or accept. He didn't speak for the Union, no matter how fancy a uniform he wore. But with any luck, if he could make his case, talk to his spacers and win them over, he just might speak for the Union's *fleet*.

Assuming he got away from his pursuers, that was. Assuming he somehow reached Confederation space before the Hegemony forces ran his fleet down and destroyed it. Assuming he got someone high up in the Confederation hierarchy to listen. Assuming he didn't miss a political officer lurking in the shadows, one with summary execution orders.

He took a deep breath that almost gave him the heaves. Assuming all that…then he would just have to learn to work with his hated enemies, and to figure out a way to defeat an enemy that outmatched both the Union and the Confederation in every measurable area, save fighter squadrons.

He'd known fleet command would be a burden when he'd accepted it, but now he wondered if it was more than just the gravity-assist maneuver trying to bring his last meal back up.

Chapter Ten

CFS Dauntless
850,000,000 Kilometers from Megara, Olyus III
Year 318 AC

The Battle of Megara – The Initial Onslaught

Barron knew what was coming. He'd faced the Hegemony forces for almost two years now, ever since the White Fleet had first encountered its forces. It had long been assumed that the Cataclysm had wiped out all human populations save those on the Rim. That logic seemed flawed now, obviously, yet he understood how it had come to be accepted fact. The Badlands closest to Confederation space had been depopulated, and system after system had been found to contain nothing but dead worlds, ancient graveyards with little to offer save for bits and pieces of lost technology.

Now, the sheer audacity of the White Fleet and its mission was evident to him, the arrogance that had sent a force so far from home, searching for scraps of ancient science and clues to the lost history of the late empire. He'd allowed himself to imagine finding some traces of survivors, if not living humans, perhaps indications that some people had at least lived beyond the dates normally set as the end of the Cataclysm.

But they hadn't found scattered survivors or their remnants.

Instead, they had awakened a giant and announced to a vast and technologically superior nation that billions of human beings still lived beyond the Badlands, on the Rim.

He'd wallowed morosely more than once, sitting in his quarters alone, imagining how many more years the Rim might have had before the Hegemony found it. Decades, even centuries. The Hegemony, too, had almost certainly taken the silent death of the Badlands as a sign that no life endured farther out.

But the audacity to reach out and explore had brought back death and destruction.

He'd watched the scanners as the energy levels raced off the charts, and then he'd stared intently at the display as ships began to appear. He'd imagined watching the enemy battleships come in. He expected they would come at high velocities, in an effort to close with the Confederation battle line as quickly as possible, limiting the time for repeated bomber strikes.

But he saw over a hundred symbols now, all of them tiny circles that represented Hegemony vessels.

And not one of them was a battleship.

The enemy had sent its escorts through, the line of modified cruisers and frigates reconfigured for anti-bomber duty. The instant he saw what was happening, he knew…and he cursed himself for not expecting it. The enemy had been developing its anti-fighter tactics for months now, and that effort had clearly continued. Confederation tactics had become rigid, its fleet maneuvers predictable. That was by necessity, born of the need to protect the heavy ships from enemy railguns, but it didn't make them any less obvious.

Why wouldn't they bet none of our heavy units would be far forward? It's only common sense. It's what we've done in every battle.

He watched as the escorts pressed forward, moving at close to two-tenths of light speed and blasting their engines at full, gradually redirecting their vectors toward Megara itself…and then as the lead units pushed into the outskirts of the minefield, and the first x-ray lasers opened fire.

The mines were simple devices, not really mines at all, but a series of high-energy x-ray lasers mounted around a thermonuclear warhead. When targets entered range, the AI firing systems locked on to the closest ships and detonated the bomb. The massive energy released was channeled into half a dozen laser blasts, nanoseconds before the atomic fury consumed the entire apparatus. If the final acts of the doomed AIs were properly executed, half a dozen beams, each one several times as powerful as Confederation primaries, would rip through space at the speed of light and cut into the targeted ships.

With devastating results.

The beams did indeed work, perhaps better than Barron had dared to expect. The targeting was spot-on, the pulses striking with unimaginable power. But the targets weren't the railgun-armed battleships Barron and his comrades had hoped they would be.

One after another, escort ships pushed into the field's targeting area, and when they did, they died. A single laser was strong enough to destroy, or at least cripple, one of the smaller ships, and even the large cruisers, new additions to the enemy's escort line, were almost spit open by the deadly blasts…and then finished off by a second hit.

Barron had hoped the mines would be effective. He'd believed they would be, in part because the deployment was something new, a threat that would be a surprise to the enemy. It was a disappointment the Hegemony heavy units had not engaged the fields, and it had dark implications for the rest of the battle, but at least Stockton's wings would have a clearer opening to attack. The enemy escorts wouldn't be entirely gone, but there were going to be a lot less of them.

But Stockton's going to have to take out even more railguns…and that means even crazier, more desperate attack runs.

Barron didn't doubt his heroic pilot would do whatever was necessary, but neither did he harbor any illusions about the loss numbers he was likely to see.

He turned his head to stare at the far end of the display, where Stockton and just over half the squadrons in the system were already launched, floating in space and waiting for the attack command.

The order Barron would give.

On the far side of the display, Alicia Covington and Dirk Timmons waited, almost another two thousand bombers in serried ranks behind them. The Battle of Megara would go down in the history books in more ways than Barron could easily count. The greatest number of fighters, certainly, almost four thousand. The largest force of battleships the Confederation had ever fielded in one spot, and the most massive deployment of all vessels. Probably the greatest fixed fortifications as well, though Barron wondered if the struggle at Grimaldi base might not retain a claim to that particular notation.

The most ships lost. The most men and women killed.

Those final two were still supposition, of course, but Barron couldn't see how such losses were avoidable. His military mind, the cold and rational part of him that made him such a successful leader, was already imagining the decision that might have to be made, the order to save what was left of the fleet and flee to fight another time. That would be a horrendous moment, and he was grateful it would be Nguyen's burden and not his own. It was a little spark of cowardice, perhaps, or at least weakness, and he wasn't proud of it. But it was real nevertheless.

The Senate would never approve a withdrawal, of course. Barron didn't doubt the self-serving politicians had imagined that the labor of billions had gone into building the fleet just to protect their own wretched hides, but Barron understood the difference between fighting for the Confederation and fighting for the Senate. Still, he'd had his fill of munity, and again, if someone in the fleet had to tell the Senate to drop dead, he was glad Dustin Nguyen would be the one to do it.

He had one responsibility of his own now, however, one given to him directly from Nguyen. The senior officer had deferred to Barron's experience facing the enemy, and given him the authority to send Stockton's people forward.

Barron stared at the display for perhaps another minute, though it seemed almost an eternity. He was hesitant to start the bloodbath he knew lay in the future…but there was no choice. And no time to waste.

"Captain Travis"—he looked across the two meters or so between them, as he had done so many times—"all squadrons are to commence the attack."

* * *

"You all heard the admiral's orders, so I don't have to repeat what he said. I don't have to go over what lies ahead of us, either. We've talked about it again and again, planned and prepared. Now it's time to do it, and I know the one thing above all others that I do not need to repeat to you all is what lies behind us. This is no longer a struggle along the frontier, nor a fight to save a strategically useful system. This is *the* battle, the one we've been preparing for since our Academy days. So, all I *will* say is: follow me. We're going straight past the surviving escorts, and damn whatever fire they throw at us. The mines blasted a decent hole in their forward defenses, but there are a hell of a lot of battleships beyond. That's all I care about. All we're going after."

Stockton took a deep and ragged breath.

"It is an honor to serve with each and every one of you." A pause. "All squadrons, power up engines…prepare to attack."

Stockton sat in his cockpit, a place that he could only think of as a second home, at least if he didn't consider it his first. Some people were born to do certain things, though not all of them found their true callings. For all the pain, the death, and the stress of his career, Jake Stockton knew he had been fortunate to find his. His work was difficult, dangerous, in many ways a nightmare. But there was nothing else he would choose, nowhere he would be, save in the tiny cockpit of his Lightning.

He took another breath, focusing on steadying himself, slamming down the cold wall that closed off distractions in combat.

He was a veteran, a legend in the fleet. His pilots spoke in whispered tones of his exploits, of his immunity to fear. Yet, for a man who was supposed to be unaffected by such things, he was finding it somewhat difficult to keep his hands from shaking. He wasn't sure how much of the fear was for himself, how much for his pilots, so many of them seeming almost like children to him, and how much for Stara, and for the others he cared about back in those ships lined up a few million kilometers behind his squadrons. He just knew one thing. It would be a hard and bloody day…or, more likely, days.

And none of those who survived would ever be the same again.

"All squadrons…attack."

* * *

"Admiral Barron has sent his wings in, sir."

Clint Winters stared across the bridge, his eyes fixed on Davis Harrington for several seconds before he responded to his aide. Finally, the words came, pushing through the uncertainty. He and Barron had agreed, and they'd both convinced Admiral Nguyen that the enemy battleships *had* to be the primary target. He knew that was a dangerous tactic, one that would almost certainly result in higher losses among the squadrons. It still made sense. There weren't enough of the new cluster bombs to arm the entire strike force, even if the decision had been made to do it…and, in the end, the enemy battle line, and its fate, would decide the fight. If they got enough railguns in close enough, the Confederation navy would be destroyed. The bombers *had* to break up that wave of battleships, and that meant gutting their way through the remaining enemy escorts, and taking whatever losses those ships could inflict.

He looked out at the rows and rows of tiny, pin-sized lights, each a squadron of roughly fifteen Lightnings. The faces of pilots slid past his eyes, as many as he knew personally and could remember. He suspected Barron had gone through a similar round of doubt.

Then he gave the order.

"Commander, all wings are to attack."

He heard the aide's acknowledgement, but it only registered as a distant, indistinguishable sound. Winters had been engaged with the Confederation almost constantly since the moment he'd answered Barron's call and rushed what forces he could from

Grimaldi to Dannith. He'd barely had time to think beyond the next deployment. But now the exhaustion was weighing heavily on him.

He'd begun fighting on the frontier, and now he found it difficult to believe his forces had been pushed all the way back to the Confederation's capital. He'd done all he could, employed every ruse, every tactic he could concoct, and yet he'd done almost nothing to hold the enemy back, or even to substantially delay their relentless advance.

Now, it's the final battle…

Or is it?

He couldn't imagine Admiral Nguyen ordering the fleet to abandon Megara…yet could the admiral allow the navy to be destroyed, to lose all hope of mounting any further resistance anywhere else? Even for Megara?

Winters didn't know the answer…and he didn't want to think about it. It was time to fight, and thoughts of defeat and retreat had no place in the forefront of his mind. He owed his people more than that.

He owed them some hope that they could win.

Even if it was nothing but lies.

* * *

"Group Beta…nav plan Green-eleven. Execute in five seconds…four…three…two…one. Execute!"

Olya Federov watched as one hundred and sixty-two Lightnings, about twenty percent of her entire force, engaged their thrust and pushed their vectors away from the dead-straight line the rest of the wings were following.

The cluster bombs were new, and there had only been enough ordnance to arm twelve of her squadrons with them. Her people were inexperienced with the new system, and there had been neither time nor spare reloads for more than a few practice runs per pilot. If the bombs performed as they were supposed to—and Anya Fritz had been surprisingly hopeful about the new system—it would be a major step forward in battling the escorts that had so devastatingly ravaged the Confederation and Alliance squadrons.

If there are enough…

Which there aren't.

The attack would be more of a test than a battle-changing event, but Federov still felt the vengeful need to see the deadly escorts blasted to hell for all they'd done to her people. With any luck, the small attack would add to the disorder the mines had already caused, and her main strike forces—and those of the other Horsemen—would get a chance to slip through and deliver their strikes on the enemy battle line.

She looked down at her screen, her eyes moving to the hazy clusters of dots. There were hundreds and hundreds of bombers—her own and Johannes Trent's—formed up side by side. It was a display of might she couldn't have imagined, even in the darkest days of the last war with the Union. She'd never seen the Confederation fleet so desperate. They had pulled fighters from every posting, regardless of experience or training level, to mass the greatest strength possible to send against the enemy. Hundreds of her pilots were out of their depth, nowhere close to experienced enough to conduct the kinds of aggressive attacks needed. It was a grim thought, and yet she knew it was the reality that her people faced.

The images on the display were complex and hard to read, too much information crammed into too small a place. The enemy escorts had been hit hard by the mines. That, at least, was a blessing. But many of them remained, the result of a shortage of mines not much different than that affecting the supply of cluster bombs. The Confederation's researchers and scientists were doing their part, racing to feed weapons into the hands of the warriors facing the enemy. But such things took time…time the Confederation simply might not have.

She had her orders. She knew what to do…and for once, she was grateful to lack agency in any of it. She would obey Stockton's orders, as she had for so long now. And she would do all she could to keep her thoughts off anything else. Losses, the importance of the battle, the consequences of defeat—she couldn't do a damned thing about any of it. So, she would focus on fighting enemy battleships.

"Group Alpha, on me. You all know the orders. We're going right through. Directly at those battleships. Full thrust, no deviation from course, no firing at the escorts. That's the Betas' job. The rest of you, let's go."

She took a deep breath, steeling herself against the impact she knew she would feel when she opened up her engines at full.

"Engage, all squadrons. Alpha Group, forward. Attack!"

Chapter Eleven

Hall of the People
Liberte City
Planet Montmirail, Ghassara IV
Union Year 222 (318 AC)

Gaston Villieneuve stared down at the report. He'd been sitting as his desk, reading the same words again and again, and he still couldn't quite bring himself to believe any of it.

Dead. Ricard Lille was dead.

It didn't seem real. The assassin—and the only one of his minions Villieneuve had ever called friend—was just too good. He'd faced countless enemies, killed more targets than Villieneuve could even guess. Lille hadn't always succeeded, especially when he'd been used for purposes beyond his core skill of killing. He'd botched the effort to bring the Alliance into the war against the Confederation, ultimately triggering a civil war that ended with the Palatians firmly on the side of the Confeds. But when Lille had been sent to kill, and only to kill, his success rate had been uncanny.

Villieneuve hadn't ordered Lille to kill anyone on Megara, though he suspected Desiree Marieles had died at his hands, despite the—almost certainly intentional—vagueness of the assassin's report on her death. The message about the agent's demise had been the last communication Villieneuve had

77

received from Lille. Marieles had done an impressive job in disordering things in the Confederation, and it appeared that she'd come remarkably close to pushing them into a full-fledged civil war of their own. That would have been a remarkable achievement, far beyond anything he'd expected when he'd sent her to Megara, but she'd been thwarted in the end by the usual cast of Confed officers and agents that had been a thorn in his side for years.

Marieles deserved better than a quick dispatch by Lille, but the more Villieneuve considered it, the more he'd come to believe it was for the best. Marieles had been ambitious, and maybe a little dangerous. Besides, the last thing he needed was for the Confeds to gather proof his people had been behind so many of their recent problems. He didn't doubt Barron and Holsten suspected Union involvement, but their cumbersome republic was run by squabbling politicians who were far less likely to get serious about sanctions against the Union, certainly without concrete proof.

Of course, they have their hands full right now anyway...

Villieneuve had hoped to hear back from his ambassadors, or even from the fleet he'd stationed at Pollux, a display of strength he'd hoped would secure an alliance with the Hegemony. He'd been patient, then distracted by news of Marieles's death and the initially unconfirmed rumors that Lille himself had also been killed. Now, he was becoming truly worried. He should have heard something by now.

Why hasn't Denisov even sent a routine report?

Villieneuve had pulled his new fleet commander from virtual obscurity, putting him in a position of power he could never have achieved on his own. Villieneuve had figured the officer retained some level of pointless idealism, but he'd also bet that Denisov would be loyal to his patron. Now, he began to have doubts, based not on logic or analysis, but on his own—usually accurate—paranoia.

Denisov is not a rebel, nor a mutineer. Besides, he's being watched. Even the watchers are watched.

Villieneuve had made sure the fleet was well staffed with

spies, a bewildering array of Political Division officers and undercover agents from the People's Protectorate. If Denisov had done anything unauthorized, even if he failed to make regular reports, Villieneuve would know.

But he didn't know. He hadn't received a word, not from his admiral, nor from the watchdogs he had surrounding the admiral.

Something was wrong.

He didn't know what, but there were two possibilities. First, some kind of Confederation action, as unlikely as it seemed while the Confed fleet was so heavily engaged with the Hegemony. Maybe they'd discovered more about Marieles's operation that he'd thought. He could see anger from that, even calls for a punitive strike. But from what he knew of the fighting, the Confeds had their hands full already. They certainly didn't have the forces free to strike at the Union's main fleet.

That left the Hegemony. Villieneuve had intended to do whatever he could to secure an alliance with the mysterious new force, but failing that, he'd planned to stay totally neutral. He couldn't imagine any power, even one as strong as the Hegemony appeared to be, would want another enemy when they were already dealing with the Confeds *and* the Alliance.

Now, he began to wonder. Was is possible the Hegemony *had* moved on Denisov's fleet? If so, the admiral had clear instructions to withdraw to Montmirail.

So, where was he? Where was the fleet? He would certainly have received word if the fleet was on the way back to the capital.

"First citizen, I am sorry to interrupt, but we have just received a communication from the fleet."

The sound of his aide's voice pulled him from his thoughts, and he felt the tension inside him relax a bit. *You're just too impatient. You knew Denisov would report…though I will discuss timeliness with him when he gets back to Montmirail.*

"On my line."

"Yes, first citizen. The transmission is encoded to Delta-Yellow protocols."

The relaxation he'd felt for a few seconds was gone. Delta-

Yellow wasn't military encryption. It was an old Sector Nine code.

The message wasn't from Denisov. It was from one of the political officers or agents in the fleet.

He felt his stomach tighten. His operatives had instructions to remain in cover unless something was seriously wrong.

He slipped his headset on—whatever he was about to hear, it was very likely highly sensitive information. His office was secure, of course, but it wouldn't hurt to take some extra care.

He recognized the voice as the message began. Decrypted messages sometimes lost some of the recognizable parts of the sender's tone, but Villieneuve knew at once who it was. Regina Descortes was one of the most senior agents with the fleet, and just about the most deeply implanted. He knew before she'd spoken a dozen words that her risking a communique could only mean something was disastrously awry.

He listened as the agent spoke, and as she did, he felt his insides tighten with panic. The Hegemony forces *had* attacked the fleet. Indeed, they would have caught and utterly destroyed it if Denisov hadn't acted quickly and decisively to pull his ships out. Losses were heavy, but the fleet remained a force, and that had been almost entirely due to Denisov's skill and talent as a commander.

Villieneuve felt a burst of satisfaction and pride. He'd finally found a capable commander and freed himself of the entrenched fools that had cost the victory in the Confederation War. He would reward Denisov when the admiral returned, even as he pushed him to prepare to defend the Union's inner systems.

But that feeling lasted only seconds before it was replaced by utter disbelief, followed almost immediately by unbridled rage.

He tapped the controls on the side of his headset, pausing the transmission, giving himself time to catch up to what he'd just heard. Denisov had indeed pulled the fleet back from destruction…but he'd taken it not on a course toward Montmirail, as he'd been ordered to do, but on a direct line across the border, toward the Confederation.

Treason!

The word rattled through Villieneuve's mind. What the hell was Denisov thinking? Villieneuve had always thought of the officer as naïve, without the political instincts to maximize his prospects in the absence of outside help. But he'd been sure Denisov detested the Confeds as much as he did. More, even. Villieneuve was a pragmatist, a man who would accept and believe anything that furthered his acquisition of power. Denisov was burdened by an integrity of sorts, and a blind loyalty to those who served with him. His hatred of the Confeds had its foundation deep in fallen comrades and battles lost, but it was genuine nevertheless.

What could have made Denisov disobey Villieneuve's orders and move toward the Confederation?

Was it possible Denisov hadn't had a choice? That the route he'd taken was the only one that allowed a chance of escape?

That *was* possible…but then again, no, it wasn't. Regina Descortes was one of Villieneuve's best people, an agent with a long track record of success and loyalty. She wouldn't have broken radio silence, risked her cover—not unless she was sure there was treachery.

Her orders…

He remembered the commands he'd given Descortes before the fleet left, her instructions in the—seemingly unlikely—event that Denisov violated Villieneuve's orders.

It was very simple, and an agent like Descortes would almost certainly carry out her orders. She was to confirm her suspicions, satisfy her own judgment that something was indeed happening. Then she was to do what had to be done.

She was to kill Andrei Denisov, assume custodial command of the fleet, and return to Montmirail.

Villieneuve hated the idea of losing the first truly talented commander he'd found in years, but even more disturbing was the realization that the fleet's return to Montmirail was now very likely blocked by the Hegemony fleet.

Descortes would almost certainly carry out her orders. She would kill Denisov, and that would leave the entire Union fleet cut off from home and pursued by a deadly new enemy.

Without the one man who could command the fleet, stay ahead of the pursuers, and find a way to survive the desperate struggle that had come upon them all.

Chapter Twelve

The Battle of Megara – The Horsemen Attack

Stockton brought his fighter around, slicing across the line of advance most of his wings had taken toward the enemy battle line. Federov and Trent were leading their wings in even as he angled his own vector to the side, instead of straight ahead toward the main strike force.

He called his senior commanders the Four Horsemen, a wink to a mysterious bit of pre-imperial literature he'd read at the Academy. Now he vowed to himself he would trust in the reason he'd given them the moniker: his complete faith in their abilities and their loyalty. Anya Federov and Johannes Trent could lead the waves of bombers against the enemy battleships, as both had done before. But the cluster-bomb-armed ships were blazing a new trail, employing a weapon they'd never used before. They needed Stockton, and even though his own ship carried a torpedo, and not a pack of cluster bombs, he'd resolved to follow them in, to stand with the small force of his pilots who'd thrown themselves at the deadly escorts with almost no concern for personal safety.

The losses had been severe, almost catastrophic, but the cluster bombs had proven to be enormously effective. Squadron after squadron had cut in, ripping toward the escorts, defying the deadly fire from the small ships. Dozens of fighters were hit. Some of their pilots managed to eject and preserve at least a chance of being rescued and returning to the fight, but most joined the ranks of their fallen comrades, the thousands of Lightning jocks who'd paid the ultimate price in the battles against the Hegemony.

The escorts were tough, even more effective than they'd been months before at Ulion, a fact that Stockton burned into his brain. If he survived the battle at Megara to fight again, he would never assume the enemy's tactics or equipment would be the same as the last time. The Hegemony was too quick to adapt, too advanced, and too capable at putting a new system into action.

But two can play at that game…

He'd watched for the last twenty minutes as the assigned squadrons delivered their payloads. The cluster bombs carried smaller warheads than plasma torpedoes…but a Lightning's bomb bay carried a payload of ten. They could be launched all together, vastly increasing the chance of scoring a hit—or the more experienced pilots could blast them out individually or in groups of two or three, extending the time they could continue their attacks.

There was just one drawback. Minimizing the size of the weapons had reduced their range dramatically. The cluster bombs had to be fired point-blank, and that meant taking an attacking ship right into the teeth of the target's defensive fire.

Stockton had left it to Federov to choose which of her squadrons would fight the holding action against the escorts, and as he watched, he realized she'd selected some of her most experienced people. The fighters sliced in and out of the disordered ranks of the escorts, hitting them while they were still coming out of the minefield.

They slammed into that disorganized mass of ships with a fury almost unimaginable. Fighter losses were restrained by the disorder in the Hegemony ranks, but increased again by the repeated attack runs. Fighters were going in three, four, even five times against enemy ships, enduring the withering point defense fire each time.

Stockton's ship raced forward, his thrust still blasting hard as he followed the last of Federov's bomb-armed squadrons in. He scanned the display, checking damage assessments, looking for a target that didn't have a squadron coming at it. He had a plasma torpedo, and he was damned sure going to put it to good use.

He nudged the throttle to the side, adjusting his vector slightly, bringing it in line with the escort he'd selected. It was one of the new cruisers. The thing seemed untouched, by either mines or by cluster bombs. Its defensive fire was utterly devastating, and Stockton felt the adrenaline flowing into his bloodstream as his ship moved directly toward it. The plasma torpedo was a powerful weapon, strong enough to take out the cruiser, or at least cripple it…if he could bring it in close enough and plant it directly amidships.

He jerked the controls back and forth, throwing his ship into a wild series of evasive maneuvers, even as he maintained a course on the chosen ship.

Laser blasts ripped past his ship, lighting up his scanner board, a few almost making his hair stand on end, they were so close. But his combination of AI assistance, talent, experience, and intuition held as he blasted toward the target ship alone.

He knew by then that the Hegemony vessel had identified him as the sole close threat. Every gun on that ship—and the cruiser had a *lot* of weapons—would be aiming at him.

He swallowed hard, again casting aside the notion that he was somehow immune to fear. He was scared to death, but, as he had so often done in the past, he was able to partition his thoughts. His focus was like iron, even as some part of him wanted to break off and run. Wanted to live.

His hand tightened on the controls, his index finger lying lightly on the firing stud. The torpedo was armed and ready, and he was well within range. But he wasn't in the range he wanted to be. Not yet.

He saw the symbol on his screen growing, the range figures dropping rapidly, his hands tightening as he slipped under five thousand kilometers. His ship was gyrating wildly, but as he moved in under four thousand, the fire almost seemed to cover every meter of space. His confidence, so often the foundation on which his success was built, began to fail him, and he *expected* a shot to hit him, despite his greatest efforts to dodge the fire.

Still, he somehow avoided every deadly burst of high-powered laser energy directed toward his ship. The crew of the Hegemony vessel knew what to expect, he was sure of that now. They understood the threat his tiny ship presented, and they were doing everything possible to take him down. A pair of lasers bracketed his ship, the closer of the two near enough to overload his portside scanning antenna. But he held firm, locked unshakably on the target.

He thought about Stara, wondered how she would feel about him sacrificing himself to take out one more enemy escort. He tried to push the thought away, but the image of her face, covered with bitter tears, stubbornly remained. She would be angry with him, devastated at his loss.

Assuming she survived the battle, something he realized was far from a certainty.

He could feel the sweat pouring down his body, the inside of his flight and survival suits becoming a slick mess. Still, he ignored the discomfort. He even managed to ignore Stara's image for an instant...and pressed the firing control.

His ship lurched hard, even as he pulled back on the throttle and struggled to get away from the rapidly approaching enemy ship. He'd scored a hit. He knew that much the instant he'd let the weapon fly, before the torpedo had even closed the distance. But it remained to be seen if he'd managed the critical shot he'd needed, the killing strike that would take out one of the enemy's strongest escorts, and probably save some of Federov's people on their trip back.

The ship remained on his screen as he decelerated to bring his fighter back around to return to *Dauntless*. He felt disappointment. Ever one for the pilot's love of the dramatic, he'd imagined a massive explosion as his torpedo cut right through the vessel's hull and broke through its containment.

But no such visceral pleasure was to be his, not this time. Though as he continued to stare at the screen, he saw the energy output of the target dropping.

It wasn't quite zero, but it was damned close. Close enough to render the cruiser a cripple. Stockton would settle for knocking the ship out, saving some of his comrades from the vessel's formerly deadly guns.

He looked up, checking the long-range scanners. Hundreds of his ships were still in action, even as many of their comrades headed back, bound for their motherships and as quick a turnaround as the flight deck crews could manage. He felt the urge to head back toward the front line, to join the ships still going in…but his discipline won out. The sooner he could get back and refuel and rearm, the quicker he could return to the fight.

And he intended to keep fighting until there was no enemy left.

Or no Jake Stockton.

* * *

"Updated assessments coming in, admiral. It looks like the enemy battle line has taken considerable damage."

Barron nodded his acknowledgment as Atara Travis finished her report. Between the two of them, that slight gesture signaled complete understanding.

He knew she was working him, too, though, trying to protect him even as he bore the responsibility of leading forty percent of the fleet's hulls into battle. She'd avoided passing on the latest fighter reports, no doubt because the losses had been catastrophic. The enemy escorts had been hit very hard, but they'd managed to dish out punishment as well as taking it. No less than a third of the bomb-armed fighters had been shot down or damaged, and a quick estimate suggested a solid fifteen percent of the pilots who had launched with cluster bombs would never return to the bays of their base ships.

Barron leaned back in his chair, analyzing the hordes of tiny dots. Some were still advancing on the enemy battleships while others were breaking off, returning to base for resupply. There would almost certainly be time for another strike. But the Hegemony would get a respite before the returning bombers hit. It would be time the enemy could use to reorder themselves and push their line forward toward Megara, forcing Barron's battleships to engage them shortly after the second bomber assault.

His eyes moved rapidly, from one side of the display to another. Clint Winters commanded the task force on the far side of the enemy, his ships positioned in the outer reaches of the Olyus system. His fighters had launched too, Dirk Timmons and Alicia Covington taking the wings forward. They were coming in on the far side of the enemy formation as Federov's and Trent's attacks were petering out. Barron had almost suggested sending them all in together, a synchronized assault of nearly four thousand small craft. But, in the end, he'd agreed with Nguyen and Winters. It was more important to keep the enemy constantly busy.

That's right—there won't be any time, no respite. If you want Megara, you bastards, you're going to have to fight every step of the way.

And Barron had something else ready—the asteroid bases. Rumors had flown among the crew until the installations had achieved mythic proportions, and they had been reverently nicknamed the "Stone Giants." They would just about be coming into range as Winters's bombing wings concluded their assaults.

"Commander, all asteroid bases are to come to battle stations and prepare to open fire as soon as the enemy moves into range."

The asteroids were something new, a testament to the driving force of desperation, and the unstoppable determination of the fleet. The bases weren't carefully designed or well constructed. The hurriedly assembled combinations of solid rock and enormously powerful weapons had been designed for one purpose only.

Unleashing pure hell on the enemy.

* * *

"The fleet will advance, commander." Vian Tulus sat on *Invictus*'s bridge. The new Alliance flagship was the first ship in Palatian history named after a preceding vessel that had lost in combat. For more than sixty years, since the Alliance had been founded by a Palatia that had just freed itself from enslavement, victory had been its mantra, a tenet followed by its society with the fervor of an ancient religion. Tulus himself had christened *Invictus*, however, in celebration of Katrine Rigellus, the lost commander of the first ship of that name. The epic battle between Rigellus's *Invictus* and Tyler Barron's *Dauntless*, also now lost and replaced by a new vessel, had set the stage for the current treaty between the two powers. That fight had been a model of skill and tenacity of command, and, through events that followed, it proved to be the foundation of a respect between the Confederation and the Alliance, one that led eventually to the powers becoming allies.

"Yes, your supremacy." Cilian Globus sat in the ship's command chair. The commander-maximus was the highest-ranking officer in the Alliance military, save only for the imperator himself. Yet, despite his lofty position, Globus had reserved the direct command of *Invictus* for himself—a tribute to Katrine Rigellus, Tulus suspected, and Globus's method of pushing the calcified ways of the Palatian warrior class forward.

Globus turned and looked across toward the row of three aides sitting at a line of workstations. He and Tulus shared the small staff, and the three officers were their conduit to the Alliance forces deployed in the Olyus system alongside their Confederation allies.

Tulus was tense. He knew the battle would be a difficult one, maybe even impossible. Yet despite his efforts to move his people to a new way of thinking, his core was still that of a Palatian warrior. He still felt the rush inside him, the call of battle drawing him forward. This fight was the dream of the old Palatian within him, a fight that would live forever in the history of the Rim. He would write some of that history, with his words and deeds, and in that, he would achieve immortality.

His more analytical side introduced a concern about just who would write that history. Would his people be remembered as noble warriors, who fought and sacrificed to hold the line against invaders? Or simply as unnamed barbarians briefly mentioned in the Hegemony annals as those swept away when the Rim was "civilized"?

Tulus hadn't received orders to move forward. Technically, he was under the command of Dustin Nguyen, the Confederation senior commander, though that arrangement, already tenuous for any Palatian forces serving alongside an ally, became infernally complex when the fleet commander in question was also the Alliance head of state. Tulus knew he could do whatever he saw fit to do, and he knew Nguyen could only request he do otherwise…and, in the end, agree to whatever he had done.

Tulus would follow Tyler Barron's commands, however, though he might choose to view them as requests from a friend. Barron was Tulus's blood brother, a bond that had never existed before between a Palatian and a foreigner. Tulus would refuse Barron no honorable request—and not too many dishonorable ones, if it came to that. To do so would be a breach of friendship, and a failure to repay the debt he still owed Barron for his aid in the Alliance Civil War.

Tulus respected Nguyen. The admiral had a distinguished career, and the two times he'd met with the officer, he'd been impressed with the man. But Tulus was slow to trust new acquaintances, and he couldn't help feeling resentment toward the officer who had supplanted Barron as overall commander. That was a slight to his friend's—to his brother's—honor, and it took considerable discipline to put such thoughts aside and respect Barron's acceptance of the arrangement.

"All landing bays are to be ready for immediate refit of returning squadrons." Tulus wished he was moving forward into battle. He ached for the final fight, the voice of every ancestor screaming in his mind for him to plunge into battle. But he knew the strength of the enemy heavy weapons, and he understood the burden his pilots carried.

"Yes, your supremacy."

His advance would place his ships closer to the enemy, but it would also cut valuable minutes from the turnaround time in launching the second strike. The fleet would definitely get the next wave of fighters launched against the advancing enemy. The real question was: could they launch a third? Tulus had run the calculations ten times, and come up with each result five of those times. It was *that* close, the final determination resting on variables he couldn't control, that even defied his efforts to guess at them.

But getting his base ships a little closer—*that* he could do.

"All ships report landing bays on full alert. All crews standing by for immediate refit operations."

"Very well, commander-maximus." He used Globus's full rank, a subtle gesture, but one that showed his respect for his immediate subordinate. Tulus knew the two of them should be on different ships. If he was killed, Globus would be the next in line to command. But to a Palatian, sometimes honor made demands that could not be refused. *Invictus* was a special ship in this fight, the heart and soul of the Alliance contingent. He and Globus *had* to be on her bridge, flying their flags together, in utter defiance of the invading Hegemony.

Tulus couldn't force himself to believe the battle would end in victory. But he was sure of one thing. His warriors would show the invaders just how Palatians could fight. Victory or defeat, any Hegemony spacers who survived this battle would carry the memory of Alliance warriors to their graves.

* * *

Federov pressed the firing stud, letting loose her torpedo, then angled her vector and blasted her thrusters at full to clear the rapidly approaching target dead ahead. The style of fighting Jake Stockton had developed for use against the Hegemony was effective, but it was also draining. She was almost as veteran as "Raptor" Stockton himself, as cool in combat as anyone she'd ever met—except for maybe old "Ice" Krill—but now she was soaked in sweat, her forehead wet, droplets streaming down her face. Her head pounded, too, some devilish combination of fatigue and tension turned into pain. It felt a lot like a drill boring through her temple.

Combat was always difficult, and she'd pounded the need for constant focus into her head. Even an outmatched enemy could take a pilot down. It only took one lucky shot...or one moment a fighter jock got distracted. But the battles against the Hegemony had all been wild, desperate affairs, taking everything she could give and demanding more. There was a breaking point somewhere for all of her people, and she'd started to see more and more signs of stress overcoming her pilots. That was bad enough, but the limit she was really worried about was her own. When she lost it, hundreds of pilots would be left without the leadership they needed to hold off their own hopeless despair.

And what about when Jake can't take any more?

She sometimes forgot to think of Stockton as a human being. The pilot had become a grim and deadly creature since Kyle Jamison was lost, like some shadow of death—invulnerable and unstoppable. But she knew him too well to believe in that view, one she suspected was shared less critically by most of the junior pilots. Jake Stockton was an unmatched pilot, she would be the first to state that as fact, but he was still only a man. There was only so much he could take, and if his resolve failed, the fighter corps was doomed.

And in this struggle against the Hegemony, if the squadrons couldn't bear their burden, the war was as good as lost.

As soon as she was clear of the target ship, she checked her damage assessments. A hit, and from the looks of things, a solid one. She felt a rush of excitement, but it was short-lived. A Lightning's scanning suite was, by necessity, limited, and that made it difficult to be sure if an enemy ship's railguns had been knocked out, or if its power generation had been severely degraded. She had come into her own fighting battles where the job of the fighters was to swarm in on and finish off damaged ships. Tactics of that sort carried with them morale-boosting visual displays of targets being blown to bits by damaged containment or left as dead, floating hulks. But war against the Hegemony demanded its own tactics, and the fighter wings were tasked with ignoring damaged ships and going after fresh ones, attacking with just enough intensity to guess the railguns had been knocked out, and then proceeding to the next target. It was a method born of necessity. If the enemy line ever got into range of the Confederation battleships with a full spread of railguns operational, the Confed line would be blasted to scrap before it got off a shot in return. But it was hard, mentally and emotionally.

She hesitated for a few seconds, trying to guess if her hit had done the job. She had it down to a coin toss, but then her eyes moved to the rows of oncoming enemy capital ships, dozens and dozens that hadn't yet been scratched. The math was simple. A one hundred percent chance was more dangerous than fifty percent…and her wings, as massive as they were, couldn't hope to disable all the enemy ships coming on.

She flipped a small switch, sending a simple message onto the combat net. The ship she'd just hit was off-limits. Her people, the few who hadn't yet completed attack runs, should choose other targets, ships coming up from the second line with no known damage.

She brought her ship around as she finished her task, and then she hesitated, checking the scanners, watching as the last of her wings blasted forward with their attacks. Her people had done well, and when the ones still going in were finished, she guessed they'd probably have hit thirty or more enemy battleships…and knocked the main guns out on at least half to two-thirds of those.

That would have been good for a day's pay, but if there was one thing absolutely, resolutely certain just then, it was this: the day wasn't over yet. Not by a long shot.

There were enough undamaged enemy ships coming on to blast the Confederation and Alliance ships to slag.

Chapter Thirteen

UFS Illustre
Emphillus System
Union-Confederation Border
Union Year 222 (318 AC)

Andrei Denisov stared into the mirror as he reached down and turned on the water. He craved sleep, almost above all things, but such a luxury seemed utterly beyond reach anytime soon. Hot food would have been nice, too, anything other than a sandwich wolfed down quickly in his command chair. But there was no use wasting time or thought on unattainable dreams. This was all he could expect, a few stolen moments in his quarters, a splash of cold water on his face. A quick change into a fresh survival suit and uniform, though without the shower he lacked the time to take, he would only be cramming his sweat-crusted body inside the fresh clothes.

He was still amazed his escape tactic had worked, that the enemy had bought wholeheartedly into his feigned retreat back toward Montmirail. Only the gravity-assist course change had made it possible to bring the fleet around and make a run for the Sauvon transit point.

The Hegemony forces seemed stunned for a few minutes, their surprise total…and then they proceeded to blast their own engines at full, struggling to match the change in vector

Denisov's people had achieved. They lacked the aid of the massive gas giant, however, and even with their superior thrust, the pursuing forces were far behind. It had appeared dicey at one moment or another, but Denisov and his people had managed to stay ahead and transit before the enemy could close to firing range.

Just.

He'd known the Hegemony ships would come through less than an hour after his own, perhaps two or three if they took time to reorder a bit before commencing the transit. So, he'd done the only thing he could think of. His ships blasted at full thrust, radically altering their vectors, doing everything he could to head away from the course of the enemy's intrinsic velocity. There were three transit points besides the one he'd entered, and any one of them would have worked. Each led to another border system, and one jump beyond any of these lines lay Confederation space.

The enemy emerged exactly as he'd expected, just over two hours after his forces had transited, and they'd almost immediately adjusted their vectors to match his. But, once again, he had a jump, and he'd chosen his next transit simply because the point was closest…and the only one his people had any real chance to reach ahead of the enemy.

They had done just that, by a margin not much better than the one by which they'd escaped Pollux, and at the cost of abandoning every one of the ships that couldn't maintain full thrust the entire way. It was difficult, leaving his people behind, but he knew the choice was between saving some and losing them all.

Denisov didn't waste a minute after his ships came through into the next system. Another abrupt course change. Another unpredictable choice of exit points. His recollection of the destruction of the units he'd left behind only drove him that much harder. There had to be a gain from such draconian tactics. There just had to be.

Another mad dash across a system. And a breaking point, a limit on what he could manage without at least a short break. He'd been sitting in his chair for far too long, enduring the high thrust levels, while simultaneously grateful for the dampeners that cut eighty percent of the pressure, making fifteen G merely uncomfortable instead of borderline deadly. It had been going on for hours without a pause, more than a full day.

His fleet's entry into the Emphillus system was accompanied by a longer-than-expected wait until the enemy followed. Two hours passed before a single ship transited. No, almost two hours, twenty minutes before there was any sign of pursuit. He'd been trying to hold back the hopefulness, the crack in his discipline that let a small part of him believe the Hegemony forces had ceased pursuit.

He wondered if that would be good.

Maybe. If they didn't just advance forward to Montmirail instead. Denisov had no particular love for the Union's capital, infested as it was with functionaries and party apparatchiks, but it was, without question, the central world of the entire nation. If the Hegemony took it without a serious fight, the Union would collapse in short order. He had no doubt about that. Then he would truly command a fleet without a home, without a nation.

He wondered if he'd made the right decision. Should he have left the road to Montmirail so open?

What else could you have done? You wouldn't have made it out at all in that direction, and if you'd tried to stay, you would have no fleet left. Montmirail would be in the same position, and the enemy would be freed of the concern about where your ships are.

There was logic in his thoughts, cold and indisputable, but still, he harbored more than a few doubts. He knew what Gaston Villieneuve was, and even though the dictator had been somewhat of a patron to Denisov, his loyalty to the man was limited. He wasn't naïve enough to expect anyone better than Villieneuve would come up through the swamp of Union politics, and while Denisov detested the brutal and corrupt government, he'd long ago fallen into a paradox through loving his country. Whatever that meant, whatever his country truly was.

What was the Union? Planets? People? A twisted and grotesque ruling class, constantly scheming for more power? Was there even logic in feeling some kind of duty to it? And what was that duty? To die in a hopeless attempt to save the capital? Or to keep the fleet alive, survive to fight another day, to keep alive some hope of ultimate victory?

His hopes—and his concerns—about Montmirail were short-lived, though. Two hours and thirty-four minutes after his last ship had transited, the first Hegemony vessel had appeared on the scanners. An hour later, the entire fleet was through and resuming its pursuit of his ships.

He shook his head as he looked at his reflection, pushing aside the thoughts. He pulled his hands up, splashing more water on his face. The coldness felt good, and it invigorated him a little. He'd taken a short break when he'd found himself unable to keep his eyes open on the bridge. He'd been shuffling his crews around, giving each shift four hours of sleep between extended periods of duty. But there was only one fleet admiral, and no one to take his place, so he'd stayed at his post almost without a break for three days now.

Three days that had seen his ship fleeing across a series of systems, constantly pursued by the Hegemony forces. He'd sent in his bomber wings again and again, each time scoring significant successes, albeit at high loss rates. He'd almost sent out another just before he'd left the bridge, but then he'd decided to hold what remained back. The fighting had left him with barely forty percent of his original force still ready for action.

If stunned pilots and battered, barely functional bombers could be called "ready for action."

He'd decided to hold back his forces, to save them for a time when running seemed hopeless, when the enemy was closing inevitably on his fleet.

For the last stand he believed in his gut was waiting for them…and soon.

He picked up a small white towel and dried his face. He'd eaten about half the food the steward had brought him, and as he walked out of the bathroom, he knew he should eat the rest. But, for all his hunger when he'd left the bridge, the first few bites had tied his stomach into churning knots. He would take another stim—though he would slip it by the chief surgeon, who'd urged him to wait at least a few more hours. He suspected if he forced much more food down his throat, he'd see it again in short order.

He turned and walked toward the door, peering out into the corridor before he stepped through. There were two guards standing there, spacers who owed their allegiance to him above all others. He hated the idea of moving around his own flagship worried about what might happen, but the truth was a stark one. He'd violated orders. His fleet was racing away from the Union. He knew there had been hushed whispers of treason, spoken in sometimes heated opposition to those backing his actions.

But it wasn't angry spacers that troubled him the most. It was Villieneuve's spies and political officers. Denisov had swept the fleet, arrested every agent he knew of and over a hundred he just suspected. Still, he knew he'd very likely missed some.

All it would take was one, a zealot committed to his role, and with the authorization to take decisive action. Denisov wasn't a coward by any means, but he didn't relish the thought dying at the hands of some Sector Nine watcher and being branded a traitor to his people.

Worse, perhaps, he'd done what he had for a reason he considered unassailable. He was preserving the fleet the only way he could devise. If some implanted agent felled him with a successful assassination attempt, he knew his fleet—the Union's fleet—would follow him swiftly into the darkness.

Then the war would truly be lost, and the long-suffering worlds of the Union would slip into foreign domination and slavery even more profound than that they'd endured under the Presidium and Villieneuve's dictatorship.

* * *

Raketh sat in the shadowy darkness of his sanctum. The dimness of the lights had been at his command, an accommodation to match his mood. He had been chasing the Union fleet for days, and his enemy had eluded pursuit through one ruse or clever tactic after another. His frustration had intensified steadily, and now it was morphing into rage. This Union admiral was an unexpected wrinkle in his plan, and now he had to make a difficult decision.

The gravity-assisted vector change had been particularly intriguing, and he had taken the brilliant stratagem as full warning that he faced a capable and wily opponent. He had perhaps been a bit careless, allowed the Confederation notes on Union capabilities to influence the urgency of his pursuit. If he had risked some overloads on the drives, pushed at least some of the fleet forward at redline thrust levels...

But there was no gain to be had in obsessing over what he might have done. He had more important things to consider. Predominantly, what to do next.

His blood was up, perhaps more so than was seemly for a first-century Master. He wanted to catch the Union forces. He wanted the battle honors, the glory he had lost when the Grand Fleet command had gone to Chronos. If he had taken Dannith, if he had crushed the Confederation forces there and pacified the planet, perhaps he would have retained the overall command. Realistically, he knew that command of something like Grand Fleet had to go to a top-ten Master, but the shame was still there.

Chronos had authorized Raketh's strike on the Union, but there had been no discussion of pursuing the enemy from the initial attack point at Pollux. That oversight gave him an excuse to continue his operation against the Union fleet, or at least the lack of orders prohibiting such a course. But if Grand Fleet needed the reserve, or if the enemy managed to get around the main force and strike at the Hegemony's supply lines while Raketh was off on his endless pursuit, things would get ugly fast.

He wanted the Union fleet. He wanted the victory, the credit for taking down the largest of the Rim nations in one massive strike, but he was nervous about the risks involved. He had limited intelligence on the systems into which the enemy might retreat. Were there fortifications, supply bases...more natural features that could be used to facilitate defense or continued withdrawal? Just how far could he pursue before he had to turn around, bring the reserve back to Dannith?

He had multiple answers, but some, he knew, were born from his desires, not from cold, logical analysis. Should he go one more system, push his ships to the limit and try a final time to compel an engagement?

Or was it too late? Was he too far in already to risk overloading engines and moving farther from his base and lines of communications?

He did not have an answer...not yet.

But he swore to himself he would before he left the confines of the sanctum.

* * *

Regina Descortes sat at the dimly lit workstation, her fingers moving swiftly over the keypad. Every few seconds, she looked over her shoulder, confirming that she was still alone. The Sector Nine agent knew something was wrong. She'd known it from the moment Admiral Denisov had initiated the course change toward the Confederation.

She'd taken a massive risk sending a message back to Montmirail, but so far, it appeared she had escaped discovery. Even if one of *Illustre*'s AIs or a routine deep scan of its information systems turned up some record of the transmission, she doubted it could be traced to her. That was good news, of course, but it still left her in a quandary.

Denisov's tactic had violated his orders, she was sure of that. The admiral had been left no option save to return to Montmirail if he'd been forced to leave the Pollux system.

She would have made her move already, but she wasn't sure Denisov had done what he had for any reason, save raw tactical necessity. The fleet would likely have been caught if it had tried to flee toward Montmirail, and if the intel she had on enemy capabilities was accurate, it would almost certainly have been destroyed. She wondered if Denisov had done the only thing he could have, if his only concern had been to preserve the fleet, and not to make a traitorous run toward the Confederation. That had been a possibility. It still was, though his choice of subsequent transits didn't bode well.

There was a route back to Montmirail from the fleet's current location. A long, tenuous path, but a way back nevertheless. But Denisov was not heading that way. He had the fleet on a course directly toward the Triton transit point...and Confederation space.

Worse, perhaps, she'd tried to access the main data banks, using an old Sector Nine back door. The pathway had been cut, and access restricted to Denisov's voice pattern alone.

Descortes couldn't be sure Denisov's actions were deliberate treason, but in the Union, proof wasn't really a prerequisite for action. Suspicion alone was almost certainly enough to authorize an execution under normal conditions. A situation involving a fleet commander this far from base required a bit more...but she had almost convinced herself there was no choice.

She closed down the workstation, entering her own codes to erase any record of her efforts. Then she stood up and reached down to her side, to the hidden pocket inside her jacket.

The gun was small, easy to hide. It wasn't the most powerful weapon she could have, nor the most accurate beyond close range. But that wasn't a problem. She only had one target, and she would get close enough to get the job done.

She would have felt more comfortable with direct orders from Villieneuve, or at least a less hazy analysis of Denisov's motivations. But she'd made her decision, and there was no going back.

There was no waiting, either. The fleet was almost into Confederation space, and if she wanted to stop it before it transited, now was the time.

She had to kill Andrei Denisov. And she had to do it soon.

Chapter Fourteen

1,450,000,000 Kilometers from CFS Dauntless
Olyus System
Year 318 AC

The Battle of Megara – The Stone Giants

Dirk Timmons inhaled deeply, savoring the scent of his cockpit. It was nothing most people would consider fragrant or pleasant, a combination of sweat mixed with a mild burning smell from his overtaxed engines and the faint odor of his new, never-before-worn, polymer survival suit. To Timmons, though, it smelled like home, and like a place he'd never expected to see again.

He wouldn't have seen it, either, not without the Hegemony invasion and their successful advance all the way to Megara. Panic had a way of overcoming foolish bureaucratic regulations. His artificial legs were wonders of science, and he was actually faster and more dexterous than he'd been with the ones he was born with. But none of that mattered to those who wrote the rules, usually with little or no regard for reality. At least not until they worked themselves up into a good, righteous fear. Then they opened the doors to anyone who offered a promise of salvation for them. In this case, foremost on that list was anyone with flight experience.

And Dirk Timmons had been well known as one of the best pilots to ever fly a Lightning.

He'd had a moment or two of doubt when he'd first lowered himself into the cockpit, uncertainty that he was, could still be, as good as he'd been. But as soon as he'd launched, it all came back like a torrent. As far as he could tell, he hadn't lost a step, either from his prosthetic legs or from the years he'd spent teaching and not doing. The throttle in his hand felt like it always had, like an extension of his own body, and every vibration, every sound took him back to his days at the head of the Scarlet Eagle squadron.

Now, it's time to let these bastards know who I am...

The bluster was one thing that came less easily than it once had. Timmons wasn't as arrogant as he'd been in his younger days. Losing countless friends and comrades, being critically wounded and almost killed, and learning to walk with new, artificial legs—all had a way of aging a man, imparting deep levels of wisdom, forged from pain. But he was still a Lightning jock at heart, and there was always a core of ego behind the driving force that allowed a man or woman to slide into a tiny ship and blast it wildly toward a target tens of thousands of times its size. There was some degree of crazy in every fighter pilot, and no amount of rational thought or tragedy could squeeze it all out.

He was still "Warrior" Timmons, and somewhere deep within him, he needed to make the enemy know that.

He was leading his second strike now. The first had pounded the enemy hard, swarming over the battleships on the Hegemony flank and hitting with over forty percent of their torpedoes. Despite the orders to focus on taking out railguns and proceeding to new targets, Timmons's people had managed to destroy three Hegemony battleships outright, the result more of enthusiasm run amok rather than deliberate disobedience.

The new wave of fighters behind him was tighter, the pilots more settled in. Between casualties, damaged ships, and stranded and wounded pilots, he had almost twenty percent fewer birds behind him this time. He mourned for every lost pilot, but he also knew the casualties had been heaviest among the least experienced personnel. There was a coldness to the analysis that didn't enhance his opinion of himself, but he knew the force he led now was better, on average, than the one that had launched hours before. It was uncomfortable looking at dead pilots as data points, but the tight order of his new formations spoke for itself.

Timmons knew this assault was likely to be the deadliest his wings launched. Far on the other side of the enemy fleet, the Hegemony ships were not only enduring "Raptor" Stockton's second wave, they were also moving into range of the "Stone Giants."

The name was entirely unofficial, of course, but it had spread like wildfire through the fleet. A dozen asteroids, towed into position and rapidly outfitted with fusion reactors and every overpowered weapon available, the "Giants" were ready to deal out death. They were a mess by any design standards, but Anya Fritz had supervised much of the work, and Timmons was sure enough that anything the brilliant engineer built would work.

He flipped on his comm unit. "Eagle Wing"—he'd named the immense strike force he commanded after the famous squadron he'd led in his younger days—"we're coming at them in one synchronized attack. Raptor is leading the other wings against the far end of the enemy formation. Those battleships and their railguns will strike our comrades with deadly force and claim their price. But this moment, right now, before they close, is ours. All you need to know is that you are here to kill, to destroy. These bastards have invaded our nation, killed our people. They would reduce us all to little more than slaves to their perceived genetic mastery. We do not need to understand them. We do not need to talk with them. We need to kill them. Every one of them. Follow me now, not as officers, not as pilots...but as avenging angels, agents of death itself."

He snapped off the comm and stared at his screens, his eyes zeroing in on the biggest enemy battleship in the group ahead of him. In that moment, nothing mattered to him, not loyalty to his nation, not camaraderie to his pilots. He only wanted to kill.

* * *

"Commander, it is time." Barron stared across the short expanse between him and his aide, his flag captain, his friend. "All bases...open fire."

"Yes, sir." Travis's voice was stone cold, the only hint of emotion a thirst for blood that would have chilled Barron to his core...if he hadn't felt the same thing.

He sat on *Dauntless*'s bridge, looking around, almost feeling the tension rising off his people. He had his battleships positioned right behind the asteroid bases, using the massive chunks of rock as cover against the enemy railguns. Admiral Nguyen had ordered the bases to be manned by the smallest possible crews, but Barron still found it painful to think of the men and women crawling through those narrow subterranean corridors, relying on weak, hastily built shielding to protect them from the massive reactors running on constant overload. That was bad enough, but Barron knew radiation sickness was far from the first concern of those gunners and engineers and technicians. The enhanced particle accelerators, giant versions of the primaries on the Confederation battleships, were still experimental. They might just as easily explode as fire, and even if they did function as hoped, the result could only be to bring down the full fire of the enemy fleet on the large but poorly armored bases.

"All bases...open fire." Travis repeated Barron's order, her voice the same echo of death it had been seconds before.

Barron leaned back and stared into the display. A few seconds later, he saw a series of flashes, the fire from the asteroids. The Stone Giants varied in size. There hadn't been time or resources to complete them all, and the dozen bases in the fight mounted between two and six of the guns dubbed "super-primaries."

The particle accelerators opened up at an even greater range than the enemy railguns, though at such distances, they struck with only a fraction of their actual power. Barron watched as two of the beams struck their targets—less than a ten percent hit rate, but not bad at such extended range. He stared as the damage assessments came in and allowed himself a passing instant of satisfaction. Even at extreme range, the deadly weapons tore into their targets, slicing through armored hulls and cutting deep into each ship's innards.

Barron knew what was happening on those vessels. However alien the Hegemony's society seemed, they were men and women, the same as those serving on *Dauntless* and the other ships of the Confederation fleet. They were dying over there, crushed by falling chunks of steel, pushed out into the icy depths of space, burned to ashes. It was a nightmare, a firestorm of human suffering…and it put a smile on his face.

Barron wasn't a brutal man by nature, but he'd seen too much war, watched too many people he respected and cared for consumed by its fire. He had no time anymore for sympathy for his enemies. He would kill them all, if that was what it took to achieve peace.

And he had never found another way to bring about that peace.

"Damage assessments coming in, admiral."

"On my screen, captain."

Barron watched the reports scrolled by, the AI's interpretation—which he knew was a fancy way of saying "best guess"—of the effects of the first hits on the enemy ships. As he was scanning the data, he caught more flashes out of the corner of his eye. It was the second barrage, and a few seconds later, new reports lit up his screen. Four hits this time, as the rapidly approaching Hegemony line moved ever closer. Damage assessments confirmed of the effectiveness of the new, heavy particle accelerators.

Perhaps thirty seconds later, the first report of a malfunction came in—a critical reactor failure on base number four. One of the smaller ones.

Barron wasn't surprised. The reactors had been thrown together, hastily set up and put into operation without any real safeguards. There simply hadn't been time for anything more. The devastating hits on the enemy battleships had been the benefit of the rushed work to put the bases into battle. Now Barron was seeing the price of that gain.

He read the reports as they scrolled by, and he imagined the situation on the base. Whole sections of the base were contaminated with radiation. Anywhere near the reactor would be well above immediately lethal levels, and any crew in those compartments would already be dead at their stations, or lying on the cold metal floors, gasping for their final breaths.

Most of the rest of the complement of Base Four were dead men walking, he knew, poisoned beyond the ability of medical science to reverse. They might live for another hour, perhaps two, though how long they would be able to continue at their posts, if they could at all, was a question he couldn't answer.

The rest of the stations fired again, and to Barron's respect and near-astonishment, two of the guns from Base Four joined that volley. The enemy ships were rapidly closing the distance, and with the reduced range, the hit rates soared. All along the advancing Hegemony line, irresistible particle accelerator beams ripped into thick metal hulls, blasting systems to scrap. In a hundred compartments on the enemy ships, Barron knew the vacuum of space was rushing in, pulling crew out to their deaths, and bursting deeper, through stressed and weakened bulkheads and hatches.

But the one-sided battle was at an end. Even as the last barrage of particle accelerators fired, a new wave of death and destruction came, this one aimed at the great asteroid bases. The chunks of super-heavy metals fired from the magnetic guns of the enemy fleet ripped through space at enormous velocities. The railguns were virtual doomsday weapons to the ships of the Confederation fleet, the only saving grace being a relatively low hit rate.

The asteroids weren't mobile, though. They'd been towed into place, and they didn't have the ability to modify their vectors. They simply floated in place, and the main guns of the Hegemony battleships blasted them mercilessly, claiming vengeance for the damage the bases had inflicted.

Bolt after bolt of metal slammed into the asteroids, and where they struck, almost incalculable kinetic energy was released.

Where base structures were hit, they vanished, consumed by the power of impact. Even where the shots missed the actual bases, they tore deeply into the asteroids themselves, vaporizing rock and unleashing massive tectonic waves and great flows of molten rock. The hastily constructed buildings, the compartments housing weapons and crews and nuclear fuel, were shaken apart. Reactor cores were torn open, spewing deadly radiation over kilometers, and underground control centers were buried under avalanches of rock.

Barron felt his teeth grinding. He knew what was happening to the people on those asteroids…the people he'd sent there. Nguyen had issued the orders, of course, but Barron was part of the command team, and he wasn't a man to hide behind technicalities. He'd been the prime mover in the creation of the asteroid bases, and that meant *he* had consigned those crews to the terrible fate unfolding on them.

Even as the bases died, their outgoing fire continued. The number of guns firing declined, almost with every shot, as more railgun hits slammed into the asteroids. Base Seven was struck by almost half a dozen shots in rapid succession, and, as Barron watched on the scanner, the asteroid itself began to break apart, a great fissure cutting through its crust and deep into its iron core. It split into two sections, and as it did, the last functioning reactors went critical. A series of fusion explosions wiped away everything the fleet had put in place there.

Barron turned away, his eyes moving back to the small screen on his workstation. The scene he was watching was a nightmare by any human standards, but the unemotional data the AIs were feeding him contained some cause for satisfaction. Fewer than forty percent of the front-line enemy battleships appeared to have functioning railguns, and he knew that Stockton's wings were attacking again…and out in the deeper reaches of the Olyus system, "Warrior" Timmons and his people were about to do the same.

Barron had to make a choice. If his line was going to pull back, it had to be now, before the last of the bases were destroyed. Before the enemy got close enough to use its remaining railguns to blast his ships to scrap.

He wanted to stay, to bring his ships around and hit the Hegemony forces as the last big guns on the bases fired. It would be a desperate gamble…and probably a foolish one. But Tyler Barron was a fighter, and pulling his big ships back constantly, allowing doomed bases and depleted bomber wings to fight his battles, sickened him. Any last stand should be—had to be—at the orbital fortresses around Megara itself.

But he couldn't issue the order. The words simply wouldn't come. He was on the verge of sending his task force forward into its final battle when the fleet orders came in.

It was Dustin Nguyen, the commander in chief, and while his voice was soft, filled with empathy for what his people were enduring, there was a strength of command there, too.

"All task forces are to withdraw to gamma positions at once. Full thrust, all units. Avoid unnecessary contact with enemy main batteries until repositioned."

Barron shook his head. He didn't want to obey. He knew it made sense; he agreed with the logic. The withdrawal would probably allow time for a third bomber strike, at least with whatever remnants of the wings that could get back and rearm quickly enough.

He hated the idea of pulling back, hated himself for doing it. But Tyler Barron always did what he had to do…and throwing his ships away wouldn't help anyone. It would be a surrender in its own way, to his anger, to his irrational rage.

And he'd reached his limit for mutiny in recent months. Nguyen was in command, and his orders had to be obeyed.

"The task force will withdraw, Captain Travis. All ships, maximum thrust. Destination, point Gamma."

"Yes, sir."

Point Gamma…directly around Megara itself.

* * *

Clint Winters stared at the comm unit, as though the message would somehow change if his gaze was intense enough.

He'd been about to order his ships forward, to take advantage of the enemy's redeployment of additional strength toward the inner system. He'd seen an opening—or what he'd convinced himself was an opening—and been about to exploit it. His fighters had ravaged the enemy battleships twice, and he'd convinced himself enough of the railguns had been knocked offline to enable his battle line to engage.

Then Admiral Nguyen's orders came in. Pull back. Withdraw to fallback positions.

Winters wanted to ignore the orders. He'd fought the war against the Hegemony with thought, with carefully devised tactics. He'd shifted fleet units, fallen back, used what cover he could. Now he just wanted to fight, to throw himself and every ship under his command at the enemy and finish things once and for all.

This was no struggle out on the frontier, around a world like Dannith, nor even a battle for a Core world like Ulion. Megara was the Confederation's capital, the planet whose inhabitants had first pushed out after the Cataclysm, forming alliances and pacts that eventually coalesced into the modern Confederation. Could that nation, *his* nation, survive the loss of its first and central world? Win or lose, was this the final battle?

He was on the verge of mutiny, of ignoring his orders. Then he saw something. It was hard to follow at first. His long-range scanners were badly affected by the enemy jamming, and his readings on activity in the inner system were jumbled at best. But he caught a glimpse. Barron's ships.

Pulling back.

Winters watched, and as he did, his insides roiled. It wasn't easy for an officer known as "the Sledgehammer" to pull back, to retreat. But there was no officer alive Clint Winters respected more than Tyler Barron.

And Barron was following the plan. Obeying orders.

Winters looked back at the display, at his fighter wings making their way back with disordered sections of the enemy battle line following. He could take those ships…he was sure of it. Well, maybe something less than sure. But he still wanted to hit them, wanted it with a raging fire inside him.

"We have our orders, commander." A pause after he forced out those words, and then a short, choked phrase following, barely pushed from his lips: "All ships pull back."

He'd helped create the battle plan, and he knew drawing as many enemy ships as he could to follow his force would achieve more than any glorious, and probably suicidal, attack could.

He'd fought the war in his own head, the battle between the sides of himself, and he knew, as much as he knew anything, that Tyler Barron had gone through the same torment.

This war wouldn't be won by heart, though it would take incalculable amounts of such fortitude to endure. It would be won by brainpower, by carefully executed plans, by men and women doing what they had to do, and not what the emotions inside them demanded.

The battle wasn't over, not yet. And the war wasn't either. The Sledgehammer didn't like to retreat, but he did when he had no choice.

He would fall back, but he would never give up.

* * *

Andi sat in the command chair of *Hermes*, feeling both at home and very out of place. She was wearing the uniform of a Confederation captain, which she now was, of course. The documents were all executed and in place, and her commission was real…as real as any in the navy.

It was something she struggled to wrap her head around. She'd spent most of her life avoiding naval patrols, if not outright fleeing from them. The journey from frontier smuggler to command of the navy's newest and fastest ship had been a strange one indeed.

Yet there was normalcy in it, too, and a strange thought that, even with all the unsettled feelings, it made sense for her to be just where she was. She was no longer the Badlands adventurer she'd been, treading both sides of the law with practiced dexterity. She was vastly wealthy, a woman with no need to risk her life for gain…or for anything else. Yet she was there, on the fringes of the greatest naval battle in Confederation history.

And that was just where she belonged.

Her friends now, everyone she cared about save for her old crew, were naval officers and Confederation spies. For all she clung to her old image of herself, she'd already become one of them—informally, at least—before Tyler Barron had handed her the two small stars of a Confederation captain and made it official.

She looked around the small, sleek deck of her ship. *Hermes* was a beautiful vessel, the very pinnacle of Confederation achievement. But it was a ship built to run, not to fight. Andi wished she had a battleship, even a cruiser…anything that would let her stand in the line of battle, alongside *Dauntless*. Alongside Tyler.

You not being there is the point.

She knew Tyler had confidence in her abilities, that he would trust her with almost any task, but he hadn't asked her to take command of *Hermes* because of her skills. She loved him, and she knew he loved her, but the two also shared a mutual respect that lay under their most passionate feelings. This time, Barron had allowed emotion to rule, to push aside his ability to look at her as a skilled captain and warrior, and to see only a lover, a woman he needed to know was safe.

As safe as anyone could be just then.

She knew he'd placed her where she was not just because he trusted her to evacuate the research teams from the Institute if necessary—but because he wanted her to be safe.

He *needed* her to be safe.

He'd managed to concoct a job for her that almost mandated that she escape, whether Megara held or fell, and it was a task so vital that she couldn't refuse to do it. If Megara was taken, the Confederation had little enough hope of survival, but what would remain was rooted heavily in the discoveries and new systems under development by the several hundred men and women she was charged with safeguarding. Combined with the industrial might of the Iron Belt, the new technology just might give whatever remained of the navy a chance of continuing the fight.

That was something Andi couldn't ignore, a job she wouldn't let herself fail to complete. However much it ripped her insides apart to think of leaving Tyler behind, perhaps to his death, she had to go.

She still felt an urge to bring her ship back to the inner system. She wanted to stand by Barron in the fight raging all across the system, and to share his fate, to meet death alongside the only man she'd ever loved.

But you would only help kill him…

The best thing she could do for the one person who'd become more important to her than any other…was to abandon him. Tyler Barron was a brilliant tactician, a leader whose people would follow him anywhere. He was going to need everything he could muster to win this fight, or at least to survive it, and she knew if she refused to go, he would worry about her. And that distraction could kill him.

Leaving him was unthinkable, but the thought of contributing in any way to his death shook her to her core.

It was painful, and unavoidable. She'd tried not to think about it anymore, and she'd just been sitting where she was, waiting.

And then the wait ended.

"Captain Lafarge, we're receiving a fleet communique via drone." A pause. "It's from Admiral Barron on *Dauntless*, captain."

Of course, a drone…there's no way Dauntless *could have burned a direct signal through all that enemy jamming.*

She could feel the tightness inside. She knew what the message said before it was decoded. Before she even listened to it.

"Directly to my line, commander." Her tone was emotionless, robotic.

I will go. I will do what you need me to do, Tyler. But please, use everything you've got in this fight—just don't throw your life away, my love…

Chapter Fifteen

Approaching Resistance HQ
Planet Dannith, Ventica III
Year 317 AC

Holcott doubled over and began coughing uncontrollably. He gasped for breath and retched as he spat up some yellowish foam, all his stomach had to offer. He'd been running, almost without stop, for what? Two days? Was that even possible?

He sucked in another lungful of air and turned and looked to either side of him. Two companions, one on his right and one on his left—all that remained of the force that had accompanied him to watch the execution of his marines.

Our marines…we are all marines…

He turned and looked behind him, as he had done every quarter kilometer or so, for the last day. He was all but sure his small band had finally eluded their pursuers, but it was the "all but" part that rattled him. If he'd missed something, led the Kriegeri search-and-destroy teams back to headquarters, he himself had been the instrument of the downfall of his forces.

What remained of his forces.

The resistance had possessed a dozen bases when the fight had begun, and forty or more outposts and safe houses, places from which action against the occupiers had been coordinated. But the Kriegeri had proven themselves to be ruthlessly efficient, and they had systematically hunted down his raiding parties, uncovered the locations of his bases, until nothing remained save the final refuge.

He'd lost most of his marines, too, and service with his resistance had proven to be nothing so certainly as it had been a path to death. As a marine, he expected endless fortitude from his people, but he was amazed that those who remained still followed him. The enemy had made repeated announcements, distributed dispatches, offered in every way to spare those who surrendered…but all to no avail. Not a single marine had left his post, nor expressed the intent or desire to yield.

He looked around again, double-checking. Or was it triple-checking? He couldn't remember. Exhaustion was wearing him down, but he wasn't going to let himself make a mistake, not this close to safety.

Or what passed for safety on Hegemony-occupied Dannith.

He moved forward, heading down the mostly hidden path that led to the headquarters. He suspected the pickets were watching him, but he knew the wouldn't show themselves, for the same reason that spawned his own caution. They would be checking to ensure that he and his companions weren't being followed, and if they spotted any sign of the enemy, they would alert the base.

As Holcott approached the hidden entrance, he allowed himself to relax, just slightly. There was still no sign of pursuit, and in just a few minutes, he would be inside the headquarters, back to the remnants of Dannith's defense force.

He slid down a steep drop on the path and turned toward the entry, pushing aside the vines that completely obscured the barely recognizable door. Just as he reached out, it swung open, and he was greeted by several marines standing just inside, rifles pointed at his head.

It only took an instant before they recognized him, and even as they lowered their guns, he stumbled down to one knee…and then to the ground.

Exhaustion took him, and even as he struggled to regain his focus, darkness came over his eyes. After a brief welcoming session, he stumbled to the pile of straw that served as his bed and slipped into a deep sleep.

* * *

"Your report sounds positive, kiloron, but any analysis at all shatters that illusion and reveals it to be a carefully concocted brew of excuses." Carmetia stood in the middle of the room, her posture rigidly erect, every movement, every glance, leaving no doubt who was in command.

She turned her head. "And you, Master Develia, what do you have to say about this?"

Develia looked as though she was trying to suppress anger, though it was unclear whether that stifled rage was directed at Kaleth, the kiloron who had pursed the rebels and somehow managed to lose them, or Carmetia, who was once again asserting her superior ranking.

"Commander…Kiloron Kaleth is correct. We may not have caught the partisans or found the exact location of their refuge, but it is very likely we have narrowed the area to—"

"Narrowed? Is that not what you have been doing for months now? Narrowing your search parameters?" Carmetia knew she was being unfair, at least to an extent. Develia had not entirely pacified the resistance, but her forces had degraded it enormously. Whatever was still out there, it was a fraction of what it had been, in both numbers and capabilities. The days of massive assaults on power plants were behind them now, and in Port Royal City, pacification operations were proceeding quite satisfactorily. If things continued the way they had been, she even imagined commencing the project to give the former Confeds the Test. She was curious how they would rank. In some ways, they seemed foolish and primitive to her, yet in others, she saw something more.

"In fairness, commander, if you look at the casualty estimates and the operations reports, I think you will see we are actually moving matters at a satisfactory pace."

"It is not satisfactory to me, Master Develia, and since Commander Chronos appointed me military governor of the entire system, my opinion is all that matters." She paused. "Get your senior officers in here now, Develia…and tell them we will be here all night, and probably all day tomorrow, too. We are going to go over every scrap of information you have, and we are not leaving here until we have a plan to crush the remnants of this pointless resistance."

* * *

"Are you sure, sir?" Clark Hoffman looked over at Holcott, at least as well as he could with his single remaining eye. Hoffman had survived the fighting, lived to stand beside Holcott in the last refuge, but he hadn't done it without paying a price. He'd lost the eye to enemy incendiary fire. The Kriegeri had a nasty weapon, a sort of shrapnel that superheated as it struck the atmosphere. Only the tiniest fragment had hit him in the face, but it had proven to be enough to burn out his entire eye.

"What choice do we have, captain? We're down to our last hideout…and that's what it's become, a place to hide. We don't have the personnel or the ordnance to conduct any meaningful operations anymore." Holcott looked up at the other marine. "Except maybe one more."

"What chance do we have of success, major? I just don't see how—"

"Would you rather sit here until they triangulate our location? Would you prefer to die in this stinking, moldy pit, exterminated like some kind of vermin? Look around, Clark. Does this look like someplace we can defend against the kind of assault they'll launch at us? Do we have the ordnance left to face those tanks, to gun down hundreds of Kriegeri?" Holcott knew the answer to his question already, and he was pretty sure Hoffman did, too.

The captain nodded and remained silent.

"We're finished, Clark. You know that as well as I do. I have no idea what's happening in the war at large, but unless a massive Confederation fleet is on its way to Dannith, the battle here is over. The people have given up, and our attacks have hurt them as much as the enemy. They probably hate us as much as they do the Kriegeri. But if we do this…well, if we have to die, this is how I would choose to do it."

Holcott stared into his exec's eyes, and he could almost see the officer imagining the operation. Launching a decapitation strike into Port Royal City, targeting the Hegemony headquarters and killing every officer in sight—it seemed insane, something only the craziest fool would try. And perhaps in that lay the one chance for some level of success.

The raid would be a suicide operation, almost certainly, but remaining in their last hole, waiting like sheep for the enemy to find them…that was just as likely to end in death. And an end far bitterer to a marine than dying on the attack, striking at the enemy with his final breath.

There were many ways to die, and Luther Holcott would choose the marine way. If his people were to face their last stand, they would do it weapons in hand, striking at the enemy in the last way they had available to them.

"I'm with you, sir…and the others as well, I'm sure. You're right. If we have to die, let us die as marines."

* * *

"You will have to come up with at least a thousand more Kriegeri for the final push." Carmetia was looking down at the table, at a map of the area two hundred kilometers around Port Royal City. One section to the northwest was shaded, approximately eight hundred square kilometers with a ninety-six percent chance of containing an enemy base of operations…and an eighty-two percent probability that refuge was the last one remaining. The forces Develia and her staff had proposed were likely adequate to trap and destroy the remnants of the resistance, but the ground commander on Dannith had underestimated the enemy before, and Carmetia was determined to see that did not happen again. She wanted the enemy destroyed, and enough troops committed to cover every possible avenue of escape. The war on Dannith would end with this operation, whatever it took to ensure that.

"That will require transferring forces from garrison duty, commander. With the first round of the Test coming, and the ongoing construction of fleet support facilities, it will be difficult to find that number." Dannith was designated as the primary support facility for the fleet, a waystation for incoming supplies and ordnance as well as the location of planned shipyards to support the efforts of the logistical fleet. "Perhaps if so many of the ground troops initially assigned to the invasion had not been so quickly withdrawn…"

"Do not try to obscure your failures with fleet policy, commander. You had ample forces to pacify this planet." Carmetia was not being entirely honest. She, also, thought Chronos had been too quick to pull forces out for his invasions of Ulion and other Confederation worlds. But there was nothing she could do about that, and she was not about to listen to Develia complain about it.

"My apologies, Master Carmetia. It is only that the enemy here has exhibited far greater endurance and tenacity than I had expected."

Carmetia did not know if Develia was trying to manipulate her or was just being honest, but Carmetia had been riding her immediate subordinate hard the past few days, and she decided to pull back on that a bit. "That is certainly the case, commander. The defensive forces here have lasted longer than I expected, as well…and I suspect nothing you could have done would have quickly or easily defeated them. This is their world, after all. They know it better than we do. And you have done quite well in controlling the citizenry. If you had not, we would likely be facing outbreaks of rebellion in a hundred places. Instead, there is little support for the resistance…and in some cases, actual resentment for the damage those forces have inflicted."

"Thank you, Master Carmetia. Your words are greatly appreciated."

Carmetia nodded. The two Masters had a tentative, sometimes difficult relationship, but Carmetia knew friction between them was not helpful to their shared mission. "It is for such reasons that I believe we must err on the side of too much force. If we indeed have a chance to eradicate this prolonged resistance, we must do everything possible to see that it is done in this final effort."

"I agree, Master Carmetia. I believe we can draw two hundred Kriegeri from spaceport security. It is unlikely the enemy would be able to penetrate the outer defenses there. We might also place several hundred on extended duty…delaying rest periods and minor medical procedures."

Carmetia nodded. She had kept Develia and her people there for almost twelve hours, and they were going to be working a lot longer. The final search-and-destroy mission on the resistance fighters would launch in thirty-six hours, and she was not about to let anything interfere with that. Chronos was deeply occupied in the assault on Megara, but she would not to let the fleet commander check on her after that fight and realize she was still fighting to secure Dannith while he had crushed the Confederation fleet and taken their capital.

"Very good…that gets us a third of the way there." She glanced up at the chronometer. It was late, and it was going to get later. A lot later. Because no one was leaving the room until the assault was one hundred percent planned out and ready.

* * *

"Keep moving. There's no time to waste. We've got to be at the target before dawn." Holcott still felt unsettled. The rapidity of the planning and the immediacy of the execution was almost overwhelming. It made the whole thing seemed half-baked, which, of course, it was. But his marines were formed up behind him, and they were with him, too, in every sense of the word. The base, their last stronghold, had been abandoned and booby-trapped. Whatever happened, it was beyond unlikely any of them were going back there.

He pushed forward, his feet moving slowly through the muck of the swamp floor, his body half submerged in the murky water. He was cold, his fatigues soaked through, the bite of the night air only adding to his misery. But none of that mattered. His mind was on the mission, on the task ahead. The plan was an audacious one, crazy even, but it just *might* work. Surprise would be on his side, at least, if only because no one would imagine he and his few survivors would try something so insane.

He looked through the reedy plants to the dry ground just ahead, and beyond, the city. Port Royal, the capital of Dannith, and home to one of the most notorious spacers' districts in the Confederation, where all manner of illicit trade flourished.

Had flourished. It felt strange for a marine to think wistfully of smugglers and criminal organizations, but if the cost of law and order was domination by the Hegemony and its Masters, he'd just as soon put up with the Badlands adventurers and small-time district gangsters.

He reached up, grabbing on to a coarse vine and pulling himself up out of the water. The swamp had to be the most miserable route to sneak into Port Royal City, but it was also the most discreet. They'd run into one small patrol of two guards, but they'd managed to take the Kriegeri by surprise and kill them before they could radio for help. One of the soldiers had cried out before he'd fallen, and Holcott had endured a tense half-hour wondering if anyone had heard the shouts. But all seemed well.

As well as they could be for one hundred and eighteen marines, exhausted and soaked to the bone, marching through a city occupied by thousands of the enemy to strike a desperate blow to kill as many of the invaders' high command as possible. He almost laughed as he repeated that in his head.

He pulled the rifle from his back and lowered it, stepping slowly forward, first through the soft, wet ground, and then up a small rise, to firmer footing. He was out in the open now, more or less, and he knew from this point on the journey would get more and more dangerous.

He looked down at his tablet, scanning the map, checking what he already knew. The Hegemony headquarters was 3.2 kilometers from where he stood. Less than an hour's march.

Then his survivors—the last, tattered remains of a planet's

defense forces—would be in position to cut the head off the enemy.

* * *

Steve Blanth sat quietly in the corner. He might have thought he was being ignored, that there was a chance to escape, or at least to strike some kind of blow against the enemy. But he'd come to know Carmetia too well to imagine the Master would be so careless, and a second glance around the room identified at least three Kriegeri who'd clearly been tasked to watch him. He wouldn't get two meters from his chair before one of them dropped him with a clean shot to the head…and he knew the Kriegeri rarely missed, at least at such short range.

Carmetia had brought him into the room, no doubt in her ever-persistent hope that she could convince him to cooperate, or at least to give something away. It was a fool's game, at least as far as getting him to knowingly help the Kriegeri hunt down his marines. But he'd come to appreciate Carmetia's keen intellect. However repugnant he found the Hegemony's system of genetic rankings, he couldn't help but realize the Masters in general, and Carmetia in particular, did seem to be highly intelligent and physically able specimens.

That made them even more dangerous enemies than he'd imagined. Though it didn't look like he'd be back in the fight anytime soon.

"The operation will commence at dawn tomorrow."

He heard the discussion, the plans for the annihilation of the few of his marines that still survived, and it cut at his insides that he couldn't warn them. He considered making a run for it again, trying to find a communication station or some other way to get word to his people. Then, even though the grimness of his despair, he almost laughed at the absurdity of it all. He'd have risked his life, or sacrificed it outright, for any kind of chance at success. But the thought of getting past the Kriegeri and finding a comm unit before they stopped him was ludicrous to say the least.

His head snapped around. He'd heard something, a distant rumble. For a few seconds, he imagined he was hearing things. Then an alarm went off, and the Kriegeri all jumped up and ran to their stations.

Any doubt he had vanished an instant later with another sound, an explosion, far closer this time. Then the sound of gunfire, just outside.

For an instant, he was stunned, confused, unsure what could be happening. Then he realized.

The marines!

Suddenly, it all made sense. They had to know the enemy was on the verge of wiping them out, so they'd decided to launch a surprise attack. Right on the Hegemony headquarters.

He felt a rush of excitement, a pride in his people, even above the dark realization that they would almost certainly all die in this last titanic effort. But if they had to die, they would at least meet their ends as marines should.

And so would he.

He scanned the room, trying to look as calm as possible, even as his heart began to beat like a drum. There were still two Kriegeri watching him, but they were also scanning the doors to the room, looking back and forth as though they weren't sure what to do.

He waited, biding his time, even as the Masters and Kriegeri senior officers present sprang into action, snapping off orders, gesturing in multiple directions. He almost leapt from his chair, but he stopped himself. *No, not yet…*

He was ready to die, but not to throw his life away pointlessly. He needed patience. He had to wait for the right moment.

It came an instant later.

The building shook as some kind of explosive, a big one, went off just in front of the structure. The lights blinked, and dust fell from the ceiling. He could hear the sounds of structural supports collapsing out in the hall, and the sounds of the injured screaming.

Only one Kriegeri was watching him now, and the soldier turned, his eyes moving toward a wounded Master stumbling into the room. Decades of subservience and dedication to the Masters made it impossible to ignore the wounded commander. The trooper turned, just for a second.

But it was the second Blanth needed. He bent low and then sprang up from his chair, throwing himself toward the distracted Kriegeri.

The soldier turned, just in time to see Blanth, but not in time to get out of the way or bring his weapon to bear. The marine slammed into the augmented soldier, and the two of them fell hard to the floor.

Blanth struck at the Kriegeri, planting his fist into the soldier's kidneys, even as his adversary shoved an arm against Blanth's neck. The fight was a brutal, no-holds-barred struggle to the death. Only seconds had passed, but it already seemed like an eternity. Blanth knew his opponent was stronger, courtesy of his implants and the controlled breeding that had created a perfect soldier. He was at a disadvantage, one growing ever direr with each passing second, as the effects of the surprise he'd initially enjoyed faded away.

The two men rolled across the floor, even as the sounds of gunfire erupted from within the building. The other Kriegeri had run out into the hall. Only Carmetia and two other Masters remained, and they'd been distracted by the attack of the marines. Now, one of them looked over toward the desperate struggle and moved to intervene.

Blanth knew he only had seconds. He reached for the pistol at the Kriegeri's side, even as his enemy tried to bring the weapon around to shoot him. His hands were on his enemy's arm, sweat streaming down his body, as he struggled desperately for the pistol.

The Kriegeri moved to the side, and the two of them rolled over...and then a shot rang out, the gun between the two of them firing.

The feeling of wetness grew between them, blood—though Blanth didn't know whose—as the sounds of the firefight grew ever closer.

Chapter Sixteen

1.45 Billion Kilometers from CFS Dauntless
Olyus System
Year 318 AC

The Battle of Megara – Enemy at the Gates

"All ships, check systems one more time. Let's make sure we're ready." Tyler Barron sat on *Dauntless*'s bridge, and he could feel the tension in the air like a dense fog. His task force had pulled back from the line of asteroid bases, just in time to avoid engagement with the enemy battleships.

The withdrawal had accomplished one thing beyond buying a few more hours until the final assault: it had made time for one more bomber strike, one last attack to weaken the enemy's front line before the final stage of the battle began.

The squadrons' losses had been heavy, many of their ships battered and flying with varying degrees of damage, but they were going in anyway. The pilots were exhausted from lack of rest, worn down from watching friends die…but they hadn't hesitated to man their ships and head out once again.

The belief that the Confederation and Alliance forces could stop the Hegemony fleet and Megara was fraying under the relentless enemy attack, but that wasn't going to stop the pilots.

"All ships acknowledge, admiral." Atara turned and looked

over at him, pausing for a moment. She'd fought at his side more times than he could easily count, and she was perhaps the most indomitable warrior he'd ever known. Now, though, he could see the cold, harsh truth. She didn't expect any of them to survive the battle.

He would have tried to convince her they were going to make it, but he didn't think they were going to get through it either. And after more than ten years as comrades, close as brother and sister, he wasn't going to start lying to her now.

"Very well, commander." He looked at the main display. Stockton's wings were about to commence their third sortie. They'd be beginning their attack runs any minute.

They just have time to finish before those big boys up front get into range. Then we'll see just what we're up against.

Barron knew his fraying hope applied only to the first line. Hegemony forces had continued coming through the transit point for almost a full day, and now, there was a second line advancing behind the first, even as a third formed up far to the rear. That was the big problem. It was possible that Barron's forces and the orbital forts could turn back the initial attack. But the second line would get there roughly six hours later, and that force would face exhausted pilots flying battered fighters, and in smaller numbers. They would not face the lost Stone Giants, as the first line had. They would close on a Megara surrounded by damaged and destroyed fortresses and the remnants of Barron's task force.

It wouldn't even be a fight. It would be a slaughter.

Barron shook his head. There was nothing he could do about any of it. Nothing, save what he'd done.

Andi will escape, at least…

He was grateful, and on some level surprised, that she had agreed to follow his orders, request…whatever it was. She was as stubborn as the core of a neutron star. He was sure she knew those scientists she was evacuating were just about the only remaining hope the Confederation had. But he suspected she'd done it in equal measure for him, because she knew she couldn't do anything to help him except go.

"Admiral…" Atara was looking over again from her station. She could clearly see that he was lost in his thoughts.

"Yes, Atara?"

"All ships report systems rechecked and fully operational. The task force is ready for battle."

I always knew they'd be ready to fight. Are they ready to die?

"Very well." Barron managed a quick, passing smile. There was no one he wanted more at his side in a fight like the one he was in, but he'd have sent her away if he could have. Atara Travis deserved better than to die in a hopeless fight.

She returned the smile, and then she put her hand up to her headset and frowned. A few seconds later: "Admiral, Senator Hoover is on the line. He wishes to speak with you."

Barron's face morphed into a disgusted scowl. "You can tell the senator to fu—" He paused, feeling no less angry, but just a touch more controlled. "Tell the senator I have no time to discuss anything right now."

Atara nodded and turned back to her station. Barron listened to her speaking with the senator, and he could see the politician was giving her a hard time. He felt guilty for inflicting that on her, but he just didn't have it in him just then to placate a scared politician. His people had been fighting—and dying—for days. What the hell more did the Confederation's puppet masters expect from men and women giving all they had to save their corrupt asses?

Barron was grateful again for the presence of Admiral Nguyen. The commander in chief had fielded most of the frantic communications with the Senate and the other civil authorities down on the ground, all of them becoming increasingly terrified about what might happen. Barron imagined that the old man had handled them with more care than he would have…and then he remembered the few times his grandfather had spoken of his old comrade, and he wasn't so sure. He'd seen the calm and softened demeanor of an old man, but apparently, Dustin Nguyen had possessed quite a temper back in his day…and if anyone could coax that out of him again, it would be Troyus City's entitled political class. Honestly, what could disgruntled senators do to a ninety-year-old admiral with no interest in a future career, even if the aged officer somehow managed to survive the nightmare that had brought him back to the colors?

Barron had a flash in his mind, an image of Nguyen telling the senators to fuck off, and through all the fear and misery around him, that made him smile broadly. At least for a few seconds.

"We're getting a communique via drone, admiral. It's from Admiral Winters, sir." Atara listened to the message. "His bombers are about to engage."

Barron nodded. That was good. The two halves of the fleet—and splitting the ships had been a huge risk, an audacious plan that somehow had secured the support of all three admirals in command—were too far apart for normal communications, at least with the enemy fleet between them, jamming all the space for hundreds of thousands of kilometers like crazy. That made drones the only way to communicate, and it also meant the fact that the two strike forces were about to hit the enemy at almost exactly the same time was either the most amazing display of joint operations imaginable, or one hell of a stroke of luck.

Barron didn't care which. He just watched the display as Stockton's lead elements went in. This was likely to be the last segment of the battle where the advantage lay with his people. Once the fighters were done, whatever battleships still had operational railguns would close to firing range, and they would open up.

Then more than just Stockton's pilots would die.

* * *

Alicia Covington was uncomfortable. She was leading her third sortie, with no more than an hour between each launch. She was covered with sweat, which poured down her back and sides over the dried crust of previous deluges. It was an endless cycle that turned her survival suit into a slippery mess, which congealed and dried into an itchy nightmare, before the whole thing started again.

She would have killed for a shower, or even for sixty seconds with a warm, wet towel—though those things were as unattainable as a hot meal or the unfathomable dream of soft bedsheets and a good, long sleep. But she was a pro, and nothing was going to stop her. Not fear, not exhaustion…and certainly not the fact that her cockpit smelled a little too much like Alicia Covington.

"Let's go. We all know why we're here, so I'm going to spare you the speeches. Whatever else you are, whatever you may think you are, right now, only one thing matters. You are killers. Remember that, whatever happens."

She cut the line. Perhaps she should have waxed more poetic. But she didn't think her pilots needed it, not just then. And she wasn't sure she had it in her. A little-known tenet of leadership was that a botched speech was worse than none at all. If she accidently let them see the fear she was feeling, the uncertainty… Well, better she said nothing at all. She was there to kill. They were all there to kill. Best they just got on with it.

Her ships were coming in on the enemy flank again. She was no grand tactician, but from what she'd seen, the attacks coming in from two sides had disordered the enemy advance. Whether that effect had been worth diverting more than a third of the available ships from the immediate defense of Megara remained to be seen. One thing was crystal clear, though: Dirk Timmons had visited hell on the Hegemony forces. Timmons wasn't actually her commander—the two each officially led half of Admiral Winters's wings—but one look at him in action told her all the stories she'd heard were true. She decided she would take orders from him any day.

She was a veteran herself, and a great pilot. She knew that. But she'd never seen anyone fly like Timmons, except for Jake Stockton. She, Johannes Trent, and a good number of the strike force's aces and squadron leaders were excellent pilots. But Stockton and Timmons seemed almost as though they'd been born in their cockpits.

"Okay, let's pick up the thrust. We need to get in there and get out." Her eyes had caught the lead row of enemy battleships, and her guts clenched as she saw each of them almost englobed by anti-fighter escorts. Her people had benefited from the devastation the minefield had inflicted on the forward escorts, but now she could see that the enemy had managed to rush up reserves from the second line, enough to surround their battleships closest to the approaching bombers.

She'd always known the attack would be costly, as the other waves had been, but now her mental calculations shifted upward. More of her people were going to die, and as horrifying as that was, it didn't matter. They had to go in, and they had to go immediately.

"Cluster-bomb-armed squadrons, increase thrust to maximum. No, override safeties and kick it up to one oh five." She'd done some crazy things in her battles, but she'd never ordered an entire force of fighters to overload their reactors. It was a violation of regulations, and probably a court-martial offense. At least back when such things mattered.

Let them throw me in the stockade if they want. If I'm still here in an hour.

If the stockade is still there…

She listened as the acknowledgements came in. Every one of her ten squadrons armed with the last of the cluster munitions replied almost instantly, with no hint of the resentment she'd expected. One by one, she watched as the designated units surged forward, jumping out to the head of the formation. She knew they wouldn't take out all of the escorts, but as she watched them approach and then begin their attacks, she couldn't take her eyes away.

The one hundred and sixteen Lightnings drove straight ahead, nothing but their evasive maneuvers to protect them from the withering defensive fire. She saw the first ship hit and destroyed in a fiery explosion. Then another. Before a single attacking ship had launched its bombs, more than fifteen of them had been destroyed or knocked out of action.

Still, the others stayed on course, not a single ship faltering, nor even cutting its thrust. They came in, their vectors chaotic but still heading toward their targets. She saw one squadron launch. Than another. Within forty seconds, every fighter still in action had sent its bombs toward the enemy escorts. The pilots were still blasting their engines on overload, but now they were flying for themselves, struggling to pull away and return to base to rearm.

As the bombs began to move in on the escorts, the Hegemony vessels maintained their fire. Fighters still died, even as they were blasting at full to alter their vectors, to get away.

We can do something about that to distract these bastards...

"All squadrons, let's follow their lead. Cut safeties and blast reactors at one hundred five, right behind me. Let's get in there and blast some battleships."

She pushed her ship forward, feeling the thrust slam into her, far above any level the dampeners could fully absorb. She didn't care. Those lead squadrons had done heroic duty, and now the rest of the wings were going to give them a chance to escape.

She stared straight ahead, watching as the cluster bombs began to impact the escorts, slamming into the waiting ships and tearing great holes in front of the battleships.

Holes the rest of her fighters were heading toward even then.

She darted her eyes down to her panel, checking the status of her torpedo. She'd picked a target already, a nice, juicy battleship that had so far escaped with minimal damage. *We'll see about that...*

She angled her thrusters, her body slamming into the side of the cockpit as the force came down on her hard. She was uncomfortable, in pain, but she held it back, a wall in her mind protecting her focus, repelling all distractions.

She stared straight ahead, her hand on the controls, her finger hovering over the firing stud, as the hulking battleship grew on her scanners. She stayed on target, every muscle in her body tight, aching. She saw the range drop below five thousand. Then four thousand.

She took a deep breath and glanced at the area display. Three of her squadrons were with her, their ships screaming in just behind. There were four enemy battleships ahead—her target, and three others that now faced the deadly assault coming in.

She pressed the controls, loosing her torpedo almost entirely on instinct, and then gritted her teeth as her ship blasted wildly, nudging her vector just enough to clear the target ship.

She'd scored a hit, she was sure of that, but the damage assessment would take a few more seconds. Meanwhile, she watched as the rest of her ships went in, the three squadrons just behind her launching one torpedo after another and scoring more than a dozen hits.

The battleships shook with the fury of the attacks, even as the remaining escorts gunned down bombers as they came in. It was a bloodbath, each side clawing at the other in an orgy of killing and devastation. Covington had fought against the Union, and she'd seen some terrible battles in that war, but she'd never witnessed anything like what she watched just then in the Olyus system.

More of her people were still coming in, but she knew there was nothing she could do for them. Her duty was clear: get back to the mothership and rearm. The wings in Admiral Barron's force in-system weren't going to get out again, not before the battleships were engaged. But Clint Winters' squadrons, half of them under Covington's command, just might manage it.

She fought off the exhaustion and the fear that kept trying to push its way in. She wanted rest, or even a few hours of quiet peace. But she had her duty, as every warrior in the Olyus system did then, and she would see it done.

Whatever it cost her.

* * *

"Get those shuttles docked, commander, and I mean now!" Andi Lafarge stood on *Hermes*'s deck. She was far too agitated to sit. Every few minutes, she had to fight off an urge to order her ship—the one she'd been given to complete her task, at least; *Pegasus* would always be *her* ship—to rush into the center of the storm.

To die with Tyler if she couldn't help him.

But that would be giving up, and Andi Lafarge did *not* give up. Not ever.

"Yes, captain. Flight control says they'll all be in place in thirty—"

"Fifteen minutes, commander. And not a damned second longer, unless everybody down there wants to float home."

"Yes, captain."

Andi had noticed some tension from her crew at first, or at least a tentative caution when they dealt with her. She understood. She didn't imagine she'd much like the idea of some smuggler taking command if she'd been career navy. But she was pretty sure she'd won them over, or at least shown them she was tough as nails, and no one they wanted to mess with. She wasn't sure which of those was the stronger motivator, but either would serve.

She'd tried to keep her eyes away from the long-range display, from the drone-relayed images of the inferno surrounding Megara...and Barron's task force. The scene looked like an image from hell, and every time her control slipped and she looked, she had to fight to hold back the tears. Barron had "Raptor" Stockton with him, probably the deadliest weapon the Confederation had against the Hegemony, and he had Anya Fritz on board to keep *Dauntless* going. He had Atara Travis, too, one of her closest friends, and probably the one person Barron needed most at his side in battle. Andi would have been jealous of Travis—and she'd have hated herself for allowing such an emotion to push its way into her mindset, too—but the relationship between Barron and his exec, and now flag captain, was so obviously akin to that of siblings that she'd put any petty concerns aside long before.

Now, she wished with all her heart the only thing she had to worry about was the two of them in some sweaty romp in Tyler's cabin. At least they'd both likely survive that.

"Captain, flight command reports that fifteen minutes is not poss—"

"Fifteen minutes better be possible, because in sixteen, somebody's going out the airlock." She didn't really care if her temporary crew liked her or not. She'd agreed to carry out one mission on *Hermes*, as a favor to Tyler. She wasn't likely to actually space any of her crew if they missed the deadline, but they didn't know that. Why not make the most of the "mysterious smuggler as new commander" thing while she could? Especially since everybody seemed to know she'd killed Ricard Lille.

She watched as the last group of shuttles lined up outside the docking bays. *Hermes* wasn't a battleship, and it didn't have the massive flight decks those behemoths did. She could only take two shuttles at a time into the inner bays, and another two at the external docking rings. Combined with the near panic the withdrawal order had caused at the Institute, especially among those not on the evac list, the entire operation had been a nightmare.

Though not as horrible, she suspected, as it would be to give the order to transit, and to leave so many of those she'd cared about behind in hell.

That horror still lay ahead of her...after she'd finished cramming the scientists aboard.

* * *

"All ships, maintain forward thrust. All primaries, prepare to open fire." Clint Winters sat on *Constitution*'s bridge, his eyes locked on the display in front of him, his hands clenched tightly in fists at his side. He'd given the order, the one that had been at the back of his throat since the battle began. The one he'd been unable to hold back any longer as he'd watched the Hegemony forces advancing on Megara, on Tyler Barron's task force and the orbital fortresses.

"Yes, admiral." A few seconds later: "All units confirm, sir." Davis Harrington's voice sounded almost like a copy of Winters's. The aide was clearly as relieved as his commander that the big ships of the task force were finally doing something.

Winters knew he was exceeding his authority, but the enemy jamming had cut communications from his flagship and Admirals Nguyen and Barron, restricting their back-and-forth to drones sent on roundabout courses. He hadn't received one in some time, and he hadn't sent one either. He didn't want to give Nguyen a chance to order him not to attack. The Hegemony would be fully engaged with Barron's ships in a few minutes, and that was when Winters knew he had to hit them. Victory seemed unlikely—the odds were just too great—but whatever chance there was, it was then.

"Admiral, *Hermes* is approaching the fleet, bound for transit point four. We've received a communique that they're transiting out."

Winters nodded. It was good to know that the scientists were on their way away from the battle, but he had no time for such things. He checked his harness and took a deep breath, as his ships moved into railgun range of the enemy. He'd soon know how good a job his fighters had done…and what hellfire awaited his ships.

Only a few seconds passed before he had the first answer. Five of the closest enemy battleships opened up, sending chunks of super-heavy metals toward his advancing battle line at hyper-velocity. The range was long, and all the shots missed, though one had come within two hundred meters of *Victory*.

He watched as the range ticked down, his ships getting closer to their own firing range. He had to run the gauntlet, race through the distance where the enemy could fire unanswered.

Time moved glacially, a long, slow crawl, even as the enemy fired again. Two of his ships were hit this time, and both were badly damaged. He glanced at the reports, but there was nothing he could do except press on.

He remained silent. His ships were conducting maximum evasive maneuvers, and their primaries were armed and ready, at least those that hadn't been damaged before they could fire. There was no point in issuing random orders. His people just had to gut their way through…until they could strike.

"Primary range in forty seconds, admiral. All ships report ready to fire."

"All vessels are to fire at will at will as soon as they enter range." The enemy railguns might be a terror, but Confederation primaries were nothing to sneeze at.

He stared ahead, waiting…and then heard the familiar whine as *Constitution*'s main guns opened fire. All along the display, primaries fired, the deadly beams lancing through space toward the enemy. The beams weren't as strong as the railguns, but they were easier to aim, and the first barrage scored four hits. Winters knew the enemy ships were huge and strongly armored, and it was hard to discern just how much damage the hits had inflicted. But primary beams gave even the largest, toughest ships more than a nudge. He was sure the shots had ripped deep into their targets, frying systems and blasting open sections of the Hegemony vessels.

A second later, his fleet had its first loss. *Banner* was struck directly amidships by a railgun. The older battleship, still carrying damage from previous fights, hung in space for a moment, floating almost peacefully. Then the stricken vessel split open like an egg, fluids and gases—and no doubt crew members— spilling out into space all along the rapidly expanding crack in its hull. The grim spectacle went on for perhaps twenty seconds, and then the ship's reactors lost containment, and she disappeared in the shocking violence of a thermonuclear explosion.

Winters was grim, but his intensity, if anything, was stronger. He added revenge for *Banner* to his list of reasons to destroy every Hegemony ship he could reach.

As if he needed more reasons.

He didn't think his people could win. They likely couldn't fight their way through the enemy to link up with the rest of the fleet. But that didn't matter to him.

All that mattered was that he was sick of holding back.

It was time to show the Hegemony why they called him the Sledgehammer.

Chapter Seventeen

Court of the Sun
Planet Elsibar, Ferrious II
Capital of the Sapphire Worlds
Year 318 AC

"I am honored, Enlightened One, that you have granted me an audience." Sara Eaton stood ramrod straight, her dress blacks pristine. She looked every bit the military officer turned ambassador she was. She hesitated for an instant, confirming from her memory that she'd used the right terminology. If her mission to the reaches of the Far Rim had taught her anything at all, it was that the rulers this far out on the galaxy's edge weren't shy about granting themselves sweeping and poetic titles.

"You are most welcome, Admiral Eaton. We have long wondered why the Confederation did not send an ambassadorial mission to Elsibar." The words were spoken by a grotesquely fat man sitting on a garish golden throne. He was dressed in fine silks, and wore more golden chains than she could easily count. She'd stopped trying at nine.

Sara nodded gently. *That's because your little strip of worlds was too irrelevant to make it worthwhile.* She kept the thought to herself, though.

"A dreadful oversight, I assure you, Enlightened One. I am afraid our knowledge of happenings so far out on the Rim is not what it should be." She stopped there. She'd almost added that most of the specific information she possessed had come from the Alliance. But the nations of the Far Rim, mostly small and fractious, shared one thing above all else: a hatred and fear of the Alliance.

The Palatians had fought wars against their neighbors farther out on the Rim, taken worlds and compelled the payment of tribute. She had gotten so used to having the Palatians as allies that she'd almost forgotten how aggressive and warlike they were. She was there to convince the Far Rim nations that a terrible enemy threatened them all…but the Palatians had been that for half a century.

"You have met with my supreme commanders, admiral. They have advised me about the threat of which you speak." The Enlightened One paused for a moment, and Sara tried— and failed—to discern his intentions. He wasn't an impressive presence, not to her sensibilities, at least, but she realized there was a certain practiced slyness to him. "Your evidence seems quite credible, admiral, and yet, you must admit, this tale of an enemy so overpowering…it is difficult to believe fully. What of your Confederation navy? Even here on the Far Rim, we know of your great battleships, and of your renowned officers—Tyler Barron, Van Striker. Your name is not unknown to us, admiral. Could you not defeat this invader?"

"Our forces fight them even now, Enlightened One, yet we have been driven back to Megara itself. And Admiral Striker, whose name you mentioned…he was killed in battle against the enemy." It was a lie, of course, but she hadn't been able to reconcile with an officer like Striker being murdered in the street. His heroic death in battle might be fictional, but it also might be useful. And that would make his death slightly less meaningless. "We will likely be defeated without aid…and if we fall, there is little chance the Far Rim will be able to endure. You will all follow our fate and become slaves to the Hegemony."

It was an aggressive argument, especially with a pompous fool whose claim to greatness was being born in the line of succession to a great-grandfather who'd been somewhat of an accomplished conqueror nearly a century earlier, at least by Far Rim standards. Sara's data on the Sapphire Worlds and other Far Rim nations had been greatly enhanced during her stop at Palatia, and she'd studied it all carefully on the voyage. The Enlightened One—and as far as the Palatians had known, that was the fool's only name—seemed like just the sort to continue the family tradition of squandering his famed ancestor's gains. By all accounts, fewer than half the Sapphire Worlds of eighty years before still remained.

"We are stronger than you might believe, admiral."

She couldn't tell if there was any resentment in his voice, or if he was just engaging in empty boasting. "I do not doubt your strength, Enlightened One. Yet the entire Confederation navy, supported by most of the Alliance fleet, has been unable to stop the enemy's relentless advance. Word of your power and renown reach all the way back to Megara, yet the Confederation is many times the size of the Sapphire Worlds. Can even your feared warriors face such a numerous enemy alone? For what else can be your fate after we are gone?"

"What would you have me do, admiral? Send my fleets far away, to the Inner Rim, while my enemies feast on my undefended worlds? What of the Alliance? The Palatians are a threat to the entire region. What guarantees can you offer that they will not seek to take advantage if we come to your aid?"

Sara had been waiting for him to bring up the Alliance. Imperator Tulus had given her a powerful tool to use in recruiting the Far Rim nations.

"Aside from the Alliance's full commitment to the fight, to which all of their available forces have been committed, I can offer this." She reached into her pocket and pulled out a miniature tablet. "Your experts may examine this and confirm its authenticity. It is an offer from Imperator Tulus, a blood oath, given on his full honor as a Palatian warrior." She knew the Far Rim nations all hated the Alliance, but she suspected they understood the place honor played in Palatian society. "Any nation that signs the treaty, that adds its forces to those defending the Rim, shall be, now and forever, friends of the Alliance, and shall never be attacked or invaded by any Palatian forces. Ever." It was an amazing gesture, a repudiation of sixty years of Alliance policy, and Tulus had given it willingly, fully aware of just how crucial it would be to any hope of uniting the Far Rim.

He had given her something else, as well.

"Imperator Tulus also vows that any nation that rejects this plea, that stands by and does nothing while the forces of its neighbors are slaughtered for lack of additional support, shall be, for all time, enemies of the Alliance, and he will himself lead his forces in the sacred war to destroy the Rim traitors."

It was brilliant, offering deliverance from the conquest all had feared from the nearby Alliance, along with a deadly and credible threat for those who failed to answer the call. She suspected the inception of Tulus's offer—and his threat—had been more straightforward than intricately woven, but it gave her the best chance at success she had. She could scare them all with tales of the Hegemony, but even with all the evidence she'd brought, a new and unknown enemy so far away would never seem truly *real*. But they already feared the Alliance. It was as real as a threat got, and much, much closer.

Still, she'd almost held back the second part. She wasn't a diplomat, but she knew showing up with dire threats along with enticements was a risky way to go. All it would take was offending one petty Rim tyrant, offending his sensibilities and his overinflated view of his own power, and that kind of aggressive effort could easily backfire. She *would* have held it back, save for one undeniable fact. She didn't have time. For all she knew, Megara had already been attacked. She didn't know what would happen at the capital—or after the struggle there—but she doubted the Hegemony was about to put its tail between its legs and return home. And that meant the Confederation needed more allies, far sooner than the glacial process diplomacy usually became. She needed to speed things along, and she'd never seen an accelerant as effective as fear.

"You carry with you interesting words, admiral, and thoughts we must consider. Stay with us for a time, and we shall discuss them in greater detail."

Sara almost snapped back an answer, a reminder that time was the one thing she didn't have to offer. But she held it back. Returning empty-handed was no better than returning late, and pompous ass or no, the course taken by the Enlightened One, and his Sapphire Worlds, would have a tremendous effect on what the other Far Rim polities chose to do. The small groupings of worlds were influenced by the larger nation, and scared as well. She'd never get some local potentate who ruled three systems to send his ships so far away if the Sapphire Worlds remained uncommitted.

"Your hospitality is greatly appreciated, Enlightened One, as is your wisdom. I urge you, however, to expedite our discussions. There is little time."

"Of course, admiral…of course. We shall reconvene tomorrow evening for a state dinner in your honor. Then, perhaps the next day, we can begin discussions in some earnest."

Sara barely held back the sigh. A day lost, and then more time wasted on pointless festivities, on some local monarch's effort to show off the richness of his kingdom to an ambassador who couldn't care less. But there was nothing she could do. She needed the Sapphire Worlds if she was going to organize any meaningful coalition on the Far Rim.

"I will be honored to attend, Enlightened One." *And, after complimenting the grandeur of your table and the brilliance of your assembled nobles, I will bring the discussion back to the treaty. I will try to save your pointless little empire in spite of itself…along with the Confederation and the rest of the Rim.*

* * *

Sara knelt before the raised dais and lowered her head as she'd been instructed to do. She found the entire process degrading, but she understood the importance of her mission to find new allies. The Sultanate was, depending on the source and its own leanings, either the most powerful of the Far Rim kingdoms, or the second most. If she could gain their support, it would likely convince several of the others to commit as well…and almost certainly the Enlightened One, still teetering on the edge of signing the treaty. The Sultanate and the Sapphire Worlds were rivals, and neither one was likely to risk allowing the other to sign a treaty with the Confederation and the Alliance without also being a part of the new power bloc. Nor could either send their forces so far while the other remained on the Far Rim in strength.

"You are welcome, admiral, to my court." The sultan's voice was deep, gravelly, and there was an arrogance in his tone. Still, the ruler's words seemed respectful enough, probably more so than he'd mustered for anyone else in a long time. The Sultanate was no less terrified of Alliance aggression than the Sapphire Worlds—though the denials of such concerns were just as loud—and the idea of the Palatians allied with the Confederation *had* to seem like some kind of nightmare.

"It is my honor to come here, your highness, as the first representative of the Confederation to make an official visit. It is something that should have occurred long ago, before desperate times forced the issue."

"Yes, admiral, it should have. For many years, your Confederation seemed to have little interest in the Sultanate, or, indeed, any of the nations on the Far Rim. Now, on this first visit, it appears you come not simply to establish diplomatic relations, but to ask that we join you in some kind of war. That is an audacious request on such short acquaintance, wouldn't you agree?"

She remained kneeling. Her advisors had been clear that she wasn't to rise until instructed to do so. She fought off the urge to stand anyway and stare down the arrogant fool sitting in front of her, to show him how Confederation admirals really did their business. But she thought of the desperate fight even then likely raging back home. Tyler Barron was counting on her. The whole Confederation was counting on her. So, she stayed in place, staring down, and said, "That is true, your highness, and yet it is born not from arrogance, but from necessity. The enemy we fight is a danger to all on the Rim—to all of humanity not already under their control. I am here not because the Confederation wishes to interfere in your affairs, but because we…need you."

She struggled to get the words out. The Confederation *was* in dire straits, but it still hurt to pander to fools like the sultan.

Duty. Duty calls. You have to succeed. You have to bring back help from the Far Rim, whatever it takes…

Chapter Eighteen

CFS Dauntless
140,000 Kilometers from Megara, Olyus III
Year 318 AC

The Battle of Megara – The Walls Crumble

"Full thrust, captain, all ships. It's time for the battle line to get into this fight." Barron struggled with all he could muster to hide the gloom building up inside him. His forces had fought well—and there were no words for what Stockton and his Horsemen had done, or for the price they had paid for it—but the cold reality that had been there since the beginning remained, as resolute and unstoppable as it had always been.

The enemy was just too strong, their numbers too great, their technology too superior. Heroism and sacrifice were powerful forces, but neither was an infinite resource. His people's morale was still strong, surprisingly so, but he knew that wouldn't last. Soaring speeches and displays of extreme heroism could work a group of warriors into a frenzy, but eventually, they would all come to the same desperate conclusion Barron himself had.

They had lost. The half of the fleet positioned with him was doomed. He wasn't going to get out of the system, and neither was Admiral Nguyen…but Clint Winters and his ships, at least, had a chance.

They could keep the fight alive, however hopeless it might be.

"Get me Admiral Nguyen, commander." Winters had to run, and he had to do it immediately. Every second that passed cut the chances of even half the fleet escaping. Worse, Tulus and his Alliance forces were positioned with Winters's task force, and Barron couldn't imagine what it would take the get the imperator to run and leave his blood brother behind.

He angled his head as he waited, glancing at the display. The orbital forts were fighting hard, most of them running their reactors—what they had left of them, anyway—at massive overloads. The platform crews were dotted with veterans, mostly experienced fighters transferring to a less demanding post than the main fleet. There were more than a few political appointees, as well. No one had expected Megara to find itself on the front lines of a desperate battle anytime soon. Still, while he'd heard reports of some problems with morale, that all seemed to be under control, and the men and women still at their posts were as deeply in the fight as *Dauntless*'s veterans.

Barron wondered if the fortress crews had figured out yet that most of them were going to die, and how they would handle that realization. Crippled forts would attempt to evacuate, of course, but the enemy railguns were still firing with deadly effectiveness, and that wasn't going to leave a lot of time to get to the lifepods. The four platforms that had been totally destroyed up to that point had lasted less than ten minutes after their last weapons were silenced, and Barron knew—but had chosen not to share with anyone who didn't—that fewer than six percent of the crews of those forts had managed to escape.

"Admiral Nguyen on your line, admiral."

"Tyler," Nguyen said, "we've got to evacuate the forces in the outer system."

Barron would have smiled if his mood wasn't so grim. He tended to think of Nguyen as an old man, decades from meaningful service. But the officer still knew what he was doing, as well as Barron did himself.

If not better.

"That's why I commed you, sir. Clint Winters isn't going to make a run for it on my orders. And I suspect it's going to take both of us to get Vian Tulus to go with him."

"You may be right, Tyler. I will send a communications drone at once. Perhaps you could transmit a personal message to Vian Tulus for inclusion."

"Yes, sir." Barron knew Nguyen realized it would be difficult to get Tulus to retreat, but he suspected the admiral couldn't really understand the immensity of trying to get a Palatian imperator to run from a battle, leaving his allies behind to die. It was almost an impossibility, but Barron knew Megara was going to fall, whether the Alliance fleet escaped or stayed and was destroyed. There was no longer any point in losing ships that could get away. He'd have ordered his own forces to retreat as well, but it was too late. The enemy was too close. His exit paths were blocked. His people would have no choice but to fight to the end.

"I will send that immediately, admiral." Nguyen was on the very edge of the Confederation line. "Sir, you might be able to make it out with—"

"No, admiral. Our forces are committed here. I'd rather fight to the end than die running."

Barron nodded gently. "Yes, sir."

He cut the line and switched his comm to record mode. Then, his voice soft, making as little spectacle as he could in the middle of *Dauntless*'s bridge, he recorded a message to Vian Tulus. A request to his friend. And a goodbye.

He sent the message as soon as it was done, and then he looked back at the display, just as the two largest forts remaining in action fired a volley. Three of their primaries caught one of the big enemy battleships within seconds of each other. The massive vessel froze for a few seconds, and then it just vanished, consumed by the massive forces of thermonuclear devastation. The explosion was instigated, Barron suspected, by the loss of containment on the antimatter pods used to fuel the railguns.

Whatever happened in rest of the battle, he drew satisfaction from one fact he considered incontrovertible. The Hegemony forces were suffering losses they couldn't have imagined. For all their technological advantage, for the overwhelming numbers the enemy had brought to bear, Barron's people were giving worse than they got...and amid the sorrow for his people's impending fate, and the fear closing in on his own mind, he felt a grim sort of pride.

He watched again as the fortresses fired, claiming yet another Hegemony battleship, and then, seconds later, a railgun blast scored a direct hit and vaporized the last chunk of what had remained of Megara's Prime Base.

There were half a dozen of the platforms still in the fight, and the need to engage them was giving Barron's battleships the chance to close to their own firing range before the enemy could focus on them. Thoughts of doom still pressed in in him, but he rallied all that remained inside and, as the range counted down, said softly, "Primaries, open fire."

The bridge lights dimmed, and he heard the familiar whine, the quad-barreled emplacement firing, in the place, in his mind, at least—and his heart—of the old *Dauntless*'s double gun. He watched, supremely confident in the skill of his gunnery crews, defying the long range of the shot. He felt pure satisfaction, but no surprise, when the weapon struck one of the lead Hegemony battleships head on.

This fight isn't over yet, you bastards...

His thoughts shifted to Van Tulus, to the communique he'd sent to the flagship for transmission to the imperator. He hoped it was good, that it would be compelling to its recipient. Because if it wasn't, one of his best friends would die needlessly, along with all his ship and warriors.

And Clint Winters is going to need the Palatians wherever he fights next. He's going to need them desperately...

* * *

"*Olympus* and *Indomitable* are to move forward and take position with Task Group Beta, at the third moon of Electra." Clint Winters's voice slammed into his officers. His determination, his raw refusal to yield, was clear in every word.

"Yes, sir."

Winters had been moving his fleet up steadily, putting all his self-control into keeping himself from simply ordering all his ships forward. Vian Tulus had been urging him to do just that for the last hour, and Winters wanted nothing more than to comply. But he had orders, and despite his reputation as something of a maverick, he'd always obeyed orders.

Well, usually…

Dustin Nguyen's orders at the start of the battle had been clear, however, and if Winters was going to ignore someone's commands, it wasn't going to be those of an officer who'd fought alongside Admiral Barron. The *old* Admiral Barron, the savior of the Confederation.

Even as Winters thought of Tyler's grandfather in those terms, he realized his respect for his own comrade was nearly as strong. He'd follow Tyler Barron anywhere, though the two were almost of the exact same rank. But right now, Tyler Barron was back at Megara, looking very much like he was trapped.

And that meant Clint Winters's forces *had* to attack. They had to break through to Barron and Nguyen…before it was too late.

Still, despite his nickname—and "Sledgehammer" didn't exactly imply reasoned and considered thought—Winters was quite meticulous in his operations. Getting his ships shot to pieces wasn't going to help anyone, and he'd been using every planet and moon in the outer system to provide cover for his fleet. He'd worked his way closer, into the enemy's railgun range, leapfrogging his ships, getting them back behind a planet or some other cover as quickly as possible.

He'd lost two ships outright, vessels caught in transit and blasted to bits by the heavy Hegemony guns, but that had been far less than he'd feared, and his advancing ships had opened up with their own fire, emerging from behind the cover of the gas giant and its moons, shooting and ducking back before the enemy targeting systems could lock on and return fire.

Usually before. His forward ships had taken a few hits,

though all but three were still in the fight, and even that trio was still active in his second line, waiting for the enemy to close. Those ships had lost their primaries, at least unless their sweating engineering teams could get them back online, but they were far from finished.

Winters watched as the two battleships he'd ordered forward increased their thrust. The pair of ships would be exposed to enemy fire for a short time—*six minutes*, he thought, with some degree of rounding in the number—but the course he'd set was an unpredictable one, and with any luck, the two vessels would reach their destinations intact. The battleships would both fire before they ducked behind the gas giant's massive bulk, and then they would sit there and recharge before emerging again for another blast.

Winters's forces were doing better than he'd dared to hope, and he knew he owed that to Barron and Nguyen for the pounding they were taking. The enemy was trying to hold his ships back with a blocking force, exactly what he would have done in their position, while they moved directly on Megara and the ships stationed there. It was the proper strategy, no question, but the Sledgehammer wasn't about to let it happen, at least not unmolested. He didn't have orders to close now—but he didn't have specific orders not to.

"Admiral, we've got a communications drone approaching. Beacon indicates it is from fleet command."

Winters froze. He *hadn't* had any order to prevent him from advancing. He glanced back to the display, to the spotty long-range readings he had of the nightmare unfolding around Megara. Things didn't look good there, which was one major reason he was pushing his forces forward. But his gut told him Admirals Nguyen and Barron would see things differently.

Winters almost told Davis Harrington that the officer had only *thought* he'd received a message from a drone, that it had actually been some sporadic cosmic energy—or any other bullshit that popped into his head. He was pretty sure Harrington would go along with him. Orders were orders, of course, but what difference did any of it make if the fleet was lost?

"On my line, commander." The words came out almost on their own, as though some disciplined part of himself had taken over, demanded he listen to the orders that drone almost certainly carried.

He listened as the sound of Nguyen's voice, shaky with age, but still strong, filled his ears. The orders were just what he'd dreaded. He rebelled against the thought of pulling out of Olyus, of turning tail and running. Abandoning Megara was unthinkable enough, but leaving his comrades trapped, surrounded by the enemy, made him want to double over and spill the contents of his stomach on the deck.

But those words were orders...from the mouth of a man who'd served alongside Admiral Barron decades before, when that famous officer had saved the Confederation from ruin.

Winters had allowed himself to imagine that the younger Barron was destined to follow in his grandfather's footsteps, that once again, a member of that naval dynasty would step in and ward off doom. But if Winters's ships fled, Tyler Barron was almost certain to die right where he was, meeting his end along with his second *Dauntless*.

Winters *couldn't* obey that order. He couldn't leave his comrades behind, leave Megara to the enemy. But Nguyen's last words struck him hard, and he leaned back in his chair, almost recoiling from their power.

"The future of the Confederation is in your hands now." The sentence rang out in his head, again and again, like the tolling of some massive bell. He longed to try to rescue Barron and Nguyen, to find a way to save Megara...but it was hopeless. He was too far away. There were too many enemy ships in the way, and too little time. He could leave now, as ordered, or he could throw away his entire task force, almost every warship the Confederation still possessed.

Or would still possess, once the fighting in the Olyus system was over.

He wrestled with himself, fighting to override every impulse he possessed, every urge that seemed even remotely natural to him. He hated Nguyen for what the old admiral had said, for placing the responsibility for the Confederation on him as he had.

He wanted to fight, to battle it out until the end, and, if need be, die right there. But duty was there again, a shadow looming over him, and behind it, billions of Confederation citizens, staring at him from the darkness, looking to him to keep the fight going, to find some way to defend them.

Winters turned toward the job that duty had thrust on him. He was morose as he calculated the retreat vectors for his fleet, and as he prepared to give the order he knew he would choke on. But there was one bright side.

He wouldn't be on *Invictus*'s bridge when Vian Tulus got Barron's plea to retreat.

* * *

"I know I place an impossible demand on you, that no matter what you do, you will feel as though your honor is lost. I ask you, as your brother, as a warrior who has shed blood with you, do not think this way. If I fall here, in honorable combat, there is no one I can rely on to continue my personal fight, no one to stand in the line where I would have...save you, my comrade and brother. I ask much of you, I understand this, and I would not do it if there was another way, if our fight was any less dire. Go, my friend, carry my respect with you, and the memories of the battles where we have fought side by side. Remember me, and if you see through to victory and return to Palatia, light the candles for me, and toast to the victories we have won together."

Vian Tulus was a Palatian warrior, the imperator of his people, a hard man who had lived a life of combat and bloodshed almost without pause since his fifteenth summer. Yet as he heard Barron's words, sitting on his flagship's bridge, he felt the walls inside him crumbling.

There was sadness, deep and unbearable, a weakness unseemly for a warrior of his stature, yet one he couldn't push back, no matter how hard he tried. Rage, too, like a force of nature, a roiling storm growing inside him, a screeching howl into the wind demanding the blood of his enemies. Honor and loyalty clashed in him, anger and obligation. He couldn't leave, flee the battle now. It was inconceivable.

But Tyler had laid the obligation on him to carry his brother's fight forward. It was a request no Palatian could refuse... yet Tyler Barron wasn't yet dead. Did such a request—could it—come before the need to come to a brother's aide?

Tulus wanted to scream, to throw his head back and howl to the gods. He wanted to let loose his frustration, the fury churning inside him, the venomous anger he felt toward the Hegemony, the enemy that had brought him—and Tyler Barron—to such a dreadful pass.

His ships were engaged, moving forward alongside Clint Winters's, leapfrogging into firing position. He'd been vaguely uncomfortable with the maneuver, some residual impulses of the old Palatian inside him crying out that such was beneath his dignity. But the tactic had worked brilliantly, and if he knew anything about Clint Winters, it was that the officer was no coward. There was victory in war, and there was defeat, and any stratagems that avoided the latter were worthwhile. Tulus's own people had experienced the bitterness of defeat, of occupation by outworlders and a century of slavery. Too many of them had forgotten the essence of that bitter lesson.

But he had sworn he never would.

I will do as you ask, Tyler, my brother, though I will never forgive myself.

Tulus stared straight ahead, and when he spoke, his tone was as cold as the grave. "All ships...the fleet will withdraw at once. Full thrust toward the designated transit point."

The bridge was silent for a moment, a delay even in Globus's acknowledgement of the command. Tulus knew what they were all thinking. He was thinking the same thing. But there was no choice. Withdrawing was the tactically correct decision. And, far more importantly, he simply could not deny Barron's request.

He sat like a statue, unmoving.

I will make the enemy pay for this...and if you are fated to die here, my brother, I will avenge you if I must cast the entire galaxy into the flaming pits of hell to do it...

Chapter Nineteen

CFS Hermes
Calvus System, Approaching Planet Craydon
Year 318 AC

"Craydon control, this is CFS *Hermes*, requesting final approach authorization." Andi was raw, her pain an open would, and it showed in the coarseness of her voice.

Somebody get up off your ass over there, before I just decide to open fire.

It was an empty threat. *Hermes* was a glorified courier ship, not a combat vessel, and no matter how useless the chunk of organic material sitting in the control center in orbit around Craydon was, the last thing Confederation personnel needed just then was to be shooting at each other.

"*Hermes*, we have cleared your beacon. You may approach and dock at gamma platform, gate four."

Andi knew her impatience was mostly her own creation, and not based on anything outside of the anger and hatred that was driving her.

She was glad to have those dark thoughts, though, because rage was the only thing keeping her going. She'd never been closer to just giving up. She'd likely lost the one person she cared most about. Worse, she'd left him behind. The Confederation itself seemed doomed, and for all the raw tenacity that ran through her veins, her intellect told a tale of seemingly inevitable defeat.

But she had something to do for Tyler, and she would die—and kill anyone who stood in her way—before she would fail to see it done.

"Bring us in, commander. And advise Dr. Witter we'll be unloading his people and their cargo as soon as the ship is docked." Andi didn't know where the Institute's researchers would end up, but she was damned sure going to see they had everything they needed, whatever that took. She had orders from Admiral Nguyen and from Tyler, but nothing from the Senate. That had just been too much of an ask on short notice, especially with every politician on Megara screaming for the fleet to drive the enemy away, or else frantically looking for some kind of cover to protect themselves if things came to an actual assault on the planet. That didn't even address those who had already fled the Olyus system in advance of the hostilities.

She wasn't sure if military commanders had the legal authority to compel planetary leaders to cooperate, but the Craydonite who gave her a hard time was going to be one very sorry bureaucrat.

She got up and walked toward the lift, then turned back to face her exec. "Advise the authorities I will be coming aboard at once to discuss a matter of the highest importance." She took another step and stopped again. "Have Dr. Witter meet me at the docking port."

"Yes, captain."

She nodded to herself as she stepped into the elevator car. She hadn't thought earlier about bringing Witter, but now it made perfect sense to her. He would support the orders she carried, help explain the importance of the research team's mission.

And he just might lessen the chance that she'd have to decorate a wall with the insides of some pompous local official who gave her shit, while Tyler and the others were back in Megara, possibly dying.

Or dead already…

It was a thought that chilled her to the bone, and she struggled to wrench her mind away from it. The battle might very well still be raging, but it could be over, too. And the implications of that were more than she could handle just then.

She reached out and punched in the code for the docking portal, and then she closed her eyes and forced herself to focus. She had work to do…work that was crucial to saving the Confederation.

To defeating the Hegemony.

She might not have been able to stay with Tyler, or to save him.

But if he didn't make it out of Olyus, if he died there with his spacers, she damned sure was going to do everything she could to avenge him.

* * *

"Those orders are from the naval C-in-C, Mr. Davidoff, and they leave no room for anything short of total obedience." Andi's face was twisted into a scowl, and she turned and gestured toward the uniformed woman standing behind her. "Captain Elvarez, here, remains your liaison to the Admiralty—however, her mission has changed somewhat. Instead of waiting while your shipyards concoct delays to create additional billings—a tradition of fraud I can assure you is over as of this instant—she will become your watchdog. One with teeth. You will now apply yourself to expediting the launch of every new ship into immediate service, whether finished or not. If it has reactors and any weapons at all, it needs to be ready for service in a matter of days."

"Captain Lafarge, that is simply not how we—"

"I'm doing you a courtesy in coming here, Mr. Davidoff. I have been on Craydon for two days, and my executive officer has discovered at least six different prosecutable offenses in your military contracting activities. I understand that you own most of Craydon's local officials, and no doubt, the planet's four senators…I believe Victoria Janus is the most senior, is she not?" She'd had no idea who Craydon's senior member of the Senate was until less than an hour before, but Davidoff didn't know that. "However, that impressive collection of criminals will no longer be sufficient to sustain your rampant overbilling and other illegal acts. I would see to it that your family's entire corporate empire comes crashing to the ground, if only out of sheer outrage, but that isn't my style." She hesitated for an instant, and then she let her hand drop to her waist. She was dressed in her still strange-feeling uniform, but the pistol she had her side was her own, trusty and well used.

The local magnate stood stone-still, clearly seething…but just as obviously, physically intimidated by Andi and her threats.

"Captain Lafarge, I must protest this—"

"You can protest anything you want, Mr. Davidoff, to anyone you want. But if you'd like to walk out of this room in one piece, you will take my request seriously." She could see the tense rustle among the magnate's four bodyguards, but Andi Lafarge wasn't the kind of woman to bring a knife to a gunfight. She had *six* marines with her, half of *Hermes*'s entire complement, and they were equipped as if they were about to launch an invasion somewhere. Killing four guards and one pompous scion of a six-generation-old family fortune wouldn't even be a warmup for them.

"Please, gentlemen," she said softly, her eyes darting toward the leader of the guard contingent. "We're here to conduct business, but if I have to kill you all, I can assure you most earnestly, I will do it, and then I will go home and sleep soundly." That was a lie. Andi hadn't had a minute's sleep since she'd left Olyus. But greasing the men standing in front of her wouldn't contribute at all to her insomnia.

"Can you assure me, at least, that all costs related to this crash launch effort will be covered in addition to previously contracted rates?"

"Mr. Davidoff, all I can assure you is that if you do everything these orders require you to do—and you don't speak more than is necessary—I will allow you to leave this room alive. All other matters, you will have to take up with the appropriate authorities via the usual channels." *Assuming there still are any.* "I trust your usual graft and corruption will lead to a speedy resolution for you, though perhaps it will be more costly than usual."

She was taunting Davidoff, but he stood, clearly enraged but just as obviously not ready to challenge Andi. She was glad that he seemed to be giving in. At least she wouldn't have to spend any more time dealing with him—and the ships in the yards would be up and ready when the Hegemony pushed out from Megara to continue the conquest of the Confederation.

Still, his capitulation only increased the utter contempt and disgust in which she held him. And, she swore to herself, if the bastard did *anything* but exactly what he'd been told to do, she would personally gut him like a fish.

"I'll expect a schedule for the deployment of all near-operational vessels by this time tomorrow."

"Tomorrow? That's not..." Davidoff paused and struggled for a moment to restrain his rage. "Yes, captain. I will see that you have it." The magnate turned abruptly and waved to his guards as he walked briskly to the door. Andi suspected his mind was full of thoughts of revenge, of how he was going to strike back at her for the way she'd treated him.

She almost felt sorry for the fool. There was no way he could hurt her. She lacked the one weakness that would require.

She didn't care. Save for her last obligations to Tyler, she didn't care about a damned thing. They were all as good as dead or slaves already...and to Andi Lafarge, that was very freeing.

It also left very little in the way of restraint to stop her from actually running her knife up the obnoxious industrialist's midsection if he pissed her off enough.

* * *

"Thank you, Captain Lafarge. This whole thing has been very...upsetting. I don't like that we had to retreat from the Olyus system, especially when we had to leave so many people behind. But we've made considerable progress on a number of fronts. If we can get a little more time, I believe we can put some new systems into production, and really make a difference in this war."

"I am glad I was able to get you here, and…*smooth out* the dealings with the local authorities." Andi had run roughshod over several Craydon officials, but, somewhat to her surprise, she hadn't had to kill anybody. If she'd been in a better frame of mind, that probably wouldn't have felt as much like a disappointment as it did. "Your work is of vital importance, doctor, and as long as I'm here, you can come to me anytime if you need something."

She *did* believe the research was crucial work. She just felt it was going to come too late to make a difference. From what she'd heard, the cluster bombs, the first system developed by Witter's team, had been highly effective in preliminary testing. But there weren't enough available, not to affect the outcome of the battle, and she had no idea how long it would take to get mass production underway.

Maybe they can come up with something in time for the next battle—assuming any of the fleet gets out of Olyus.

She wanted to believe the fleet would manage to escape, that Tyler would get past the enemy and pull his forces back to Craydon. Andi saw Tyler's logic in the choice of a fallback position for the fleet. The Confederation's Core consisted of seven systems, all wealthy and highly developed, but their days as industrial powerhouses had long since passed. Megara and her six sisters were dominated by information technologies and the like, and it had been years since busy shipyards and bustling factories had surrounded any of them.

Craydon was different. The planet, like the fifteen other planets in the Confederation's Iron Belt, wasn't quite as heavily fortified as Megara, but it was still well armed by any normal standards, and its productive capacity far outmatched that of the Confederation's capital. Notwithstanding morale and political considerations, the worlds of the Iron Belt were actually more vital to the Confederation's continued resistance and ability to wage war.

The Iron Belt worlds treated commerce and production almost as religion, and the great industrial families dominated the planets and their populations, exerting almost total control over the politicians, government agencies, and, of course, the people. Fraud and abuse were common occurrences, but such things had been ignored for at least three generations, during which the sixteen heavily industrialized worlds had been the true powerhouses of the robust Confederation economy…and provided the raw output to fight three wars against the Union.

"Dr. Witter, I don't know how much longer I will be here." Andi had no other orders, no place to take *Hermes*, but she wasn't sure what was next for her. She wasn't a naval officer, not a real one, no matter how authentic the commission Barron and Holsten had handed her, or how attentively her crew had followed her orders. She *was* a fighter, in every way one could be, but she didn't know what would happen if Tyler and the others she cared about, those she'd left to fight in Olyus, didn't return. Andi had fought her way through one struggle after another with grit and tenacity, and she'd won her deadly duel with Ricard Lille, arguably the most capable assassin the Rim had ever known. But she knew herself well enough to understand one thing.

She was close to being used up. She'd pursued things her entire life—success, wealth, the ability to help those she cared about…even vengeance. But now there was nothing left. She'd done what she'd promised Tyler she would do, and now all that remained was to wait to see what happened at Megara.

And who, if anybody, survived the titanic struggle there.

Chapter Twenty

The Battle of Megara – "Barron's Breakout – Part One"

Tyler Barron was staring at the display, his hope slipping away with each passing moment. *Dauntless* was deep in the fight, along with his entire line. The Confederation battleships had fought hard, even as the remaining enemy railguns tore into the big vessels, knocking one, then the next, from the line...and into oblivion.

The Hegemony forces had copied his tactic of seeking to cripple, not destroy, their targets, to knock out the Confederation primaries before the long-ranged weapons could inflict more damage on their own battered line. There was a perverse satisfaction in realizing the enemy had such respect for the particle accelerators of the Confederation line, but it didn't change the calculus in any material way. The enemy first line was likely going to crush his fleet, albeit at a horrendous cost... and, if somehow Barron managed to escape that fate, there was another force coming forward, dozens and dozens of virtually untouched Hegemony capital ships. When they closed to railgun range, things would be over very quickly for any Confederation survivors. There was a point where massive firepower became invincible, where no tactic or countermove could make up for the sheer destructive fire coming in.

"Admiral, I have Captain Fritz on the line for you."

Barron was a little startled. He hadn't expected to hear from Fritz, and when his longtime engineer had needed to reach him in the past, she'd generally commed directly. *Dauntless* had been extremely fortunate so far in the battle, escaping any serious damage, so he wasn't sure what she needed. But he knew any time Anya Fritz had something to say, he was ready to listen.

"Fritzie, what is it? Some problem in engineering?" Of course, Fritz wasn't *Dauntless*'s engineer anymore, at least not on the official OB. She was responsible for all technical operations fleet-wide.

And Barron wasn't *Dauntless*'s captain anymore either. If there was a problem with the ship, Fritz would have contacted Atara.

"It's something I've been working on, captain...I mean, it's experimental, and probably damned dangerous, but it just might be what we need if you want to."

Barron was confused. He couldn't remember ever hearing Fritz so tentative. "What is it, Fritzie? Just say it."

"I've programmed an operational sequence for the reactors, for any of our reactors. I think it can increase output massively, at least for a short time. The wear and tear on the systems will be brutal, and fleet-wide, we'd almost certainly see some catastrophic failures, but it just might give us enough power."

Barron was still struggling to follow her. "Enough power for what, Fritzie?"

"To break out. To get the fleet through the enemy lines... and out of the system."

Barron was silent for a moment. The Hegemony forces were closing in all around. There was no escape route remaining that could accommodate a fleet the size of the one formed up around Megara. Barron had twice urged Dustin Nguyen to make a run for it himself, to try to get to Craydon with a few ships and reorganize the fleet, but the old admiral had answered that he would remain with the rest of the force at Megara, whatever fate awaited it.

"What are you talking about, Fritzie? We're almost surrounded."

"I didn't say around the enemy. I said through them. If you're willing to take some chances—insane, dangerous chances—I think I can get you eighty-G acceleration, at least for a short time."

The reality of her words hit him hard. The Hegemony forces were moving toward Megara. If his almost stationary fleet could accelerate at that rate, they could close rapidly and push beyond the enemy's range on the other side. It would take time for the Hegemony forces to decelerate and reverse their vectors to pursue.

Would it be enough time to get away, even if Fritzie's wild claims proved to be accurate, as they always had before? And how much of those massive G-forces could the dampeners absorb, even if he overloaded them alongside the reactors? Would his ships get through, only to fly through space full of dead and dying spacers, crushed by the pressure of their own wild escape?

"It's a gamble, Tyler," Fritz said. He couldn't remember the last time she'd used his first name, and the fact that she just had truly scared him. "Maybe a bad gamble, but as far as I see it, we've got no chance otherwise...of holding Megara or of escaping. Unless you have another plan."

He didn't have a plan other than fighting to the bitter end. But he couldn't save Megara no matter what he did, so his crew's deaths would serve no purpose. If there was any chance to get even a portion of the fleet out...

"Fritzie, do what you have to do. You've got maybe twenty minutes to get every ship ready for whatever you've got planned...after that, it'll be too late anyway. Is that even possible?"

"I'll have to make it possible, admiral." She sounded unsure of herself, and *that* scared the hell out of Barron. But any chance was better than none at all.

"Do what you have to, Fritzie, but have it ready in time, or there's no point."

"Yes, sir." She cut the line.

Barron sat for a few seconds, still trying to process what he'd heard. Then he realized there were two things he had to do.

He had to get Stockton's fighters back out there. The thought of sending them out yet again, without rest or food, horrified him—and he suspected that if Fritz's plans worked, some of them would end up left behind, unable to catch up with the retreating fleet in time. He tried to tell himself they were going to die anyway, that anyone who survived would be an improvement. But that was cold comfort.

He had to talk to Stockton…but first, he had to get the whole crazy idea approved. He wasn't in command, and whatever else he might do, he wasn't about to order the fleet into an insane flight across the system without Dustin Nguyen's approval.

"Get me Admiral Nguyen, Atara. Right away."

* * *

"You've all done well, beyond what I or anyone else had the right to expect from you. You've fought like demons, and you have paid the price, but our job isn't done yet, not by a long shot, and I need every one of you to dig deep, to pull up everything you have left. We need to punch a hole in the enemy line. We need to help the fleet break out, to escape this trap and prepare to fight again another day."

Jake Stockton's voice was raw, his dry throat feeling as though a blade sliced across it with each tortured word. His hands ached from gripping his throttle. His body was sore and covered in bruises from the endless G-forces. His heart ached for those he'd lost, no small number of friends among the legions of dead pilots, and he still struggled to face the fact that the fleet was abandoning Megara. All he could hope to achieve now in the capital's system was to extricate some portion of the fleet.

The center of the Confederation was gone. The Hegemony was on the verge of doing what no enemy had ever done before, and even the seemingly invulnerable Jake Stockton felt something that seemed like the end.

"We're going in hard, and we're hitting every ship on our frontage. We're going to launch torpedoes, and then we're going to do strafing runs…until every ship we've got in this system is through. Then we're flying for ourselves, a race to catch our landing platforms, because any battleships that get through aren't stopping and waiting, not even for a lifeboat full of senators, and damned sure not for some pilot too slow to catch up before they jump."

He paused, trying not to think about how many of his people were likely to be left behind to the enemy. He'd always hated the reality of such things, but he'd never been able to argue against the maxim that a battleship that took three years to build, with a thousand crew members, shouldn't rate higher than a few battered Lightnings and the pilots flying them. Still, the harder his people fought now to clear the way, the less chance they had of escaping themselves. It was the kind of profound unfairness that existed so often in war.

"Jake…" He could hear Stara's voice, and a quick check confirmed it was coming in on his private command line. He didn't respond, not immediately. He wasn't done with his pilots yet.

"Leading these wings has been the greatest honor of my life. I thank you all for your tenacity, for your skill. You are the best the Confederation and Alliance have ever produced, and what you have done here will always be remembered. Go forward now, all of you, and know I will be there until the last of you have broken off and headed back to base."

Stockton closed the line and stared at the comm unit, at the blinking light that signified Stara was still waiting. He knew why she had commed him. She loved him, and he loved her, but the odds that both of them would make it out of Olyus were impossibly long. He wanted to say things to her, things he might never have another chance to utter…but he couldn't, not now. Not when he was so deep in his combat mentality. The last thing he wanted to do was hurt her, to speak words to her that were unkind, and that might be the last she ever heard from him.

But the brutal reality was clear. This might be the last time they spoke.

"Stara, I'm sorry. I was sending the wings in."

"I know, Jake. I listened. You were perfect. It's no surprise those men and women will follow you anywhere." Her voice was shaky, but she was clearly trying to hold it together.

"Stara…you know…"

"I know, Jake. I didn't call to distract you. That's the last thing I want to do. Go and fight. No one knows how to do that better than you." She paused. "I love you, Jake. I just wanted to say it once."

The words were simple, quick, intended to preserve his focus, but they hit him like a hammer to the gut. He felt his emotions twisting inside, and he barely managed to respond. "I love you, too, Stara." He couldn't close the line, couldn't bring himself to do it.

She took mercy on him. "Take it to them, Raptor. You can do it. I know that. Your pilots all know that. Now, you go and show the enemy." She cut the line immediately, before he could respond. He knew that had been difficult for her, that she'd done it for him. And he knew he had a job to do.

He flipped back on the main line.

"All wings, full thrust. Let's go remind these bastards just who we are."

* * *

Anya Fritz stood outside *Dauntless*'s reactor control room, staring at the thick metal door. She paused as she moved to enter the space, held back by something unseen, but definitely felt. She'd been in the chamber dozens of times before the fighting around Megara had begun, but the last time she'd entered the space in an emergency, she'd almost died there.

Walt Billings *had* died.

Fritz was a cold fish, a fact she'd always known about herself. But now, she felt fear and remorse, and she struggled to step into the haunted space, cleared now of the radiation that had so poisoned it, but not free of the spirits of Billings and the others who had died there.

Those who had died following her orders.

Those who had died when she had lived.

She walked across the large room, her boots clicking on the polished metal floors. To any observer, she appeared as resolute and unshakable as she ever had. But inside, she was hurting.

The room looked immaculate, almost untouched by the battle raging through the system, and by the usual desperate damage-control efforts of stringing cables and equipment across an already battered chamber. Fritz had seen many combats, and she'd come to realize the factor randomness and luck played in each. She'd served aboard two ships that carried the name *Dauntless*, and both had been desperately damaged in some of their fights. But this time, so far, at least, the enemy's fire had found other targets, and Admiral Barron's flagship had avoided all but light and superficial damage.

So far.

That couldn't last, she knew. If her plan didn't work, if she couldn't get the ships of the fleet out of the trap springing all around them, *Dauntless* would be blasted to scrap, as would every other Confederation ship in the system. Megara was as good as lost. The only question that remained was if the fleet was also lost.

She stopped in front of a massive control panel and paused, for just a second. She'd run her calculations a dozen times, and she was as sure as she could be it would work. But the margin was slim, the exact levels of the fuel feed and the reaction control almost like threading a needle. If she erred on the low side, nothing would happen, or the reactors would just shut down. The fleet would face the advancing Hegemony forces, and it would be destroyed.

If she pushed just a bit too hard, the reactors would jump right through the redline, and systems would start to overload. Catastrophically. As in ships vanishing in the fury of unleashed nuclear fusion. She'd always been sure of herself, but she'd never done something as wildly desperate as this.

She sat down at the lone workstation on the wall, turning toward the half-dozen engineers standing behind her as she did. "I'm going to set up the coded sequence and transmit it to the other ships of the fleet. Klein, Verity, I want you to check out every circuit in these reactors, every conduit. If there's so much as a crack or a slightly misaligned section, it has to be fixed. Now."

"Yes, sir," the two engineers replied almost as one, and turned, rushing out of the control room to muster their crews. Fritz knew her orders were impossible. There was no time, not to do anything properly. But if the fleet didn't break out in the next ten minutes, fifteen outside, there would be no point in any of it.

"Pierce, I need you to transmit this sequence to every ship in the fleet. It has to be followed *exactly*. There is no room for error in this."

"Yes, captain." The officer turned and jogged across the room, sliding into a workstation along the far wall.

Fritz turned back and stared at the code on her screen. Tyler Barron had relied on her in dozens of tense and dangerous situations, and she liked to think she had earned his trust. But she'd never been more worried about an operation she'd proposed that the current one.

Or more desperate than she was just then.

I hope I don't let you down, admiral…

* * *

Barron watched as Stockton's fighters sliced once more into the enemy formations. The Hegemony battleships were engaged with the Confederation line now, and, despite their massive power generation and sophisticated AIs, that meant some level of distraction for the enemy vessels. Either they could focus primarily on the Confederation line, or they could divert their attention to the incoming bombers. They couldn't do both, not at maximum effectiveness.

They pressed on, pounding at Barron's battle line. That was

a mistake, he thought, though one he understood. The enemy could smell victory, and they knew Stockton's pilots would be as good as dead without any place to land. The orbital forts were just about gone, and none of the few scraps still functioning with one or two active guns were capable of landing fighters.

Stockton's wings were driving in, closer even than they had before, taking advantage of the reduced effectiveness of the enemy's point defense. There were still escorts active, and where the small vessels remained in the fight, they extracted a grue-some toll. Even the battleships remained dangerous, despite most of their energy and targeting capability being tied up in the duel with Barron's big ships.

Barron had watched his fighter squadrons in action for years, back to the days when Jake Stockton commanded a single squadron of fifteen instead of thousands of Lightnings. Yet, each time, he felt the same. All his people risked their lives in battle, and in his career, and no small number had died at their posts, whether in the squadrons or manning some station on *Dauntless* or another battleship. But there was something about the fighter pilots—thousands of kilometers away, encased in a tiny chunk of metal, driving in on a behemoth fifty thousand times larger. He's always respected his pilots, and they retained a special place in his heart.

Now, he watched even more of them die, fighting desper-ately to open a corridor and give the fleet a chance to escape.

A chance for Anya Fritz's desperate plan. A chance to give us a chance.

How did we ever get so desperate?

He looked ahead as the wings tore straight at their targets, engaging now to destroy Hegemony ships, and not just knock out railguns. The fleet needed a hole in the force moving in all around, a route it could take to the exit transit point, and a momentary respite. Barron understood the magnitude of the defeat the Confederation had suffered, the implications of the loss of the capital. He'd been besieged by desperate comms from the surface, repeated demands from terrified politicians that he *do something*.

What the hell do they want me to do? *We may yet all die here, but if some portion of the fleet can escape to join the others at Craydon, we've still got a chance.*

He looked at the comm unit. Stockton's people, against all odds, seemed to be driving through, opening up the corridor the fleet needed. It was time. But he'd heard nothing from Fritz.

He'd almost commed her half a dozen times, but he'd held back. She knew what she was doing, and she knew there was no more time. Barron didn't pretend to fully understand the technical aspects of what she was trying to do, but he knew he'd never heard her as tentative as she'd been suggesting the maneuver. It chilled his spine to think of Fritz being afraid of what she was doing, and he had no illusions of the danger the fleet would be in when she gave the signal that she was ready.

Dustin Nguyen had given the okay for the operation, relieving Barron of some portion of responsibility if things went badly. For what that was worth. There really hadn't been any choice. Staying in place meant the fleet would be obliterated. The only thing left to fight for would be taking a few more enemy ships down before the end came.

Barron shifted in his seat. If Fritz wasn't ready soon, there would be no point. *Republic* had just taken a railgun hit. The battleship was still there, but even a quick glance at the damage reports made it clear she was done for. Her engines were down, and there was no time for any repairs. The breakout, if it happened, would have one less battleship, a thousand fewer spacers. And every moment that passed would add to that toll.

The comm crackled in his ear. "We're ready, admiral."

Barron took a quick breath. Nguyen had given him authorization to commence the operation, to lead the fleet as it made one, last desperate attempt to break out of the trap even then closing all around it.

"Do it, Fritzie. Get us out of here."

Chapter Twenty-One

Andrei Denisov stared at the bank of screens on *Illustre*'s bridge. Union vessels lacked the massively expensive 3D displays that dominated the center of Confederation battleships' control rooms. The Union lacked many of the luxuries and cutting-edge technological goodies their longtime enemies enjoyed, but that was the reality of an economy like the Union's matching up with one as dynamic as that of the Confederation. A Union battleship probably cost half what a Confed one did, and maybe less. Still, the Union had equaled, and for many years surpassed, its neighbor because it was double the Confederation's size.

He still thought of the Confeds as the enemy. He despised the corruption and brutality of the Union government, but he was also a patriot, and dedicated to the navy. It was a force that retained its pride, despite having seen its share of defeat and even humiliation at the hands of the Confederation.

You have to stop thinking that way. Whatever this Hegemony is, it's a deadly threat to the whole Rim. There is no place anymore for old grudges...

His fleet had just crossed into Confederation space, officially an act of war. The Hovan system was nothing much to speak of, a few marginal mining stations, and one harsh, but lightly inhabited, planet. The total population was about a million and a quarter per the latest Sector Nine estimates, and, as with all the border systems on both sides, it was devoid of any fixed defenses.

There was a small cluster of system patrol boats around the planet, six at last count, the largest no more than five thousand tons. They were putting on a good show of preparing to defend the world, but Denisov figured the Confeds in those tiny tin cans would be just as happy when his fleet passed them by, leaving them unmolested.

He just hoped there were no suicidal fools in those ships, ready to open fire on a Union fleet five hundred times more powerful than they were. He really didn't know what he'd do if that happened—shooting at Confed ships, even pisspot little patrol boats, wasn't the best way to try to mend fences. Dead Confed spacers, even local ones, were likely to upset their naval peers, and pointless hostility between Union and Confed forces was the last thing the Rim needed just then.

The threat of the vastly outgunned Confeds forcing a fight, as unlikely as it seemed, struck him hard, and he realized just how difficult what he proposed was going to be. The Confed Senate had made the peace after the last war, but he couldn't imagine that had gone down well with the naval types. The Confeds had suffered terrible losses in the war, as had the Union. They were on the brink of pushing their advantage, of invading a Union that was prostrate and unable to resist...when their own war weary politicians stopped them. Denisov knew the resentment *he* would have felt, and he didn't guess that Tyler Barron and his compatriots would feel much different.

And you're not even here as the Union. Hell, if you go back to the Union, you'll be lucky if you just get shot. There are far worse ways to go in those Sector Nine cells.

Denisov had the fleet, at least at the moment. They had seen the Hegemony forces, as he had, and such things tended to make an impression. Still, he had no idea how long he could sustain his position, or how his people would react to allying with their longtime enemies. Assuming he was even able to find the main Confederation force, and somehow convince them he'd brought his fleet deep into their space not as enemies, but to join them as allies.

He looked around the bridge. His officers were busy at their posts—edgy, of course, about being in Confederation space, but otherwise with him. Still, he knew that wasn't the case for all. With thousands of spacers on the fleet, some of them were bound to oppose what he had done. Most would remain silent and do nothing, but perhaps not all.

He'd rounded up all the political officers he could find, and anyone he'd suspected of ties to Sector Nine or any other intelligence-gathering operation. But there were almost certainly some conspirators out there who would try to stop what he was trying to do.

The question was, how many? How capable were they?

And how far would they go to try to stop him?

* * *

Regina Descortes swore under her breath as she twisted her body through the narrow conduits and pulled herself up, a few centimeters at a time. She was sore, bruised, and tired. Her knowledge of *Illustre*'s layout, not just the corridors snaking through her decks, but the tubes and pipes and passageways that wound through the ship's innards, had proven invaluable. She'd studied the schematics Gaston Villieneuve had provided her, the details of every out-of-view way to get around the giant battleship. It had taken her some time to decide exactly how to proceed, and in the end, she'd waited until Denisov had actually crossed the border and entered Confederation space. There had been no doubt left at that point, at least none in her mind.

Denisov was a traitor, and there was only one thing she could do.

She wriggled her way up and then climbed to the side, pressing her face against the ventilation duct and looking cautiously out into the room. It was semi-dark, only a single light on, and, at least as far as she could see from her difficult vantage point, there was no one there. She'd been pretty sure the room would be empty. She'd managed to confirm that Admiral Denisov was out on the bridge. He'd been spending a lot of time there, no doubt focusing on interactions with the Confeds. That gave her time.

She pulled a small wrench from the kit she carried at her side and carefully removed the covering screen. It almost slipped out of her grasp—a crashing sound she didn't need just then—but she managed to hold on to it. She angled her body, pulled her legs out of the conduit, and then, with a deep breath, dropped down to the floor.

She spun around, pulling the small pistol from the waistband of her pants. She'd managed to stay fairly quiet, but she'd been trained not to take chances. If anyone heard her, or even happened to be coming through the door, she had to be ready.

Her eyes darted around the room, checking every dark space and potential hiding spot. She was alone.

Good. She'd expected to come into an empty space, to have time to set up and prepare for what she had to do. But she was standing in Admiral Denisov's private office, and it wouldn't have been shocking to find him at his desk.

She reached up and put the grate back into place. When Denisov came into that office, whether in five minutes, or five hours, she didn't want a thing to look out of place. Descortes was a highly effective killer, trained by none other than Ricard Lille, and she wouldn't need long. Denisov was no fool. Doubtless, he suspected there were undercover agents in the fleet beyond those he'd already rounded up. He would be edgy, watching out for anything suspicious.

She walked over to the control panel and entered her overrides. A screen appeared, a black background with light blue text, a view no one in *Illustre*'s crew had ever seen.

It was a routine Sector Nine had placed in the battleship's AI programming when the vessel was still in the shipyard. She punched in a series of codes, and then even the small light that had been on winked out.

Then she turned and walked over to the desk, feeling her way through the darkness. When she reached her destination, she crouched down behind the heavy desk and looked toward the room's only entrance—save, of course, for the unorthodox one she had just used.

She would wait now, for as long as it took for Andrei Denisov to come into his office.

Then she would kill him.

* * *

Denisov walked slowly down the corridor. He'd been on the bridge for hours. Twelve, fourteen… He couldn't remember, but he knew he needed a break. Sleep was out of the question, of course, the soft cot in his quarters no more than a distant dream. But he needed to close his eyes for a moment, and to take something for the raging headache that felt as though it might shatter his skull like an egg at any moment.

He walked down the familiar corridor, and as he reached the door to his office, he stopped and froze.

He heard something. Footsteps. Coming up behind him.

He spun around, his hand dropping to the sidearm he'd always carried at his side, but that he'd now checked and rechecked a dozen times. He was about to pull the pistol out when he saw the shocked face of one of his aides.

"Apologies, admiral, if I startled you." The man looked scared, his eyes locked on Denisov's hand resting over the pistol's handle.

Denisov's hand loosened almost immediately. The aide was one of his, a spacer he trusted completely. "What is it, lieutenant?" He was annoyed at the needless tension, but he tried to hide it as well as he could.

"We have received a communique from the Confederation forces. They are demanding we stop and power down, and wait while they signal to their fleet command for instructions."

Denisov was relieved the Confeds were at least talking to what had to seem an invasion force to them. *Though what real choice do they have? If we were here to attack them, they'd all be dust clouds already.*

Denisov stood in the corridor, silent for a moment, thinking. If he ran past the small defense force, more than likely they'd just let him go. Even if they opened fire, he might just be able to ignore them. They might damage a ship or two as the fleet passed by, but they couldn't do much more than that.

Still, *if they kill any of my people, that's going to make it that much harder for us to find a way to cooperate. My people are scared of the Hegemony, but they hate the Confeds, too. If we have any fatalities, will I be able to maintain control?*

There was logic to all of that...but he just couldn't sit there on the border and wait. He had to get to someone of a high rank, and he had to speak to them himself. Directly, in the same system and not by days or weeks long communication trails.

No. He couldn't stop.

But he didn't want to ignore the attempt at communication, at peaceful resolution. He didn't know how persuasive he could be to some border defense officer, but he had to try.

"Come with me, lieutenant. I want to respond to the Confed communique." He turned, pressed his hand over the locking plate, and stood to the side as the door slid open.

He gestured for the lieutenant to step inside, and then he turned to follow. "Lights." It seemed odd. The AI was programmed to put the lights on as he entered.

And I'm sure I left the desk light on...

A panic gripped him almost instantly, and he swung his body to the side, pulling his pistol out, just as he heard a loud crack... and then he felt warmth, wetness on his face. The aide dropped hard to the floor right in front of him, and Denisov realized the officer's blood, and a good bit of his brains, were all over him.

He cursed himself for his carelessness, even as he reached out his arm and fired his pistol. He got off one shot, two.

Then he felt an impact on his chest, hard, and his legs slipped out from under him. He was falling, and then he was on the ground. He could hear sounds from outside now, heavy boots, either his marine guards rushing to save him...or more assassins coming to finish the job.

Not that the one who'd been waiting for him couldn't do that all alone.

You're a damned fool.

It was all he could think, the only thought that would stay in his mind.

You're a damned fool...

Chapter Twenty-Two

The Battle of Megara – "Barron's Breakout – Part Two"

Tyler Barron sank deep into his chair's cushioning, struggling to endure the G-forces bearing down on him. He could feel the pressure on his face, on his arms, and deep inside his body. Everywhere the scars of an old combat wound remained, healed breaks and patched-up cuts radiated with new pain. He almost yelled out. He wanted to scream, but he knew he had to set the example for his people.

Besides, he wasn't sure he could suck enough air into his tortured lungs to manage it.

The fleet was on the move, a desperate, insane effort to accelerate past the approaching Hegemony fleet. The highest G-force reading he'd heard from the AI was eighty-three. He had no idea how much of that the overloaded dampeners were absorbing and how much was slamming into him and the rest of his crew—all his crews, on every ship—but he was pretty sure it was the heaviest he had endured in his career.

All of his ships were blasting through the enemy fleet, save two battleships and six smaller craft that had suffered catastrophic failures in their reactor systems when they'd implemented the plan. Fritzie had told him the procedure was dangerous and untested, that there *would be* losses if he attempted it. But Barron would still have done it, even if he'd known over three thousand of his people would be killed in a matter of seconds. The breakout wasn't about whether he lost any spacers, but about whether any survived. And, at that moment, most of his people were still alive.

He knew there were, that there had to be, casualties from the acceleration on the surviving ships. Broken bones, internal bleeding, and, very possibly, some fatalities, but, again, the alternative was for all of them to die…or, unthinkably, to surrender to the Hegemony. That was an order that he would never have given, nor one he could imagine coming from Nguyen's mouth, but more than likely some of the last vessels remaining, after the flagships were gone, would have chosen such a route. The idea appalled Barron, who would choose death for himself a hundred times before yielding, but he couldn't fault anyone who might have sought to survive once the fight was clearly over. The Barron legacy weighed heavily on him, and sometimes he remembered just how much feelings of obligation to the family name guided his actions. He didn't want to die, to sacrifice all he might live to do and see…but disgracing the Barron legacy, being a disappointment in his perception of his grandfather's judgment, was unthinkable.

Dauntless was last in the line. He'd held his flagship back, waited to pick up lifeboats from the shattered hulk that had been *Republic*. Endangering a thousand of *Dauntless*'s crew to save one hundred and three didn't make mathematical sense, notwithstanding also risking himself, the second-in-command of the fleet. But he'd done it anyway.

His own worth, and how it greatly exceeded that of an average spacer, was something he'd never been able to evaluate objectively. Besides, it wasn't about math. It was about the bond between the men and women who'd followed him into battle, who'd fought with everything they had. He knew he would leave thousands behind, dead, captured. But there wouldn't be a single spacer in that total that he could have done something to save.

Dauntless shook from a hit, her luck finally running out as she raced past the gauntlet. Barron felt an instant of panic, an image in his mind of the engines or reactors giving out, stranding his fleet in the middle of the enemy forces. But the thrust didn't slack off, not at all, as far as he could tell.

The Hegemony ships had been taken completely by surprise by the unorthodox move. Not only had there been no sign of a breakout attempt before it actually happened, but as far as they could know, Confederation and Alliance ships were not capable of the thrust levels they were currently employing.

The Hegemony probably had extensive files on Confederation systems and capabilities, but Barron smiled, or as close as he could manage, thinking to himself that what they really needed was a file on Anya Fritz.

He tried to turn his head enough to look over at the display, but he gave up after ten seconds of fruitless effort. The discomfort and pain were getting worse, and he felt as though his ribs were going to burst through his chest. All he could do was lie back in his chair, wondering how the enemy was reacting, waiting to see if *Dauntless* was hit again as it tried to flee…and hearing the moans and muffled shouts of pain from his officers and bridge crew.

Seconds went by, and the pressure continued. Somehow, and Barron wasn't sure how, *Dauntless*'s engines endured under the stress of twice the thrust they were designed to produce. He imagined fractures in the super-hard metals, cracks in the fuel pressure pumps, waiting to split, with tragic consequences. No doubt, some of his ships *had* given out, their overtaxed engines and reactors failing, leaving them at the mercy of the enemy.

Or going supercritical in spectacular explosions that killed all concerned.

Barron wanted to give the order to cut the thrust, to reduce the reactor output and make the relentless force go away. He felt as though he and his people were pushing their luck, almost asking for the worst to happen. But he'd done the calculations himself, and he knew how long the thrust had to continue if his people were going to have any real chance of escaping the system. If each added minute, ten minutes, thirty minutes, increased the death toll from out-of-control G-forces, then so be it. If none of his ships escaped, the entire enterprise, and all the suffering it had caused, would have been for nothing.

He shoved his head to the side slightly, enough to get a look at the chronometer. The AI would warn him when they were down to the ten-minute mark, but he'd begun to believe the system had failed to notify him, that there couldn't possibly be more than ten minutes left of the hell he and his people were enduring.

His mind was reeling, and around the periphery of his vision, hallucinations began to gather. He told himself what he'd seen on the clock was wrong, that his eyes were failing. Then he realized he'd read the thing right.

Almost twenty minutes remained at full thrust. A third of an hour of pain, of hellish torment.

And a third of an hour where, each second, any of his ships could fail. If the engines stopped, a ship's crew would die. If the reactors redlined, a ship's crew would die.

If the dampeners overloaded, a ship's crew would die.

And if everything went exactly right, his people had, maybe, a fifty percent chance of getting to the transit point in time and making the jump.

But those were better odds than they'd had formed up around Megara, waiting for certain death.

* * *

"Pull those throttles all the way back, all of you. We're not worried about formations now, we're not worried about enemy fire—we're not even worried about getting to the right ships. Just catch up to any battleship you can that has a berth, and land…before it's too late." Jake Stockton was in the rear of the giant formation, the last fighter to break off and make a mad dash for a landing slot before the fleet transited. He'd seen to every one of his squadrons, every lost pilot, and only then had he set his own course and blasted at full, chasing after the fleet.

He could see the flashes on his screen, fighters in his wings being picked off by enemy fire as they zipped away from the pursuing Hegemony formations. He felt a passing regret at his choice of words, of not worrying about the fire killing his people as they raced after their fleeing motherships. But he'd meant it, every word. Reality gave no alternative. His people had a much better chance running the enemy guns that they did if they watched their motherships transit without them.

Taking a fighter through a transit point jump was a difficult maneuver, and for those in ships with damage or whose shielding had been worn or battered, it could be fatal. He'd done it himself, many times, and he knew just how many of his people would die in the attempt, especially since most would be running out of fuel just as they reached the transit point.

He also knew just how little most of the survivors would stand to gain for their success as they emerged with dry fuel tanks, just through the point, only to watch the fleeing battleships continue their flight before the Hegemony fleet could reform and pursue. That would save them from dying at the hands of the enemy, of course, but Stockton wasn't sure suffocating or freezing to death were better options.

Catching the fleet while it was still in the Olyus system was the best chance any of them had to survive.

That was going to be a close race for most of them. Closer still, because he'd kept his squadrons on the attack after they'd launched their torpedoes, conducting strafing runs and doing everything else possible to delay the enemy pursuit of the fleet. That had been successful as a way to aid the retreating battleships, but it had left his fighters far behind and struggling to catch up.

Stockton angled his vector slightly, an instinctive move to add some evasive maneuvering to his course, but he'd also mostly stayed on a direct line. He didn't have the time or the fuel to waste, any more than any of his people did. He would just have to take his chances and hope the rapidly increasing range from the firing batteries was enough.

He glanced down at the display. The pursuing Hegemony forces were accelerating. It had taken considerable time for the ships to reverse their vectors toward Megara, and for a large portion of their line to come about to pursue Barron and the fleet, but now, they were blasting at full thrust. Meanwhile, the fleeing Confederation vessels had cut back to thirty G or less. That was still fast, but it was a lot slower than the Hegemony ships chasing them. Stockton had been surprised the fleet had managed to maintain the massive overloads as long as they had, and yet disappointed they couldn't manage it further. Another fifteen minutes would have eliminated any possibility that the fleet, or even part of it, would get caught still in the Olyus system. Right now, the whole thing was too close to call. Some ships would almost certainly get through, but there was a good chance some would get hit before they could transit.

Or they just might all make it through. Stockton tried to analyze the data, to come up with his own estimate, but it was just too complex. Some of the fleeing ships had battle damage; others had suffered malfunctions during the reactor overloads that had made the breakout possible. Over a dozen ships of various classes were strung out behind the fleet, unable to keep up, doomed to almost certain destruction if their sweating damage-control teams couldn't repair their engines quickly enough.

Stockton had run the calculations on his squadrons as well, and the results were no less frustrating. There was, in theory, time to get all his people landed before the fleet transited. But theory and reality were different things, and human error, damaged landing bays, and a hundred other factors clouded his view.

One thing he knew almost for certain, though, was that he had the longest odds. He was too far back, and even redlining his reactor and drives could still leave him behind when *Dauntless* transited.

And he knew Tyler Barron well enough to guess that *Dauntless* would be the last ship to go through, the last chance to get a ride out of Olyus.

If Stockton missed that, he'd have to take his damaged ship into the point and hope his dwindling fuel reserves held out long enough to take him through…and to get him back onboard.

Otherwise, he might make it through, only to watch the fleet pull away as he waited for his life support to slip slowly away.

* * *

"Admiral, we're out of time." Moments before, Atara Travis had accepted Barron's orders to decelerate at maximum thrust. It was a wildly risky maneuver, but one she understood. There were still fighters trying to catch the fleet, several dozen of them. While Barron and Nguyen had agreed the fleet could not slow down to wait for the last of the squadrons, Barron had issued the command almost immediately after the senior admiral's ship had transited. It was technically mutiny, though Travis doubted anyone would see it in such severe terms. She understood Barron's attachment to the fleet's pilots, his recognition and appreciation of all they had done, in Olyus, and in previous battles.

And she also knew that Jake Stockton was still out there.

Stockton had served under Barron—and her—for over a decade, and the two of them had watched him grow from a wild and somewhat crazy, if extremely talented, squadron commander, to an almost legendary leader, and arguably the one man who had done the most to push back against the Hegemony. She didn't like the idea of leaving him behind any more than Barron did…but she'd checked the numbers five times, and he was just too far away. If *Dauntless* stayed long enough to pick up Stockton, none of them would get out. The battleship would be caught against the point, with at least half a dozen railgun-armed enemy warships in range. It likely wouldn't take more than one hit from the deadly weapons to slow *Dauntless* down, at least enough to allow the rest of the Hegemony forces to close and fire again.

She'd started to run the numbers. Then she'd tried to stop herself, but her brain didn't work that way, and it continued over her own internal protest. One chance in six. It was rough, based on considerable supposition, but in her gut, she knew that was close to the mark.

Dauntless had a one in six chance of escaping if the ship waited for Stockton to land.

She was as fond of Stockton as Barron was, as loyal to the pilot she called one of her closest friends as anyone. But there was no justification for risking almost a thousand crew on the battleship, *and* the fleet commander she considered most likely to find a way to defeat the enemy. Not even to save Jake Stockton.

Barron hadn't answered her, so she repeated herself. "Tyler, we *have* to reaccelerate and transit now." Even as she spoke, fighters were landing on *Dauntless*'s flight decks, some of her own, and others from different ships, strays and refugees seeking any place to go. Even if Barron gave the order now, pushed the thrusters back to full acceleration, most of the ships out there were close. They would be able to get aboard, at least if the flight crews could cram them all in the bays somehow.

All except Stockton, and maybe seven or eight others…

She knew Barron had heard her, and despite their close friendship, she rarely repeated herself. Pushing too hard came close to insubordination, but she knew he needed a push now. He needed her to help him leave Stockton behind.

She just wasn't sure how hard she could pressure him. The thought of abandoning her friend tore her guts out, and more than a small part of her wanted to say, "Damn the odds—let's stay until we've got everyone on board."

She stared across the short space toward Barron, her gaze locked on to the side of his face. Finally, he turned toward her, and she could see the pain in his eyes.

"I know, Atara. I just…"

She realized she didn't have the strength to push harder, to continue the argument to leave her friend, and one of the fleet's great heroes, behind. She knew it was her duty. She owed it to the crew of the ship, *her* ship. But she was tired to the bone, and the fight in her was just about gone.

Then she saw the light flashing on her board, an incoming communique. She paused for a second, confused. *Dauntless* was the only ship still in the system.

She flipped the controls and Stockton's voice filled her

headset.

"*Dauntless*, what the hell are you doing?" His voice was hoarse. It was clear it took all the strength he could muster to force the words out. "Why are you decelerating? Are you insane? The whole Hegemony fleet is right behind you."

"Jake." She knew she had to respond, but she didn't know what to say. "We've got to…"

"You don't have to do anything, not here in Olyus. I can make the transit…and I can get the others through, too."

He was trying his best, but she could tell immediately he was far from sure he could do what he claimed. At his best, he'd done it more than once. Now, he was exhausted, almost out of fuel, nursing a battered ship. With seven other pilots to lead through.

"Admiral, I've got Jake Stockton on the line." It wasn't her proudest moment, but she pushed the matter to Barron. It was going to be his decision anyway.

"Jake, we're cutting our thrust, but you've got to get here—"

"Forget it, admiral. I'll never make it…and, if you wait, you won't either. Reengage your thrust, sir, I'm begging you. Don't make me watch you all die waiting for me. I'll make it, and I'll bring the last stragglers with me. You *know* I can do this, sir."

Atara was still listening, and she could still hear uncertainty in Stockton's voice, despite the words he'd spoken. She was one hundred percent certain he was planning to make a herculean effort, but just as sure he rated his odds of success probably right around fifty percent, and probably less to get the others through.

"Jake…" Atara could see the pain in Barron's expression, but she also realized Stockton was giving him a way out, enough of a push to do what he already knew he had to do.

"Admiral, you know me better than anyone. I can do this. We'll get through, and there will be time to pick us up on the other side. The enemy formation is a mess, and they've got Megara sitting behind them. They're not going to follow, not yet." Stockton sounded sure of himself, more so than Atara suspected he was. But his logic was sound.

Barron was silent, but even as he sat there, he turned toward Travis, and she could see he'd made his decision. She felt relief, and the same fear she knew Barron was feeling.

"I'm taking your word for it, Jake, but I damn well better see you follow us through that transit point." It was a pointless statement, but she knew why Barron had to say it. If it helped him believe he wasn't leaving his friend behind to die, at least long enough to get *Dauntless* through, it served its purpose.

"I'm right behind, admiral. All of us are."

Travis looked out over the bridge, hearing Barron's words before he even spoke them.

"Full thrust forward, Atara. Take us through the point."

"Yes, sir." She worked the controls, leaned back as the thrust cranked up to maximum, and ran some quick calculations. "Transit in one minute, ten seconds, admiral."

She turned and looked at the display. She had a minute before the jump and nothing to do, so she stared at the Olyus system, and at the symbol representing Megara, now almost two billion kilometers distant. She'd never had a second thought about the capital—or, for that matter, given two shits for the nest of pampered and corrupt politicians—but now it struck her how deeply wounded the Confederation was, how close to defeat, even with a good portion of the fleet escaping.

It was hard to see a route to victory, a way to defeat the invader. But even through the exhaustion and the grief, there was still a spark inside, a flicker of what made Atara Travis herself. She looked at Megara on the display, and she had one thought in her mind, one vow, and as unlikely as it seemed, in that moment, she believed it with all her heart.

We'll be back.

Chapter Twenty-Three

Hegemony's Glory
Orbiting Planet Megara, Olyus III
Year of Renewal 263 (318 AC)

The Battle of Megara – The Landings

"Our course now is clear. The enemy navy has been critically damaged, and what remains has fled the system. We will pursue and secure their surrender—or their total destruction—in due time, after we have repaired our battle damage and resupplied our forces." Chronos knew he was oversimplifying the enormity of the tasks of which he spoke. Once again, the escorts had suffered appalling losses, and he needed to convert more of his existing small vessels to the anti-attack craft configuration. His battleships had been badly hurt as well, and the magnitude of ordnance expended was almost incomprehensible. If it not for the logistics fleet, he would be stuck at Megara for a year, even two. Worse, he would be dependent on a long and tenuous supply line subject to interception at multiple points. But a preliminary survey of the system confirmed what his previous intelligence had suggested. There were adequate resources in the Olyus system to produce everything his fleet required.

Everything but antimatter. He still had stores of the precious resource, enough to keep the fleet's railguns firing for a while, but he was becoming highly dependent on receiving new shipments from home.

"The Confederation capital lies below us, stripped of its orbital defenses, open to our invasion. We will waste no time, and when the resistance on the surface is crushed, the war will be all but over. The Confederation government will surrender, and we can begin the long process of integrating their people into the Hegemony, and even enlisting them to aid us in absorbing the remaining Rim nations."

Chronos *was* confident, but he was not *that* confident. The Confeds had proven to be a more difficult enemy than he had imagined, and, truth be told, he was a bit shaken, both by the ferocity of the defense and the losses he had suffered. Still, morale was crucial to any military operation, even to Masters, and others of high military rank, and he needed the best his people had to give. Early scans suggested the ground defenses were old and dated, and that some had been all but abandoned for many years. It seemed like Megara had been strong and warlike in the early stages of its return to interstellar relations, but that its years as the sheltered capital of a large nation had sapped that early strength.

He still suspected the troops on the ground would fight hard, and that his own forces would be hampered by his desire to capture the enemy capital intact, or as close to that as possible, but he was hopeful he could wrap things up fairly quickly, especially if he could convince the civil authorities there was no point in resisting. The Confederation Senate had already attempted to contact him, but he wanted to get his forces on the ground before he responded. Better to bargain from maximum strength. He was willing to deal a bit if that brought things to a swift conclusion, but there was no negotiability in the area of reordering Rim society by genetic ratings. That was the source of the Hegemony's strength, and so it would be on the Rim.

Though he could offer those currently in power certain guarantees regarding their own positions and physical comforts under the new order. He could not make someone a Master if they lacked the genetic makeup to be one, but that did not mean the old political class could not enjoy a gilded retirement in obscene luxury until they died out.

Megara itself was an impressive world, worthy to take its place as part of the Hegemony. It restored Chronos's belief that the campaign had been worth the effort and the cost…and even the risk of leaving the home sectors underdefended for a time. The Hegemony would double in size and strength when the Rim dwellers were fully integrated, and that was a strong positive for the future of humanity.

"Let the invasion begin. The landings shall commence at once. Orbital bombardments will be held to minimal levels, and only utilized against the strongest positions. Go, all of you, and fight for the Hegemony, for the future of all mankind."

Chronos stood in the control room, his white robes flowing all around him, ornamented with platinum chains and other adornments, as befitted the commander of the Grand Fleet and the eighth most perfect human in existence. He detested the garb, and all the fuss that went with it, but he knew its value, too.

He would use every weapon, every tool he needed for the victory he had come to attain. Because, for all he told himself the Others were a threat of the past, that they were a nightmare more fit to scare children than panic adults, he felt the need to finish matters on the Rim.

Quickly.

* * *

Bryan Rogan stared at the map, and at the rows of figures on the large tablet he had just set down. Tyler Barron had ordered him back up to *Dauntless* just before the enemy arrived, but the marine general had asked his longtime commander, and his friend, to allow him to stay. He was a warrior, and his career had been spent fighting the Confederation's battles. The defense of the capital, the effort to defeat the enemy's troop landings, was something he *had* to be part of.

Even though it was likely to be his last fight.

Barron had sounded as though he was going to refuse, or

at least argue, but then he just wished Rogan luck and bade his friend goodbye with sadness in his tone, and a hint of finality. Rogan suspected Barron understood, in a way few could, why he had to be on Megara, with the tens of thousands of marines stationed there. The enemy was irresistibly strong, but the ground forces on the capital dwarfed those on a frontier world like Dannith. The marines might not be able to win in the end, but they would make the Hegemony, and their cyborg Kriegeri, pay for every meter.

What had stunned Rogan was the order he received a few hours later, the one naming him commander in chief of the entire defense.

"General Rogan, the positions outside Troyus City are ready. The missile bases in the Western Hills are active and on full alert. The reinforcements you ordered to cover the approaches to Abellus and Pierpont City are en route. They should be in place within two hours."

"Thank you, colonel." Daniel Prentice was proving to be quite a success as Rogan's senior aide. He'd found the officer rotting away in a semipermanent capital-area posting and assumed the worst. Such places didn't tend to produce the best fighters, not even when those in question were marines. But Prentice had been spot-on from the start, and he didn't seem to lack any aggressiveness or marine spirit. Rogan fell back to assumption number two: Prentice was in a backwater job because he'd pissed off someone powerful enough to take vengeance on his career. Rogan despised that kind of thing, but he knew it happened all too frequently.

This time for the better. This is going to be a nasty fight, and I need all the good marines I get can get.

Prentice turned abruptly, his hand moving up to his earpiece. Rogan waited, letting his aide listen to whatever message was incoming. It wasn't good, he knew, as he watched the scowl harden on the colonel's face.

"A communique from the Senate, general." A pause, as though Prentice was having trouble forcing the words from his mouth. "We are ordered to remain in our defensive positions, but we are to stand down and not engage enemy landing forces unless we are fired upon."

"What?" Rogan was usually soft-spoken for a marine, but this time, his roaring bellows seemed to shake the very foundation of the command post.

Prentice didn't respond. There was no need. His face told Rogan the aide agreed completely. And handling the Senate was firmly within the commander in chief's sole dominion.

"They can't order that. It will be suicide." Rogan could barely restrain the trembling from his anger. His best chance to hurt the enemy was during the landing, and in the hours immediately after. The Hegemony forces, now virtually unopposed anywhere in the system, save on the very dirt of Megara, were massive, overwhelming. Rogan had kept himself from analyzing the long-term chances of holding the planet—which he knew were nil—and focused on the immediate future, on making the enemy pay for every meter they occupied.

Now the Senate wants me to just let them land? Let them form up and get their heavy ordnance deployed so they can sweep us away?

Of course, because they're thinking of surrender, not of digging in. They'll just look to see if they can get some guarantees about their own perquisites, see that their own asses are covered, and then they'll sell out the billions who live here.

Thoughts went through his mind, dark and terrible images of what the savage that lived deep inside Rogan thought should be done to collaborators. He was a disciplined marine, but he was far from sure he could maintain that posture if he was faced with Megarans aiding the enemy.

"Send a response, colonel. Advise the Senate that we cannot possibly have received their transmission correctly. We are prepared to resist the enemy invasion at every pass, commencing with the initial landings...which I expect to begin at any moment. I suggest they retreat to their bunkers where they will be safe." *Relatively safe, at least.* Rogan doubted "safe" existed anywhere on Megara just then.

"Yes, sir."

Rogan stared again at the map, trying hard to keep his anger in check. He'd always been one to follow orders scrupulously, and he was keenly aware that the Senate could relieve him of command, even strip him of his rank. But, for the first time in his professional life, Bryan Rogan didn't care.

He didn't even come close to giving a shit.

They could make all the pronouncements they wanted to over in the Senate hall, and they could pass whatever resolutions their fear and their bruised egos demanded.

But they couldn't stop Bryan Rogan from fighting the enemy to his last breath.

Alone, if he had to, though he suspected many of his marines—*many* of them—would feel the same way.

* * *

"Watch your fuel, Jake…you're right on the line."

Stockton shook his head, trying to rid himself of the annoyance he felt at Stara's constant reminders and advice. He'd made emergency landings before, probably more than any pilot in the fleet. He damn well knew he was almost out of fuel. Why the hell did she think it served any purpose to remind him yet again?

He didn't want to vent at her. She was just scared. No, not just scared. She was worried to death about him. He appreciated that, but he was scared too. He was coming in low on everything, and, to be honest, he had no idea what was keeping his engine output going, because as much as he could read from his instruments, his tanks were bone-dry. All she was doing was focusing his attention on things he couldn't affect.

"I've got this, Stara. Just sit tight and make sure you get this all on vid. They'll want this one at the Academy to show the newbs how it's done." He knew Stara would see through his bravado, even though he'd done a masterful job—if he did say so himself—of sounding serenely confident. He also suspected it would irritate the hell out of her, but any way he could distract her now was worthwhile. He told himself he'd manage to pull off the landing, mostly because he always had before, but just in case he lost it this time, anything that could distract her from staring at the scanners as he came in—from watching him die—was worth the effort.

Whatever happened, he had one bit of satisfaction, and it warmed his otherwise cold and shivered insides. He'd gotten all seven of his pilots through the transit point and onto *Dauntless*'s flight deck. He hadn't really believed he could pull it off, and he smiled just a bit as he thought of his people safe.

Or whatever passes for safe these days.

Getting seven damaged ships through the transit point had been a tough enough prospect, and he was sure his comrades would carry some nightmares with them from the experiences. His own hallucinations had been worse than those during any of his last transits, and if he made it into *Dauntless*'s bay in one piece, he suspected he'd wake up screaming more than one night in the future.

Still, getting seven other pilots through, and all of them into the bay, was a major victory, whatever happened to him. He hadn't tried to calculate the odds on getting everyone through, and while he was sure Stara had at least taken a stab at it, she'd so far taken enough mercy on him not to share the results.

He looked straight ahead as *Dauntless* loomed before his ship. He was coming in too fast, and he blasted his thrusters, cutting his velocity. Miraculously, the engines responded, still drawing fuel from somewhere.

He released the throttle. He was still moving faster than he liked, but whatever was left in those tanks—or, most likely, just residue in the fuel lines—he was going to need it as he entered the bay. If he came in a little too hard, well, he could survive that as long as his entry angle was on line.

He'd done it before.

He counted down to himself, eyes darting back and forth from the range display to the forward screen. He'd flipped off most of his extraneous systems, anything to save a drop or two of fuel.

His view of space was gone, replaced by *Dauntless*'s looming hull. Tyler Barron had held the battleship back while the rest of the fleet continued its retreat. It was daring, even reckless, and if the enemy had pushed through the point in any force at all, Stockton's landing would be irrelevant. He'd be as good as dead in the landing bay as he would be in space.

But the Hegemony forces hadn't pursued. There were reasons for that, Stockton knew. The battle had been hard on them as well, and they were no doubt exhausted, and overwhelmed with damaged ships in need of repair. They also possessed the Confederation's capital system, a great victory by any measure, and no doubt they were focused on gaining control of Megara itself.

They will come, though. Soon.

The thoughts of the enemy blanked out, as his ship moved toward the opening in *Dauntless*'s hull leading to the landing bay. He was still coming in too fast, but he didn't dare feed any fuel to the engines. Not yet. It would be enough of a miracle if he had what he needed. He would wait until the last instant.

The ship streaked into the bay itself, and Stockton immediately saw Lightnings, battered, scorched from combat, lined up anywhere there was space. He had no idea how many ships Barron had taken onto *Dauntless*, but he guessed it was over a hundred.

Significantly over.

He was maybe three meters over the deck, with about two hundred meters in front of him before the looming bulkhead. It was time. If he had enough fuel, he just might make it.

If not…well, he could see the fire-containment teams already deployed. Barron had waited for Stockton, taken great risks to give him a chance. He couldn't take offense at the admiral putting some precautions in place.

He flipped the breaking control, an almost instinctive move…and the positioning jets fired. His body lurched forward—*hard*—and a wave of pain took him across his chest, and in his neck.

He writhed for a few seconds, unsure what had happened. Was he badly hurt? Dead?

Then he realized. His ship was still, sitting on the deck about five meters from the bulkhead.

And while his body hurt like hell, he could move all his appendages, and he could breathe, if with a bit of mild distress.

He'd made it.

Somehow.

* * *

Bryan Rogan looked up at the cold dawn sky. He couldn't see anything yet, but there was no mistaking the scanner data. The landings had begun.

It wasn't Rogan's problem anymore, at least not in an official capacity. He'd listened to the transmission himself as, he suspected, half the marines on the planet had. He was relieved of command and under arrest. He was to surrender to the nearest marine authorities, pending later action by the Senate.

He was amazed by the politicians' timing. Now was the time to hurt the enemy, to make them pay a price. And the Confederation Senate had intentionally paralyzed the entire defensive operation.

He turned and looked at Prentice. The colonel had been silent since the Senate's orders had arrived, but now he stared at Rogan and said, "To hell with the Senate, Bryan." It was the first time he'd used Rogan's first name and not his rank. "I'm with you, and I'd bet my last credit most of the marines are. Tell the politicians to drop dead. We've got a world to defend, a battle to fight...and we can't do it without our leader."

Rogan waged war with himself. He would fight, of course—there was no authority that could command him to surrender himself, and he suspected many of the marines would feel the same way. Still, they'd be disorganized, scattered, with no real way of making a difference.

Can I do this? Will they even listen to me?

The obedient marine inside him was giving way as he stood there, replaced with raw defiance, patriotism. Suddenly, he knew what he had to do.

"Get me a force-wide line, colonel."

"Yes, sir!" Prentice's enthusiasm was nearly uncontainable. He worked his hands over the portable unit, and then he nodded to Rogan, gesturing toward the general's headset.

"All marines on Megara. All defensive forces, whatever affiliation, this is General Bryan Rogan. I am—was—the commander of all defensive forces, but I have been relieved because of my refusal to stand our defenses down, to facilitate the craven and cowardly surrender the Senate is currently negotiating."

Each word pushed strength into him, and anger. He damn well *wasn't* going to give up, and he'd lead any man or woman who would follow him into battle. He would fight until the enemy put him down...if they could.

"I call on all of you now to stand with me, to fight the enemy, to defy calls for surrender. Though I warn you, those who stay with me risk court-martial, or worse. Rallying to my cause will be called mutiny, even treason...but I ask you all to decide the true meaning of duty, of patriotism. Is it surrendering, putting down our arms so our leaders can save themselves? Or is it fighting with our last breaths to preserve all we hold dear? I am a marine, and I will die as one...and today, if need be. But I will never surrender!"

He shut down the line and turned toward Prentice. "We'll see what happens now."

"I'm with you, general, all the way. And after that speech, I don't want to even look at the marine who isn't."

"Well, Dan...let's see how we did. We'll start with the missile bases and see how convincing I was to them. We've got landers inbound, and I'd damned sure like to shoot some of them down before they reach the surface."

Chapter Twenty-Four

Hegemony Headquarters
Port Royal City
Planet Dannith, Ventica III
Year 317 AC

Shouting, crashing, the sounds of gunfire all around.

Blanth pushed hard, shoving the bulk of the Kriegeri trooper off him. The last minute or so had been a hazy mess. There had been a fight for the Kriegeri's gun...and Blanth had lost that, his hand slipping off the grip just as the two landed on the ground.

Some kind of instinct had taken hold of him, guided his hand to the large combat knife hanging from the man's belt, even as he heard the loud crack.

As he felt the strange feeling, more pressure than pain. It took a few seconds for him to realize he'd been shot, and in that time, he'd somehow managed to grab his enemy's blade...and drive it up under the trooper's armor plate.

He hadn't been sure how badly his opponent had been wounded, but the trooper's body hit the ground with a dense thud, and he remained stationary. Blanth turned to the side, tried to pull himself up, but he didn't have the strength. As he looked down, he could see his shirt was covered in blood.

He lay back on the floor, gasping for breath, trying to gather the strength for another attempt to get up. The noise all around was getting louder, and the gunfire closer.

It was Holcott and the marines. It had to be. They were launching a decapitation strike.

He felt a moment of excitement, but it quickly faded. An assault into the city was almost certainly an act of pure desperation, one with almost no chance of succeeding. It was a signal he couldn't deny. The resistance was finished. It was expending its last flash of energy, even as he lay on the cold floor listening to it all.

He'd expected one of the Kriegeri to come over and finish him, but the seconds turned into minutes, and still, he lay where he was, ignored, as the shouting grew louder and more urgent, and the gunfire drew ever close.

Is it possible? Can they really do it?

He sucked in a deep breath, wincing at the pain it caused. Then he gritted his teeth and tried one last time to push himself up.

He didn't know if his marines had a chance, but he knew they needed him in the fight.

* * *

Luther Holcott pushed himself forward, whipping around the stairs and angling his rifle upward, hosing down the landing above and catching one of the Kriegeri in the deadly blast. The Hegemony soldiers were fearsome adversaries, as Holcott knew from bitter experience, but the attack had taken them by surprise, and they were pulling back, upward into the building.

The enhanced soldier dropped where he was standing, and a quick glance confirmed he was dead. Holcott didn't waste any time and continued to race up the stairs, his marines right behind him. There was no time to waste. Whatever edge his people had gained by the pure, unfiltered daring of their desperate attack, it wouldn't last. Half the troops stationed in the city were almost certainly already on the way, and that meant his marines had only minutes left.

At best.

He ran up another flight, gesturing to the side and snapping out orders as he did. Five marines burst through the door and onto the fourth level, as they had on each that had come before. Holcott and the rest of his people continued upstairs. He had no real reason to believe the real brass would be at the top, but it seemed the likeliest place to look. His people couldn't take the whole building, or, at least, they couldn't hold it. But they just might manage to scrag a few Masters and shake up the occupiers. There was nothing they could do anymore to save Dannith or drive the invaders away, but Holcott would damn sure prefer to die on the attack than he would crawling around in some hole somewhere like a scared rodent.

He ducked back around the corner, an instinctive reaction. His gut was right, and the area just ahead was blasted with enemy fire. At least three or four Kriegeri, he guessed, and they were firing on full auto.

The top commanders are *up there.* The enemy troopers were on the top floor, and they certainly seemed to be desperately trying to hold the line at the stairwell. He turned toward the marine behind him, reaching out. He didn't say a word. He didn't have to. His marine knew what he wanted…and she handed him the small sphere.

It was an explosive, assembled from what few supplies remained, and he'd hoped to use it when he found something like a control room. But his people weren't getting any farther unless they could clear that top landing.

He didn't hesitate. He just set the bomb for a five-second delay, leaned forward, and threw it up the last half-flight of stairs as hard as he could.

He ducked back, and the makeshift grenade exploded, sending chunks of debris flying all around. But he didn't wait to see what damage had been done, or even if the top of the stairs was clear. He just raced forward, climbing up as quickly as he could, firing as he did.

* * *

Carmetia was snapping out orders as she fired into the swarming mass, her perfect vision quickly picking out the resistance fighters from the Kriegeri. She had put down four already, even as she sent out the call for reinforcements and directed the defense all around her.

Develia was fighting, too, and she was also giving out orders. Carmetia was upset that her comrade had done such a poor job of bringing an end to the last of the resistance. The fact that the few survivors of the Dannith defenses, a ragtag group of marines low on weapons, ammunition, and probably even food, had managed to mount what was clearly a decapitation strike—and one that might still succeed—did nothing to alleviate her anger. She was a firm believer in the genetic rating system, but she had long been concerned that too many Masters claimed rank by virtue of their birth and their genes, while they lacked the experience to do their jobs effectively.

Develia would be lucky to be directing a colony of Defekt miners on some radioactive moon, though, when this was all through.

Assuming any of us make it out of here.

She turned her head, remembering Blanth suddenly. She glanced back to the chair where he had been sitting. It was gone, splintered into a hundred pieces, and there was no hint of the marine. Had he gotten caught in the crossfire? Or had he escaped and jumped into the melee? She had come to respect Blanth, and even like him after a fashion, but she did not doubt he would join his warriors, given the slightest chance.

A chance like the one he just got…

She spun back around. She was worried about the marine, about what he might do, even that he might get himself killed. But there was no time to look for him now. She had two thousand Kriegeri on their way, but none of that would matter if her people could not win the fight there, or at least hold out for a while longer.

She turned again, scanning the room one more time for targets.

* * *

Holcott's eyes darted back and forth, identifying one target after another. The fight had turned into a melee of sorts, and his people were mixed in among the Kriegeri, exchanging fire, even fighting hand to hand in places.

The few of his people that were left, that is.

He could hear the sounds of fighting coming from outside now, as well, and he knew the marines he'd left on the first level were struggling to hold back the reinforcements the enemy had no doubt called in from everywhere. They were doomed, of course. Every man and woman down there knew their purpose was to sell their lives as dearly as possible, to buy a few more minutes for Holcott and the others to finish what they'd come to do.

He turned and caught a Kriegeri in his sightline. The hulking trooper was faced off against one of his people. He brought his rifle around, just as the enemy soldier saw him. It became a race, the Hegemony warrior moving quickly, trying to dodge the shot, and Holcott firing. Once, twice…both misses. And a third time.

A hit. The high-powered bullet sheared the top of the trooper's head off, leaving a wild spray of blood all around. Holcott exchanged glances with the marine he'd just saved. He was still looking when the man's face twisted into a horrible grimace, and his chest exploded into a bloody mess. Holcott had saved the marine for all of five seconds.

The fight devolved into a desperate exchange, a wild, deadly melee. For a moment or two, it seemed almost as though no one would survive. But even as he pressed on, fought with all he had to give, Holcott could feel his assault had crested. The Kriegeri were as good as his marines, maybe better. That was a bitter pill for a warrior like him to swallow, but it was one he couldn't dispute, not after months of battling against the Hegemony fighters.

Then he saw something. A figure on the far side of the room, standing almost eerily erect, waving her arms and directing the Kriegeri all around her. She had no implants, and only a pistol in her hand. She wore a uniform, and while Holcott had never seen the insignia she wore, from what he'd learned of Hegemony nomenclature, she was a high ranker…and certainly a Master.

He brought his rifle up, his focus locked on his target now, no longer scanning the room for threats. He sighted the weapon, and his hand tightened on the trigger.

* * *

Carmetia saw the marine…and she immediately knew he was someone important, perhaps even the commander. Her rifle snapped up, but it was just an instant too late.

She saw the whole thing unfolding almost in slow motion before her. Develia, unaware at first, snapping orders to a pair of Kriegeri standing next to her. Then recognition, as she saw the marine's weapon aiming at her, and tried to escape.

Too late.

The Master's head lurched back, as a bullet tore through her neck, leaving a jagged and bloody path of tissue damage in its wake. The gun was an assault rifle, and at such short range, it almost decapitated her. Develia was dead, Carmetia suspected, before she even hit the floor.

But her killer did not have long to celebrate. Carmetia's shot was no more than half a second behind the marine's, and it struck him in the side of the head. His rifle flew out of his hands, and he stumbled backward and slammed hard into the ground.

Carmetia ran forward, cautious, but as soon as she took her second step, she could tell he was dead. Then she saw another wounded marine. Blanth. On his knees, looking at the marine she'd just killed—*definitely their commander*, she thought after seeing Blanth's expression—struggling to bring a Kriegeri rifle to bear.

He has me. The thought ran through her head like a fast-moving train, and for the briefest instant, she thought she was dead.

But Blanth did not fire. He held the weapon in place for a second, and then he let it drop and fell to the ground right after it.

Carmetia didn't know if Blanth had tried to shoot her and lacked the strength to fire…or if he had hesitated, if some part of him had not wanted to kill her, and that had delayed his action.

She was still wondering that as she realized the fight was dying out. The marines had made a desperate fight of it, and they had even killed the planetary commander, enough by most standards to call it a successful decapitation strike.

Though Develia was on her way out one way or another.

It was not a victory for the marines. At best, it was only a more satisfying way to die. The resistance on Dannith was over, and the planet was as good as pacified.

And Carmetia did not even have to share credit with Develia.

A pair of Kriegeri stood over the wounded Blanth. She was not sure if he had spared her or not, and his immediate usefulness had declined with the end of active resistance. But as she saw one of the Kriegeri raise his weapon and prepare to fire, she waved her hand and shouted, "No. See to that one's wounds. He is still needed for questioning."

She was not even sure why she had saved him.

Maybe she believed she could learn more from him, understand how to better fight his people.

Or maybe she just thought enough people had died that night, and over the last months. The Hegemony was there to rule, to show the Rim barbarians the way to the light of civilization. When they allowed that mission to descend into savagery and pointless killing, they had turned down the road the empire had taken.

Then again, maybe she just liked the marine, despite the fact that she knew he was her enemy.

Chapter Twenty-Five

"The Core is the heart of the Confederation, but it's been a long time since it's been the driver of its strength. The Iron Belt has served that role for generations now, since the second war with the Union, at least." Clint Winters was freshly showered and wearing a spotless new uniform, but his attempts to create a look of "normal" were hindered by the three visible wounds he carried from the recent battle. The most obvious was the fifteen-centimeter gash across his forehead, now covered with a bandage crusted over at its edges with dried blood.

Tyler Barron stood on the observation deck next to his friends and comrades, staring out through the clear hyper-polycarbonate windows. The grayish-blue disc of Craydon lay in the lower field of view, and directly outward, there were three other massive platforms visible, not even a tenth of the more than thirty industrial behemoths orbiting the Iron Belt world. Factories, shipyards, refineries...the industry of Craydon ran the gamut, both on the surface and in orbit. Raw materials from the system's asteroid belts and outer planets poured into the great industrial machine, and all manner of manufactured products came out, filling a dozen freighters a day. But the most important production just then was in the planet's orbital shipyards,

205

and in the dozen munitions factories accompanying them.

"Perhaps." Barron's voice was soft. He'd felt a burst of excitement when he'd managed to extricate his task force from almost certain destruction—some of his task force, at least—and the rescue of Stockton and the last seven fighter pilots had actually put a smile on his face. But it hadn't lasted. He hadn't been in command at Megara, just as he still wasn't at Craydon, but he blamed himself for the defeat anyway.

I'm sorry, Grandfather. You were the man who saved the Confederation…and I am the one who lost its capital.

Barron knew that wasn't entirely fair, but he didn't care. He couldn't see any way to avoid final defeat in the war, and he was in no mood to let himself off the hook for any failings, actual or invented by his own raging mind.

"Admiral Winters is right, Tyler." There was a somber tone to Dustin Nguyen's voice, and something else. Barron couldn't place it at first, but then he realized the admiral sounded *old*. He *was* old, of course, but now there was a frailty and a quiet sadness that hadn't been there when the officer had first reported for duty and taken command. "I remember those days. Your grandfather was all history makes him out to be, Tyler, but if he were here, he would be the first to admit that it was the astonishing production from the Iron Belt that enabled him to win the war. The spacers of the fleet earned their glory, but the laborers and engineers of the Iron Belt deserve at least as much credit." Nguyen took a raspy breath. "If we can hold the Iron Belt, we're still in this war. We still have a chance."

Barron heard the words, and his head believed them, at least to a point. But in his heart, there was only defeat.

He also knew the situation was far more complex than a simple "we lost the Core, but we hold the Belt" assessment. The Hegemony had only occupied two of the seven Core worlds, Ulion and Megara. But the other five Core worlds had been more or less abandoned to their own resources by the fleet when it withdrew to Craydon. That was more than forty-five billion human beings, abandoned, left to wait and see if the Hegemony would come—or, more accurately, *when* they would come.

Even a decision to "hold the Belt" was a commitment to a vague and fuzzy strategy. The systems were often spoken of together, but they were located roughly in a ring around the Core, which meant that some worlds of the Belt were actually closer to the Hegemony forces at Megara than they were to the Confederation fleet at Craydon.

"We will fight here, of course." Barron didn't have any real hope of victory, but the idea of not fighting to the end never entered his mind. "Anything these shipyards and factories can produce before that battle comes will only help."

"Additional forces will be arriving from Palatia within the next week." Vian Tulus sounded defiant, unbowed. Whatever effect the loss of Megara had on his Confederation allies, it was clear the Alliance imperator was ready for the next fight…and nowhere near giving in. "Commander Globus confirmed the communique, and he also received news of Admiral Eaton's stop at Palatia. I am pleased to report she made quite an impression. The treaty between our peoples started amid difficultly, but we are now as one. Your battle is our battle, and we will not stop until the enemy is driven from the Rim. Indeed, the time will come when we pursue them back to their own worlds, and show them of what we on the Rim are made."

Tyler nodded toward Tulus. He respected his Palatian brother, and counted him among his closest friends, but he didn't share the almost unbreakable optimism the imperator enjoyed. He wondered if Tulus would sound so defiant if Palatia had been lost instead of Megara.

Gary Holsten had stood silently next to the three admirals and the two Palatian warriors, but now he spoke up. "We must fight here, and this time, if we lose, it may well be the last fight. At least the last resistance of any consequence. The Hegemony is overpowering, and we have no hope at all to defeat them without the Confederation's industrial might. If we're driven back from here, if we fall back on the Far Rim, we are lost, whether we stage a token fight someplace like Archellia or not."

Holsten turned toward Tulus. "Even Palatia could not stand against this tide." Barron understood what the spy chief was trying to say, but he hoped it hadn't offended the imperator or Commander Globus. Holsten had meant no disrespect to Alliance arms, but the Palatians could be touchy and difficult to predict at times.

"You speak the truth, Mr. Holsten. It is no shame to admit this enemy vastly outnumbers us…and we are still far from restoring Palatia's defenses after the damage done during our recent civil war."

Damages that Tyler had done, fighting alongside the Gray Alliance forces and attacking Red-held Palatia.

"So, we all agree. We fight here, and this time there will be no retreat. We will stop them at Craydon…or the war will end here." Tyler still had his doubts, grave doubts. But he knew what he had to do, what the fleet had to do.

And Tyler Barron never ran from his duty. Even when he saw the specter of his own death in it.

* * *

"I'm not sure what to say, Dr. Witter. What you've accomplished in such a brief time is nothing short of amazing." Tyler Barron stood in the large room, a storage area, he guessed, recently transformed into a makeshift laboratory and test facility. "I'm particularly excited about the particle accelerator improvements. If it is truly possible to match the range of the enemy railguns, that would be an enormous tactical factor." Barron was impressed, but he wasn't sure excited was the right word. He still felt a deep sense of gloom, and he didn't see anything happening that would allow the Confederation and its allies to defeat the Hegemony. The enemy was simply too strong.

There was something else, too, another impetus behind the despondency he was trying to hide. He'd commanded the White Fleet. He'd brought this nightmare down on the Confederation. The White Fleet expedition had not been his idea, nor had he been an early supporter of the operation. He had joined with his comrades in hope that the needs of the exploration mission would slow down the Senate's rapid decommissioning of ships after the end of the war. Still, he blamed himself, and he'd stared into a bitter irony that existed only in his own mind. His grandfather had saved the Confederation…and he was going to lose it.

"All of this needs more testing, of course, but—"

"No." The answer came from the part of Barron that would never yield, however morose his view of events got.

"Admiral? I'm not sure I under—"

"There is no more time for testing. We need to get what we can into production and deployed as widely as possible. We have two months, maybe three." Barron had no idea how long it would take the enemy to follow up, but his experiences with the Hegemony gave him a good guess. Any conventional invasion force, so far from home and so battered by a desperate fight, would be stopped in place for a year, probably more. But the enemy's logistical supply train was so vast that everything Barron thought he knew about such things was irrelevant in this war. They had stopped at Ulion for three months, and he felt somewhat confident that they would need at least that long at Megara. Bryan Rogan was in command of the ground defenses, and he would put up one hell of a fight. And the fleet had battered the Hegemony forces even harder at Megara than they had at Ulion.

Yes, he felt reasonably sure they had three months. Counting on any more than that felt more like a prayer than reasoned analysis, though.

Witter stared back, an incredulous look on his face. "Admiral, that's just not possible."

"You're going to have to make it possible."

The scientist looked dumbstruck. He turned toward Andi Lafarge. The smuggler turned navy captain had become somewhat of a friend as she'd ferried his people to Craydon. But her expression offered him no support. It was clear she agreed with Barron.

"Admiral, captain…it will take months' more testing before we can even think of mass production, much less installing systems in our active warships. If we move too quickly, there could be a hundred problems, dangerous flaws, malfunctions that could cripple a ship, even destroy it."

"I understand that, doctor. What you need to understand is that this will very likely be the last battle, at least the last one of any consequence…unless we can find a way to win it."

"And what if we install new systems in your battleships, and they fail? Or worse?"

Barron stared coldly back at the scientist. "How much worse than total defeat can we get, doctor? How much worse than death?"

He took a deep breath and continued, "We are past nightfall now, Dr. Witter, and deep into the darkness. Dawn will never come unless we are able to find a way to defeat the enemy. Your research is almost certainly our best chance, regardless of the risks involved."

The researcher looked as though he was going to reply, but Barron kept going. "We will face them here with fewer ships than we had in Megara, and a smaller complement of orbital defenses. We will almost certainly lose unless we are able to deploy something new. Your new weapons offer us at least some shred of hope. I don't care about danger. I don't even care about odds of success. I will settle for the *chance* of success, however remote."

"Ah…Mr. Davidoff. Just in time. Thank you for responding so…promptly," Andi said as a man stepped into the room. He was smartly put together, perfectly manicured from head to toe, and wearing probably two years of the average spacer's salary in stylish clothing. Barron recognized an Iron Belt oligarch when he saw one, and somewhere in the back of his mind, he seemed to recall that the Davidoffs were Craydon's preeminent family.

That explained the fine clothes and the air of relaxed superiority. It didn't explain the strange look on his face, like some kind of cold fear wrestling with a lifetime's practiced arrogance.

One glance at Andi told Barron that she was most likely responsible for that. She'd carried the initial orders for the shipyards to launch any space-worthy vessels, and he didn't doubt Davidoff had seen easy pickings in some random cruiser captain delivering him requisitions. He almost laughed through all his doom and gloom, imagining how Andi had probably unloaded on the unsuspecting fool. The only real question in his mind was how literally had she described the man's impending dismemberment to him.

"How may I be of assistance?" Barron could hear the hatred, and he knew that was directed toward Andi. The fool wasn't as good as hiding it as he probably thought he was. He was rich and powerful, and no doubt used to dealing harshly with those who got in his way. Barron made a note to tell the magnate, one day when they were all alone, that Captain Andromeda Lafarge wasn't only enormously wealthy in her own right, and a stone-cold fighter from the Badlands, but she was also the one who'd killed Ricard Lille. The Union assassin had been known throughout the Rim.

"Thank you for coming, Mr. Davidoff," Barron interjected. Andi had secured the man's attention, and likely his grudging cooperation, but Barron figured it would be best if he took it from there. "We have a number of new systems we need to put into immediate production"—he paused, staring at the man, only scarcely less coldly than Andi had—"and I cannot stress how literally I mean 'immediate.'"

* * *

"The enemy appears to be well into conducting repairs to their front-line forces. I'm sure intensive review of the scanning results will yield more data, but I can summarize a bit if you wish." Stockton stood in the front of the conference room. He was looking out at all the senior officers present, but he was mostly focused on Tyler. Barron wasn't the overall commander, nor Stockton's direct superior anymore, but the pilot had served under him for a long time, and there was a strong bond between them.

Tyler nodded. "Please, Jake." He'd sent the fleet's strike force commander on a multi-system trip back to Megara, three transits each way in a fighter. It was a grueling run, and while Barron hadn't expressly ordered Stockton to go himself, he'd had no doubt that the legendary Raptor would make the run. Stockton had tried to go alone, but Barron had insisted he take two other pilots with him. One of those, at least, had made it back with Stockton.

"Well, sir—sirs—there are mining platforms and refineries around the asteroids and some of the outer system moons. There are factory ships and mobile shipyards, and they are all operational, working at what appears to be an almost unbelievable rate. I couldn't get any real data on how many ships have been serviced, or how much ordnance replaced, but my gut is they'll have the whole fleet in decent shape for a fight in another month…and damn closed to fully operational in two."

Stockton stood silently for a few seconds. "Of course, that's all guesswork. I fly fighters. I don't analyze fleet logistics."

Barron appreciated Stockton's flash of humility, but he was ready to take the pilot's analysis at face value. He'd always admired Stockton, but he was beyond impressed at the grim and capable leader this once-brash, young pilot had become.

"I, for one, don't have any problem accepting Admiral Stockton's analysis." Barron still had trouble believing the rank Stockton had achieved, the rank he had chosen to give his old squadron commander, and even more, just how much he knew Raptor deserved it. It had leapfrogged Stockton over hundreds of more senior officers, but there was just no escaping the fact that the pilot commanded thousands of fighters in every battle. The fighters were not only a massive force, but also the most vital one to preserving any hope of victory.

"Aside from the admiral's proven capability as a scout, it fits with our own estimates—albeit, unfortunately, with the more pessimistic ones." Which had been the only ones Barron had even considered. The Hegemony might kill him, but he'd sworn they would never take him by surprise again with their capabilities or dynamism.

"I think we all consider the admiral's report to be reliable, Tyler." Dustin Nguyen was staring down at the table as he spoke. The stress of the battle in Olyus and the unending workload since the fleet had arrived at Craydon were noticeably wearing down on the old officer. "I think the real question is, what can we do about it? This war has been like no other we've ever fought. We've had no significant respite, and they don't even have any vital supply lines that offer a vulnerable spot to attack. Yes, of course the enemy still must have ordnance moving forward from the distant home worlds, but with their mobile logistics, their ability to mine raw materials and refine them into what they need, there is nothing we can cut them off from that will cripple them...save, perhaps, for antimatter. And as crucial as that resource must be to their main guns and other key systems, it is not large. A single freighter can carry enough to sustain their operations through the complete conquest of the Rim. For all we know, they may have—probably have—enough in that vast fleet of freighters to keep them going to the end of the war."

No one spoke for a moment. The room was silent, save for the distant hum of some machinery. Then Tyler Barron's voice cut through the eerie quiet.

"We have to destroy it."

"Destroy what?" Clint Winters was sitting opposite Barron. "There are no normal supply lines to hit, no convoys we can intercept to hurt them, at least not enough."

"Their logistical support fleet is their true strength in this war. It's the one thing we haven't been able to counter, and the single resource that has denied us almost every defensive tactic that might have helped us, bought us time." Barron paused. "When they advance to meet us here, to crush us once and for all, they will almost certainly leave the support ships behind, as they have in every instance of this war. The freighters and mining ships and mobile shipyards will be in Megara when their battle fleet moves forward against us. We have to destroy it."

"Destroy the logistics fleet? Is that even possible?" Gary Holsten was the sole occupant of the room who wasn't regular military.

"Possible? Yes. Probable?" Winters said. "I don't see how."

"The stealth units." There was no detectable emotion in Barron's tone.

"I understand what you're thinking, but they're untested... and we've only got sixteen operational units. Assume you're right, that the logistics train is left in the Olyus system, and the enemy main fleet moves on us here. They will still leave some kind of garrison, both to support their conquest and occupation of Megara and to defend the supply fleet. How can we possibly expect to use sixteen stealth generators to get there with a fleet large enough to pull this off?"

"The answer is simple, Clint. We put the generators in our sixteen newest and biggest battleships...and we send them to Megara. We have more than one way to reach the capital without going through enemy-held space, or anywhere the Hegemony battle fleet will pass on its way to Craydon. And the stealth units will safeguard against running into some random patrol."

Winters stared across the table, an expression on his face the likes of which was rarely seen on a man called "the Sledgehammer." "You can't be serious," he finally said.

"I'm deadly serious. What else can we do?"

"Tyler...first, aside from the fact that even our sixteen best ships constitute a woefully inadequate fleet to send against whatever garrisons the enemy leaves in Megara, do you realize how badly it will weaken the fleet here to detach the force you're talking about?"

"I realize that. Does it matter?"

Winters just stared at him.

Barron knew they all thought he was losing it, but for all his cold-blooded pessimism, he knew exactly what he was proposing.

"We lost in Megara, Clint...with Prime Base, the capital fortresses, even the asteroids we armed and towed into place. We're weaker now, down twenty percent in hulls, and over a quarter in fighters. Everybody under arms is exhausted and demoralized. We're not going to win here, my friend, no matter what strategies we concoct, what desperate plans we put in place. Craydon is *not* the primary battle in my plan—it's the diversion. Hitting the logistics fleet in Olyus is the main attack. The mission of the ships deployed here is to entice the enemy battle fleet out of

Olyus, to give the raiding force a chance to get around and hit those supply and repair ships hard."

"The attack on Olyus will still be very close a suicide mission, Tyler. Especially if those stealth units fail to function perfectly. You know that."

"I'm willing to take that risk."

"You? Who decided you would lead the ships back to Olyus?"

"It's my plan. It's on me to take the chances. You and Admiral Nguyen can command the fleet here…and once the enemy is clearly deployed, you can decide what to do, fight it out or pull back. I just need those heavy units busy while I hit the support fleet."

"You should be here with the main fleet, Tyler," Winters said. "Even with the sixteen best heavies gone, it's still far and away the largest force." A pause. "I will lead the flanking force."

Barron stared across the table at his comrade, his friend. "No, no way. It's too dangerous."

"But it's not for you? We're way past worrying about danger now, aren't we? We're teetering on the edge of the abyss here, and you're right. This may be the only way to stop the enemy, at least for long enough for us to deploy more of the new technology, and get some new ships in the line. A chance, at least… which is more than we've got now."

Barron was about to respond when Nguyen slammed his hand down hard on the table. "That's enough from both of you. Let's figure this out, make sure the plan is even practical. We don't even know if those stealth units can be installed quickly enough, and without them, this really *would* be a suicide mission, and a pointless one at that. We work out the details, together. Then *I* will decide who leads the raiding force and who takes field command here at Craydon."

The old admiral glared at both of the younger officers. "You wanted me in command, and that's what you got…and that's just what I'm going to do. Command."

Chapter Twenty-Six

UFS Illustre
Hovan System
Union-Confederation Border
Union Year 222 (318 AC)

The pain was intense, and it radiated out from Denisov's chest to every extremity of his body. There was blood all over him, his own now, mixed with that of his murdered aide. He was on the floor, though it took him an instant to realize that, and he didn't remember actually falling.

He was still screaming at himself inside, railing against the carelessness that had caused him to walk into an assassin's bullet. The aide's face flashed through his memory. If the young officer hadn't chased him down with a last-second report, if he hadn't gone in first, Denisov would be the one lying dead on the floor, his brains blown across half the room.

Instead, he was just critically wounded, and his assassin was still there, somewhere in the darkness of his office, no doubt ready to finish the job. His fortune, if that was the word for it, had bought him a few seconds more of life, nothing beyond that. He'd led his people into mutiny, put countless loyal officers into the sights of Gaston Villieneuve's murderous paranoia. All for nothing.

He waited for his death, expecting it any second. But it didn't come.

I'm behind the lieutenant. He'd fallen hard, and the dead aide was on his side right next to him.

Blocking me?

He imagined his office, trying to guess where his killer was positioned. *Behind the desk.*

Of course.

And the body next to him was right in between him and his desk.

He might have a chance after all…but even as he tried to move, to reach for the gun, he realized he'd dropped it and it had skittered out of reach. The brief flash of hope drained away, and despair settled in again.

He caught a glimpse of something, not a visual sighting so much as a soft sound, the rushing of air. The assassin on the move.

Now, it's over…

He heard a crack. No, a loud succession of shots. Some kind of automatic fire, and a second later, a bright light shining across the room.

He wrenched his head around and saw a figure dead center in his field of view, caught in the middle of the shaft of bright light. A woman. She had a pistol still in her hand, but as he watched, it slipped down to the ground. She wore a normal spacer's coveralls, but they were covered in small red dots.

Not dots…gradually expanding circles of crimson. She fell to her knees, and in her face, he could see pain and determination. She still looked as though her only thought was to kill him, even as her strength slipped away, and her own death came for her.

He heard the sound of loud boots on the deck, and he knew his guards had come. They had made it in time. Just.

Or not quite. He wasn't sure. The pain was almost unbearable. He was badly wounded.

Very badly wounded.

He felt hands on him, saw the hazy image of a guard. There were words, but they were soft, far away.

And then not there at all.

* * *

"He will probably survive, though if you'd asked me an hour ago, I might have said otherwise. He's tough as nails, but even so, if it had taken another three or four minutes to get the artificial heart in him, he'd have died right there on the table."

Denisov could hear the words, and on some level, he could understand them. But they still didn't seem real.

He was lying down, as he had been before, but now he wasn't on the deck. He was in a bed. And the pain…it was gone. He felt nothing. Almost as though he was floating.

But the words…they were still there.

Where am I? he said. Or, at least, he'd tried to say it. It took a few seconds to realize that he'd heard the words in his head, but his raw and parched throat had not managed to force out anything audible. He moved his hand, though that, too, was far more difficult than he'd expected.

He took a breath. It didn't hurt, not exactly, but there was a strange feeling. Pressure? Tightness?

He tried to move his head, but he couldn't. His midsection was covered with something. Metal. Some kind of apparatus.

I'm in sickbay. I was shot.

Artificial heart? The words echoed in his mind, realization setting in. He knew he'd been badly hurt, but now he realized just how close he'd come to death.

How close his assassin had come to success.

He tried to move his arm again, and to force something audible from his mouth. He managed a grunt, not very communicative, but enough to get the attention of the doctors standing just inside the doorway to the room.

They came running over, one of them turning to check the bank of monitors next to the bed, while the other leaned over him.

"Admiral, I am very pleased to see you awake. You've been through quite an ordeal, but I am confident you will survive."

There was considerable sincerity in the doctor's tone. That meant two things to Denisov. One, he probably *was* going to make it. And two, the man tasked with seeing to that result was a supporter of his, and not an officer harboring closeted resentment about the choices he'd made for them all.

He tried to speak again. He slowed his words down, concentrating on each one as though its utterance was a herculean task. Which each of them was. "Thirsty…"

"Of course, admiral." The doctor turned and snapped a command to one of the medical technicians who'd entered the room. "I was reluctant to allow you any water in case I had to take you back into surgery." He looked at the other doctor, who turned from the readouts and nodded. "But your stats all look very good, so I am optimistic you are past the worst of it. You will need a substantial recovery period, of course, and there are some realities of living with a robotic coronary pump you will have to adjust to, but in the end, I am sure…"

Denisov stopped listening. He didn't want a pep talk on how well he was doing. His fleet was in enemy space, at least what had been enemy space for a century. He was on his way to try to forge an alliance with people who hated him, who despised the Union and its spacers as much as he and his people hated them. He didn't have time for "substantial recovery periods," and he damn sure didn't understand why doctors had to make everything so complicated. Did they think "robotic coronary pump" sounded better than "artificial heart"?

"No time…" He'd managed to get a better handle on forcing out words, but he stopped when an assistant came up to the bed and held a small canister next to his face. He opened his mouth and wrapped his lips around the small straw extending out.

The feeling of water, cool, crisp, wet…it was indescribable. For a few seconds, it was his universe, all he cared about, all he could imagine he would ever want.

He drank and drank…and then the container ran dry. He looked up, his eyes finding the doctor's, his expression as clear a communication as any oratory could deliver. *More.*

The doctor shook his head slowly. "I'm sorry, admiral, but after what your system's been through, we have to go slowly. You can have another canister in half an hour."

Denisov felt a wave of anger, of pure, unfiltered, elemental rage. He wanted water, damn it. Now! It faded quickly, and his rational mind understood the situation.

"I need to get out of here, doctor…as soon as possible." His speech had recovered considerably from the hydration, and, while not exactly loud and commanding, his voice was now completely audible.

"Admiral, that's not possible. I'm afraid—"

"You know where we are, doctor. You know the situation. I *have* to get out of here and back to the bridge…as soon as humanly possible."

"I understand the situation, admiral. Do you understand that if I disconnect you from the med support system right now, you will be dead long before you can reach the bridge? Will that help the fleet in any way?"

Denisov saw unintended complexity in that last question. He was far from sure his presence had done a damn thing beneficial for his people, at all. But he was determined to finish what he had started.

"Then we need to set up a command station down here. I need my aide, and we'll need a direct comm link, and some portable scanners." He looked up at the astonished doctor standing next to him. "And I'll need some help staying awake, doc, so have some stims ready. I'll go as long as I can without them, but—"

"Admiral, that is out of the question. You need rest, and the—"

"Is it better if I die because the Confeds attacked us? Or if the Hegemony forces are still following us, and they hit us when we're not ready?" The doctor was only looking out for him, and Denisov knew that. But reality was reality. "There is no choice, doctor. I'll try to get some rest, but that's not going to happen unless I have all the data I need down here. Help me get everything I need set up, and I will stay as calm as possible."

The doctor looked unhappy—astonished, even. There was little doubt Denisov had stolen the crown as his most difficult patient. But there was realization in his expression, too. He clearly knew Denisov had spoken nothing but the truth about their situation.

The doctor nodded, looking defeated. "Okay, admiral...but you have to take it easy when there isn't a crisis. You won't help any of us if you push yourself too hard and relapse. You could still die if we're not careful, so keep that in mind."

Denisov nodded, or came as close as he could. He would try to remember that.

It seemed like a damn difficult thing to forget.

Chapter Twenty-Seven

Orbital Platform Killian
Planet Craydon, Calvus System
Year 318 AC

"The technicians have finished installing the upgraded stealth units. The sixteen battleships are ready to go…but, I must say again, those units were not tested to any reasonable standards. They *may* work. They *should* work. But there are a hundred things that could go wrong."

"We understand that, Dr. Witter, but I think you can see that there's no choice, and very likely no time to waste," Barron said. "Destroying—or even badly damaging—the enemy logistics fleet is just about our only chance to slow them down, to buy some time. Time you can use to complete and test more of the devices your teams are working on." Barron understood the scientist's concerns. He even agreed with them. Sixteen ships. Sixteen separate stealth generators. And all it would take was one of them failing at the wrong time, and the entire operation would be compromised. The raiding force was strong—the main fleet felt gutted without those ships—but its target was vast, and whatever the Hegemony sent to Craydon, there was little doubt they would leave at least some defensive forces behind.

None of that mattered. The fleet was busy preparing to defend its latest stronghold, but Barron knew they were going to lose. He didn't share those thoughts, at least outside the circle of top commanders, nor did he behave in any way other than defiant and determined. But the Hegemony forces were just too strong, and detaching sixteen of the fleet's best battleships only made things worse for the impending fight at Craydon.

But it also gave something the fleet didn't have otherwise. A chance. The forces at Craydon wouldn't be fighting to save the planet, or even the Iron Belt. The combined might of Confederation arms was a decoy, their primary purpose to lure as much of the Hegemony's force as possible from Megara, and allow the raiding force to strip them of their logistics support.

If the enemy's supply and support ships could be hit hard enough, they would have to pull back from Craydon, maybe even from Megara. They were at the extreme end of a very long supply line back to their bases, and Barron knew his attack on those supply ships could do more than any noble stand at Craydon to stabilize the situation.

At least, he hoped it would be his attack. Admiral Nguyen had been silent on his thoughts, about whether Winters or Barron would lead the raiding force. The other would serve as Nguyen's exec and help command the main force at Craydon.

"As soon as the stealth units are installed, the teams will begin to add the mods to the primary batteries." There was hesitation in the scientist's voice again. The upgrades to the primaries were really just mods to the power transmission and flow parameters. In essence, trading safety and reliability for power. And range. The modified beams would be effective up to twenty percent farther out, and that took away more than eighty percent of the range advantage of the Hegemony railguns.

It was only a guess what the cost would be for that…in disabled weapons and even critical failures. But all three admirals present had agreed the changes should be made was quickly as possible.

"Doctor, when can your people have the raiding force ready to go, with stealth units and enhanced primaries operational?" Nguyen sounded tired. Hell, Barron couldn't imagine how exhausted the admiral was. He was about to drop himself, and

Nguyen had more than fifty years on him. But the fleet commander was still going, and keeping up every step of the way with his younger comrades, confirming to Barron again that he'd been the right choice for the job.

"Three days, admiral. Maybe four."

Nguyen was shaking his head before the scientist even finished. "The raiding force has to leave in two days, doctor. We've waited too long as it is." Barron had been thinking the same thing, and he suspected Winters had too. "You have to be finished in forty-eight hours, doctor. I don't care what you need. If it exists on Craydon, I will get it for you. But those ships have to be underway in forty-eight hours."

Witter looked like he was going to argue, but he glanced back and forth at the three admirals, each wearing a similar stony expression. Finally, he said, "I will do all I can, admiral."

Nguyen stared back. "Make sure that is enough, doctor. Forty-eight hours."

* * *

"I want to thank you again, Andi, for bringing the researchers from the Institute here. I know you only did it because I asked you to." Tyler paused and looked at her silently for a few seconds. "And I also know you did it because you knew I'd be worried about you, that it would distract me."

Andi wasn't surprised how well he understood what she had done and why. No one had ever known her like Tyler Barron, and it sometimes shocked her, as accustomed as she was to being mostly a mystery, even to those close to her, like *Pegasus*'s longtime crew.

"As a loyal Confederation officer, what else could I do?" She smiled at him and reached over, running her palm softly over his cheek and back through his hair. She was happy they'd found some time, a little, at least, to be together, amid all the stress and work preparing for yet another desperate battle. But that happiness was a false veneer, she knew, and inside her was a black pit of sadness and despair.

She knew Tyler as well as he knew her, and in his words, in his body language, in everything she could see and hear around him, she knew he didn't expect to survive the coming battle.

And, possibly worse, she didn't expect him to make it either.

The pleasure she felt at spending time together was quickly eradicated by the realization that these few stolen hours could very well be their last together. She and Barron had always had an on-again, off-again kind of relationship, one of constant affection, but staggered by a realization that their lives were simply too different, that they were constantly pulled in different directions.

Andi could never imagine herself as the dutiful spouse of an admiral, and she couldn't quite get her head around one of the navy's top officers married to a smuggler and a Badlands adventurer, either. *I guess I'm a stone-cold killer now, too.* Word of her battle to the death with Ricard Lille had spread throughout the fleet, despite the fact that she'd never spoken of it to anyone.

Regardless, she'd always resolved to enjoy what time she and Tyler had together, and to leave it at that. But her emotions had betrayed her; the stony toughness that had always shielded her like armor had developed a weak spot. She loved Tyler Barron, and she had resolved to herself, somewhere in her subconscious, at least, that once this was all over, they would be together, whatever it took. Forever.

Except there wasn't going to be any forever. The Confederation was losing the war, darkness was falling all around, and nothing save for a few desperate plans stood between all of them and the abyss. And even if the Confederation somehow survived, she knew Tyler Barron too well. He'd come through more than his share of battles, but she had a bad feeling about this one.

She lay next to him, enjoying the warmth of his body as she always did, and, deep inside, she believed it would be the last time. She wanted to burst into tears, to scream and beg him to run away with her, to find some planet where they could hide, from the Confederation, the Hegemony. From everything.

But she knew the man she loved could never grant such a

request, not even to her. She had to let him fight his war, and die, if that was his fate. And there was nothing she could do to stop it.

She pushed back hard on the despair, refusing to feel sad, to give up the joy of those last few hours together. She slid closer to him and pressed her face against his, and then she kissed him.

If they only had hours left, she would make the best of them…enough to last a lifetime if it had to.

* * *

"So, we're all agreed on the route. It has an extra transit, but it's probably the least likely to be patrolled in any way by the enemy, and the entry point is the closest to the logistics fleet, or at least our best guess on where those ships are deployed."

Barron just nodded. They'd discussed the topic for hours. But the plan had survived every attempt to tear it down. It was a shitty option, dangerous as hell and with an unknown, but probably small, chance of success. But it was better than all the others they had.

"The question is, how much velocity do we want coming out of the transit point?" Clint Winters was standing across from Barron, staring down at the tabletop display. "If we're right about where the logistics fleet is, we can save a lot of time and hit them quickly. And despite what Dr. Witter says, I don't believe that blasting the engines hard won't make it easier to spot the ships, even with the stealth generators going at full power. Any thrust we can blast before the transit instead of after helps our odds, in my view."

Barron nodded. He'd been thinking exactly the same thing.

"If we're wrong, though, the ships will need that much *more* thrust to change their vectors." Nguyen had been playing devil's advocate during the entire meeting, putting his two top commanders in the position of defending the plan…or abandoning it.

So far, both had stood steadfast.

"We're not wrong." The words were out of Barron's mouth

almost involuntarily. "Their mining ships need to be at the most resource-rich planets and moons, and the mobile refineries need to be close to the mining platforms. It's just a guess that the freighters and the shipyards will be there too, but I'm willing to take that bet. They'll be trying to keep their repair and refit operation moving as quickly as possible, and having to haul things all over the system would just slow them down."

Winters nodded. Nguyen was silent for a moment, and then he said, "I agree. It is decided, then. The fleet will set out in nine hours, and it will follow the agreed-upon course."

The aged admiral stood in place for a minute. Then he looked at both admirals and nodded.

"I've given a lot of thought to which of you should lead the raiding force, and which should stay here at Craydon and help me command the fleet."

Barron looked right at the fleet commander, as did Winters. They both wanted to lead the raiding force, Barron knew, though remaining with the fleet was, by all normal standards, the senior posting.

"Both of you are more than qualified for either position, but I have finally come to a decision." Then he told them what he had decided.

Chapter Twenty-Eight

Planet Megara, Olyus III
Year of Renewal 263 (318 AC)

The Invasion of Megara – The Clouds Gather

"We will do no such thing, senator," Bryan Rogan said into his comm unit, struggling to remain civil as he did. Dealing directly with senators had been nowhere in the job description when he'd graduated from the Academy so many years before. There should be someone he could hand that duty off to, some senior commander more adept at such things.

But there wasn't. Rogan was the top Confederation military commander on Megara—at least, he had been until the Senate relieved him.

The senator was clearly scared to death by all that was happening. As well he should be. *We can put up some resistance, but we're pretty much screwed in the long run. At least unless the fleet manages to return soon.*

Which is why these cowards want to surrender now. At least there's some negotiating value in not making the enemy go through an entire campaign to pacify the planet.

Rogan didn't give a shit what the senator and his pack of lying colleagues wanted, not anymore.

"As I said, senator, my forces—all volunteer partisans, by the way, since you fine gentlemen relieved me of my official command and, I believe, ordered my arrest—will resist the enemy at every opportunity. Resisting the landings is crucial. And Troyus City may be key to our strategy." He'd added that last bit in a burst of spite. He had no intention of remaining within the city limits long enough to dare the enemy to blast Troyus from orbit, nor to tempt the Kriegeri in and fight a desperate, building-to-building battle that would leave the city as wrecked as a bombardment would.

But he had every intention of keeping his forces in place while the landings were still going on. The Hegemony forces were coming down in massive strength all around Troyus. Clearly, taking the capital quickly was high on their list of combat priorities. Rogan wasn't ready to commit too much strength to hold the city. It was shockingly unproductive, at least in terms of anything militarily useful, and he suspected feeding its vast population would become a critical problem almost immediately. He didn't trust the Senate either, not at all. Certainly not in terms of staying in the fight.

The politician on the other end of the comm line was angry. Rogan was astonished at the man's arrogance. The Senate had ordered him to stand down and let the enemy land, and then they'd fired him and issued an arrest warrant. *And now this fool is incredulous because I won't do what he wants me to do...*

"Senator, I do not have time for this foolishness. If you and your colleagues find your spines, I will be happy to work with you. Until then, I have a world to defend, and a large force of patriots who have rallied to my cause." Almost all the marines had responded to Rogan's call to arms, and a surprising percentage of the other defense units as well.

Rogan cut the line and then walked back toward the small building he was using as a makeshift command post. The enemy had cut his satellite links, and that greatly restricted his communications. He'd expected it, though, and had deployed independent commanders to a dozen different sectors on Megara, each with total autonomy. He'd taken the capital area command himself and commandeered every civilian aircraft on the planet.

They would enable him to maintain some kind of links to his various commanders, at least until the enemy landed enough force to gain air superiority. That wouldn't be terribly difficult for the invaders. Megara's defenses were astonishingly short on atmospheric combat craft.

Rogan didn't care. He'd fight the enemy with missiles, with artillery, with guns.

With knives and sticks and rocks if need be.

But he'd be damned if he'd give up, if he'd let the Confederation down.

Or if he'd fail the man who'd been the prime mover in giving him his current command.

No, Admiral Barron…I will not fail, not while I still draw breath.

* * *

"I trust that the capitulation of the Confederation Senate will quickly bring resistance on the surface to a speedy conclusion." Chronos sat on his pedestal, looking out over the officers he had summoned, both those present and the ones down on the surface and attending the meeting in the form of holograms. The fleet commander was not one for such pretentious nonsense, and normally, he would have conducted the meeting in one of *Hegemony's Glory*'s conference rooms instead of in his sanctum. There was a place, though, for spectacle, and he had decided it would not hurt to remind his people, Masters and Kriegeri alike, that no less a personage than Number Eight was watching them conduct the invasion.

The war had already taken too long. Total pacification would require years, of course, even if he was able to compel mass surrenders instead of taking each planet one by one. But once he managed to destroy the main fleets of the enemy, he could send most of the Grand Fleet back to the Hegemony homelands, now so dangerously stripped of their normal defenses.

"Commander, the Confederation Senate *has* surrendered, and they have ordered their forces to stand down, as per the terms set forth, but…" Illius was not normally one to mince words, but the megaron hesitated, something that didn't escape Chronos's notice.

"Speak freely, old friend." Chronos had not intended to address anyone so informally, but Illius was one of his oldest friends, and a man he truly respected. He would likely have ignored apparent concern from most of those present, but if Illius was concerned, things were probably not going quite as he might have hoped.

"There are a considerable number of enemy positions still active, firing on our landing forces. I also have multiple reports of ground units attacking landing zones, almost immediately after the vanguards have disembarked. One LZ has actually been overrun, and another is barely hanging on."

"Treachery?" Chronos wondered if the Senate had some- how tricked him, if their capitulation had been a ruse of some kind.

"I do not believe so, commander. All indications are that a substantial number of enemy troops have laid down their arms. Our best intelligence suggests, however, that these units consist heavily of local militias and reserve forces. The vast majority of the enemy's heavily armed ground troops appear to remain in the field, actively attacking our own forces."

Chronos had received similar reports from Dannith, and he had always responded by reminding those involved how little he cared for their excuses. But now, he was hearing it from one of the few officers he relied upon.

The Kriegeri were bred for war, most of the best specimens taken into training facilities in childhood and raised to join spe- cific regiments. They endured multiple rounds of painful sur- gery to install the implants, and they took their places in a life of endless military service. The best specimens would breed the next group of Kriegeri, but there would be little contact with their breeding partners after copulation, nor any of note with their offspring. They had little contact with anyone outside immediate comrades. Even those destined for high rank would remain almost entirely focused on military matters.

By all accounts, the Confederation soldiers were nothing like the Kriegeri. They were recruited or drafted as adults, and they fought with no implants or physical upgrades of any kind. They were not a match for the Kriegeri, not in an even fight…but they were a *lot* closer than any enemy the Hegemony had yet encountered. Any save for the Others.

"Are you suggesting that renegade soldiers refusing the orders to surrender constitute a significant threat to our landing forces?" Chronos knew that was just what the megaron was saying, but he wanted to hear Illius explain it.

"I am, commander." Chronos appreciated the blunt honesty, and he listened intently. "The enemy appears to remain active in considerable numbers, far more than I had anticipated. We face a considerable challenge in forcing our landings and getting enough strength on the ground and formed up to conduct our breakouts."

Chronos would have admonished any of his other officers, but Illius was not one to be easily shaken by enemy action, or to ask for resources he did not need. "What are you proposing, Megaron? I assume you have something in mind."

"Yes, sir. I understand the restrictions on ground bombardments, and I completely agree with the mandates to take control of the enemy capital intact. I believe we need to support our landings with targeted orbital bombardments. Just until we can get significant heavy forces on the ground and in formation. I believe we can limit the damage mostly to sparsely inhabited areas…though the enemy is deployed in strength around the capital city, and there will likely be some impact to sections of the urban area."

Chronos took a deep breath. His impulse was to refuse the request, even though it came from Illius. The conquest of the Rim was intended to bring new worlds into the Hegemony, to tap into massive populations that were mostly untouched by the mutations and genetic damage so prevalent in the coreward regions. The more brutality he was forced to unleash, the more difficult it would be to assimilate the ex-Confeds into the Hegemony.

And if he authorized the use of too much force, if his fleet began nuking cities and unleashing other devastating weapons, he could very well destroy the one thing that made the Rim populations so extraordinary: the absence of mutations and genetic damage in the chromosomal pools.

"Very well," he finally said, "but conventional ordnance only. No nuclear weapons, no chemical or biological agents."

"Thank you, commander. I will closely monitor all attacks and ensure that the minimum needed force is applied."

"You may all go." His voice was suddenly deep, imperious. "Except you, Illius. You remain." It was a demand that took the others by surprise. But they quickly obeyed. Few in the Hegemony were slow to respond when Number Eight issued an order.

Chronos waited until only the two of them remained. "Illius, my old friend, I trust you to exercise caution. We need to take Megara without inflicting too many civilian casualties or too much damage to the infrastructure. The planet will likely become the regional capital of the Rim, and it will need the facilities to serve in that capacity. Besides, we still want to assimilate these people as smoothly as possible. The fewer martyrs and the less brutality, the faster we will achieve that."

"Yes, commander. I will obtain your specific approval for every planned bombardment before—"

"No."

"Commander?"

"I will not be here, Illius. Enough time has elapsed since the survivors of the enemy forces fled. Too much time. I must take the fleet now in pursuit and finish things. The next fight will likely be the last one. The Confederation forces have been impressive in both their abilities and their tenacity, but they have suffered very heavy losses. We have located their new position, three jumps from here. I am leading the fleet out tomorrow… and leaving you in command here. Do what you must, but be cautious, deliberative. Look not just to the victory, but to the future beyond, and remember, these people are tomorrow's strength of the Hegemony. The industry here on the Rim is more dynamic and productive that anything coreward. We need these people, their energy…even as they need us to guide them."

"Understood, commander. I will not let you down."

Chronos nodded. "I know you won't." And he meant it.

Illius was the only officer in the fleet he was not worried about.

Chapter Twenty-Nine

"Admiral Barron, we're getting energy readings from the Crawford transit point."

Tyler Barron's head snapped around. "Details on my screen, as soon as they come in." He wasn't expecting anything from that direction, but a few scattered ships had come in over the past two months, stragglers rallying to the main fleet from various frontier postings. The Crawford point was the last place he expected any Hegemony forces to emerge.

Barron had been sitting quietly in the control center. Actually, he'd been brooding, though he wasn't about to admit that to anyone. Admiral Nguyen had made it clear that his decision to send Clint Winters to command the raiding force had not come from any lack of confidence in Barron's abilities. Quite the contrary—Nguyen had based his choice on whom he thought he most needed with him to command the main fleet. Barron even believed that. Still, he knew the fight at Craydon was a lost cause, and while he wouldn't have gone so far as to say the raid on Megara could win the war, it was just about the only hope to keep the fight going, and possibly even to force the enemy to retreat from the capital.

You've always been the one to lead the desperate and crazy missions, and you don't like being left behind. Being the old man, in charge of the staid, old-school tactic...

Barron had never considered himself an egotist, but he realized he'd bought more into the legends that had grown up around him than he wanted to admit.

"Put it through the AI, commander." Barron didn't know what could be coming through, but he wasn't overly concerned.

Crawford is on the line out to the Union...

There was a time that would have concerned him, but he longed for the days when Union fleets were the worst thing he had to worry about. The Union was still his enemy, but fortunately, they weren't ready for a return engagement. They couldn't be.

"It looks like a single ship, admiral. It's through." Another moment passed. "AI says it's a fast cruiser, admiral." The officer looked toward Barron. "It's a Malikov-class light cruiser, sir. A Union ship."

The words hit Barron, and it only took a second for the reality to coalesce. It *was* a Union ship.

"Battle stations, commander. All fleet units and orbital platforms at full alert." He felt anger welling up inside him, renewed hatred for the Union. The entire Rim was fighting for its life, and the reality of what he was seeing became starkly clear. The Union was taking the opportunity to strike at the Confederation while it was engaged with the Hegemony.

His mind was dark, and he hated the Senate almost as much as the Union. He blamed them for stopping the fleet from finishing the endless series of wars between the two nations once and for all. The politicians had caused this, and now, whatever chance his people had was gone. Even if Winters somehow completed his mission, there was no way the fleet could fight two enemies.

"Admiral, we're getting a communique." The officer turned around again, a stunned look on his face. "They are requesting a line to the fleet's commander."

Barron was unsure what to think. It was a Union ship, and

that made him suspicious. But he couldn't see what a single ship could hope to do. Issue a threat? Or something else? "Commander, I want full active scanners on that transit point. I want to know if so much as a cloud of dust is about to pass through on the heels of that ship."

"Yes, sir."

Barron took a deep breath. He almost passed the job off to Nguyen, but the admiral had finally gone to his quarters for a rest, and Barron didn't want to disturb him unless he absolutely had to. The old fleet commander had driven himself almost to death over the past few weeks, and Barron was going to see that he got some sleep. Nothing short of the whole Union fleet coming through that point was going to change that.

"Put them through, commander." Barron was trying to keep his hatred for the Union in check, but memories of what Ricard Lille had done to Andi, of the nightmare she'd been put through, kept pushing their way into this mind.

"On your line, admiral."

"This is Admiral Tyler Barron. You are violating Confederation space, in violation of the treaties in effect between our nations. You have committed an act of war, and I order you to power down at once and prepare to be boarded." He didn't expect the Union ship to do as he demanded, but he didn't really care. Honestly, he'd be just as happy to blast them to atoms… and this time the Senate wasn't going to save them.

"Admiral Barron, this is Captain Raymonde Chanticleer of the cruiser *D'alvert*. Our intrusion into Confederation space is not an aggression against the Confederation. I am here to offer a treaty of alliance, between the Confederation and the Union fleet."

Barron was stunned. He felt as though he'd been sucker-punched. "Excuse me, captain? You invaded our space to request an alliance?" Barron was actually angrier than he'd been at first. He didn't know what kind of game this captain was playing, but he knew better than to believe anything anyone from the Union told him. *And what does he mean, "Union fleet"?*

Barron waited while the signal traveled to the Union vessel, and the response returned. It was always annoying to try to communicate with a thirty-second delay between each answer, but this time, Barron was especially raw.

"Admiral Barron, I assure you, this is not the way I—or Admiral Denisov—would have chosen to handle this matter. We had no choice, and I urge you to listen to what I have to say."

"Captain Chanticleer, I don't know what you mean by 'no choice,' but there are numerous ways to initiate diplomatic negotiations without violating our borders. Now, I will repeat, one final time. You are to power down at once and prepare to be boarded. If you do not comply within one minute, you will be destroyed. I trust this is clear enough to you."

"We were attacked by the Hegemony, admiral. That's why we're here."

Barron was startled by the what he was hearing. Then the captain's words truly sank in. "The Hegemony? You fought Hegemony forces?" Barron didn't know if he believed the officer, but something in his gut told him it was true. Was the Hegemony moving against the Union as well? It made sense. They almost certainly wanted the whole Rim, and not just the Confederation.

But that would mean they had even more ships than those deployed against his forces. The mere thought of that made him nauseated. He didn't want to talk to some Union officer. The whole thing was anathema to him. And he was still suspicious of a trap.

But there was no choice. He had to know whatever he could about the Hegemony. And he damn sure had to understand why there were Union ships in Confederation space.

"Yes, admiral. The Hegemony. The same enemy you are currently fighting."

The captain's response came through the comm, even as Barron was formulating his own next move. "Captain," he finally said, "you will approach Craydon at one-tenth thrust levels, and you will come to a dead stop at three hundred million kilometers. You will then take a shuttle and come to me here. You will receive further instructions as you commence your final approach. If you deviate from the course transmitted to you, or if we detect any energy spikes, on your shuttle or on your ship, you will be destroyed. Is that understood?"

Barron waited, wondering if he'd been too aggressive, if he'd allowed his hatred toward the Union to control him too deeply. But the answer, when it came, told him that was not a problem.

"Your terms are acceptable, admiral. We will begin our approach at once."

Barron leaned back in the chair, his mind reeling at the officer's quick acceptance. *What the hell is going on?*

He didn't know, but he was damn sure going to find out.

He was sure about one other thing: this was definitely a reason to awaken Admiral Nguyen.

* * *

"I know you wanted more time for testing, doctor, and I understand why you were pushed to move forward without it. I'm inclined to agree with the admirals. They need everything they can get. I just wanted to ask you what you think. What you really think. Without pressure, with no one else listening. Will all this stuff work?" Andi stood in *Dauntless*'s engineering section, watching as Witter supervised the modifications to the battleship's primaries. She'd already said her goodbyes to Tyler, at least for the next few days. She was still *Hermes*'s commander, and until she relinquished that position, she was going to take it seriously. She'd been away from her ship for several days, and it was time to check up on things. If the wait for the enemy attack continued, if things were still quiet in three or four days, maybe she could get back and they could steal a few more moments.

"That's a difficult question to answer, captain. Do I believe that generally, if one of these weapons is fired, that it will function? Yes, almost certainly. Similarly, the stealth generators will work as long as they are operated properly." The scientist paused for a moment. "The problem isn't most of the time. The problem is achieving the levels of consistency that are necessary. Stealth generators can function on sixteen ships for extended periods of time, but just one of them failing at the wrong time, for even a few seconds, could be devastating. A battleship can fire a hundred shots, but if one of them fails catastrophically, the energy feedback could cripple the ship, even destroy it."

Andi listened. She knew everything Witter was telling her… and it wasn't what she'd asked. She wanted numbers. She wanted to know what the chance was that one of the stealth units would give out when Winters's ships were in Megara, or how likely it was that *Dauntless*, or any of the other battleships, would experience a disastrous malfunction.

She was about to ask him again, more pointedly—and with considerably more aggression—but something stopped her.

He isn't evading answering you. He just doesn't know.

That made sense, of course. It was one of the big reasons Witter had argued so hard for more testing. The scientist had been right. Those systems weren't ready. They weren't reliable enough to count on.

But Barron and Nguyen and Winters had been right, too. None of that mattered. They needed whatever they could get, regardless of the risk. If they couldn't count on something, they would gamble on it. Things were *that* desperate.

She just nodded to Witter and extended her hand, shaking his. Then she turned and left to catch her shuttle to *Hermes*. As she walked down the corridor, one though settled in her mind.

Would this amazing new tech save Tyler? Or would it kill him?

Or would it make no difference at all in what was about to happen?

* * *

"I don't trust them, admiral, not one bit. It's as likely they're in with the Hegemony as sincere about joining us against them. And what about this story that the fleet took off into our space without permission, and in violation of orders? I don't know everything about service in the Union, but Sector Nine is no mystery to any of us. Could a Union admiral really do something like this, and pull it off?" Barron hesitated. "I just don't buy it."

Nguyen had been silent, calm, listening to Barron's rants. He knew the admiral's memories of facing the Union in battle were far fresher than his own, that there'd been less time for the wounds to heal. He also knew about Andi's experiences, at least what Gary Holsten had told him. That wasn't everything, he suspected, but it was enough to explain Barron's incendiary hatred for the Union.

"Tyler, you're the smartest officer I know—mostly likely that I have ever known, your grandfather included. But you're letting your anger blind you here. I know you haven't deluded yourself on our chances at Craydon. The fight coming our way was hopeless before we sent Clint Winters off with sixteen of our best ships. We may be able to pull back, retreat again, but where will we go? Losing the Core was one thing. That was bad enough, but it didn't cost us any real production. If we can't hold the Iron Belt, or a good part of it, what are we going to do? Throw rocks at the enemy?"

Barron stared back at Nguyen, and it was obvious from his expression that he understood what the admiral was saying, even that he agreed. But he was still having trouble accepting the logic of it all.

"I understand, sir, but can we afford to count on such an untrustworthy…ally?"

"Can we afford not to? If things are hopeless anyway, what do we have to lose?"

Barron fell silent for another minute, clearly deep in thought. Nguyen suspected Barron was trying to analyze the situation with some rationality, but prejudices like those he had against the Union—like almost every Confederation spacer had against the Union—were hard to overcome.

"We need the help, admiral, I can't argue with that. But the Union?"

"Can we be picky, Tyler? Do we have any real choice? And does it seem that difficult to believe that the Hegemony has taken action against the Union as well as us? We never had any reason to believe they had deployed all their strength against our forces. They are larger than we are, and more powerful. Considering the forces we have faced, are you really so convinced they don't have even more? It wouldn't take another fleet the size of the one we've been fighting to give the Union a run. You know how battered they were in the last war, and in the subsequent near-collapse they suffered."

Barron just nodded.

"So, what do we do? If they are secretly allied with the Hegemony, if this is all some kind of trick, why would they even bother? We can't beat the Hegemony forces alone…with the Union ships added in, it would be even more hopeless. If we send them away, we can't stop them from coming on anyway and attacking us. We don't have any strength to detach. If the Union wants to invade, if they want to blast dozens of our planets to radioactive ash…*we can't stop them*. So, what do we have to gain by not believing them, by not working with them?"

Nguyen paused, but Barron remained silent, so he continued, "I understand your reservations, Tyler, and I share them. But I don't think we can afford to pass up the chance this is real. I don't have up-to-date intelligence on Union fleet strengths, but I'm willing to bet they'd replace the ships Admiral Winters took. More than replace them. And it will be a force the enemy doesn't expect. I'm not saying it will be enough for us to win, but we'll be a damn sight better off."

Barron stayed silent and still for another moment. Then, at last, he nodded slowly. "You're right, admiral, of course."

Nguyen wasn't sure how sincere Barron was, but it was progress, and he'd settle for it.

Barron took a deep breath, and then he surprised Nguyen with the words that came out of his mouth. "We should send Captain Chanticleer back at once to rendezvous with Admiral Denisov. If we're really this desperate, if relying on the Union keeping its word is all we have left, we can't waste any time."

He took a deep breath. "Because even if they're sincere, it's still a crapshoot on them getting here on time."

Chapter Thirty

Planet Megara, Olyus III
Year of Renewal 263 (318 AC)

The Invasion of Megara – The Fight for the Landing Zones

"Keep up that fire!" Seth Alivari was hunkered down behind the wreckage of an old building, now no more than a pile of twisted metal and shattered masonry. But it still served as cover, which was something that the Kriegeri his marines were facing didn't have in abundance.

The orders had been clear. Hit the landing zones and don't let up. The Kriegeri were well armed, technologically advanced, and enhanced with multiple implants that made them stronger and faster than normal human beings. If they broke out of the LZs, they would be ten times harder to stop.

Alivari was a battalion commander, and his people were stretched out across a five-kilometer front. It wasn't so much a "front" as a semicircle surrounding one of the biggest landing zones. Major Truscott and his battalion linked up with both of his flanks, completing the circle of almost a thousand marines pounding on the enemy forces as they emerged from their landers.

Before they landed, even. The supply of anti-air ordnance

was far lower than Alivari—and certainly Bryan Rogan—might have hoped, but what was available had been used well. The landscape all around the LZs was littered with the wreckage of landing craft, some of them still marked by great plumes of smoke, rising like dark gray towers against the midmorning sun.

Alivari wanted to feel good about things. Certainly, the battle had gone well so far, but he knew that wouldn't last. That it couldn't last. Megara was blockaded, and by all accounts, the fleet had bugged out. The enemy forces were vast, and they were supported by complete orbital control. Megara wasn't exactly a center of military production, even assuming any factories that existed could still function once the battle was truly underway. That meant the marines were eventually going to run out of ammunition and supplies.

Bryan Rogan was a capable commander, a true hero of the marines, but he wasn't a magician. He'd gathered up everything he could, and he'd stored it in the most secure locations. But when it was gone—used, captured, or destroyed—the marines would be down to knives and clubs.

Such weapons weren't much good against automatic rifles and artillery, not to mention giant tanks of the sort Alivari had heard about. Stories of the massive armored vehicles had made the rounds among the marine units, and the size of the war machines, grew, Alivari suspected, with each retelling.

He hadn't seen the things himself. None of the enemy landing forces had managed to bring the heavies online yet, and he hadn't been involved in the fighting on Dannith. But word of things like *that* spread, and when the enemy could get a meaningful number of the tanks deployed and on the loose, the marines would have no choice but to pull back. That meant deploying either into the cities, to dig in and fight to the last and risk staggering civilian casualties, or fleeing to the hills, to the rugged areas far from the urban regions.

That choice, even though it would be Brian Rogan's when it came, was one hell of a reason to keep up the pressure, to pen the enemy in, keep them bottled up in their landing zones.

His head snapped around, moving toward the sound he'd

just heard, the one still ringing in his ears. An explosion, there was no mistaking that. And close.

His eyes darted around and focused on the column of smoke rising, perhaps half a kilometer from where he stood. *That's Company D's ground…*

He waved his arms toward his aide. "Get Captain Corrigan on the line right…"

He finished the command, but neither he, nor the aide, heard it. Two more explosions, within perhaps a second of each other, had hit with deafening roars, both closer than the first had been.

Alivari knew something was going on, and he had a good idea what it was. The hope he'd felt a few seconds earlier was gone, and he knew his people would be on the move soon, opening the way for the enemy to form up and begin their advance. If those explosions meant the enemy had opened up an orbital barrage, the effort to keep the enemy penned in was almost over.

* * *

"Damn." Bryan Rogan was in his command post, his eyes darting from one scanner to another. The flow of incoming data had been shrinking steadily. His satellites were all gone, of course, but now he was losing ground stations, and all around the LZs, the enemy was doing everything they could to jam his communications. And what he *could* see wasn't good.

His people had been performing well, extracting a gruesome price from the enemy advance forces and keeping them penned up in their LZs. Everything had gone exactly as he'd planned. As he'd hoped.

For a while.

He was a victim now of his own success. The enemy's inability to break out of their beachheads had forced them to escalate. It was a strange form of poker he was playing, fighting such a dominant enemy. He could push, his marines could fight well… but if they were too successful, they compelled the enemy to bring out the bigger guns.

In this case, orbital bombardments.

The Hegemony fleet could blast Megara into a lifeless, radio-active wasteland, of course, if that was what they wanted. But it was clear they planned to take the Confederation's capital intact, or as close to that as possible.

They're going to get it a little less intact now…

He could see the streaming video coming in from the LZs.

His positions were being blasted, and his marines, who'd had the invaders penned and suppressed in most locations, were now diving into whatever cover they had. The bombardments were heavy, though Rogan immediately noticed there were no nukes, no mass drivers, no true weapons of mass destruction. Just conventional bunker busters and other ordnance…in massive quantities.

Casualties were mounting rapidly. His people had kept losses fairly low in the first hours, but now that was all shot to hell. He didn't even have casualty reports from almost half his deployed units. Between jamming and disorder, he'd lost contact with a large number of battalions.

He stood where he was, barely listening to the reports his aides were shouting at him. It was all nonsense, pointless information that had nothing to do with the crucial decision he had to make. He had reserve units ready to send forward, to back up the marines at the LZs. That had been his first impulse, and he almost issued the order. Then he hesitated.

Anything I send out there is just going to get blasted. We can't stand up to that kind of bombardment intensity.

He knew his best chance to defeat the enemy was to hold them at the LZs. But was that possible anymore, in the face of the bombardment? And would he just compel the enemy to increase the intensity, widen the target areas, even add nukes and other really nasty stuff to the mix? He was angry at the Senate, but was he willing to risk being the reason millions of Megarans died?

The Hegemony forces were ignoring unfortified urban areas so far, but they *were* blasting the perimeter of Troyus City, where he'd positioned some of his forces. Anyplace he sent his people, the enemy would very likely bombard. That made the open areas deathtraps, and the potential urban battlefields virtual abattoirs for the millions who lived there. There was military advantage in fighting for the cities, at least as long as he didn't think the enemy was ready to glass the planet, but on a world like Megara, the cost in lives would be almost incalculable.

The Confederation's capital was a heavily developed world, but there were still considerable remote areas, mountains and deep forests, the kinds of places his people could defend for a long time against even aggressive attacks. He would be giving up the initiative, but he'd begun to realize that was gone already. His forces had held the enemy as long as they could, and they'd inflicted what could only be horrendous losses on the invading enemy's lead units. But if he left his people out there, they would be massacred.

The time had come to play the long game, to hold out, give the enemy a hundred different places to subdue. It would give him tactical flexibility, allow him to choose when and where to strike out against any areas the enemy left vulnerable.

But it meant giving up the population, allowing the cities to be taken and occupied by the enemy. That was the kind of thing a marine like Rogan never thought he'd consider. He'd imagined he would give the orders to hold and fight, stand in the line with his people and battle to the death to save the civilian inhabitants.

But that very act would consign billions of them to almost certain death.

No, he couldn't make the cities his battleground. He would leave forces behind, certainly, special forces teams hidden, ready to strike behind enemy lines and do everything possible to disrupt Hegemony operations. But the main force would pull back.

He hesitated for a minute, and even in those few fleeting seconds, he could see the situation deteriorating rapidly. He had to get his people away from the LZs and into cover.

And he had to do it now.

"Captain," he yelled. "Get me a line to as many command posts as you can raise, and get runners ready to go to the others. We're pulling back from the LZs...and we're doing it now."

Chapter Thirty-One

CFS Constitution
Alvion System, Midway Between Transit Points
Year 318 AC

"Admiral, passive scanners confirm contacts at 203.124.011. Three vessels, estimated tonnage below twenty thousand each."

Winters was nodding as he stared at the display, but then he turned toward the tactical station, his eyes meeting Davis Harrington's. "Any change in vectors or thrust?" He wasn't sure how complete the data coming in was. *Constitution* and her fifteen companion vessels were limited to passive scans while in stealth mode, and the contacts were at the extreme edge of maximum range.

"Keep the passive scans on it, commander. And get the AI crunching the data. Maintain course and thrust levels." He felt an urge to cut the fleet's thrust, but he held it back. Witter had assured him the stealth generators could hide the engine output from detection by all but the very closest scanners, but he still felt like the ten G his ships were blasting at was as good as waving a flaming torch on a dark night.

There wasn't time for caution, though. He had to get to Megara, and the sooner his ships arrived there, the better chance they had of completing their mission. If that meant risking detection, there was nothing he could do about it except trust to the new tech Witter and his people had installed in his ships.

"No sign they've detected us, admiral. They've got their active scanners on full, but no course changes, so sign of alert status or power surges in engines or weapons…at least as far as our passive scans can pick up at this distance."

That was the rub. Everything Davis just mentioned *could* be happening on those ships, and just slipping by the passive scan readings.

No, not everything. We'd see any vector changes, at least. Though it wasn't like three scout ships were going to alter vectors to engage sixteen battleships, even if they could see them. Or even one.

"Send a pulse comm to every ship, commander. Stay on course until further notice." He didn't love the idea of using ship-to-ship comm, even with the almost-undetectable direct laser pulses. But he liked even less the chance that one of the fifteen ship captains could get unnerved and do something fool-ish. He'd been clear about procedures for the operation, but he'd been a flag officer for long enough to realize how differently people could interpret situations.

"Yes, sir."

Winters looked back at the display. The scout ships were definitely still on the same course, not a hint of any change. If they'd spotted any of his ships, they were being some very cool customers. His stomach was tight, his fingers clenched around the armrests of his chair as he watched. But he saw a positive to it as well. This encounter was his first test running into enemy ships, and if his sixteen battleships slipped right by them…well, maybe they *could* pull the whole crazy thing off after all.

The fleet had gone through two systems already, with no sign of any Hegemony presence. The one advantage of the ene-my's lightning advance to Megara was they hadn't had time to broaden the axis of their advance. Their attack had been a spear wound to the Confederation's heart, but even two transits from Megara, there were systems devoid of any Hegemony presence.

Alvion was the last star before the transit to Olyus, before Winters's ships emerged in Megara's system and made the desperate run toward the enemy support fleet. He'd managed to keep from thinking about what happened after that, about how the hell his ships would escape after they'd blasted the supply and support vessels. That depended, of course, on just how strong a defensive garrison the enemy had left behind, and how well the stealth units held up. There were many ways things could go into a shithole, but Winters had stopped thinking about them after he'd hit number twenty.

"Admiral, the scout ships appear to be decelerating."

Winters looked at his screen, confirming what his aide had just reported. For an instant, he was sure the Hegemony ships had picked up his ships, or at least one of them, but their maneuver didn't suggest a response he would expect in that case. There was no movement back toward Olyus, no apparent drone launches, no sign of an attempt to send back a warning. No concentration of active scanners around his fleet's position.

The longer he watched, the more he realized what was happening. The scout ships were taking position in the center of the system. They were pickets, flank guards, positioned where they were to watch for precisely the type of operation he was leading toward Megara.

But they didn't appear to be aware of his ships.

Winters still felt like an icy hand was gripping his spine, but through the deep and cold stress, hope began to poke through. He wasn't sure he believed his people were going to make it to Olyus…but he was beginning to believe it was *possible*.

And that was a start.

* * *

"Transit in one minute, captain. Stealth systems at full power."

"Very well, commander." Captain James Eugene sat bolt upright in *Tenacity*'s command chair. The battleship was one of the Confederation's newest and most powerful, like most of the others assigned to what had become informally known as Operation Midnight. The ship had quad mounted particle accelerators, enhanced with Dr. Witter's upgrades, plus over two dozen heavy laser batteries. She was a killing machine, the very best Confederation science and industry could create. That made her an unlikely scout ship.

But that was exactly the function she was serving at that moment.

"Thirty seconds to transit."

Tenacity was at battle stations, and Eugene was sure every member of his crew was well aware of the danger of their mission, and its almost indescribable importance. They'd all fought the Hegemony forces, and they knew what they were up against. The Confederation had no chance to match the enemy's numbers or, in the short term, technology. But if the Hegemony logistics fleet could be destroyed, or sufficiently degraded, it was just possible the principles that defined war on the Rim for more than a century would reassert themselves.

And the enemy that had driven straight through to the heart of the Confederation and seized its capital might be forced to withdraw along their enormously long supply lines.

With only sixteen stealth units, there had been no room to waste generators on scouts, or even escorts or cruisers. Admiral Winters needed all the firepower—and all the fighters—he could get.

That meant sending a battleship through as a scout. A single ship to confirm that the enemy didn't have warships sitting in wait just on the other side of the point, and to check for mines or any other traps or weapons that might interfere with the fleet's transit.

To go through and see if the transit itself gave away the ship's position, to determine if the fleet could actually get through without being detected.

Eugene sat stone-still as his ship slipped into the still poorly understood tube of the transit point, and traveled through the strange alternate reality of whatever lay between the departure point and the destination. In normal space, 5.5 light-years separated the stars Alvion and Olyus, a distance that would take a lifetime for a vessel to traverse in normal space. In the strange otherness of the transit point, that journey took less than a minute.

The blackness of regular space reappeared as he was still thinking about the network of transit points and imagining the amazing technology that had gone into their construction. There were stars again on his screen, and gradually, the display updated, showing the familiar stellar geography of the Olyus system.

"Passive scanners only. Thrust at one G." Eugene knew the transit was the most vulnerable moment, the instance when enemy scanners, ineffective against the stealth field protecting his ship, could pick up the energy spike at the point. He'd almost *expected* to be detected, or at least for the enemy to know *something* had come through. But there was no reaction at all.

At first, he thought the enemy might be laying some kind of trap for him. But then, as the data from his scans continued to flow in, he understood. His people had been fortunate. They'd slipped through while the enemy was distracted.

He stared at the display. The main Hegemony battle fleet, clear across the system, was moving steadily through another transit point, the very one *Tenacity* had traversed months before, along with the rest of the fleet, in the ignominious retreat from Olyus.

My God…

Though he'd known the enemy would almost certainly advance on Craydon and engage the fleet again, the reality of watching it hit him hard. Enthusiasm, patriotism…such things could alter thought, overwhelm analysis. But as he watched the enormity of the fleet moving out of the system, all hope that Admirals Nguyen and Barron could hold Craydon vanished. The enemy had repaired massive numbers of ships, and the force now on the way to fight the climactic battle was even stronger than had been feared. The fleet was doomed. The Confederation was finished.

Unless Admiral Winters and the other battleships could destroy the supply and support ships.

For an instant, Eugene felt a wave of panic, a sudden fear

that the logistics train would move out with the battle fleet to reposition itself somewhere along the line to Craydon. That hadn't been the Hegemony's prior methodology, but the concern gave Eugene an unpleasant few minutes.

But the supply ships were not moving. They were positioned in the middle of the system, not too far from his current position. The mining vessels were clustered around the system's middle planets and their moons, and the refinery ships were strung out nearby, no doubt processing the ores as quickly as they were mined.

And deeper out, between the orbits of the seventh and eight planets, sat the great mobile shipyards, each one of them surrounded by those damaged ships still unrepaired after the last battle.

Eugene was glad to see that even the Hegemony had ships still backed up and waiting for repair. The fleet at Craydon certainly did, and he knew no small number of his comrades would go into battle in battered and partially operational vessels.

If we can keep the surprise, hit them hard before they can react...

Eugene knew the fleet escaping had never been a major part of the plan. It would be good, of course. The fleet didn't need to lose more battleships or seasoned crew, but *Tenacity*'s captain knew the primary mission was to destroy those enemy support ships...whatever the cost. Even if it meant every ship in the fleet was blasted to atoms.

He understood that, and it scared him, at least in ephemeral sort of way. But his mind was focused on the mission, and he'd been ready for death for months now. He knew his duty, as he was sure Admiral Winters did, and every other spacer in the fleet.

Eugene watched as the enemy ships continued to transit. His orders were clear: report back at once. Winters had the fleet on alert, ready to come through the instant *Tenacity* came back through and transmitted the situation.

"Captain? Should we return to the transit point?"

Eugene was silent for a moment. Then he answered, his voice like a hammer on an anvil, "No."

"Sir?"

"We got lucky coming through, commander. It doesn't look like anyone picked up our transit. But we can't count on that if we go back, and any drone we launch will be outside the stealth envelope." He turned and looked again at the enemy ships transiting. "No, we've got to let that battle fleet finish moving out of here, or they just may turn around and come after us." The fleet had a chance of hitting the supply ships, but not if a massive force of enemy battleships turned around and remained in the system.

No, *Tenacity* couldn't go back. Not yet. They would stay right where they were.

Eugene wasn't going to move. He wasn't going to take any risk of being detected, not while there were still masses of enemy warships in the system. He could be patient—when he had to be, at least.

He just hoped Clint Winters was just as patient, and that the admiral trusted his captain enough to wait. Because if another ship came through too soon, it might not be as lucky as *Tenacity*. And any tip-off at all to the Hegemony forces would probably unleash those queued-up battleships in the rearmost columns back into the system.

And right after Winters's entire attack force.

Chapter Thirty-Two

CFS Dauntless
Orbiting Craydon
Calvus System
Year 318 AC

"Admiral Denisov, I intend to be blunt in our conversations, as I do not believe diplomatic niceties serve us in any useful way." Barron looked across the table at the Union admiral, and though he was still driven by his hatred of the Union, Denisov's condition disarmed him considerably. The officer was ghostly pale, and Barron could see it was a struggle for him even to sit upright.

"I wouldn't have it any other way, admiral. I am a blunt man myself." Denisov was clearly trying to look as strong as possible, but it was obvious with every word he forced out that he was exhausted and in almost constant pain.

Barron had remembered the admiral's name when he'd heard it, though the man he'd recalled from the fight against the Pulsar had been a captain, one who'd come close to thwarting his efforts to destroy the deadly imperial relic. The officer he'd remembered had been dynamic and aggressive, not inflexible and bureaucratic, as most Union commanders were. But when he'd seen the size of the admiral's entourage in the landing bay, he'd been ready to revise that analysis.

Until a moment later, when he realized the crowd consisted of doctors and medical technicians, and not superfluous guards and clusters of personal aides. Then he saw Denisov. The admiral had been in a power chair in the shuttle, but Barron had watched as he waved off his attendants and rose painfully on his own, walking forward, slowly but steadily, with only a cane to help stabilize him. Barron could see his legs shaking from the exertion, even as he extended his hand, first to Admiral Nguyen, and then to Barron himself.

A showing of personal stamina, even grit, was always something Barron respected, but it was far from enough to overcome his deep-seated hatred for the Union. Still, he found it difficult to direct that animosity at Denisov himself…and even harder to maintain his intense suspicion and cynicism toward the officer. In spite of himself, Barron found the Union admiral to be credible from the start. As a man, at least. He was still far from comfortable accepting help from Union "allies." Not only did he *not* trust them, but Andi's ordeal had forged his rage into something far more intractable and powerful than it had been before. For all his softened feelings toward Denisov himself, he could never forgive the Union for what their murderous agents had done to her.

On some level, he wasn't even sure he wouldn't rather die fighting an overwhelming enemy attack than accept the Union as allies to fight at his side.

"If I might ask, Admiral Denisov, how were you wounded?" It was a direct question, and one Barron thought was perfectly relevant concerning an officer who'd led his ships on a trek across Confederation space, supposedly without engaging in any combat.

"An officer on my flagship shot me, admiral." Denisov's answer was direct, disarmingly so. No hesitation, no attempts at obfuscation. It took Barron by surprise. It was the last thing he'd expected from anyone wearing a Union uniform. "You must know that Union ships are usually seeded with political officers and Sector Nine operatives. Certainly, no admiral is dispatched without being accompanied by minders, both openly and under cover. As I disclosed in my initial communique, I speak only for my *fleet*, and not for the Union. My presence here is not only unauthorized, it is, to many, treasonous."

Barron was silent for a moment. If Denisov was trying to craft some kind of deception, it was the strangest one Barron had ever heard. Somewhere inside, he knew almost immediately that the Union officer was telling the truth.

"You were so moved by our plight in battling the Hegemony that you decided to commit mutiny and bring your fleet on a desperate run to our aid?"

"No, Admiral Barron. Certainly not at first. My orders were to form up along the border and prepare to invade the Confederation…as an ally of the Hegemony."

The tension level in the room ratcheted up, the officers all around Barron shifting in their chairs. But Barron was like a statue. Denisov's statement had seeds in it to grow anger and rage, but it was also almost certainly the truth. And that was what mattered to Barron.

"How did you transition from preparing to violate the treaty your nation signed to coming to our aid?"

"We were attacked by the Hegemony, admiral. Nothing came of Gaston Villieneuve's efforts to arrange a treaty, save a surprise attack from Hegemony forces. They attempted to eradicate our defensive capabilities in a single fight. I'd guess our ambassador is dead, or a prisoner. I was able to extricate my fleet by transiting toward Confederation space instead of back toward Montmirail. Our maneuver caught the enemy by surprise, and gave us enough time to make the transit. They chased us for a time, but we were able to escape…mostly because they ceased pursuit."

"So, this idea of an alliance with us is very convenient for you, isn't it? You can't go home, not without the Hegemony forces blasting you to dust. And even if you did manage to evade them and return to Montmirail, you'd be very likely to trade your command chair for a Sector Nine cell somewhere. So, suddenly, joining with the Confederation navy seemed like a better idea than attacking it."

"I don't know what you want me to say, Admiral Barron. I

was against any hostilities against your people, if for no other reason than we were far from ready for such a conflict." Denisov had been very calm, but now there was a touch of anger in his tone. "But I won't lie to you. I don't like the Confederation. You have been my enemy since I was a cadet, as I have been yours. I have lost more friends than I can count in battles against your forces. I am not here because I crave your friendship, or your forgiveness for what you perceive as the Union's sins. I am here because I do not believe we can win alone. Survive alone." He paused, gasping for air and steadying himself in the chair. "And I don't think you can either."

Barron felt a flush of anger, but he clamped down on it. He'd wanted blunt talk, and Denisov couldn't have been blunter. For all Barron's hatred for the Union tried to color his view, he knew the officer was right: the Confederation didn't have a chance alone.

"How many ships do you have?" Barron and Nguyen had insisted that the bulk of the Union fleet remain on the other side of the transit point pending the conference. Denisov had agreed, and he'd come through in his flagship alone.

There was a short pause. Barron suspected it came no easier to Denisov to trust him than it did for him to rely on the Union officer. There was something in that, maybe. A path to…certainly not friendship, but maybe to a way to work together.

"I have one hundred and eight ships, admiral. Including twenty-eight battleships."

Barron was stunned. First by Denisov's willingness to answer. And then by just how weak the Union fleet was. He knew they'd been hit hard in the war, and in the disruptions that followed, but if Denisov had been telling the truth earlier, the ships with him were essentially the entire Union navy.

Another thought quickly formed. It might not be enough to make a difference. Even with everything Denisov had brought, even if they fought alongside the Confederation ships, steadfast and without treachery, Barron's gut told him the Hegemony could still win.

But the arrival of another hundred ships was a very welcome

development, even if Barron had to take Union crews and officers with them. He turned toward Admiral Nguyen. The old
officer nodded, almost imperceptibly.

"Admiral Denisov, you have been honest, brutally so, and I
will return that courtesy. I do not trust you. More specifically, I
do not trust the Union, or *any* of its people. I will admit that I do
find you, yourself, far more credible than I expected." He stared
across the table at the admiral, trying to find a way to accept the
officer, but in his mind, he was imagining Andi's experiences
when she fell into the clutches of Sector Nine. She'd never told
him much about it, and he had never asked. But he'd seen what
it had done to her, the single-minded creature it had made her,
willing to sacrifice everything for the vengeance she'd convinced
herself was the only way to wash it all away. He knew Denisov had nothing to do with Sector Nine, or with Ricard Lille.
Indeed, the Union officer seemed to be yet another victim of
the deadly spy agency. Still, it took all Barron had to continue.

"Let us get to the heart of this, admiral. It really doesn't
matter if I want you as an ally, or if I believe everything you
have told me. There is only one factor that matters, and that is
indisputable: we can't win on our own. I speak differently to my
spacers every day, lie to them, struggle to give them hope where
I know there is none. I don't know that I can trust you. I am not
sure you will not betray us at the first chance you get, or that
you will even be able to control your fleet, protect it from those
who see you as a mutineer. But whatever chance there is that
your forces fight honorably at our side—and whatever power
the added force provides—is better than nothing."

It was a caustic, brutally honest response that would have
sent career diplomats into epileptic fits. But it was clear, and it
was truthful. And that was the best Barron had to give.

Denisov winced. Not from his words, Barron suspected, but
from the exertion it took for him to sit upright for so long. Any
concern that the expression was related to Barron's hard-edged
response vanished a few seconds later.

"I feel very much the same way, Admiral Barron. We have
long been enemies, and it is difficult for me to envision a future

where we are friends. But we share an enemy now, one that is stronger than either of us, and one that seems intent on conquering the entire Rim. You are my enemy's enemy, as I am yours. I believe we can forge a useful partnership on that basis. I will not promise you a great future of cooperation and peace. But I will give you my word, if you will take it, that until the menace of the Hegemony is defeated, I will fight at your side, along with all my ships and spacers." Denisov gripped the sides of his chair and pushed himself up to his feet, his face twisted into a scowl of pain as he did it. He looked across the table at Barron and extended his hand.

Barron waited for a few seconds, and then he stood. He looked across the table, his eyes locked on Denisov's, and then reached out and took his old enemy's—and now, for a time at least, his ally's—hand.

"I will take your word, admiral. And I will offer mine. The Hegemony threatens both of us. Let us fight them together."

The two men stood, gripping each other's hands for a long moment. Then, just as Barron began to pull his arm back, the klaxons began to sound.

It was an alert, and that could mean only one thing.

The Hegemony had arrived.

Chapter Thirty-Three

CFS Constitution
Alvion System, About to Transit into Olyus
Year 318 AC

"Transit in twenty seconds, admiral."

"Very well, commander. All ships at battle station, ready for action as soon as we emerge."

Clint Winters was tight. No, he was twisted into knots, struggling to stay focused even as his body began to show the strain of enormous tension. He'd waited, doing nothing for hours, while *Tenacity* was in the Olyus system. He trusted Jim Eugene, as he did most of his people, but it had become increasingly difficult not to believe *Tenacity* had somehow been destroyed or crippled the instant it transited. He'd come close to ordering another move through the point, but he'd been torn between committing a new scout…or just blasting through with his whole fleet. It didn't really matter if there were a hundred Hegemony warships waiting just beyond the transit point. He'd come to try to destroy the support fleet, and he was going to go through with it, regardless of the odds.

But still, he'd waited. And then, at last, *Tenacity* had come back through.

The enemy fleet—the massive force of Hegemony warships—had just departed from Olyus. Winters had expected them to be long gone, on their way to Craydon and the fleet under Nguyen and Barron that was there waiting for them. That battle wasn't likely to go any differently than the others that preceded it. The enemy was just too strong. But if his sixteen ships could complete their mission, perhaps the losses the fleet suffered would not be for naught. A Hegemony unable to quickly repair its damaged ships and refit its worn fleets would be a different enemy. Powerful, yes, and dangerous. But at least there would be time to try and develop a strategy.

Winters wasn't sure if he'd be a part of that. He tried to tell himself his people would make it back, but the whole thing looked a little too much like a suicide mission for his tastes.

That hadn't stopped him from wanting the posting, or feeling satisfaction when Admiral Nguyen had placed him in command. He knew he was a skilled leader, but he didn't imagine he could match Tyler Barron…and, if one of them had to be lost, better for the Confederation it was him.

Winters had felt the urge to go right in after he'd gotten Eugene's report. But he'd held back for several days. *Tenacity*'s transit into Olyus seemed to have gone unnoticed, and he didn't want to take a chance the enemy might recall the fleet that had just left. His ships were going to go after those logistics units, and they weren't going to let anything stand in their way. But if the entire enemy fleet returned to the system, things would get ugly. Fast.

He sat quietly, doing his best to ignore the various, and often uncomfortable, effects of interstellar travel, and then he felt normal again as *Constitution* emerged into normal space.

We're back in the Olyus system…

It had only been a couple of months since Winters had last been there, but it felt like an eternity.

He sat, waiting, his eyes darting to the screen every few seconds. Then, finally, his station came to life. *Constitution*'s systems were coming back online, rebooting after the disruption of transit-point travel. The scanners came on, and the display began filling up with circles, triangles, rectangles, all manner of icons representing the vast array of ships and stations and other designated points in the Confederation's capital system.

"Commander, fleet order. All ships, execute designated nav plan alpha-one. Full thrust."

Winters knew where the targets were. *Tenacity* had done her job well, and returned with intel of enormous value. There were enemy garrison ships present, but they were mostly cruisers and escorts. The smaller vessels could hurt his battleships, but the stealth generators would give them on hell of a time in targeting, even after Winters's vessels had opened fire and given away their presence.

His targets were dead ahead…and nothing the enemy did was going to keep him from them.

* * *

"Kiloron, we're picking up energy readings from transit point four."

Sestus had been analyzing a routine report, but the instant the scanner technician spoke, his head snapped up. "Intensity?" The invasion of the Confederation had been so fast, the progress toward the capital so relentless, that some remote worlds that didn't know what had happened. There had been several ships, routine freighters and the like, transiting into the Olyus system, unaware that the Hegemony forces were in control.

"Significant, kiloron. In excess of ninety techons."

Sestus had barely been paying attention, but the response grabbed his full focus. Ninety techons was well above the output from a routine cargo ship, even a small group of such vessels. He didn't know what was coming through that point, but the Kriegeri knew one thing.

He had to get a Master involved.

"Put the sentinel units on full alert, and order them to investigate any vessels emerging."

"Yes, kiloron."

The officer thought for a moment. His first impulse was to contact Megaron Illius. The Master was in total command of the system now that Chronos had left with the fleet. If the contact was an enemy attack, if the Confederation had assembled a new fleet somehow, or if the force Chronos thought was at Craydon had actually snuck back to Olyus, such a leap up the chain would be warranted.

But if it's just some group of freighters or tankers stumbling into the system unaware, you'll look like a fool…

"Send a transmission to system command, hectoron. Include all scanning data, and advise that we have put the sentinel units on alert."

"Yes, sir."

Sestus sat quietly for a moment. Then he added, "And get me an updated report on ships under repair that are capable of action."

"Yes, kiloron."

Sestus didn't know what was about to emerge into the system, but despite his impulse not to overreact, he had a bad feeling about it.

*   *   *

"Power readings from the nearby vessels suggest some kind of alert status, admiral. But there is no sign of any hostile movement." A pause. "They're just sitting there. It looks like they're expecting something, but it doesn't look like they've spotted us."

Clint Winters leaned forward, his eyes fixed on the floating dots in *Constitution*'s display. The specks of light represented the Hegemony warships, mostly light escorts, deployed in the immediate vicinity of the transit point. There were almost two dozen ships, enough to give his fleet a hard time, but not to really stop it. His tactical sense told him to engage them, to take them by surprise and eliminate the threat, but he knew his time was limited, and minutes he wasted fighting a force of pickets was time and ordnance wasted, resources lost to the ultimate attack on the logistics fleet.

"Prepare to transmit nav plans to all ships. And commander, make damn sure those direct laser pulses are *tight*." Winters was concerned enough that the enemy would pick something up when his ships blasted their engines at full thrust. He didn't want to give anything away with comm traffic. He'd have preferred total communications silence, but hadn't been able to finalize his orders until he'd seen the system scans himself. He was breaking his fleet into three groups. Five battleships would move against the massive mobile shipyards, probably the most important target of all. Another five would hit the mining and refinery ships that were scattered throughout the outer system. The other six ships would target the vast armada of supply freighters that had kept the Hegemony fleet moving steadily forward, almost without pause.

Winters had imagined there would be a vast number of empty cargo ships, their payloads long since expended to support the ongoing war effort. But as he looked out at the intricate web of mining craft, ore-processing ships, factory vessels... he knew those freighters were refilled almost as quickly as they were emptied.

He realized, with even more certainty than before, that the mission he'd come to complete was the only real chance the Confederation had. If the enemy could continue to rearm and repair their forces so quickly, there was simply no way to hold them back. He *had* to succeed, whatever the cost. If he could destroy, or at least badly damage, the enemy logistics train, it would be worth losing every one of his ships...and every spacer on them, himself included.

He didn't think lightly of casualties, nor of branding his operation a suicide run. He would fight like hell to get his people through this, and to lead them back out of the system to join their comrades, at Craydon, or wherever they were by then. But he wouldn't allow thoughts of escape to interfere with his decisions. There was one priority and one alone, and it came before all things.

Destroy those support ships. Whatever the cost.

* * *

Alicia Covington leaned back and stretched her spine, rolling her head around on her shoulders. She'd been in her fighter for four hours now, waiting, ready to launch at a moment's notice. She knew the situation. The enemy pickets were looking for the fleet, pinging all around with their active scanners, searching for the cause of the transit point energy spike.

So far, they hadn't found anything. At least, they showed no signs of closing on the fleet.

They had called for reinforcements, though, that much was clear. There were over a hundred ships moving toward the general area, as with the initial garrison units, mostly cruisers and escorts. Despite the lighter ship classes, that was a lot of firepower coming in, and she knew she might have to divide her forces, send some squadrons to engage the approaching enemy warships while the others went in as planned against the logistics fleet.

She understood why Admiral Winters had ordered her people to man their ships so early, and she also realized why they had been held back so long. The instant they launched, they would be detected, and that would tell the enemy there were ships in the system. It would also provide a starting point for them to search. It would degrade her assault plan for hitting the supply fleet if she had to engage the warships as well, and her squadrons would waste a lot of time and fuel modifying their vectors. But there was nothing to be done about that.

The waiting was getting to her, and she knew it had to have her pilots on the verge of insanity. They all knew, to varying degrees, just how little chance they had of getting back to the fleet, and making them sit in the silence of their cockpits for hours was a form of torture.

Still, they would do what they had to do. They all understood, as she did, just what was at stake. They'd lost friends, comrades. They were all veterans. Even those who'd been green going into the battle at Megara were far from raw now.

Covington was ready. Her people were ready.

She just needed the launch order. She had to get her people out there, doing what they did best.

Before they all lost their minds.

* * *

"Admiral…"

Winters knew as soon as he heard Harrington's tone that something was wrong.

"We're picking up *Resolute* on our scanners."

The words hit Winters like a ton of bricks. His ships were closing on their targets. But they needed more time. Time it looked like they weren't going to get. Not if *Resolute*'s stealth unit was down.

Damn!

"Direct laser comm to *Resolute*. I want a report right now. And get Captain Fritz on my line. I want her in on this." Tyler Barron had sent his famous engineer with Winters and his fleet. He suspected it had been painful to part with an officer who had served with Barron for so long, but, short of sending Dr. Witter himself, there was probably no one else in the fleet more qualified to keep the stealth systems operating than Fritz.

She had done so flawlessly, monitoring every generator almost constantly. As far as Winters could tell, Fritz hadn't slept since the fleet left Craydon. But the communications blackout had cut her off from the constant stream of data. Winters had known that would be a risk, but he'd hoped he would get lucky, just for a few more hours.

That was a damned fool mistake he'd never repeat again, at least not if he somehow got out of the mess he was in.

"Give the launch order, commander. Direct laser signal. Operations plan two." He didn't like that last order. Plan two split up Covington's wings and only took strength away from the attack on the real targets. But if he didn't manage to hold back the enemy garrison units, the ones even then angling their vectors toward the new contact on their screens, his whole fleet could end up in a straight-up fight. He needed time, and Covington could get it for him.

He hoped.

"Launch orders issued, admiral. Captain Fritz on your line."

"Captain, I need you to do what you can. It looks like *Resolute* has lost its generator." His eyes darted to the side, toward the display. He could already see symbols on the move, more Hegemony ships blasting toward his fleet's location.

He was out of time.

"I will do what I can, admiral."

"Do your best, captain." Winters turned his head, cutting the line as he did. His attention was diverted, and he knew he'd have to rely on Fritz to do what could be done. She was an engineering genius, but he was a tactician, and the enemy knew his fleet was there. He had to hit the logistics train, and he had to do it fast.

"Commander Harrington, all ships are to increase reactor levels to one hundred ten percent. I want every G of thrust we can get." He'd been reluctant to go in at full thrust, concerned about energy leakage through the stealth fields. But that was far less of a concern than it had been moments before. Nothing was as important as time. He almost felt as though he was trying to hold on to precious seconds, like water in his hands.

"We've got a race to run, and we're going to win it. We're going to blast the hell out of those support ships, and nothing in Olyus or the Rim, nothing in the whole damn galaxy, is going to stop us."

He wasn't sure if the words were for his bridge crew, the whole fleet…or for him.

He felt a distant vibration, then another. And another.

The fighters were launching. He closed his eyes for an instant, a silent wish for Covington and her people. And an acknowledgement that he'd just done as much to give away the locations of his ships as *Resolute*'s busted stealth generator.

He turned and stared at the display, even as the pressure from the increased thrust levels hit him. "All weapons at full power. All gunnery stations ready to fire on my command."

Chapter Thirty-Four

CFS Dauntless
Orbiting Craydon
Calvus System
Year 318 AC

"Here they come…"

Barron's head snapped around, his eyes scanning the room for the source of the words. There were more than thirty officers on the great battleship's bridge, and after a cursory look around, he decided it didn't really matter who had spoken. His people were on edge—hell, they had to be scared out of their wits. He wasn't about to enforce minute regulations about who was authorized to say this or that. It was a waste of time.

And it wasn't his job anyway. *Dauntless* was Atara's ship, its crew her people. He'd reminded himself a hundred times, and he did it again, as he pushed back once more against the urge to slip into the captain's role. It was Atara's call how to handle her bridge crew, and he had total faith in her ability and in her wisdom.

Whatever else he might say about the unidentified officer's remark, he couldn't argue against it on fact. It was one hundred percent correct.

He looked at the display, watching as the column of ships continued to emerge into the system. Only a dozen had come

269

through so far, but he knew from bitter experience what lay beyond, in the strange reality of the transit tube, and beyond, queued up light-years away, waiting to move forward.

The time at Craydon—preparing the fleet for another fight, even spending a few stolen moments with Andi—had seemed somehow to pass by in an instant, and also to last forever under the grinding tension of waiting for the enemy. Barron was seeing nothing new—at least, nothing he hadn't imagined a hundred times over the preceding weeks.

He was as ready as he could be…and not ready, too. He was prepared to fight, though he couldn't get completely past the exhaustion—both physical and emotional—that weighed on every decision, every move he made. He was anxious to face the enemy again, to strike at his deadly foe, but he couldn't entirely banish thoughts about whether this would be his final fight.

Whether he had seen Andi for the last time.

He felt the urge to issue orders, but there was no need. Dustin Nguyen was in command, and the fleet already had detailed orders. Every ship captain knew what to do. Every squadron leader was ready to lead his or her fighters into the maelstrom. All Barron could do was sit and wait. And watch the carnage unfold.

He looked to one side on the display. The Alliance ships were formed up in perfect order, *Invictus* in the forefront—the only place a Palatian flagship could be. Barron was grateful for his Alliance allies, and he knew they would fight hard, that they would die before they would desert him.

His eyes shot over in the other direction. Another force lay there, also formed up and ready for action. But this ally filled him with mixed emotions: hope that they were the added strength the fleet needed to have a real chance at victory, and concern, because these new "friends" were just another enemy, an old enemy. He tried to think only of the fight ahead, but he couldn't drive the old memories away, a lifetime of looking at the Union and seeing an enemy.

He watched as more and more enemy ships transited. He'd considered trying to hit them as they came in, an effort to bottle them up at the transit point. But he didn't have the minefield he'd had at Megara, nor the great asteroid fortresses. His fleet was weaker, diminished by the losses suffered at Megara and the detachment of Winters's sixteen heavy battleships. The fleet needed to concentrate its strength. It needed a simpler battle plan.

That was just what Barron and Dustin Nguyen had put together. With any luck, the newly arrived Alliance reinforcements and the Union fleet would surprise the enemy, throw them off their game. It was little more than hope, but Barron knew his people needed something.

He needed something.

"Admiral, I have the flagship. Admiral Nguyen says you may issue the orders when ready."

Barron nodded toward Atara, and then held her gaze for a few seconds. It was time. "On my line, captain," he said softly to her, knowing she'd understand what he wanted.

"On your line, admiral."

"Jake…I just wanted to talk directly with you before you launch. I won't bother with a speech. You're too old a veteran for that, as am I. I just wanted to say good luck to you, old friend, and to all those who fly with you." Barron could feel a shakiness trying to take his voice, but he resisted. Stockton was a friend, and a man he admired hugely…though he remembered the young version of the hero giving him fits on more than one occasion. He wondered if he would ever see the pilot again.

"Thank you, admiral. It's been the greatest honor of my life serving with you, sir. Whatever else they say about us in the years ahead, we definitely made our mark. Good luck to you, too, admiral."

Barron listened to the words. He understood a goodbye—when he said it and when he heard it. And both had just happened. He wasn't sure he would die, that Stockton would die. But he was damn sure worried about it, and he knew Stockton was, too.

"Admiral Stockton, you may launch your wings when ready."

"Yes, sir." Stockton had always been somewhat of a discipline problem, but the words that came through Barron's comm were sharp, perfect, like an instructional video at the Academy. Barron could almost see the crisp salute in them, and he knew it was a last show of respect.

Then, no more than thirty seconds later, he felt the first launch. He knew Jake Stockton as well as anyone did, save perhaps for Stara Sinclair, and he'd have bet the stars on his shoulders that his strike force commander had been the first one to go.

* * *

"Maintain position, commander." Andi Lafarge sat in the center of *Hermes*'s bridge, looking in every particular the part of a Confederation captain. Inside, she'd never felt more out of place.

"Very well, captain." She heard the response, and some part of her mind acknowledged it, but her thoughts were mostly on other things. The battle, what would happen, the last words she'd spoked to Tyler...and whether they would actually be the *last* words the two shared.

And she thought about how she'd ended up in a crisp new uniform on the bridge of a Confederation naval vessel. She'd come to expect the unexpected, but she'd never imagined the actual reality she faced now, either of the Confederation's grim struggle for survival, or her place in the ranks of the warriors fighting that battle.

Her orders were clear. Stay in position at the rear of the fleet and await further instructions. Tyler hadn't come up with a new task as an excuse to get her away from Craydon and out of the Calvus system, but she didn't doubt he would try to get her to run if things began to fall apart.

This time, she wasn't sure she would obey, though. She knew as well as the career admirals did, Craydon was likely the Confederation's last chance to stop the enemy. The Iron Belt was essential to any hope of building and repairing ships, and implementing the new technologies. She had no doubt some ships would escape from a defeat at Craydon, flee to the frontier to make yet another defensive stand. But a loss at Craydon would take all hope of victory away. The war would be over, in all meaningful terms, and she believed one thing with unswerving certainty: Tyler Barron was not going to survive a defeat at Craydon. She loved Barron, and she knew him in ways no one else did. There wasn't a doubt in her mind.

If he was going to stay, she was going to stay, too. *Hermes* was no real addition to the fleet's fighting power, but that didn't matter to her. There were times one had to draw a line, and say, "This far and no farther."

This was that time.

Victory or death at Craydon, and no other option. None she would accept.

* * *

"Dragons, Sabers, Red Waves, with me. We're going in one after another, a long line. Target Gamma two, three, and four. Wolverines, Black Stars, Silver Hawks…you've got Gamma five, six, and seven. These things are huge, and we've got to take them out, now. They're target priority one." Stockton tapped his throttle, adjusting his vector to a direct line in on the huge battle wagons at the front of the Hegemony line. They were the biggest things he'd seen yet, larger by half than any of the enemy's other ships, and well more than double the size of the Confederation's *Repulse*-class monsters. They had railguns, he would have bet anything on that, and maybe even a larger battery of the deadly weapons than normal. There was no way he could let those things past him and into range of Barron's and Nguyen's ships.

Stockton didn't know if the big ships were some kind of reserves sent from the Hegemony home worlds, or if they'd just been held back in the earlier fights, but either way, it was damn depressing to see even more powerful Hegemony ships streaming in from the transit point. The enemy already had countless advantages in the fighting, and his fighters were just about the only edge the Confederation possessed. He was glad to have the monopoly on fighters—the Confederation would have been conquered already otherwise—but it was a terrible burden and a drain on morale and stamina to bear such responsibility battle after battle.

He'd heard the acknowledgements coming in, all six squadron commanders answering almost as one. He didn't really pay attention, though. The six squadrons formed up behind him were among the fleet's very best, and he didn't doubt for an instant their pilots would follow his instructions precisely.

He knew it was a little ridiculous for the overall commander of more than three thousand fighters—*no*, he thought, *over four thousand again*. Admiral Denisov had placed the Union strike force under Stockton's command as well, and their numbers had replaced his losses from Megara, and then some. He was glad to have reinforcements, of course, but he'd struggled a bit with it, too. He didn't trust the Union…and, truth be told, he didn't think much of their wings either. But he needed everything he could get, so he'd sent the Union squadrons straight toward the enemy battle line. He would have ordered them to engage the Hegemony escorts—it was cold, perhaps, but he'd rather lose Union pilots than his own—but they didn't have the new cluster bombs. And over a thousand of his Confederation and Alliance birds did.

He was coming up on the target, his torpedo armed and ready. He watched as his range dipped down, under five thousand, to four thousand.

Three thousand.

He launched his torpedo and then pulled back hard on the throttle, blasting his engines at full to clear the target, just as his computer registered a hit. He felt his fists tighten as his ship lurched hard into a wild spin. Half his instruments shorted out in a wild burst of sparks, and acrid smoke filled the cockpit.

He felt a pain in his side, and then he realized there was blood pouring down…and he heard a loud hiss as air began to escape from a crack in his cockpit.

He'd been hit, and even before he checked any of his equipment, he knew it was bad.

You damned fool…that was light fire, and you blundered right into it…

Two battles in a row. He'd let himself get hit in two battles in a row. He'd been pushing himself to the edge, desperate to do whatever he could to sustain the fight against the enemy. His cockiness had always been there, telling him no matter what, he would make it through. Now, he felt the armor of that assuredness slip away, as he gasped for air and winced at the pain in his side.

He'd pulled himself out of more than one mess before, but even as he reached down and tried to work what was left of the controls, he knew this was going to be bad.

You're in trouble now, Jake…

* * *

"Stara…" It was Admiral Barron's voice on the comm, and *Dauntless*'s flight-control chief knew what it was about. She'd been watching Stockton's ship approach for the last few minutes, struggling the entire time to maintain her focus, and not to think about what if…

"Admiral, I've got his ship on my screen." She knew what the admiral was calling about.

She wasn't even sure how Stockton was coaxing the thing back to *Dauntless*. Her screens showed that every guidance circuit was fried, every flight control blown, even the AI knocked out. All blasted to scrap. However Stockton was flying that thing, it had to be ninety percent raw instinct.

"What can I do to help, Stara?" She could hear the tension in Barron's voice, the anguish. Stockton was Barron's friend, there was no question about that, but she knew there was more to his concern. Stockton was a vital component in the fight against the Hegemony, and she knew the admiral was also worried about losing one of his most potent weapons.

She found that upsetting, and she struggled to hold back a surge of anger. Stockton was more to her than some killing machine to continually unleash against the enemy. She knew she was being unfair to Barron, but it was hard to feel any other way.

"There's nothing you can do, sir. Nothing I can do. He's cut out of the net; his circuits are burned to hell. I can't even get a comm link to him. He's going to have to bring that thing in all by himself."

If anybody can do that, it's you, Jake. Please…

"The ship's yours, Stara. If you need to reorient or adjust our positioning…"

"Thank you, sir."

She stared at her instruments, and even as she checked everything for the second or third time, she realized she'd told Barron the truth. There was nothing she could do, absolutely nothing, except clear out the bay and hope Stockton came in soft enough to walk away.

As he's done more than once…

She already had the bay on alert. Med teams, fire control crews…all were standing by. There was nothing she could do in the bay herself.

But there's nothing you can do here, either.

She jumped up and ran down to the corridor leading to the flight deck. Her presence wouldn't make a bit of difference to what happened, but it didn't matter.

She had to be there.

* * *

How the hell many times is this going to happen?

Stockton had made it through more than one emergency landing, so many that he wondered for an instant why he had such a reputation as a master pilot. The answer was quick in coming, though, shot back by the side of his brain that housed his ego. Hundreds of combat missions, against disastrous odds. Repeated sorties, beyond the norms of human endurance. The need to set an example, with ever-more insane displays of skill and courage. Battles against the enemy, against fatigue, against damage and equipment failure.

He'd had more than one close call, certainly, but stacked up against the number of times he'd blasted out from the flight deck to face the enemy—the various enemies—his record was pretty damn good.

That may have been true before, but this time you just screwed up. You underestimated the enemy, and you got distracted, hit by a shot you should have easily avoided. It would serve you right if this was the time you lost it all...

He'd made it back to *Dauntless*, but even he wasn't quite sure how. His scanners were shot to hell, and the data he had coming in was something comparable to a blind man feeling his way back home through a hundred kilometers of dense jungle. A lot of gut had gone into it, along with all the analysis he'd been able to muster.

Now, you've got to land this thing...

The throttle was still responding, at least partially. It was sluggish, and it had gone dead three or four times on the way back, but whatever spirit of fortune had followed him for so many years had brought the controls back.

He was coming up on the landing bay now, and he was approaching far too quickly. He tapped the throttle. Nothing. Then again. A short pause, and then his engines fired, decelerating sharply as he moved closer, and the great grayish-white hull of *Dauntless* filled his field of view.

He'd slowed down some, but his velocity was still too high. He tapped the controls again. Nothing. He tried again, and then three or four more times. Nothing. No thrust, so sign of any response at all.

The spirit was gone, and he was on his own. And at the speed he was coming in at, there was no piloting trick that would save him. Especially with no thrust.

He was dead. He believed that, completely...for a few seconds. Then he had an idea. He just wasn't sure there was time.

His ship was moving toward the landing bay entrance, and he turned, looking away, his eyes locked on a small control board off to the side.

The ejection system. He should have bailed out when he

was closing on *Dauntless*, but he'd told himself he could land his mortally wounded ship. Now, he would pay the price for that hubris.

Unless he could eject in the landing bay.

It sounded crazy, and he was sure his instructors back at the Academy would have said it was impossible. It wasn't impossible. To the part of Jake's mind that made him who he was, nothing was *impossible*. It would take precision timing, certainly. He didn't have time to do the calculations, but his best guess was that he'd have a window of about one-third of a second.

If he could hit that instant of time, he might make it. If the system was functioning perfectly in a ship clearly shot to hell. If he got lucky and he didn't slam into any of the vehicles or stacks of the ordnance laying around the bay.

If he could make all that work…then he'd just slam into the bay floor with enough force to break every bone in his body.

But it was the only chance he had. He watched for another few seconds, as the fighter slipped inside the bay, and then he pulled the controls to initiate the escape sequence.

Chapter Thirty-Five

CFS Constitution
Olyus System, 3.2 Billion Kilometers from Megara
Year 318 AC

Alicia Covington stared straight ahead at the row of mobile shipyards. The structures were immense, like nothing she'd ever seen before, long cylinders with great arms protruding in all directions, creating docks for the ships under repair. She'd knew the situation in general terms, realized that the enemy had been able to quickly return its damaged vessels to service, but she hadn't really understood until she laid eyes on the things.

She had six hundred and eleven fighters under her command. That was several hundred fewer than Winters's sixteen battleships could carry, but the strike forces had taken terrible losses, and there hadn't been nearly enough squadrons based at Craydon to make up for the shortfall. There had been talk, she knew, of transferring units from some of the other ships, but the fleet had already been facing almost hopeless odds against an enemy everyone agreed would attack Craydon. In the end, Winters had insisted he would take his ships with their own complements, and nothing more. Covington had supported that decision, at the time. But the instant she saw the size of the things she'd come to destroy, she wondered if that had been a mistake. She wasn't sure her ships had the firepower to take out the vast constructs, and there were only so many targets the fleet's sixteen battleships could hit.

If she'd had six hundred fighters, she'd have felt better, but she'd sent two-thirds of her wings to meet the enemy warships rapidly approaching Winters's fleet. The garrisons were a bit lighter than she'd expected. No, not lighter, but more spread out. She'd been afraid there would be warships mixed throughout the support fleet, but that hadn't been the case. At least, not for the most part. But the job of holding back the enemy reserves, of keeping them at bay while Winters's ships pounded the mining and supply vessels, had fallen squarely on her squadrons.

The enemy had called on every ship in the system, including battleships that had been in orbit around Megara, no doubt for surface bombardment missions. Most of those appeared to be older ships with varying degrees of damage, and preliminary scans suggested there were no railgun-armed ships in the system, save for those attached to the shipyards and under repair. That was good news, and not entirely difficult to understand. The Confederation battle plan, at least where the fighter corps was concerned, had been based almost entirely on targeting those fragile weapons, knocking them out before they could close to firing range and blast their Confed counterparts to scrap. The enemy would want every railgun they could get in the force attacking Craydon, and that meant, with any luck at all, that Winters's ships would be spared the single greatest danger they might have faced.

"Let's go, teams Alpha, Beta, Gamma…you've got your designated targets. Now, let's go in and get the job done."

She was going in with the Alphas herself. She'd almost led the bomber wings against the approaching Hegemony warships, but in her gut, she knew the mobile shipyards were the most important targets. The fleet had come back in Olyus to deprive the enemy of their supplies, denying their foe the time to dig in, rebuild, bring up reserves. And nothing in the logistics fleet was as crucial to that as the repair facilities. Replacing the mobile platforms would take at least a year, maybe longer, and it would tie the Hegemony forces to a fixed base of operations. That would offer the Confederation forces the only real respite they'd seen since the war began. It would also open up the enemy's very long supply line to disruption.

Assuming she and her pilots *could* destroy the monstrous things.

There were ships docked with all of them, in varying stages of repairs—and serving as obstructions to incoming attacks. Covington didn't care about the ships. She wanted the shipyards, and that meant getting to the long cylindrical structures at the center…and blasting them to bits.

She glanced at the closest structure, designated "Alpha," the one her team was attacking. Most of the ships at the docking ports were escorts, in various stages of reconstruction, but two were battleships, big ones that undoubtedly had railguns. The ships were in various stages of repair, and it didn't seem likely they had their main batteries back online yet.

Still, Hegemony battleships were dangerous, and for more than a year, they'd been her primary targets. She felt the temptation to send some of her bombers against the vessels, but she resisted it. Picking off a couple of heavies would be a nice addition to her list of kills, but she couldn't risk leaving the shipyards functional. "Stay on target, all squadrons. We're not getting distracted by those ships. The shipyards are our targets. We hit them now, and we make it count."

She gripped the controls tightly, and her eyes narrowed on the targeting display. She was coming in hard and fast, and that meant she'd have a short window to take the perfect shot. The shipyards were huge and slow-moving, perfect targets…but Covington didn't want to hit an attached ship or some peripheral appendage, a docking port or something similar. She wanted a direct hit to the station's rotating midsection. She wanted all her people delivering torpedoes to the core structure of the great shipyards. Nothing less would be enough to destroy the huge constructs.

She drove her ship in, noticing that several of the escorts had broken free and were firing. The point defense fire was getting fairly heavy, but nowhere near the worst she'd seen in her battles against the Hegemony. She thought about increasing her evasive maneuvers—and ordering the squadrons with her to do the same—but shook her head grimly and put the thought aside. She *had* to take out those shipyards, and she couldn't afford to sacrifice accuracy for more variability in her approach vector.

She watched as the range dropped, her tension ramping up as the defensive fire steadily increased. She was soaked in sweat, uncomfortable…and damn scared. But she knew her duty, as she was sure all her people did.

The shipyards had continued to launch escorts from the repair docks, and there were a dozen active in the immediate area, all firing, though at various levels of effectiveness. Some were clearly only partially operational, while others mounted something closer to full broadsides of their weapons. The overall intensity was increasing, however, and she was beginning to lose ships. One incoming shot came close—too close—to her own ship, but she shrugged it off and continued in.

She continued to ignore the enemy fire, even as another of her ships vanished from the display, and then, seconds later, two more. She hated losing anyone, but the casualties were still light compared to those in the recent assaults on the enemy battle lines. The shipyards had been lightly defended, especially before they began to deploy the vessels in their docks. Winters's fleet had caught the enemy by surprise, just as they had hoped to do.

They're used to pacifying half-primitive survivors of the Cataclysm. They haven't had to deal with the kind of initiative to launch behind-the-lines attacks like this. Maybe, just maybe, we can actually pull this off…

Her hand tightened further, and she adjusted her sights… and let loose the torpedo.

She pulled up, blasting at full thrust, struggling to get enough of a course change to clear the great bulk of the shipyard rapidly growing on her screen.

Her ship streaked across the top of the massive construct, clearing it by less than a kilometer, even as her screen displayed the preliminary damage assessment.

A hit. A direct hit.

There were massive explosions erupting from a great gash in the monster ship's hull, where the blob of plasma had impacted, and she felt a rush of excitement. One hit wasn't going to take out the giant vessel, not even close, but as stared at her scanners, the squadrons formed up behind her came in, planting hit after hit on the great platform

She allowed herself a little smile. The fight in Megara, the battle to cripple the enemy's logistics…it had just begun, and she knew there was a long and desperate road ahead over the next several hours.

But her people had drawn some blood, and she felt a rush of excitement, satisfaction.

She'd be damned if her pilots were going to let even one of those shipyards escape.

She angled her ship around and blasted back toward *Constitution*. "All ships," she yelled into the comm, "no hanging around and watching. Get back to base as soon as you've launched your torpedoes. We've got to rearm and get the hell back at these bastards."

Before the enemy can get all the ships they have in-system out here…

* * *

"All ships, I said full thrust, and that's just what I meant. Strip off all safeties, and get me everything those reactors can give." Winters was standing next to his chair. That wasn't a particularly safe or smart thing to do going into battle, especially at the thrust levels *Constitution* was putting out. One malfunction in the dampeners, or one particularly rough evasive maneuver, could send him to the deck. Hard. But he was too edgy to sit, too anxious waiting to see if his ships could close with their targets before the warships blasting out from around Megara arrived.

He'd sent some of his battleships against the massive fleet of cargo ships, but he'd kept a most of them with him, and they were bearing down on the outer-system asteroids and moons, where the enemy mining ships were hard at work, digging out thousands of tons of raw materials and feeding them to the clusters of refining vessels positioned nearby. The whole thing was an astonishing display of engineering and ingenuity, and he was amazed by it. The raw productive capacity the Hegemony forces had managed to set up in just a couple of months exceeded anything he could have imagined. The immensity of the logistics fleet, the hundreds of billions of man-hours that had no doubt gone into its construction…it all filled him with amazement. It was an incredible example of human ingenuity and dedication.

But he was going to destroy it all anyway.

He'd had a passing thought, a morose feeling on the waste of it all. What could humanity achieve with such industry if it wasn't always so hellbent on fighting with itself?

But that combat, that self-immolation the human race seemed to prize so greatly, it had been his career, his life. It was what he did, and by God, he was going to do it now. Billions of Arbeiter had labored to build the Hegemony's gargantuan repair fleet, and now he was going to destroy it with just sixteen battleships, whatever it took to see that done.

"We're entering range, admiral."

Winters hadn't needed Harrington's report, but the aide was just doing his duty, so Winters humored him. "Very well, commander. Fleet order, all ships. Cut thrust to twenty percent." A pause. "Open fire."

Constitution's primaries fired no more than a few seconds later, along with the familiar distant whine, and the short-lived power drain that were almost trademarks of the weapon system. Winters tightened his fist in excitement, and then again, after a quick look at the display confirmed his other ships had fired as well. Forty-eight heavy primaries lanced out across the thousands of kilometers, and a few seconds later he saw that, even at extreme range, seven of them had hit.

Confederation primaries had always been powerful weapons, but those fired by Winters's ships were enhanced, powered up according to Dr. Witter's specs. Winters knew he was taking some chances, that most likely he'd see some failures in the systems before the battle was over. But he'd been able to open fire from a much longer range, and that meant he had more time to blast the enemy support ships before the bulk of their warships could arrive.

He was far from sure his people could destroy all the target ships quickly enough, but one thing was certain as he watched two mining ships explode and saw streams of damage assessments coming in on two others.

He'd caught the enemy unprepared. And that meant his people had a chance, at least.

Maybe a good chance.

Chapter Thirty-Six

Stara Sinclair screamed as she saw Stockton's ship rip into the landing bay and slam into the bulkheads on the far wall, erupting into a massive fireball as it did. For an instant, even as she watched the fire teams working to control the conflagration, she was sure he was dead. No one could have survived in that inferno.

But there was a shadow in her mind, something she'd seen but not completely processed. Her eyes had caught it even as the fighter came tumbling onto the flight deck and then, perhaps twenty seconds later, she realized what she'd seen.

Just as the med teams started yelling and an emergency vehicle went racing down the flight deck, weaving its way around the chunks of flaming debris.

He'd elected. Jake had ejected from his fighter just before it crashed and exploded. It hadn't quite made sense to her, even as she saw it, because it was something she'd never seen done before.

Never even heard of being done. Ever.

The timing, the focus it would take to pull something like

286

that off…it was almost impossible.

But that was Jake Stockton's specialty, at least when he wasn't going after the *completely* impossible.

She felt a burst of hope, but she clamped down on it. Timing the eject sequence, launching it with the required precision, was only part of the problem. Eject systems had been designed for deep space, not for the confines of a landing bay. She tried to imagine Jake being tossed out from his fighter, the velocity of the ship mixing with the force of the ejection.

She looked across the bay as she ran, and saw that he was lying against the far wall. He'd been sent flying across the deck and slammed into the bulkhead with a force she couldn't imagine. She'd thought for sure—*again*—that he was dead, as sure of it as she'd been when the ship exploded. It was hard to imagine anyone surviving what he'd just been through.

Then she saw him moving.

Not just moving, but… Was it possible? Getting up? On his own power, more or less?

She broke into a dead run and covered the rest of the distance in five or six seconds. "Jake," she cried as she stumbled to a halt just outside the ring of medical techs surrounding him.

He turned toward her, and she saw the side of his head, already blackened with bruises and half covered with a sheen of bright red blood. He was battered, banged up almost beyond easy recognition…but he was standing up on his own, and barking out orders to the techs trying to check his wounds.

"I need a ship ready to go immediately."

Stara heard the words, but she couldn't believe them, even from Jake Stockton.

Then she realized he was dead serious. He was beaten up, in pain, no doubt, and luckier maybe than he'd ever been. But "Raptor" Stockton was okay. He was in one piece, and Stara knew her biggest challenge would be keeping him out of a Lightning…at least until the doctors checked him out.

* * *

"I am pleased to hear that Admiral Stockton survived his landing. While death in battle is always a fitting end for a warrior, we have great need of the admiral, still."

Tulus flipped off the comm unit, cutting his line to Tyler Barron. His blood brother was too occupied for idle talk, though Tulus appreciated the update on Jake Stockton's condition. The methods of war necessary against the Hegemony were difficult ones for a Palatian to accept. Holding back, waiting for fighters to knock out as many of the enemy heavy batteries, swung too close to cowardice for some, especially those with views deeply steeped in the early lore of the Alliance. Though the Palatian pilots had never been so awash in glory as they were been in the current war...nor as deeply blooded in one vicious fight after another.

Tulus didn't especially like sitting back in his flagship, waiting to engage the enemy...but he understood the need for such tactics. And he recognized just how much Stockton had done, how crucial the master pilot had been in keeping the war going. It was almost impossible for a Palatian to honestly assess a combat situation and acknowledge that his forces would have been defeated, but without the sacrifices of the fighter corps, and the leadership of Jake Stockton, the war would almost certainly be over, the proud Alliance reduced—as the Confederation would be—once again into bitter slavery.

"I want the fleet ready to move the instant we receive the go ahead, commander."

Cilian Globus turned toward Tulus and nodded, a respectful gesture between the commander-maximus and the imperator. The two highest-rank Palatians were completely in sync regarding what they had to do to fight the Hegemony. It was difficult for both of them, and they'd had to spend considerable time dealing with less enlightened officers, who saw only fear and disgrace in a failure to simply move forward and engage the enemy with everything. Tulus knew such tactics would be suicidal, that any who pursued them would fail in the highest and greatest duty to defend sacred Palatia. Still, Tulus found it a constant strain to hold back everything he'd been raised to believe, all he'd been trained to do.

"All ships prepped for maximum thrust, your supremacy. All weapons online and ready."

"Very well, commander." Tulus turned his head and looked toward the main display. It wasn't time, not yet. But it would be soon. And he was ready. To fight the enemy, to defeat them and send them fleeing back to their home worlds far beyond the Badlands.

Or to die in the fight. To die like a Palatian.

* * *

"He's alive!"

"Warrior" Timmons was on the force-wide comm. There wasn't a pilot in arms, not one wearing a Confederation uniform, or Alliance colors—and even, perhaps, those in Union greens—who wasn't relieved to hear that Jake Stockton had somehow landed his battered fighter.

Stockton's comm had been down, and for the last hour or more, the pilots of every squadron in the system had struggled to stay focused, wondering what would become of their revered leader. Some of the pilots had picked up Stockton's ship on their scanners, and the word spread that it still appeared to be at least partially functional, and heading back to *Dauntless*. Timmons had tried to interject several times, struggled to keep the wings focused on the fight. He'd had some success, mostly through dirty tricks like telling them Stockton was counting on them. He didn't hesitate to share the first good news he'd gotten on the subject.

It was time for the strike force to cut loose. Time to take vengeance for what had almost happened to their leader. "All ships with torpedoes, with me. We're going to hit that battle line, and we're going to do it with everything we've got. Squadrons with empty bomb bays, back to your motherships. Load up and get the hell back out here."

Timmons brought his fighter around, nudging his vector toward the row of enormous, but battered battle wagons just ahead. Stockton's people had hit the new enemy heavy units hard, but there were still six of them moving forward. They were monsters, bristling with weapons and massively armored. Stockton's people might have knocked out all the railguns, but Timmons didn't know. And those ships looked like they could easily mount double spreads of the deadly weapons.

He *had* to be sure.

"Blue squadron, Yellow squadron, Scarlet Eagle squadron, with me. We're going to hit those lead ships, the ones Raptor attacked. We've got a score to settle with them…and we owe it to Raptor to finish what he started."

He listened as the squadron leaders acknowledged, struck by the lack of familiarity of any of the voices. There had been enormous turnover, of course, since Timmons had served on *Dauntless* years earlier, and almost every pilot who'd been in that battleship's veteran squadrons then had moved on. Some were dead, he knew…more than he wanted to think about. Others were badly wounded and retired from the service, as he had been. Still more were commanding their own squadrons now, or even full wings.

He'd checked the Scarlet Eagles' roster when he'd first reported to *Dauntless*, and there wasn't one pilot left from his days commanding the celebrated formation. It was the nature of things, he knew, but it still triggered a sadness inside him, a melancholy for the loss of his youth, a longing for days he now looked back on fondly.

In his ship, at the head of the formations, nostalgia didn't matter. Memories didn't matter. Only the battle raging all around him. The ships behind him might not be the Scarlet Eagles he remembered, but the squadron itself would always be *his*. And now he could lead them in, a new generation, with Stockton's old Blues and *Dauntless*'s Yellow squadron as well.

He glanced at the screen, checking on the other formations, shouting orders into the comm as he directed the various wings scattered across the system. He wasn't officially Stockton's second-in-command, but he'd seized that place, and not a pilot out there had resisted his doing so. They would follow "Raptor"

Stockton anywhere, he knew, but Timmons fancied that most of them would be willing to fly alongside "Warrior" into some pretty dark places as well.

Timmons was going to lead them there...at least until Stockton got back out. He owed that to his old rival, and his friend. He would watch the squadrons, see that they did what they had to do.

He had Stockton's back, and he took that duty very seriously. He stared at the screen again. He had squadrons to command, wings to refit and lead back to the fight, formations to reorganize.

But first, he had six battleships to blast to atoms...

* * *

Tyler Barron stared at Atara for a few seconds, and then he nodded. He could see she was struggling with the whole thing, and he'd almost activated the comm and done it himself. But *Dauntless* was her ship, even though Jake Stockton was a fleet-level commander now, who actually outranked her.

That was a technicality, Barron knew. Atara deserved her own stars, and if they lived long enough, he intended to make sure she got them. In the meantime, she had been clear that she was content to serve at his side, as she had for so long, and that she actually preferred that duty, at least until the war against the Hegemony was under control. Barron was deeply relieved by that. The fight his people were in was enough without losing his right arm.

He watched as she leaned forward, activating the comm. "Flight deck Alpha, Admiral Stockton is cleared to launch." She'd barely choked out the command.

They were words Barron couldn't have imagined, even an hour before. He'd watched Stockton come in, and for a short while, he'd been sure the pilot wasn't going to make it. Then they'd heard the news. Stockton was in...and fine. Well, close to fine. Banged up a bit, but not seriously wounded.

Barron had felt a wave of relief amid the stress and terror

of the battle, and it lasted perhaps thirty minutes, the extent of the time Stockton had given to humor the doctors in sickbay. He was fine, and he told that to anyone who came within earshot. Then, when he had endured all he could take, he just got up and walked out of sickbay and back to his quarters. Ten minutes later, he walked back out into the corridor, wearing fresh survival and flight suits to replace the shredded and damaged garb he'd been wearing.

Then he went right to the flight deck and began terrorizing anyone he thought might be able to find him a fighter to fly. Stara tried to stop him—half the flight crew tried to stop him—but he was a force of nature. Barron's recollections were secondhand, of course, but he knew Stockton well enough that he was one of the few who weren't at all surprised.

Barron had been a bit shocked at his own response when Stara Sinclair called him and asked him to intervene. He refused her, though seconds before, he had intended to agree. He still wasn't sure where the thought had come from, but suddenly it became clear he couldn't deny his hero pilot the chance to get back out with his fighter wings. If this was to be the final battle, Stockton deserved to fight it alongside the men and women he'd forged into such a deadly weapon. And they deserved to have him there with them.

Atara knew that, too, though she clearly had some trouble actually authorizing the pilot to launch. Barron understood, and he imagined Stockton down there, ready to launch in a dusty previous-generation Lightning, the only ship still on *Dauntless* even potentially capable of flight.

Whether it was or was not *actually* capable remained to be seen.

Barron sat quietly, waiting. With anyone but Atara, he would have intervened and given the order himself, but he didn't have the slightest doubt she would do what she had to do. He'd never seen Atara Travis allow herself to be defeated by anything.

Her voice was a bit shaky, but it had been loud and crisp when she said, "Cleared to launch."

Barron took a deep breath and, seconds later, felt the distant vibration. Jake Stockton was back out there.

Back where he belonged.

Chapter Thirty-Seven

Bridge - CFS Dauntless
20,000,000 Kilometers from Craydon
Calvus System
Year 318 AC

"Admiral, there's no other choice. We're getting the fighters back out there as quickly as we can, a squadron at a time, even half a squadron. But it's just not enough." Barron had been watching the battle, watching as the battle was being lost. His people were fighting like demons, and the relentless self-sacrifice of the Palatians had stunned him like nothing he'd seen before. Even the Union forces were fighting well and bravely, though he'd found that rather more difficult to acknowledge. It was going to be a fight to the finish, and Hegemony casualties would be beyond anything in any other battle of the war. But it wasn't going to matter. None of it. The enemy was just too strong. The invaders were going to be the last ones standing.

Barron had beaten himself up, questioned the tactics he and Nguyen had employed, even wondered if the sixteen battleships sent to Megara with Clint Winters might have been just enough force to give a chance of actual victory at Craydon.

He craved an answer that would let him push the torturous thoughts aside, but the one his mind gave him was profoundly unsatisfying, either for the side of him that sought relief, or the one that desired self-flagellation.

Maybe.

It was *that* close. Barron had even managed to convince himself a few times there was still a chance, even with the forces present. But he'd never been good at self-delusion, and the armageddon happening all around Craydon was quickly slipping into the realm of pure mathematics.

The fighters had fought like wild predators, and they'd knocked out more than three-quarters of the enemy railguns, but the losses had been astonishing, worse than anything Barron had seen or even imagined in his worst nightmares. Forty percent of the bombers were gone, and a third of the pilots Stockton had launched with at the start of the battle were dead now.

The battle line had not been spared the carnage, and three separate groups of enemy heavy units had closed, raking the allied ships with the railguns that remained operational. They'd gotten a surprise this time, though, when Barron had ordered the Confederation ships to open up with their own augmented main guns. The new weapons almost matched the range of the railguns, and they ripped into the Hegemony ships with nearly as much destructive force.

Witter's warnings about the untested weapons had proven prescient, however, and despite the damage inflicted on the enemy, the weapons had taken their toll among the firers, too. Barron had been staring right at the display when *Indefatigable*'s batteries erupted in a massive explosion that blew the front of the battleship completely off. He had ordered nearby units to try to save the crippled vessel, but the enemy concentrated fire, sensing an easy kill. About a hundred of the crew had managed to get out in the lifepods in time, but the other ninety percent had been lost when the ship lost containment and vanished from the display.

Indefatigable had been the only total loss from primary battery malfunctions, but three other battleships had lost their main guns in less catastrophic ways—and, in two of those instances, the damage had left the engaged ships in combats they could no longer win. *Integrity* drove forward with all her engines could give her, bringing her secondaries into range and blasting away at the enemy, but the damage she'd taken on the way in had just been too severe. Her containment had endured through one critical hit after another, but she was a floating hulk, without any energy production and, almost certainly, any survivors from her crew.

Halcyon's end had been more dramatic. Barron had watched in stunned amazement as the battleship, stripped of all her weapons, blasted her thrust at full directly toward one of the largest enemy vessels. He'd opened up a comm line, intending to order Captain Barrett to alter his course, but stopped just before he spoke. *Halcyon* was doomed, with no hope of escaping the enemy ships closing on it. He couldn't save her crew, and he wasn't going to deny them some meaning in their deaths.

Fate, however, had been less merciful, and the big ship lost containment less than one minute from completing its ramming run. The explosion had been massive, but too far from any enemy vessels to do any damage.

He was amazed at the heroism he saw all around, and even at the way Denisov's Union forces fought selflessly at the side of their old enemies. The Union ships were less advanced than their Confederation counterparts, their fighters nowhere near as sophisticated. They suffered even more severely at the hands of the invaders, but they held, standing in line, fighting a hopeless battle against the oncoming enemy.

Barron was still troubled at the presence of Denisov's forces. They'd been his enemy as long as he could remember. They'd been his grandfather's enemy. And he still held them responsible for Ricard Lille, and what had happened to Andi.

Though they tried to kill Denisov, too…and now he and his people are here, fighting at your side.

He didn't have time to understand his conflicting opinions. All he needed to know was that his forces would likely have been defeated already if they'd had to fight without the Union fleet.

They were all together there, in that moment…the three greatest Rim nations. Whether they'd been friends, enemies, both, now they were fighting to save all their homeworlds.

And they were losing.

* * *

"Black Fist squadron, you're the last unit out here with torpedoes. We've got two enemy ships coming on strong at 140.111.302…right for the center of the Alliance line." It felt strange to Timmons to be so worried about Alliance ships, but the Palatians had been dedicated allies in the war against the Hegemony, and they'd suffered horrendous losses at both Megara and Craydon, fighting to save Confederation planets.

Timmons respected his allies and their spirit in battle. The Palatians weren't the only ones with honor.

"You've got to hit both of them, and it's got to be now." Trying to take out the railguns on two large Hegemony battleships with a single squadron was a difficult enough proposition, but there were only eight Black Fists left in action, and the acting squadron leader was a pilot who had launched as fourth in command. But that was eight more torpedoes than all of the combined thirty-two squadrons in front of the Palatian line. The weapons had been well used, and they'd done their damage… but they'd fallen short.

The Palatian battleships were strongly built, but they lacked even unenhanced versions of Confederation primaries. They were massively outranged by the Hegemony forces, and that meant their unwavering courage had mostly led them to slaughter. Three of their battleships had managed to close enough to open fire with their broadsides, and they had drawn some blood, taking out two of the enemy battleships before all three of them were blasted to plasma. But most of the Alliance ships were knocked out of action before they could get close enough to strike back.

Timmons watched as the eight fighters swooped in, attacking with the courage and determination he had seen all across the battle line. They closed to almost insane ranges, losing two of their number on the way in. Then they launched.

The closest ship took two hits, adding to damage it had already absorbed. The vessel shuddered, and there was a noticeable drop in power output. The point defense systems were still active, and they inflicted yet another casualty on the Black Fists as the attacking ships tried to come around and return to base. Timmons didn't know for sure, but he'd bet the Hegemony ship had lost its heavy guns in that attack.

It had been costly for the pilots who'd come in at the ship, but at least they had succeeded.

The attack on the other ship hadn't gone nearly as well. One torpedo scored a hit, but it slammed into one of the vessel's extremities, too far from the vital systems to do more than superficial damage. As if to dispel any hope Timmons might have had that he was wrong in that assessment, the ship fired its dreaded railguns almost immediately after the torpedo impacted...and scored a hit on one of the largest Alliance battleships, splitting the enormous vessel open like an egg.

Timmons stared at the spectacle for a moment, realizing that what he saw as a small dot flickering out of existence had, in actuality, been hundreds of Palatian spacers dying. Some, no doubt, went quickly, incinerated before they even knew what was coming. Others had clung to life, while the ship itself began to split apart. Some compartments would have retained integrity longer than others, and even in the cold vacuum of space, death was far from instantaneous. He'd spent so much time with the squadrons, watching pilots wiped out by the hundreds, that he'd forgotten just what a nightmare it was when a battleship's entire crew died, almost as one.

He stared at the enemy ship, the only one with functional railguns still remaining in range of the Alliance battle line. If he could have taken it out, he could have bought some time for the Palatians to regroup, perhaps even for some of their squadrons to rearm and meet the next Hegemony wave.

But that one ship would wreak havoc. It wouldn't close, and before the Alliance battleships could advance to bring their own weapons into range, more of them would be destroyed. Timmons didn't know if it would be one more, two...five. But each one represented almost a thousand trained spacers.

He wondered, for a terrible instant, if a suicide run could

take out the ship's heavy guns…if he could save thousands of his allies if he sacrificed himself. He wasn't sure if he was seriously considering it or not, but, as the thoughts drifted through his mind, he realized how profoundly he believed he would die right there in the Calvus system. The battle was lost, and perhaps none of the Confederation or Alliance spacers there would live to see another fight anyway.

Is another hour of life—or three, or five—worth letting thousands of other spacers die?

He was still thinking that when his comm crackled to life.

"I always knew you wanted my job."

Timmons couldn't believe what he was hearing. He'd been relieved at the news Stockton had somehow survived his crash landing, but he'd never imagined his friend would launch again less than an hour later. It was a shock…one more line to etch into the legend of Jake Stockton.

Something for future generations to debate, to wonder whether it actually happened, or if it was just some old space tale.

If there even are future generations…

* * *

"You did one hell of a job, Warrior. Let me see if I can finish this last bit." Stockton was struggling to sound strong, but it was an act. Every centimeter of his body ached, and his fatigue almost laughed at the high-dose stim he'd just taken. Whatever images of hell he'd imagined in his life, he knew it couldn't be much worse than how he felt as he blasted his fighter toward the target, one tiny ship and one man, coming in at an enemy behemoth bristling with weapons.

But there was no choice. He'd had a bad feeling, a frigid coldness down his spine that told him Timmons had been about to do something crazy. And why not? It wasn't hard to decide there was no chance anyway. But Stockton wasn't quite there yet, at least not in the part of him that housed his spirit.

"Thanks, Raptor. That means a lot. I'm surprised to see you

back so soon. Damned glad, but surprised. Still, that's a rough run for only one ship. Let some of us go in with you, take off some of the heat."

Stockton jerked his hand wildly, trying to make up for the lack of thrust and maneuvering power in the obsolete ship. He was going to respond to Timmons, to tell him, "Thanks, but no thanks," but he was too late. Warrior was already on the line, rounding up nearby pilots to make another run, one without torpedoes. One with a single purpose—to draw fire from Stockton.

Flying down the throat of a Hegemony battleship was just about the last thing Stockton wanted to do, but watching his comrades do it alongside him with no role, save as targets, was even worse.

But he realized nothing he did or said now would ward them off, so it was time to go in, and see what he could do. The ship he was flying was a pig, but it had a plasma torpedo in its bomb bay, and he had a target. Everything else was window dressing.

"It looks like we need one more hit in just the right place…"

Stockton continued toward the target, pitching his ship wildly back and forth in a desperate attempt to avoid the incoming enemy fire. His makeshift wingmen were coming on in an even crazier pattern. None of them had to worry about aiming a torpedo.

Pulses ripped by all around, at least half a dozen coming within two hundred meters of his fighter, but they missed…his ship, and those of his comrades.

Somehow, they all missed.

Stockton was flying in as wildly as he could, putting every bit of his considerable skill into piloting the fighter. The other ships were drawing off at least some of the fire, but he knew his greatest ally was luck. He'd been cocky as a young man, but age had brought awareness with it, even wisdom. He was doing what he was doing because there was no choice, not because he didn't think he could be hit. He knew all his experience and ability would mean nothing if fortune deserted him, even for an instant.

He came right at the enemy ship. It was close, and getting

closer every second. The fire was almost impossible to avoid, every battery on the giant ship targeting the small cluster of fighters. He still came on, through the nightmare of fire, down to the closest point-blank range he'd ever seen.

Then he loosed his torpedo and struggled to clear the rapidly approaching target...zipping by no more than a hundred meters from its gray hull, even as the damage assessment confirmed he had hit the target just where he'd intended. The damage was clearly considerable, but it was just a guess as to whether he'd taken out the railguns.

Whether he'd save three or four thousand Palatian warriors, or if his risky—crazy—attack had been for nothing.

Chapter Thirty-Eight

Bridge - CFS Dauntless
20,000,000 Kilometers from Craydon
Calvus System
Year 318 AC

"We'll have the bombers ready to launch again in twenty minutes, admiral...but I'm afraid the situation is highly variable across the fleet. We'll get maybe thirty percent of the total birds out this side of an hour. The others will trickle out one squadron at a time, assuming the damage-control crews can get the bays back to some level of functionality."

Tyler Barron heard Stara Sinclair's words. Sinclair was the best he'd ever seen at what she did. He imagined she had already unloaded on the deck chiefs on the other ships, probably far more aggressively than he would have. In the end, you could push just so hard, and then reality stood in the way.

"Very well, captain." He didn't have to say a word to her. He knew she would do everything possible no matter what. But it came out anyway. "See if you can push them a little harder."

"Yes, sir."

He cut the line and leaned back in his chair.

"It's over," he mumbled to himself, the words coming out far more audibly than he'd intended.

Atara looked over. He could see her thoughts were the same

as his. The enemy's third line was advancing, and there was no longer any doubt. The battleships would come into range before he could get another sizable bomber assault out.

He'd have to send the bombers back out in small groups, as each three or four ships finished refit. That would make the whole thing far more dangerous for those going in without the benefits of mass.

But he would do it anyway. It just wasn't going to make enough difference.

At least not to save the fleet, or save the battle.

"Atara, better make sure *Dauntless* is ready for close combat. And then check on the other ships. We're going to be in the shit, probably before we even get the first squadrons back out."

"Yes, admiral." She turned back to her workstation, but he could feel the coldness in her, the resignation, as the same thing began to take over his own body.

He was scared. He didn't want to die at Craydon, nor watch all the rest of his people killed. He considered contacting Admiral Nguyen, discussing some kind of last-minute retreat plan. It was just possible the fleet could make a run for it. Everyone wouldn't get away, not even close, but some might. The idea of living a bit longer, maybe long enough to see Andi again…

But there was no point. If they couldn't stop the enemy here, they were only going to have a harder time farther out, where they would lack the fortifications and production of the Iron Belt. They couldn't face the enemy again with a fraction of the strength they'd had at Craydon.

He might have ordered the fleet to run for it if there had been some real hope, but the allied forces of the Rim were at Craydon in strength, and even the unexpected arrival of the Union fleet had proven to be too little to hold off the terrifying power of the Hegemony. A few hopeless, bleak weeks or months were of no value, and he suspected there would be more pain in that than in dying right there and then.

He felt pain for his people, and for the Palatians, and even, to his surprise, for the Union spacers. Admiral Denisov had been true to his word, and his people had fought steadfastly alongside their old enemies.

And now they will die with us…

Barron had never imagined he'd be watching a Union fleet blasted to pieces and feel only sorrow.

He sat silently for a moment, listening as Atara moved from addressing *Dauntless*'s gunners to relaying his orders to the entire Confederation fleet. He was overstepping, he knew, but Nguyen was on *Bastion*, all the way at the far end of the formation, and if the fleet was going to fight to the last, it was time to get ready to do just that.

Barron turned, about to tell Atara to send a communique to Nguyen's flagship, but she spoke first…and eliminated the need.

"Incoming comm from fleet command, admiral. We are to initiate Plan Black at once."

Barron nodded. He would have grinned if anything approaching a smile could have penetrated the grim and morose cloud surrounding him. Nguyen had come to the same conclusion he had. Plan Black. The orders the two of them had prepared for just such a situation.

For the fleet's final battle.

"Pass on the admiral's order, Atara. All task forces, prepare for Plan Black."

"Yes, Tyler. I'll see to it."

Barron sat listening as his aide, his friend, worked her way through the task forces, all the way to the Union fleet, with a respectful "suggestion" to Admiral Denisov to join with the rest of the forces in one last, well-ordered struggle.

She turned and looked back at him. She'd contacted all but one of the fleet's sub-commanders. And Barron knew why she had paused. There was one contact he had to make himself.

Nothing less would serve where his blood brother—and the Alliance imperator—was concerned.

"Get me a line to *Invictus*, please, Atara." His voice was soft, but inside, he was marshaling his strength. This would likely be his last communication with Tulus, and he'd be damned if he'd sound anything less than the defiant warrior, worthy of a Palatian's respect and ready for whatever was to come.

* * *

"Go to battle with honor, my brother, and if it be our fate to die here, then let us see it is well done. We will fight until the last breath escapes our bodies. It has been my privilege to find a friend and brother so far from home. Die well, Tyler Barron… and remember, you go into battle not only as Confederation officer, but as a Palatian as well."

Tulus cut the line. He would have preferred to speak with Barron for the last time in private, but there was no time. The Hegemony battle line was rapidly approaching, even as the scattered groups of bombers made what runs they could. The squadrons had fought like lions, and Tulus nodded in silent respect to all of them, Alliance and Confederation alike.

Even the Union wings, he thought, with some surprise. They weren't as good as either the Confederation or Alliance wings by any measure, but they had displayed unwavering courage, and that was enough to win a full measure of his respect.

"Are you ready to die, old friend?" he asked, looking over at Globus. "It has been a long road for us, yet I think we have reached its end."

"A Palatian is always ready to die with honor. We have fought well, your supremacy. If we must die, this is as good a place as any"—the commander-maximus looked around, his eyes moving across the bridge and over the screen displaying the other ships of the combined fleet—"and this company fitting for a warrior to die among."

Tulus sat for a few seconds. Then he took a deep breath and said, "All Alliance ships prepare to advance at full." Tulus's ships didn't have Confederation primaries, not even the unenhanced versions. They had a much longer gauntlet to run before they could deal out death to the oncoming next wave of their enemies…and Vian Tulus wasn't going to die in some one-sided exchange, watching helplessly while an untouchable foe obliterated his ships.

He was ready to die, but he would take the blood of his

enemies with him. The Hegemony might prevail, defeat the Alliance and the Confederation, but they would pay such a price that men and woman yet unborn would speak of it in hushed tones. Even the descendants of the victors would feel the chill of death through the generations.

"All ships ready, your supremacy."

Tulus's face tightened, turning almost to stone.

"Advance, commander. To battle, and—if it be our fate—to death."

* * *

"All ships forward, commander."

"Yes, admiral. As you command." Guy Lambert's voice cracked a bit, but the aide managed to hold it steady. Denisov knew his tactical officer was as aware of the situation as he was.

Andrei Denisov was sitting in his chair in the center of *Illustre*'s bridge, shooting a glance over at Lambert. The battle had been brutal, a wild, vicious struggle that had gutted the forces on both sides. But it was almost over now, something Denisov knew very well as he looked out at the main screen, at the lines of Hegemony ships pressing forward.

Denisov was sore, too. More than sore. Every millimeter of his body ached. He'd shifted every way he could manage, turned and leaned forward, and even gotten up half a dozen times. Nothing he did relieved the pain. And the fatigue was indescribable. Even the slightest exertions brought on near fits of hyperventilation. He should still have been in sickbay, as the doctors had reminded him, what, fifty times? It seemed like fifty.

That wasn't an option. He'd come to Confederation space to try to ally with the Confederation, and he had succeeded. The old enemies had battled together, side by side, and they had given the Hegemony one hell of a fight. But it hadn't been enough. The enemy was just too strong. Denisov's ships had been battered, and no small number destroyed already, and he knew he had just given the order that would send the survivors to their doom.

He'd considered retreating, slipping away with what he could extricate from the line. But the Confeds and the Palatians were standing firm, and he decided his people would do no less. Both of his new allies looked down on Union arms, he knew, but they didn't understand the damage poor leadership had inflicted on the campaigns of the past wars, how badly the gifted officers that existed were constrained by fear of Sector Nine or by jealous, and better connected, superiors. A Union spacer could hold his own in any fight. Denisov believed that with all his heart, and he felt certain his people had shown that at Craydon.

He found himself hoping that Tyler Barron had noticed as well, even as he cursed himself for caring. His people had followed him bravely, despite the fact that doing so had almost certainly put them all at grave risk, and almost guaranteed they couldn't go home.

He hoped some of his people did manage to survive the battle somehow, though he didn't know what would be left for them once the Hegemony conquered the entire Rim. He just knew he wouldn't be there.

He wouldn't leave Craydon in defeat, to hide until the Hegemony hunted him down. No, he would die where he was.

He was scared, though the familiar feeling of his heart pounding was absent, replaced by an odd, steady rhythm, the artificial pumping action that kept him alive.

For a few moments longer, at least…

* * *

"I need those primaries back online, now!" Atara Travis shouted into the comm, her hard words directed at her engineering teams. *Dauntless*'s engineers were highly skilled, as were all the battleship's spacers, but Barron knew the ship, Atara's ship, was weaker than it had ever been in terms of damage control. He'd sent Anya Fritz with Clint Winters's force, in the hopes the brilliant engineer could keep the stealth generators working long enough to give the attack on the Hegemony supply fleet a chance. Walt Billings had become a brilliant engineer in his own

right, and the head of *Dauntless*'s team when Fritz wasn't there…
but Billings had been killed in the battle at Ulion months before.

As Barron watched Travis pushing her crew, he couldn't help
but think about how many people he'd served with were gone,
how many skilled officers had been lost in battle after bloody
battle.

Dauntless's primaries had remained in action for far longer
than Barron had hoped, but finally, the battleship took a solid
railgun hit. It wasn't as bad as it might have been, but the impact,
and the secondary explosions it caused, had torn up huge sections of the power feeds that kept the heavy weapons functioning. It had taken *Dauntless* out of the fight, save as a target, but
that would only last for another two minutes. Then the broadside of secondaries would be in range, and if the ship could
avoid taking another hit until then, she would be able to resume
dealing out death to the Hegemony invaders.

Barron almost told Atara it was pointless to try and get the
primaries back, that the teams would never be able to make
repairs before the ship entered secondary range. But he kept his
silence, let Atara run her ship.

A few seconds later, she came to the conclusion herself, and
she ordered the teams to abandon the main guns and focus on
keeping the broadsides in action. The two of them were in sync
again, as they had been for so many years.

Barron waited as *Dauntless* closed the distance to the enemy
line, the battleship gyrating wildly, her nav teams doing everything possible to offer the most difficult target possible to the
enemy railguns. One of the great shots ripped by, less than half
a kilometer from the ship's hull, but nothing stopped *Dauntless*
from pushing on.

Barron thought about the battle, about defeat. About the
end.

He had fought. He had done everything he could…but it
hadn't been enough. His grandfather had been the hero of the
Confederation, the man who'd saved it from destruction.

And Tyler was the one who'd lost it.

He thought about what his grandfather would say to him

if he could be there. And he thought about Andi. He'd almost tried to get her to leave, as he'd done at Megara, but something had held him back. It cut through him like a blade to think of her dying at Craydon. He wanted her to run. But, he realized, there was nowhere to go. For her, escape would only prolong the agony. Barron had found himself hoping, even expecting, that most of the people of the Confederation would adapt to being virtual slaves to the Hegemony, that they would adjust to the loss of the freedom few of them had ever truly appreciated anyway. He believed most of them would manage to eke out some kinds of lives under the rule of the Masters.

But he knew Andi Lafarge well enough to realize she would never be one of them. She would fight, he knew, with her last breath…and he respected her too much to try to tell her what to do again. He would let her decide—and from the position of the lightly armed *Hermes*, advancing even then at full thrust, he could see she had made exactly the choice he'd expected.

She would die in Craydon, just as he would. He only hoped he went first. It was selfish, a small mercy for himself. But it was a weakness that pushed through the wall of strength he'd erected in his mind.

"Admiral, we're picking up energy readings at the transit point."

Barron sighed hard. More enemy forces? Was it even possible? "I don't suppose it matters much now if they get reinforcements, Atara, do you think?"

"No, sir…not the enemy entry point. The Axella point."

The words bored into Barron's skull, but it was twenty seconds before he truly understood them. The Axella point was directly behind the fleet, on the opposite side of the system from where the Hegemony forces had entered.

If they have ships out there, things are worse than I thought…

It seemed unlikely, but he couldn't imagine who else it could be, what force could be coming through that transit point, even as the massed forces of the Confederation, Alliance, and Union faced the final struggle.

Then he saw the symbols on the display. He was confused at first, uncertain. Then he just stared in stunned disbelief.

Chapter Thirty-Nine

SWS Enlightened One
Just Inside Axella Transit Point
Entering Calvus System
Year 318 AC

Sara Eaton sat in the seat to the right of the immense—throne was the only way she could describe it—where the Enlightened One sat, and she looked straight ahead, eyes on the screen as the scanners rebooted and began to display the situation in the space around Craydon.

It was nothing short of apocalyptic. There were floating clouds of debris everywhere, and, about thirty million kilometers from the planet, the two battle lines were standing toe to toe, firing away at point-blank range. It was a stage of battle no fight against the Hegemony had reached—had been allowed to reach—at least not in such scale. The cost of it was evident everywhere she looked.

We got here just in time.

Or just too late...

She wasn't sure which it was, but she knew there was no room for delay.

"Enlightened One, with your permission, I would give the fleet order to attack." Sara suppressed the sigh her body desperately wanted to expel. Her military career had put her in situations she'd never have imagined as a young cadet, but none quite as utterly surreal as pandering to some petty Far Rim despot with delusions of near-divinity. One who'd not only given himself a ridiculous moniker—she hesitated to call it a name—like the Enlightened One, but also named his flagship after it. It turned her stomach every time she had to humor him, but she knew her duty.

And it's not like the sultan is any better…

She'd split her time between the flagships of the two dominant Far Rim powers, trying to appease the vanities of both rulers, and realizing just how fragile the alliance she'd somehow cobbled together truly was. If either the Sultanate or the Sapphire Worlds withdrew their fleets, she'd lose the other as well, and most of the minor powers, too. The whole thing was built on a precarious balancing act where each nation felt secure sending its fleets so far away, precisely because their rivals were doing the same.

She'd had a headache for weeks now, one apparently impervious to all known forms of medication.

The Sultanate and the Sapphire Worlds had long been enemies, rivals for dominance on the outer reaches of the Far Rim. They'd casually despised each other for generations, but they'd avoided having any real conflict beyond a few small skirmishes. That had been accomplished through one simple expedient.

Cold, stark fear of the Alliance.

The Palatians controlled a much larger empire than either of the Far Rim nations, and the Alliance worlds, while still rough and far out in the wilds of the distant Rim by Confederation standards, were vastly more populated and cosmopolitan than the fringe borderland systems of the Sultanate and the Sapphire Worlds. That had long been something the Alliance had not hesitated to exploit, and each of the Far Rim powers had fought three losing wars against the Palatians, shedding a dozen systems between them in a series of shameful treaties. Still, not once had they resolved their differences and joined to face the Alliance as a united bloc. The allure of watching their rival smashed by Palatian arms had always been too compelling.

The ruler of the Sapphire Worlds had been silent for a moment after she spoke. She suspected he was thinking, considering options…though she wasn't sure what there was to consider after traveling through two dozen transits and arriving even as the battle was raging.

He's just a coward. He's trying to pull himself together…and probably wondering if there is a way he can pull the flagship back from the fighting without losing face.

I can save you time, "Enlightened One"—there isn't.

"By all means, Admiral Eaton. Assuming our Sultanate… allies…are ready for a fight as well."

"They are, Enlightened One." She didn't like the sultan much more than she did the ruler of the Sapphire Worlds, but she had to admit, he seemed to be made of somewhat sterner stuff.

He's probably imagining making his mark, and gaining Confederation support in the future. The Sultanate's been number two out there for a long time, and I suspect that's been a burr in his ass for years.

She reached down to her controls and activated the fleet-wide comm channel she'd prepared even before the jump into Craydon's system. "All ships, it seems the fight is already on…" *And almost lost, from the looks of things.* She decided to leave that part out. "Full thrust forward. Let us advance and engage, and drive the enemy back where they came from."

She turned and nodded toward Enlightened One.

He turned toward his primary aide. "All ships will advance, commander. All weapons armed and ready."

* * *

Tyler Barron was staring at the display in utter disbelief. He'd suspected the inbound ships were some kind of Hegemony force that had found its way to another entry point into the system. Then when he saw the ships, all unfamiliar designs, he imagined it was some kind of new Hegemony fleet, perhaps the forces of some types of satellite nations, reserves brought forward to finish the conquest of the Rim.

Then he heard the voice on the comm.

It was difficult to hear; the static from the Hegemony jamming had blocked most of it. But it came in on the fleet's priority channel, and suddenly, a few seconds of clear transmission fought their way through. The voice was immediately familiar.

Sara Eaton.

Was it even possible? He'd been part of the group that had convinced Eaton to go out to the Far Rim to try to recruit new allies. He'd believed she might succeed, for about a day, when he'd given her the blood oath signed by Tulus, guaranteeing eternal friendship with the Alliance to any powers that joined her and came to fight the Hegemony—and perpetual enmity to all those who refused. It was a potent offer to Far Rim nations long victimized by Palatian aggression, and even the Alliance's enemies knew Palatian imperators did not violate blood oaths.

Still, his hope had quickly faded. It seemed too much to seriously expect that Eaton—a brilliant naval officer, but, by her own admission, no diplomat—could forge such a coalition in so little time. He'd come to regret his support for sending her so far away, wishing she was with him, helping to command the fleet.

The connection slipped again into the static of the Hegemony jamming, but those few seconds had been enough to tell him all he needed to know. Eaton had done just what she'd been sent to do…and she'd arrived back just in time.

"Atara, it looks like we have some reinforcements, against all odds. We'd better make the best of it. It's time for the final push. Get a comm out to any ships you can reach through this jamming. Reactors on one hundred and fifteen percent. Safeties off all weapons. We're going to pour everything we've got into these bastards, and damn the consequences!"

"Yes, sir!" He could hear the burst of energy in her voice, and he felt it in himself. He was far from sure even Eaton's reinforcements would be enough to turn the looming defeat into a victory—that would depend, he suspected, on just how much of a stomach for losses the Hegemony commander had.

But whatever chance his people had to outlast their enemies, it was far better than it had been just moments before.

He would take that.

* * *

"Bring us forward, commander. You heard the fleet order. Cut all safeties and fire up the reactor. We may not have many guns, but we're going to make the ones we do have count." Andi Lafarge's voice was like the clang of a hammer on steel. She was hard, immovable, and her determination to participate in the battle, to add whatever meager amount of strength *Hermes* could to the combined effort, was almost irresistible.

"Yes, captain."

She nodded and turned back to the display. The symbols representing the fleet were changing, some of them flickering and moving about as the Hegemony jamming interfered with *Hermes*'s scanners. But she saw what she'd been looking for, a blue circle, right up at the front of the fleet, in the thick of the fight.

Dauntless.

She wasn't surprised at all that Tyler was right at the forefront of the battle, leading his spacers in their most desperate struggle. She hoped he was occupied, too focused on other things to see her small cruiser moving so far forward. She didn't want to worry him—or worse, distract him—but there was just no way she could leave him again, blast off in the fast cruiser he'd given her and run away while he stayed behind, to win or die.

She would stay too. She would also win or die, and if it was the latter, she would do it fighting next to him, her only true regret that she wouldn't get one last chance to see him before the end came.

"You heard the fleet order, commander. We've only got four guns, but we're going to strip off every safety and pour as much energy as we can through them. With any luck, they won't consider us a threat, and we'll be able to get close enough."

Close enough to kill some Hegemony spacers…

* * *

"You are authorized to launch."

Jake Stockton slammed his hand back, ready to blast his engines at full, even as the catapult hurled his ship down the launch tube and into space. He'd been far from sure he'd get back out again, that *Dauntless* would endure the enemy bombardment long enough to launch yet another sortie. But the arrival of whatever reinforcements Sara Eaton had brought had disrupted the enemy somewhat. Eaton's ships were coming in more or less against the Hegemony fleet's flank, and the enemy had been compelled to reposition some of its ships to meet the new force.

Now they would face another attack by Stockton's fighters. It wouldn't be anything like the massive assault waves early in the battle. Casualties had been immense, and hundreds of fighters were sitting damaged in the bays, incapable of launching. Beyond that, the fleet organization was in tatters. Fighters had returned to their base ships squadron by squadron, or even in mixed groups. Bombers were being refitted, even as other squadrons launched attacks, and Stockton knew he'd be lucky to get a few hundred ships together for the attack he was leading out now. They would be a disorganized mix of Confederation, Alliance, and even Union ships, with varying levels of damage, and almost universal exhaustion among the pilots. But he knew, in many ways, it would be the most important strike of his life.

"Jake?" It was Admiral Barron, coming through Stockton's comm. There was some static, but he was still very close to *Dauntless*, so it was clear enough to understand.

"Yes, sir."

"I know I don't have to tell you this, my old friend, but this is the time, the attack we've been readying ourselves for all these years. It's our first real chance to beat these bastards." There was a slight pause. "I know I can count on you. Hit them, Raptor. Hit them as hard as you can."

Stockton felt his emotions stirring. He was already raw, a raging predator out for blood, but the idea of letting Admiral

Barron down…it was *unthinkable*.

"I won't fail you, admiral. You can count on my wings."

Stockton moved the controls back, kicking up his thrust, pushing forward, even as he watched his thin, patched-together strike force begin to form up.

He thought of Kyle Jamison, wishing his old commander could be there in the next fighter. He missed his friend with an ache that had never diminished, but one aspect of his grief that had long plagued him was gone. He no longer wished Jamison was there to take the burden of command from him. He had long felt out of place, as promotions had moved him up the chain and placed him at the very top of the strike force organizational chart. He was tense, as anyone would be in the same situation…but the discomfort of command was gone. He was where he belonged, and he'd ascended vastly farther along that climb than Kyle Jamison had ever had the chance to reach.

He didn't know if his people would make a difference, if the reinforcements would give the fleet a chance of finally defeating the Hegemony. But he was damn sure going to do everything he could. It was time to truly show the invaders what fighters and veteran pilots could do.

* * *

Repulse shook hard, and Sonya Eaton knew her ship was badly hurt. She'd been in the line, trading volleys with the Hegemony ships for almost an hour. She was exhausted, struggling to dig up the strength to give her people what they needed from her.

Then, suddenly, Sara returned with reinforcements. More than fresh ships, Sonya's sister had somehow, against the odds, come back with something even more powerful than hulls and laser cannon. Hope.

Sonya felt energized, and she could see her crew did, too. *Repulse*'s primaries were long gone, but that didn't matter at such close range, and she still had about half her broadside operational. Power was going to be a problem soon, at least if her damage-control teams couldn't get reactor B back online—but, all things considered, the battleship was still in the fight. That was about all she could ask, and it was a boast that many ships that had started in the battle line days before could not match. Casualties had been massive, so utterly brutal that she'd given silent thanks that her position didn't require her to keep track of such things.

She'd been on the verge of giving up even the small vestiges of hope to which she'd desperately clung, but now, her face twisted into a strange little smile.

Welcome back, sister. Well done!

She didn't have a real feel for whether the forces Sara had somehow brought back would be enough to turn the tide, but they'd damn sure been enough to reinvigorate her spirits. Victory was far from certain, and perhaps not even in reach…but it was a hell of a lot closer than it had been minutes before.

Sonya scanned the display, staring at the two enemy battleships firing at her ship. One was closer than the other, but the more distant of the two was badly damaged. She might be able to take it out…before its companion blasted the rest of *Repulse*'s broadside and put the battleship out of the fight. Or worse.

"Commander, give me twenty percent thrust, course 105.230.355…and all weapons, shift targeting to target beta. We're going in…"

She stared straight ahead.

"Right down their throats."

* * *

Stockton's finger tightened, and his fighter shuddered as the torpedo lurched forward from the bomb bay. His hand clenched on the controls, pulling the throttle back and blasting his engines hard, as he zipped past his target. There were two dozen Lightnings stacked up behind him, coming in at the same enemy battleship. The fight had changed, and with it his orders and the mode of his attack. The battle was now a test of wills, and the goal was simple: put the enemy to the test, see what losses they could endure before they turned tail and ran.

The Hegemony spacers were not cowards, far from it. Even through his hatred, Stockton could see that. But they lacked one thing his pilots possessed, that the entire fleet did: desperation. There would be no retreat for the Confederation forces, no fall-back to another defensive location weaker and more helpless than the current one. The forces arrayed at Craydon would turn back the enemy…or they would die where they were.

That was a potent force in battle, and Stockton ignored the sweat pouring down his forehead, the tense jumble in his gut. There was no time for fear, nor for thought, only time to kill. He thought about returning to *Dauntless*, trying to get his ship rearmed. But Barron's flagship was at the forward edge of the fleet, engaged at point-blank range with Hegemony battleships. Whatever happened, however the Battle of Craydon ended, it would that finish would come before Stockton could land, rearm, and launch again.

So, he activated his lasers, listening to the soft hum as the secondary weapons charged up to fire.

He watched on his screen as the fighters he'd led in planted torpedo after torpedo into the targeted ship, and finally, as the vessel shuddered, and great geysers of gas and liquids burst through the wounds in its hull, instantly freezing in the icy cold of space.

The ship hadn't lost containment, but Stockton would have bet his last credit the hulking wreck was close to dead. Stockton had always been very precise when it came to the damage his forces inflicted, but he'd lost count long before. The Hegemony fleet was badly battered, worse than it had been at Megara, and he began to wonder if it really was possible. If the enemy might actually retreat.

If the fleet could hold Craydon.

Hold the Iron Belt.

He paused as he saw a badly battered Hegemony ship, one with multiple large breaches in the hull, and he angled his thrust, nudging his vector toward his next target.

If he could drop a laser blast into one of the gashes in the hull, maybe he could do some meaningful damage.

The battle wasn't over, and he had no idea how it was going to end.

But he knew one thing without the slightest doubt.

Every kill counted.

More than that—every hit counted.

Chapter Forty

Chronos stared at the giant display in the center of his flagship's control center. He had resisted the urge to retreat to his sanctum, to the relief of solitude amid the indescribable carnage embroiling both his fleet and the forces of the Rim dwellers. The battle had been all but won, the enemy on the verge not just of defeat, but of annihilation. Then, somehow, reinforcements had arrived.

The new ships were of various types, unlike any his forces had faced before. He suspected they were from the minor Rim nations, about which he knew little more than the mere fact that they existed. The new fleet that had arrived was not *really* that strong, not relative to the massive forces that had contested at Megara, and again, at Craydon. But they were fresh, and they had arrived at a critical moment, blasting in from the transit point, almost directly at one of his flanks.

Chronos had been determined to avoid ruinous losses to Grand Fleet in the Rim campaign, but somehow, despite his intent, he had seen the great force, built up over generations, savaged, its numbers drastically reduced. It was still a massive force, and when the ships damaged at Craydon were repaired, it would remain stronger than its enemy's. But it was not nearly as powerful as it had been, and if the Others, so long little more than memory and legend, ever did return, his expedition against the Rim could well prove to be the Hegemony's undoing, instead of the conquest that doubled its size and power.

Worse, however, than taking such losses would be to suffer those casualties for no gain. The Rim was massively productive, far more so than even the most aggressive estimates before the invasion. The records seized at Megara provided an insight into the industrial might of the group of systems called the Iron Belt. Integrating the Rim would vastly increase the Hegemony's strength, and proper harnessing of the industry of the Confederation, in particular, would allow the fleet's losses to be replaced in a matter of years.

Still, he hesitated. Should he should fight it out to the bitter end, to a victory he was almost sure his forces could still achieve? Or fall back on the logistics fleet at Megara and refit and rearm his ships for the final battle another time?

No…he was there, the fleet was there. He would not withdraw. The enemy had committed to battle, and he would destroy them.

"Commander, there is activity at our entry transit point."

Chronos was not expecting any reinforcements. Perhaps the logistics fleet had sent a force of repaired vessels forward. He had not left any such orders, but he had not left any procedure at all for the deployment of vessels coming out of the shipyards.

It was a welcome development. Whatever forces were coming, they would be helpful. Anything that allowed him to defeat the enemy more quickly, to end the savage battle sooner, and with fewer losses, would be most welcome.

* * *

"It looks like we've got some kind of Hegemony force inbound, admiral." Atara was clearly trying to hide the horror in her tone, with far less success than she usually managed.

Barron just stared at the display. He'd been trying to decide if he thought his people had any kind of chance, at least assuming the Hegemony commander stood in place and refused to retreat. If it came down to a fight to the very end, to the moment only one side had any ships left, who would that be? And if it was the Hegemony, would they retain enough of a fleet to complete their conquest of the Rim? If not, he knew there could be a victory of some kind for his people, even in death.

But if the enemy was getting reinforcements...

Any hope he'd been nursing quickly slipped away, and he could feel the blackness of despair coming on him.

"Wait..."

He snapped his head around. There was something about Atara's tone. He paused for a few seconds, but when she didn't elaborate, he asked, "What is it?"

"The readings are sporadic, admiral...it's that damned jamming. But there's just something...about the mass figures, the energy readings..."

"Attention...ederation fl...this is...inters..."

The signal was weak, the words hard to understand, but Barron's eyes darted back to the display. There were six contacts, and while the reported mass sizes varied, yet another effect of the enemy jamming, he quickly calculated an average.

It was within five percent of *Dauntless*'s mass...for all the incoming ships.

Is it possible?

"Atara..."

"On your line." Travis's near-telepathic link to him was clearly in full force.

"Vessels entering the system, please identify yourselves immediately."

Nothing. Just static.

"Attention—"

"Sir!"

Barron turned toward Atara.

"We're picking up fragments of beacon signals, admiral... Confederation beacons! I think one of those ships is *Constitution*!"

Barron was stunned. Was it even possible?

"I need that confirmed!" He grabbed the sides of his chair as *Dauntless* shook hard. Whatever was coming through that transit point, his flagship was still in the middle of a fight, and another hit had just rocked the battered vessel.

Seconds passed, a minute. Atara was hunched over her station, her hands flying all across the controls. "It *is Constitution*, admiral! And five other battleships. *Confederation* battleships."

Barron felt a rush of excitement. If Winters was back, did that mean his fleet had completed its mission? Or been repulsed and chased all the way back to Craydon? Were there Hegemony ships on his tail? Barron didn't know…and he wasn't sure it would matter. It would take at least two hours for Winters's ships to close with the enemy, and Barron wasn't sure his fleet had two hours left.

He could hear the excitement spreading around the bridge, nevertheless, the sounds of officers talking in animated tones.

"Enough!" he snapped. "We've got a fight here, and unless you want to get blasted to plasma before those ships get anywhere close to us, focus on the work at hand. Bring us in closer, captain. All ships. I want us close enough to reach out the airlock and hit those bastards with a club!"

* * *

"Full thrust, all ships." *Or whatever passes for it.*

Clint Winters sat on *Constitution*'s bridge, amid the twisted metal and charred wiring. His flagship was in rough shape, though he knew she looked worse than she actually was. His damage-control teams had worked wonders, and there was no mystery to him about that. Anya Fritz. He'd heard about Barron's miracle worker, of course, about the famous engineering savant who had played such a role in his victories. But he hadn't really believed all the stories.

He did now.

She had worked nothing short of magic in his estimation, and beyond repairing *Constitution*'s damage at an astonishing rate, she had spent hours on the comm, mercilessly driving the engineers on the other ships to their limits and beyond. Barron had loaned him Fritz to keep the stealth generators working, but she had done far more than that. He didn't think a single one of his ships would have made it out of the Olyus system without her wizardry, much less all the way back to Craydon.

Constitution's companions, the five other battleships limping in-system, were all that remained of the sixteen he had led to Megara. Losses like that always hurt, but this time they were tempered by the fact that the mission had been a complete success. Half the Hegemony mobile shipyards had been destroyed, and the others critically damaged and put out of operation for a considerable time. The reduction in mining, refining, and general stores of supplies had been over seventy percent, eighty by the most optimistic projections. The enemy would have one hell of a time trying to repair the damage it appeared to have suffered in the fighting at Craydon, and that realization told him, at least, that his people hadn't died in vain.

"Vector change, commander. Thrust at…thirty percent." He figured all his ships could manage thirty percent, though it was a good bet at least half of them couldn't go much higher. He felt the urge to rush right at the enemy fleet, to hit them from the rear as Barron and Nguyen engaged from the front. But his ships were too badly damaged for that. They would join the fight— the Sledgehammer knew no other way—but they would hit the enemy flank, where they could limit the number of enemy ships they engaged. Getting his half-dozen battered ships blasted to atoms wouldn't do a thing for the fleet, or for the battle.

"Navigation orders locked in, admiral." The tactical officer looked over and nodded. "Executing now…"

Winters felt the pressure from the thrust as it overwhelmed *Constitution*'s damaged and barely functional dampeners. His people were going into battle again, and he knew this one would be to the end. The fleet would hold Craydon…or there would be no fleet.

And no Confederation.

* * *

Chronos was stunned. How was it possible for Confederation forces to come through that transit point? There was nothing between Craydon and Megara, not along that route. Nothing save two virtually empty systems.

How could Confederation forces have come through the Olyus system?

He felt his chest tighten. No, it was not possible. There were garrison forces there, enough to protect the logistics fleet.

But had they been ready? On the alert? No one, including himself, had expected anything as wildly audacious as a move on the supply ships back at Olyus. He was not sure how it was even possible. His scouts would have detected anything heading for Megara.

He tried to convince himself there was no way...but then he looked out at what remained of the enemy forces. He could finish them, he still believed that. But it would cost. That had been acceptable moments before, when he had been confident he could take the time to repair his damaged ships, to bring his fleet back to combat ready status.

Now, there was doubt. Suddenly, his very long supply line seemed tenuous, vulnerable. He had already gambled bringing the Grand Fleet so far from home, committing to battles that had inflicted such losses. Did he dare double down, not knowing the status of his supply and support units?

He analyzed the situation from every possible angle. He considered percentages, force ratios, tactical options. It was close. If he had not been so far from home, if he had been more certain of his supply situation...if he had not been plagued by concern about how naked the Hegemony was with so much force deployed to the Rim...

He turned slowly and looked over at his chief aide. "Megaron," he said, struggling to sound as the eighth most genetically perfect human being in the galaxy should sound, despite the blackness he felt inside. "Command level order. All units are to disengage immediately and retreat on our entrance transit point." A pause, long and uncomfortable. "We are going back to Megara."

Epilogue

Hegemony's Glory
Olyus System

Chronos sat in his sanctum. He normally considered the elaborate domains to be wastes of space in warships, and needless enhancements to Master egos that were already far too inflated. But now he *needed* the privacy, the silence.

He had been defeated at Craydon. He knew many of his fellow Masters would have characterized it differently. The Hegemony fleet was, almost certainly, still in far better shape than the decimated forces of the Confederation and its allies, and his retreat had ensured his force would remain at least somewhat in condition for the next fight, something his enemies would have difficulty matching.

Now, he had much to consider. He would proceed with the war, certainly. That much he had decided almost immediately. There was no choice. Too much had been lost to stop with no gain. The need to conquer the Rim was greater than ever. But he had been unprepared for the damage to the logistics fleet. He had suspected the enemy had conducted some kind of raid when he saw their ships emerge behind his fleet, that he would find some damage and destruction when he returned to Megara. But his first warning that things were far worse had come when the fleet had encountered a courier ship bound for Craydon with dispatches for him. He had listened to the reports of devastation to his supply and support ships, and even then, he had assumed they were exaggerations from shaken subordinates.

When *Hegemony's Glory* transited back into the Olyus system, and he saw for himself, he realized it was far worse than his subordinates had acknowledged. He had nowhere near the supplies or repair capacity to service the fleet after the epic battle at Craydon. He would have to look elsewhere for support. The reserve, certainly, though the thought of committing even more of the Hegemony's massed strength only fed his tension and fear.

He hoped Carmetia had gotten things under control at Dannith and made some progress on erecting shipyards and fleet support facilities there. That would be helpful, though a supply line stretching even from Megara to Dannith would be long and vulnerable.

He cradled his head in his hands. He was tired, exhausted beyond measure. He would rest. Whatever happened next, the Confederation forces were damaged worse than his own. It would be months before they could make a real threat out of themselves, and that gave him time.

Time to develop a new plan. Time to prepare for a final offensive, one that would succeed. One that would conquer the Rim.

But first, he needed to sleep…and he needed to think.

CFS Dauntless
Orbiting Craydon

Andi Lafarge stood in the doorway, looking across the room at Tyler. She was exhausted, as she knew we was…had to be. But she hadn't waited. She couldn't wait. She had to see him, for many reasons, but most of all because she'd so been absolutely sure she never would again.

He moved across the room toward her, and she stayed still… for a second. Then she raced toward him, and the two embraced.

"I am so glad you're okay." She held on to him tightly, and

she pressed her head against his shoulder.

"I'm glad *you're* okay," he replied. "When I saw *Hermes* advancing…" He didn't continue, and she knew why. She loved Barron for many reasons, some of them stunningly obvious, but what had truly set him apart from anyone else she'd known was how matter-of-factly he'd always accepted what she was, who she was. From their first moments in each other's presence, he'd never treated her as anything less than capable and independent—save, perhaps, for his periodic efforts to keep her from danger. Even those, she knew, had only to do with his affection for her, and because he thought she couldn't take care of herself.

Theirs was a union of equals, and while they were very different from each other in many ways, it had become clearer and clearer to her that they belonged together. She had fifty reasons why it couldn't work, but she had no more use for any of them. She'd never allowed obstacles to stop her before, and she wasn't about to start now.

"There's something I need to say, Ty." She'd been thinking about what she wanted to say, but, speaking to him, she changed everything, forgetting most of what she'd planned. "I know you have duty stretching out in front of you farther than the eye can see…and I'm part of that fight as well. But when all this is over…" She resisted the urge to say "if." Andi had been a cold realist her entire life, if not an outright pessimist, but she figured it was about time to try and embrace the bright side for once, to reach out and grab at some shreds of hope. "…I'm never letting you go again."

Grand Hall
Craydon Assembly Building

Barron sat at the immense table, some monstrosity of carved Balsacan wormwood, or some other stunningly rare and staggeringly expensive material. It had been brought to the Assembly building for the great summit meeting. Barron had just come through the costliest and most exhausting battle he'd ever fought, but he dreaded another session of relentless droning by dozens of pompous diplomats more than he did an enemy railgun aimed at his forehead.

It was very simple to him. They all banded together and fought as one to save the Rim. Or they died. Or became slaves. The Hegemony had been beaten back for now. The forces of the Rim had secured their first victory. But the cost had been almost unimaginable, and any real triumph in the war seemed as far away as ever. The victory, such as it was, bought some time, and nothing more.

He detested the work involved in rallying nations to an alliance, pandering to rulers and politicians and ambassadors more focused on their own egos than the problem at hand. But he couldn't argue against Sara Eaton's results. She'd saved the fleet from annihilation. It was that simple. For all her military skill, she'd never made as stark a difference as she had as an ambassador. If her force hadn't arrived—or if it had gotten there *just* a little too late—the battle would have been lost. The war would have been, for all practical purposes, over.

Barron's head was splitting, and his mind raged against the pointlessness of the whole foolish circus. The nations present would all remain in the alliance, and they would do it for one reason and one reason alone.

Because they were all scared to death of the Hegemony. The framework of the agreement had already been laid out, and the pact combining the forces of eleven different nations even had a prospective name...

Blood on the Stars will Continue with

The Grand Alliance

Book 11

Appendix

Strata of the Hegemony

The Hegemony is an interstellar polity located far closer to the center of what had once been the old empire than Rimward nations such as the Confederation. The Rim nations and the Hegemony were unaware of each other's existence until the White Fleet arrived at Planet Zero and established contact.

Relatively little is known of the Hegemony, save that their technology appears to be significantly more advanced than the Confederation's in most areas, though still behind that of the old empire.

The culture of the Hegemony is based almost exclusively on genetics, with an individual's status being entirely dependent on an established method of evaluating genetic "quality." Generations of selective breeding have produced a caste of "Masters," who occupy an elite position above all others. There are several descending tiers below the Master class, all of which are categorized as "Inferiors."

The Hegemony's culture likely developed as a result of its location much closer to the center of hostilities during the Cataclysm. Many surviving inhabitants of the inward systems suffered from horrific mutations and damage to genetic materials, placing a premium on any bloodlines lacking such effects.

The Rimward nations find the Hegemony's society to be almost alien in nature, while its rulers consider the inhabitants of the Confederation and other nations to be just another strain of Inferiors, fit only to obey their commands without question.

Masters

The Masters are the descendants of those few humans spared genetic damage from the nuclear, chemical, and biological warfare that destroyed the old empire during the series of events known as the Cataclysm. The Masters sit at the top of the Hegemony's societal structure and, in a sense, are its only true full members or citizens.

The Masters' culture is based almost entirely on what they call "genetic purity and quality," and even their leadership and ranking structure is structured solely on genetic rankings. Every master is assigned a number based on his or her place in a population-wide chromosomal analysis. An individual's designation is thus subject to change once per year, to adjust for Masters dying and for new adults being added into the database. The top ten thousand individuals in each year's ratings are referred to as "High Masters," and they are paired for breeding matchups far more frequently than the larger number of lower-rated Masters.

Masters reproduce by natural means, through strict genetic pairings based on an extensive study of ideal matches. The central goal of Master society is to steadily improve the human race by breeding the most perfect specimens available and relegating all others to a subservient status. The Masters consider any genetic manipulation or artificial processes like cloning to be grievously sinful, and all such practices are banned in the Hegemony on pain of death to all involved. This belief structure traces from the experiences of the Cataclysm, and the terrible damage inflicted on the populations of imperial worlds by genetically engineered pathogens and cloned and genetically engineered soldiers.

All humans not designated as Masters are referred to as Inferiors, and they serve the Masters in various capacities. All Masters have the power of life and death over Inferiors. It is not a crime for a Master to kill an Inferior who has injured or offended that Master in any way.

Kriegeri

The Kriegeri are the Hegemony's soldiers. They are drawn from the strongest and most physically capable specimens of the populations of Inferiors on Hegemony worlds. Kriegeri are not genetically modified, though in most cases, Master supervisors enforce specific breeding arrangements in selected population groups to increase the quality of future generations of Kriegeri stock.

The Kriegeri are trained from infancy to serve as the Hegemony's soldiers and spaceship crews, and are divided in two categories, red and gray, named for the colors of their uniforms. The "red" Kriegeri serve aboard the Hegemony's ships, under the command of a small number of Master officers. They are surgically modified to increase their resistance to radiation and zero gravity.

The "gray" Kriegeri are the Hegemony's ground soldiers. They are selected from large and physically powerful specimens and are subject to extensive surgical enhancements to increase strength, endurance, and dexterity. They also receive significant artificial implants, including many components of their armor, which becomes a permanent partial exoskeleton of sorts. They are trained and conditioned from childhood to obey orders and to fight. The top several percent of Kriegeri surviving twenty years of service are retired to breeding colonies. Their offspring are Krieger-Edel, a pool of elite specimens serving as mid-level officers and filling a command role between the ruling Masters and the rank and file Kriegeri.

Arbeiter

Arbeiter are the workers and laborers of the Hegemony. They are drawn from populations on the Hegemony's many worlds, and typically either exhibit some level of genetic damage inherited from the original survivors or simply lack genetic ratings sufficient for Master status. Arbeiter are from the same general group as the Kriegeri, though the soldier class includes the very best candidates, and the Arbeiter pool consists of the remnants.

Arbeiter are assigned roles in the Hegemony based on rigid assessments of their genetic status and ability. These positions range from supervisory posts in production facilities and similar establishments to pure physical labor, often working in difficult and hazardous conditions.

Defekts

Defekts are individuals—often populations of entire worlds—exhibiting severe genetic damage. They are typically found on planets that suffered the most extensive bombardments and bacteriological attacks during the Cataclysm.

Defekts have no legal standing in the Hegemony, and they are considered completely expendable. On worlds inhabited by populations of Masters, Kriegeri, and Arbeiters, Defekts are typically assigned to the lowest-level, most dangerous labor, and any excess populations are exterminated.

The largest number of Defekts exist on planets on the fringes of Hegemony space, where they are often used for such purposes as mining radioactives and other similarly dangerous operations. Often, the Defekts themselves have no knowledge at all of the Hegemony, and regard the Masters as gods or demigods descending from the heavens. On such planets, the Masters often demand ore and other raw materials as offerings, and severely punish any failures or shortfalls. Pliant and obedient populations are provided with rough clothing and low-quality manufactured foodstuffs, enabling them to devote nearly all labor to the gathering of whatever material the Masters demand. Resistant population groups are exterminated, as, frequently, are Defekt populations on worlds without useful resources to exploit.

Also By Jay Allan

www.jayallanbooks.com

Made in the USA
San Bernardino, CA
22 May 2020

72134352R10212